SHADOWS OF THE PAST

By Annay Dawson

Shadows of the Past is a work of fiction. Names, characters, places and incidents are the products of the author's imagination or are used fictionally. Any resemblance to actual events, locales, or persons, living or dead, is entirely coincidental

ISBN: 978-1-4303-0588-0
        Published By Lulu

Copyright © 2006

Chapter 1

All she could hear was the relentless beeping in her ears and damn, it hurt. It was her first realization of being alive, full awareness was still far from her grasp. Something had gone horribly wrong and now she was paying the price of being stupid. She was still struggling to figure out what had happened from the murky darkness that was once her mind. Slowly and carefully she took in a breath and felt a welcome jab of pain. From the pain she felt she knew some of her ribs were broken, but knowing that information did nothing to make the pain in her chest easier as she breathed. Somewhere in her past she remembered having broken ribs before but that was where it stopped. She thought the pain in her head had been bad until that breath. Now she chose to focus on the beeping sound to take her mind off the pain in her ribs. Next time she would try a shallower breath, hoping there was a next time. With no memory of what had happened, it was hard to know if there would be another minute in her life. The beeping continued; it seemed to be never ending. Not knowing what else to do she listened closer to the beeping. It seemed as if it was some kind of warning. Slowly she sucked in a shallow breath of air. This time the breath she took hurt just as much as the first one that she remembered taking, but she was ready for the pain. Focusing on the sounds around her she was able to push aside the pain to take in shallow breaths as she began to realize that there was pain in almost every part of her body. 'Oh great!' she thought as the beeping sound never failed to remind her she wasn't anyplace she could remember. That worried her. Even thinking was causing her pain as if her mind had been assaulted as well. Just when she thought she could grasp a bit of what had happened the screeching siren erupted, keeping any memories she may have had at bay.

She had now fought her way back to a dizzy awareness of her surroundings. Without moving the rest of her body, she waited for her eyes to open not wanting to make the situation any worse than it was. The question pounded her mind again. 'What had happened?' the next breath cleared all her thoughts and brought back the pain that lingered in her chest, arms, legs and head.

Heavy and swollen from what she could tell, she slowly tried forcing her eyes to open just enough to let in the barest glimpse of light or clue. Her eyelids seemed glued into place, and for a moment, she actually hoped that wasn't the case. 'Now wouldn't that be just the icing on the cake,' she thought. Slowly and with an effort she knew was far more than it should be she opened one eye just a little. 'Nothing, nothing to see at this angle,' she thought as she lay helpless on what she could only assume was cold concrete, and the sound seemed to continue its warning that she could not heed. Nothing else seemed to be working well but her ears. And they only picked up on the tormenting sound of the beeping. Searching her mind she tried to figure out what it was trying to tell her? Her nose caught a faint familiar smell; smoke. She was sure she could smell smoke. 'Could it get any worse?' she asked no one in particular.

The automatic call came through from the fire alarm at the factory. The dispatcher looked at the address without feeling and emotion and chose the closest station to respond. The factory in question had been closed for a year and a half and falling apart for two before that. The owners had put at least three hundred people out of work when they had decided to move their business overseas for cheaper labor cost. Her brother-in-law had been laid off. He had not taken the news well and it hadn't been long until he had left her sister and her two children to disappear to who knew where. Secretly the dispatcher was glad that the factory was finally coming to a fitting end. At least it wouldn't be there anymore to torment her sister with all the 'what might have beens'.

Her brain seemed vacant and empty as the smoke began to fill her lungs. Everything and nothing told her she had to move, to get out of here. 'But why?' It was the urge; the need and desire to escape that were overwhelmingly powerful. Trying to move, though, was another story. Nothing seemed to be working. If the eyelids seemed impossible to open, the arms and legs were more than impossible for her to lift. Steel beams would have been easier for her to move. Nothing she did could encourage them to work with her fuzzy brain. Ignoring the increasing amount of sweat trickling down her face and dropping to the concrete floor as she worked to move anything, she searched her mind for any answers. She looked for any reason that she could think of that would have caused this paralysis, pain, or her yearning to flee. For that matter, an identity to the incessant beeping that threatened to make her head explode at any minute. But it was like looking into empty rooms of a house you never knew. As she tried to move her arms again she could feel her heart start to beat a little faster and then faster as the need to flee fed the realization of the impossibility of the action. She couldn't let panic set in.

Another wave of fear hit her. She didn't even know who she was. The question, 'Who am I?' rang through her brain only briefly as she came to the conclusion that this might be, should be, and would be better answered later. Funny thing was that she couldn't remember much that had gone on in the last week, month, and maybe even the year through the haze of pain she felt numbing her brain. Panic took hold of her. 'Was it getting hotter?' not a great time for amnesia she chastised herself. The thumping of her heart filled her chest, overflowing into her ears, competing with the annoying beeping, and making it nearly impossible to think. The rhythm of her beating heart began to resound louder in her ears, louder and louder until, with panic, it drowned out the incessant beeping she had first heard. Then she heard something or someone move near her. As she once again tried with every amount of strength she had left to move, she discovered that it was just as fruitless as the first time she had tried it. With every ounce of strengthen she tried to scream and only mustered a voice barely audible to her ears. The voice that did emerge from her lips was a flat, feeling-less voice she barely recognized, 'At least I can recognize the sound of my own voice.' The thought drifted quickly through her mind as the allure of unconsciousness toyed with her brain through the overwhelming pain she felt and that did very little to calm her nerves. A small hopeful thought drifted through her mind as she waited for the stranger to say something. She wanted them to know, 'I'm alive.'

"She's awake." a voice, not one she knew, but one that filled her with anger and fear.

"Let the fire finish her off. I won't do it. I owe a friend at least that much. I've gotten all the useful information I could from her," somewhere in her mind she knew this speaker, but it wasn't the calming thought she thought it might be or should be, "She's just like him. Did you find what we needed in the car?" She never heard the answer from the other voice. Although her mind tried to tell her just who was standing near her, logic kept arguing that it couldn't be him. She felt him focus on her again and her head began to feel as if it would explode. All hope seemed to leave as the blackness finally claimed her. It was a blissful release from her current world of pain and agony, floating in a black nothingness, weightless, wantless. Thoughts were not a part of this world she had entered, and neither was anything else.

"Jan ... Jan, can you hear me?" the voice came from nowhere, and from no particular direction that she could tell as it floated to her ears. First things first, she sniffed the air. All she knew was that she couldn't smell smoke anymore, it wasn't hot anymore, and she was lying comfortably on her back in a soft bed. She began to feel a little safer, whether or not she really was didn't seem to matter.

It seemed to have been years since Jan had heard any voice, but especially this voice. That voice was familiar. The clouds that still lurked in her mind threatened to hide all that surrounded her and drag her back into the abyss she had just left as she tried to think. They must have her on some kind of drugs because the pain, although there, didn't seem half as important now. Even though she was thankful for them she knew for some reason that she needed to be off of them as soon as possible.

Something from her past told her that it was a friendly voice and she fought to stay in the present and conscious. 'Jan, yes this was her name,' the thought drifted through. The panic had long subsided, and became only a distant memory. She tried to speak, and found that it still took great effort.

"Who's there?" she barely recognized her own voice. It sounded fragile, strained, flat, and only a fraction of the volume that she had expected for the amount of effort it took. Once again, panic began to eat away at the corners of her memories as she tried to move, to open stubborn eyes, to look at the person who owned the voice her ears had faintly recognized but her eyes had yet to see. Her eyes still seemed to fight her, refusing her every effort to open them this time. Jan tried to move her hands to her face. This time her arms were less like steel beams, more like granite rocks, but still refusing to move without tremendous effort that she didn't feel like exerting. Giving up, she realized that it had not been years since she had heard a voice, but the correct amount of time had escaped her. At least breathing seemed easier than what she had remembered from before, and the beeping in her ears was somewhat different.

"Jan, it's Rob, Rob Brown, do you remember me?" without even waiting on the reply he continued, "Do you remember anything?" His voice held a touch of concern, or was it panic. There was another beep in the room. Now just for a split second, Jan was able to recognize the beep as an institutional sound of some kind.

"Maybe," it was all Jan could get out. So many questions pressed through Jan's mind. It was impossible to determine which one to ask first, and this seemed to be adding to the cloud that already existed, and making it grow into a full-blown storm. Something in the back of her mind wasn't sure yet if she should ask or answer any questions, some memories were beginning to play at the corners of her mind taunting her, not clear, yet not fuzzy, but certainly not where she could access them. None of the pieces she wanted to share with only a faceless voice she seemed to have some recognition of from a past of which she had no memory. And it seemed as if it was a distant faceless voice from her memory at that.

Without being taken aback by the answer, in fact, it seemed that he had not really expected any answer just yet, Rob went on, "Jan, you have had a small accident. You are in the hospital, and have been here for about two weeks. Your condition seems to be stable now, but you have had some injuries to your eye area, among other problems. That is why you can't see anything right now. The doctors still have your eyes bandaged as a precaution, so don't try to open them yet. Your attackers thought you were dead, and left you that way. It happened about two hours after the trial. Kevin was killed, no one has yet been charged, identified, or found. You are the only witness." He took a small breath before beginning again, "We haven't got much time. They said you could only have a visitor for a couple of minutes. Do you remember anything?" a small bit of urgency crept into his voice. He didn't have time to tell her that he was glad she was still alive or that he had notified a friend. Business was first; humanity was sometimes second in their line of work.

The clouds in her head that had been threatening to storm now began to build again. The pain returning to Jan's head was now worse than before. The little information she had darted between the lightning bolts and mixed with the ominous darkness that spun, and threatened to turn into a tornado. The more that Jan tried to remember the less she could focus on anything. The smell of antiseptic was now registering in her nostrils and with that nauseating her, it nearly initiated a fit of coughing. She tried to clear her mind, push away the storm for just a minute, 'Who was Kevin?' 'Was she some how responsible for his death?' she had no memory of him at all. The beeping started again pushing out all thought, but this time it was clear to her that it was a hospital beep. Obviously, it was no small accident if she had no memory of the last two weeks or any part of her life that had existed before now. Someone had died during this time. Someone was dead whom she was supposed to know. Nothing made sense. 'If only I could see' rang through her growing storm cloud, 'maybe then I could fit some of the pieces together.' It all sounded so official, a trial, being charged. Jan began to question who she was and just what she had done in her life before this moment. She wondered if she was the one on trial, the jailor, the juror, or just who she could be.

Jan could hear the door scrape on the floor as it opened. The dark storm cloud churned with every thought as Rob began his questioning again. Jan, not knowing any more than she did, and not wanting any more information to increase the size of what now could be now classified as a full blown hurricane managed to force out a word, "Stop", before it could swallow up what she could just manage to sort out. Plain and simple, she needed to know more about herself first. Then maybe the rest would somehow become important. The trauma had been significant; the present, past, and even the future, was unknown. Now, more than ever, she began to realize that she needed to remember who she was, all the details, and not rely on others that she didn't remember as of yet, 'Why is that so important to me? Why can't I trust this voice? I somehow recognize from somewhere in my past?' Too many questions, not enough answers, and from somewhere deep inside her she decided that she could not trust anyone just yet. Footsteps echoed throughout the room on the tile floor. They were lighter footsteps and it was clear to Jan when the voice spoke.

"Time to leave, she needs rest," it was a woman, a nurse probably; considering she had been told she was in a hospital.

"I have already waited two weeks to get some answers. I won't leave yet," Rob directed the comments toward the footsteps that had entered the room, and away from Jan. His voice was quiet, yet impatient, demanding.

"I'm sorry, I have my orders that the visit was to be short no more than five minutes. It is clear that the patient is agitated and needs to rest. If ...." the nurse's calm, clear, but firm voice was interrupted by Rob's agitated one, and Jan could only imagine what the conflict looked like.

"Then just get new orders," there was restraint in his voice, "I need to find out who did ..." this time it was Jan who interrupted.

"Leave," in a voice she could hardly call her own, she again spoke the words on her mind, "I need time to think."

"Just tell me this, do you know who you are?" It wasn't a demand, yet it was, and she could feel his presence nearer to her almost wishing the information out of her. There had been something else in his voice as well, concern she thought.

The question couldn't have more poignant, or well timed. Yes, she now knew her name and could even remember small bits of trivial information. But it was only trivial. What was still needed hovered only on the outskirts of her mind just out of her reach and taunted her with what she so wanted to know. She knew that it wasn't as it important to know that her hair was brown, and that her favorite color was orange. It was a start though and something to build on. Even more things were becoming clear, but not as fast as she needed, or wanted. The things that still escaped her were the biggies. She wanted to know what she did, how did she live, where did she live, did she have friends, family, a lover, or a pet? The questions began to fire from all directions in her brain and the hurricane began to swallow her up.

"Go away!" she shouted at no one in particular, and this time she meant it. She needed time, more time than this Rob wanted to give her right now. The effort of the conversation, and the raging storm in her head, were all making her tired. The idea of the dreamless unconsciousness she had just escaped was teasing and tempting her. Its darkness waited again to claim her, rescue her from this existence, and take her back to a world filled with no thoughts, no memories, and no worries. She could hear the nurse, if that was who she was, pulling Rob out under protest as she drifted back into that wanted peace unconsciousness had once been.

As peaceful as the unconsciousness had been before, it was now just as terrifying. Her dreams were haunted with explosions and with visions of death, and dying. Not hers, but others. Most of the images were just that, images, unknown faces. The dreams were relentless. First she was on a plane, next being shot, then jumping out of a different plane, next meeting with faces at places she knew but names she could not retrieve, and then finally she could see steel pipes swinging at her again and again. She was part of the dream, and yet she was also an observer and commentator. She could feel the pain all over again. She wondered about the reality of it all, 'Had she really experienced this once?' She noticed another pipe coming toward her in the dream, or was it. She fell to the ground rolling away from the next hit. The other person was not as lucky. He took the full force against his head. Jan remembered, 'Yes, it was a memory, real, but now just a memory,' the sound of bones breaking, the sickening sound of the thud of the pipe as it connected with the other person's head, and the lifeless pile that had been left after the attack. Dream mixed with reality, and Jan had a sickening feeling that she now knew the name that belonged to the victim in her dream as her thoughts interrupted trying to clarify what she was seeing. Jan felt herself receive another blow from a faceless figure behind her. It wasn't the same person that had attacked the man that now lay lifeless on the floor, so there were at least three people there, 'That could be Kevin, or was it Keith, that now lay lifeless on the floor.' There was something about her attacker, but in the dream Jan didn't get a chance to get a good look at him. In the dream though, she just caught a glimpse of the other man that now approached her. He seemed familiar, but no name came to mind. The dream took over again and she felt another blow and then another from behind. As she lay helpless on the floor the man facing her spoke in a low and threatening voice his eyes seeming to burn straight through her, "You're almost worth saving, but I have my orders," and instinctively she knew that the saving would not be any type of rescue at all.

In that one moment, and only for a moment, she knew who her attacker was. Not only did it surprise her, she wasn't so sure that she hadn't seen a ghost. It seemed as if he reached into her mind with his and within a wink of an eye all thoughts and memories were gone. Memories she thought were there forever, who she was, friends, and the name of her attacker. It felt as if her brain was being sifted through, and shredded. She fought back as best she could, who could do this? The pain in the dream, though not real, began to increase to the point at which she awoke stifling a small scream in the process. Jan could feel the sweat on her brow slowly dripping off to the side of her head and into the bandages around her eyes. The pillow and her hair were already soaked with sweat she noticed as she gasped for air. It seemed the closer she got to knowing who she was, and who hurt her, the farther away the memories traveled. She wondered why, how, and who had locked the memories so far away from her conscious thought.

Jan listened to the noises in the room, waiting, and hoping that no one was near. She could hear the beep of the machine that she had heard earlier, but the rest of the room was silent. The beeping was faster; it seemed to match the beating of her heart. 'Logical,' she thought. She listened for breathing, not just hers, but of anyone that might have been left to watch her. If they were hoping she could tell them about the attack, which she could now clearly remember more of, pain and all, would they have left someone in the room, or just outside of it? Most likely just outside the room from the woman's earlier reaction. The hurricane that had once been her thoughts and dreams now started to clear again. The woman that spoke earlier was right, rest was what she had needed, but somehow she didn't think it was the right type of rest that she had gotten. Her dreams also led her to believe that she needed the answers they were looking for and she wanted them sooner, not later. Somehow she didn't think that patience was her strong point. She was sure that here in the hospital if they were not the good guys, at least they were not the bad guys that had those large poles. That or their tactics had drastically changed. What did Rob, or was it Bob, say, 'two weeks had gone by'. That was a lot of time to be unaware of where, who, or even what she was. That was now beginning to change. Thoughts, memories, and even feelings were returning, this time in a coherent form, one she could organize into a picture, she hoped, of who and what she was, or had been. There were still many holes, too many, but with time that would soon be solved. 'Bob,' Jan wondered where that name had come from, was it someone she had known. Her head began to hurt again as she tried to focus on the name. She began to wonder what the extents of the injuries were that she had received from the beating.

They had told her that her injuries to her head and face were, or had been extensive. That was what Jan had attributed to the cause of the memory loss. What they hadn't told her was if she could see or not. Slowly she thought back to the dream and the attack to try and remember, even though her mind fought her efforts, the moment she first regained consciousness, 'Yes, there had been light, even some color.' The damage must not have affected her sight too much, or at least that was the premise she was going to work on.

Next, she started wiggling just her fingers and toes. Stiff, sore, and in general twice as heavy as she remembered, but they still seemed to work and respond to her orders, or at least she thought they were. Now, she decided, for a damage report on her hands. Rotating the hands slowly at the wrist she winced. It seemed that in the right hand there must be an IV and on the left hand there was a definite restriction, it must be a cast. But there was pain so she was sure that the information she was getting from her body was reliable. Slowly, and conserving movement where she could, she got a greater understanding of the extent of her injuries. There was definite tenderness to the trunk of her body, probably had been internal injuries, hopefully most of which were healed, or healing by now. She concentrated hard, she could remember the pain taking a deep breath had caused and this reminded her that the possibility still existed of broken ribs. Her hand responded slowly, but respond it did, to feel for the tape that Jan knew would be around the trunk of her body. The left and right ankles and up the legs were also in casts, or restraints, a problem for getting out of here in any hurry, and her neck was in a brace. All in all, the outlook didn't seem good, but she was still alive, and now she could remember a bit more in an organized fashion. This could be important.

Now it was time to discover what was left of her sight. She was almost sure that patience was not her strong point by now. Moving both the right and left arms with a slow and steady effort, she touched her face. At first she didn't seem to recognize it as a face. It was swollen and tender in most places that her hands could touch, and bandaged the rest of the places.

Nothing seemed to be broken, and from what she could remember that could only have been a miracle. She let her fingers investigate the bandages over her eyes. Simple, yet effective to keep the light out, as well as keeping her from knowing where she was. Rob, yes it was Rob, had told her where she was, but she couldn't be sure that was the complete truth. She was also pretty sure that they didn't want her knowing everything yet. Jan's fingers had now become used to moving again and a little more nimble. It seemed that only the cast caused any restriction. Jan noticed that her fingers were also a bit swollen but not enough to keep her from starting to undo the bandages that kept her from seeing her surroundings. She stretched out the gauze around the eye pads so that she could easily slide it up and down. Carefully she slid it onto what she would call her nose, swollen and sore, but probably not broken.

Fear gripped her again. It was not like before. It was a new unknowing fear, one that she had never felt before, 'What if I can't see? What then?' Throwing caution to the wind, and knowing that whether it was now or later, the truth would still be the same, she took a breath and carefully removed the one pad from the right eye. The eye responded by opening only halfway. Light streamed into her eye. Light, the blinding, beautiful light of the rays of the sun assaulted her eye. The florescent light in the room only added to the pain. There were more lights and colors from where ever else it might be coming from in the room. Her right eye shut just as quickly as it had opened, but now Jan knew one thing, she could see. This time, more slowly, she opened up her eye and was greeted with a welcome barrage of light and colors, mostly white. She took off the pad from her left eye and with the same care slowly opened it. With a sigh of relief, she greeted the light and color seen painfully by the left eye, with a smile. She blinked and took the next step, focusing. As her eyes watered and she blinked away the tears the first thing she could focus on was the institutional like ceiling of sound absorbing squares. With a slight smile she began to move her head as much as the brace around her neck would allow her to survey her surroundings.

The room was small, just enough room for a bed, desk or table, and a chair, which to her relief was empty. Monitors stood beside the bed and even though she could not move her head enough to see what they were reading; she knew that someone outside the room was monitoring her vital signs. A dramatic change in Jan's condition would bring someone to the room and that was the last thing she wanted. Jan took another relaxing breath. The door was located out of sight at the foot of the bed. A small but adequate mirror was on the wall opposite the monitors along with what might be a small table or desk, unknown as she could not move her head to determine which it was.

Jan was all of sudden interested in what she looked like. It was vain, yes, but more of a curiosity. She let her hands feel for the bed's controls and, finding them with her left hand. She slowly tried the buttons until she worked the bed to an upright position to better assess her condition as well as see what was left of the room in the mirror. Pain had figured into the equation, but Jan fought off the initial reaction, breathing in a relaxed manner she didn't feel, and continued. Figuring that she might have drawn attention to herself by now, she quickly visually checked what she was able to see of her body. Sighing, and realizing that her first assessment had been correct she then turned and looked at the mirror just before the door opened. She gasped as she looked at what was once a fairly familiar face. It was now swollen to three times its size and with a number of butterfly bandages and bruises that made it nearly unrecognizable as a face. She turned carefully to see the face of a woman enter the room, the nurse.

"I think that is quite enough of a sneak peak for now," it was the same female voice she had heard before, but now she could place not only a face but also a job to it. Yes, she was the nurse. She went over to the mirror and removed it placing it face down on the desk. "I will need to get the doctor now that you have decided to remove your own bandages. You have been very naughty," the nurse turned back to look at her, "Are you seeing all right?"

The concern was real, and deserved a considerate response, "My eyes seem to be working fine," but not ready to volunteer any more information Jan decided to feign tiredness, "I do think I may have done too much though. Could I rest before the doctor comes in? I promise to close my eyes and be good." The voice sounded better than before and it was only partially a lie about the tiredness. The nurse settled Jan back to a resting position and then left the room agreeing not to send the doctor in just yet. Jan's eyes closed and bits of memory started to flash through her mind again.

Moments later, Jan was aware of someone on the other side of the door. It was only the gentle sound of the door opening that disturbed her thoughts. The person that entered, Jan assumed was the doctor, but when there was barely any sound as he moved through the room she knew it wasn't. Jan left her eyes closed as terror gripped her heart. She took one calming breath pushing away the fear that filled her and waited. It seemed to be a conditioned response. Help was only seconds away, yet it really didn't feel to her as if she needed the help. The waiting seemed like forever. The feelings she had didn't seem to be hers. Instead they were feelings of compassion, hurt, caring, love, and fear. The last one was unclear as to where that feeling was coming from. It wasn't until the voice spoke, so soft and low, gentle and warm by her ear that she released the air from her lungs. She felt a reassuring hand on her head, smoothing her hair gently away from her face as the voice whispered in her ear.

"Ahh Babs, what did you get yourself into this time?"

"Didn't get much," Rob paused, "She had just gained consciousness for the first time when I went in there and she didn't seem to remember much of anything," Rob leaned his five foot ten inch frame against the wall as he talked into the phone with his back to Jan's room. He was well proportioned, and very fit for his age. "Doctors say the trauma was pretty severe. They can't be sure if she will even remember what happened," in his mind he wondered why she would want to remember any of it. It might only get her killed the next time. There was a silence while he listened to the person on the other end of the phone, and he pushed the fingers of his other hand back through his short black hair. The warmth of the cell phone on his ear matched the heated words he was hearing, and he didn't like the tone of it at all. He had known what they had thought, but to hear the implications spoken out loud unnerved him. Rob was sure that all the allegations were unfounded, or at least the ones that left her on the wrong side of the law. He had also been sure of it with another coworker a while back, and who had left this line of work, in what some would say was on unfavorable terms. "The nurse assured me that I would be able to see her again after the doctor's been in, and Okayed it. I'll report back after that or tomorrow, whichever comes first," he rang off quickly without any formalities.

He went back to watching the door to the room. His windbreaker was old with the logo of the sports team unreadable, and his shirt standard white-collar, button up. As he sat in the waiting room on the dirty orange chairs with the attached Formica table, his cold coffee sitting next to him on the chair, he mused over the past ten years. He had known Jan for all those years. They had worked together and had been friends most of the time, good friends. He was ten years older than her, and had taken her as a partner about two years after the department was officially formed. Over those years he had become protective of her, as a father would be to a daughter, even in her life outside of the job. That was part of his job anyway, to make sure that there was no life outside her job, nothing to pull her away from the team, and in that he knew he had failed. Once he had become her friend, he had allowed her more freedom. It was that freedom that now threatened to incarcerate her forever, guilty or not.

When he found her after the attack, he had half-expected Jan to be dead, although he knew if there were any way to have escaped it, she would have. He heard the call go out on the scanner in his old Camry. It was reported as a factory fire out on First Avenue and Highway A-1. It was a deserted, disintegrating area at best. The years had left the area abandoned and neglected after the factory had closed. It was now the type of area for drug dealers, drops and a place where the netherworld inhabited. It hadn't been the first time he had been to that warehouse on this assignment, and when he heard the call go out he immediately turned in that direction fearing the worst.

Rob and Jan had known that this attack might happen, that was why they had chosen to relocate Kevin, but didn't think it would be right after the trial. Jan was good at her job, and the only thing left in his mind, at the time he had heard the call, was that Jan had been removed from the picture permanently. How had they missed the warning signs? He wondered how she had, knowing just what she could do. He had not known nor could he understand it, and that still remained the mystery, and looked to stay that way for a while. When he got there the firefighters had just removed the two bodies and had been surprised to find anyone in the building. They were also surprised to find that one of them was still alive. So was Rob.

Kevin hadn't had a chance, his head was no longer round, and only a gross approximation of a head was left. They had just kidded themselves that they might be able to offer him some protection from that group, but now that the worst had happened there were even more pieces to be put together. Kevin had been threatened that if he testified he would be killed, but this was truly more than that. Kevin wasn't even recognizable, but when he had seen who the other body was, he had his fears confirmed. It had been Jan, but somehow she was still breathing and alive. It surprised him that she had made it through such an ordeal. Then again, Jan didn't give up easily. It must have been some fight, and Rob wondered if Jan had even gotten a good look at them. Most likely she had, and that would be the problem. Even if Jan never remembered, Rob wasn't sure if that would matter to her attackers. It would be easier to hide her and keep her safe if she had no knowledge of her past. On the other hand, Jan would also have no memory of how to deal with things as they came up, and could he protect her forever? The bosses might frown on that one. No one devoted his life to protecting another agent, not in this race. At best she was damaged goods, at worst a liability.

Rob flipped through an old magazine, glancing back and forth at the door. For right now he felt pretty sure that Jan was safe. The newspapers had reported two deaths at the factory. This was important for the time being. In fact, it may have been the truth for all Rob had known; it was touch and go for a couple of days. She had been registered under the name of Casandra Hughs. A name she had used from time to time when needed, but was truly unknown to most people. Only one other person knew this name, and he wasn't too worried about him just yet. This gave the department time. Since she had regained consciousness it was now becoming apparent that something would need to be done.

Rob dropped the magazine on the table and walked toward the door. The nurse was just leaving the room, and as he approached her she held up a warning finger. "Just checking to see if I could go in yet?"

"I'm afraid Miss Hughs has tired herself out, and will be asleep for a while yet," and the nurse, putting her hands on her hips, gave Rob one last look as if to say just try and get past me. He decided he'd rather take on the entire Marine Corp than this nurse.

"Guess I should get a fresh cup of coffee then," as he turned he felt that Jan would be safe with 'Sergeant Major Nurse' on duty for the moment. The next morning, once he was relieved of door watching duty for a while, he would have to pick up the surveillance equipment and wire her room. He had won the argument on video equipment at least, and it would only be sound. The thought of the conversation with the director he had just had angered him. Rob was unsure that this was the best way to protect her. He didn't want any unexpected visitors in Jan's room, but the department seemed to think this plan may smoke out those involved if they let out the information that she was alive, or worse yet, prove that she was implicated. And it was that part that scared him, that and the thought of drinking more hospital coffee.

An orderly was standing off to the side of the nurses' station and looking through the charts at hand. He stood about six-foot although it was hard to tell the way he slumped over the charts. The hospital cap hid all but the ends of his hair, and the tan on his well-defined arms drew no attention to him as Rob walked past. Once Rob had turned the corner, the orderly counted the seconds it would take for him to reach the elevator. Once the time was up, he looked around for the nurses. It was at that moment that the orderly, Ward, slipped the charts into the bin and moved quickly to the door of Jan's room entering silently. Taking in all aspects of the room with a single glance, he knew that there was nothing here yet to let them know that he had shown up. Good. He then dared a look at Jan. 'Shit.' She had been in rough spots before, but never this bad. He stared for just a moment, noticing that the breathing had tensed up. He smiled knowing she must be aware of someone in the room. That was a good sign. She was at least conscious. He walked over to her slowly, not wanting to scare her. He bent over and moved his hand gently across her head, "Ahh Babs, what did you get yourself into this time?" He rested his hand gently on her forehead.

The voice was not so much familiar as the feelings it evoked. Jan had a sense of true warmth and caring from the touch and the intonations in his voice. The hand resting on her head only added to the pleasure, yet she wasn't sure she could place any of it, or why she felt that way. At best she could only remember snippets of her life right now, and somehow this person didn't seem to be a part of those snippets. It seemed that she had only lived in the shadows, and somehow either gotten into or out of trouble most of the time. Jan could remember vague silhouettes of people that she worked with or helped, but mostly their faces and names remained somewhere out of reach. This person was different. He seemed to fit into both categories, but there was something else. There was something about him that touched her memory. And if he was a person she worked with, then why be so sly about coming into her hospital room, he had barely made any noise. It seemed to her as if she could feel his feelings of worry, and that took her off guard, how did she know what his feelings might be, did she know him that well, or was it all just guessing from the tone of his voice? One thing still bothered her, why did he feel the need to sneak in. Her head began to ache again with all the thoughts going through it.

"Don't honestly know yet. Who are you?" was all the reply she gave and then opened her eyes slowly. Best at this time to keep everyone guessing, even herself. He didn't remove his hand, he only moved closer. To most people this might have made them uncomfortable, to Jan, she only felt reassurance. She could see him clearly now. In fact, he had made a point to move into her line of sight so that she could. Jan could only guess that his height was around six foot, and weight, well it didn't look as if he had a problem with that, as she got a clear view of well toned muscle down the front of a very baggy hospital shirt. His face, although hard and chiseled with experience, was not threatening, and in fact she could see worry lines at the corners of his dark green eyes. Not a bad face to look at, and one Jan knew had featured in her dreams recently. She only wished she was able to make a direct connection to any specific dream, name, or lifetime.

"Shh. I really didn't expect you to respond. You've been through a lot of nasty stuff. The doctor will be here for rounds in about ten minutes so I'll have to be fast," he gently took his hand from Jan's head. "Name's

Ward and we have," there was a slight pause, "worked together at times. Right now, all you need to know is that whatever you remember, which I'm guessing is very little at this point, it is important to keep it to yourself until you can get your wits about you, and remember who is who." This time he stood up, "This may be the hard part, trust no one, not even me Babs until you remember them," at this he smiled and touched her hand. The name Babs rang a bell way off in the distance and the touch brought back emotions of love and warmth. Jan tried to smile, and Ward caught a glimpse of it. With his mind's eye, he also saw something else. "Do you trust me?" Jan just stared at him, unsure, "Close your eyes, and look with your heart," never once moving his hand, Jan felt safe and closed her eyes. All at once the pain in her head cleared and a thought drifted through her mind. It was his face, and his hand in hers, and they were together. The thought was hazy, and the why even hazier, but she was sure it was the two of them. Jan wondered how this man fit into the picture she was getting, and just why he was able to help her clear the storm long enough to get a clear thought of the past through it. Many things began to tumble through her mind and all she heard was a quiet, "Shh... all in good time." Jan opened her eyes to his smile, "one thing always to remember, you have to know who your friends and enemies are, and I think you still might be trying to remember who you really are. Rob's a good guy, but he is still just following orders," letting go of her hand, he moved toward the door. After looking through a little crack as he opened the door, he continued, "I'll be back soon, but by that time they'll have your room bugged and humming. It'll be harder to talk then, but I'll find a way to answer any questions you have." The door opened wider, "Take care Babs, I'll see you again soon, I promise," and he was gone. There was something unspoken, something she could not put a finger on, only a feeling, and that scared her in a very different way than the events prior to today have.

    One thing was true; she was still trying to put all the pieces together.

But this person, Ward, had asked her for nothing, and said he'd be willing to answer her questions when he could. He also seemed to be the only one concerned about how she was doing, besides the doctors, not wanting to know what she could remember. Only one thing bothered her about Ward, his desire not to be seen by Rob, or by anyone else by the look of things. This brought up some very interesting thoughts. His voice and mannerisms seemed to evoke only good feelings in her, whereas Rob's presence had done neither. Nor did his presence bring a sense of fear or of mistrust, she seemed to trust Rob but she didn't know why. The cloud was beginning to grow again, swirling relentlessly in her head. The fact that it seemed to have quieted while he was in the room and allowed her to see a bit of what he was feeling made this Ward character more interesting. Had she just imagined that? How many times had he been in here? Maybe she had just imagined it all, and was dreaming again, hoping so much for a normal life beyond this room that Ward had appeared as a part of her subconscious. She still had no real sense of self, or of any reality. She made a mental note to ask for as much reading material as possible to catch up on current events, learn about her surroundings, and to figure out her life.

If it was true and she was in a hospital, she still didn't know where the hospital was, or even where she lived. At the present time, even if she felt the need to, she could not escape. Except for the nurse, everyone she had seen, at the grand total of two now, she had somehow known, and neither person had elicited a fear response from her. That was a good sign. Kevin, the mystery man in all of this, was dead. Jan also knew she looked and felt like the inside of a sausage, and that the throbbing in her head had started again and was about to claim her sanity. She looked to the door expecting someone to open it just as the doctor walked in and started what was soon to become a regular routine to check on her progress.

Chapter 2

It was a week later when Jan was finally sitting upright, the collar off her neck for the first time, the IV removed from her arm, and the throbbing in her head beginning to clear completely. There was still no memory of the past, or who or what all these people meant to her. Ward had not been back at all during this time and she was beginning to believe he had been a hallucination. Rob had been in everyday. Most of the time had been spent just sitting and watching her, quietly from the chair in the corner of the room. At times she pretended to be asleep, and even with her eyes closed she was pretty sure that Rob was content to just come in, question her, and then to watch her. Not much conversation had gone on. Jan had secretly watched him wire, or bug, the room even though he thought she was sleeping. Every morning it had been the same routine, but not today. Today they just sat and looked at each other for a long time before Rob began the same old questioning routine.

"Has anyone else been in to see you?" this was a question that he hadn't asked before. He waited patiently for the answer.

"Only the doctors and nurses assigned to me," no need to bring Ward into this since she still wasn't sure that he wasn't a figment of her imagination. After all no one else had seen him.

"Are you sure?" It sounded as if he really didn't believe her.

"No one," she said calmly.

"Do you remember anything more about your attackers?" Rob always started there. When Jan chose not to say anything again this time, he continued in the same routine as before, "What were you doing there?"

"Where?" it was a valid response since Jan generally knew it wasn't in a well traveled place, but still had no memory of where the attack had accord.

"Jan, you know that I'm only trying to help here. How long have we known each other?" She could hear his exasperation, and she felt the same.

"By my calculations," Jan had not many choices where to look, but in answering this question she would make direct eye contact, "one week."

The questioning would end there today. Much to his disgust though, she opted to tell him nothing. Not even of her visit from Ward. Unsure of who was who in this game yet, it would be wise to keep all the players still guessing. This seemed very natural to Jan, like she had done this type of deception, and played this game before. Part of the reason for all this deception was that she herself only remembered bits and pieces of the events that had happened that day, and even more frightening, she only remembered pieces of her life. She wondered if she was the good guy, or the bad guy?

"My turn," gently raising the bed with the remote, "Let's try something easy. Where do I live?"

"That's not important right now, you could be in real danger," it wasn't a good sign, Rob turned away from her face deliberately, his voice betraying how worried he truly was. She could clearly see the short-sleeved white business shirt in need of ironing, and his crinkled tan pants. This meant to Jan that, who ever she was, she was important enough for him not to leave the hospital too much. He had probably slept in that shirt the night before. It was also plain to her that he was struggling with something and she wanted to figure out what it was.

"The problem is Rob, that's what's important to me right now. I have to find some of my own answers first, before I can uncork what happened. If you really knew me before then why not give me some of the information that I desperately need and want?" the question hung in the air, heavy. Rob turned slowly, the pain in his eyes visible to Jan. Frown lines between his eyes deepening. As he looked at her the pain seemed to transcend the room and enter into her feelings as well.

"Not yet. It could put you in danger," his gaze stayed on her, "and I won't do that."

"Have you ever thought that not knowing could put me in danger," their eyes locked and silence threatened to swallow them up. Until now Jan had really been at the mercy of all who surrounded her. Now she was ready to start taking charge. Jan felt the pull to look toward the door. Over time she had gotten use to knowing that someone was about to enter the room, but this time, it was not a well timed visit. The doctor entered the room before anything could be settled. With the silence broken, Rob went to sit down in the straight back chair again. Stalemate.

"Today we start therapy. Just for the neck and back. Cast should come off in about one to two more weeks," he flipped through the chart, "We will keep you here," and with that he paused to look at Rob. Rob gave a nod of approval and the doctor continued, "The loss of memory still has me concerned and I would like to keep you closely monitored. Run another CAT scan. I have another doctor that I would recommend come in and visit with you about any anxiety you might be feeling about the memory loss if that would be okay," and he looked again toward Rob, "Any questions?"

Jan's first thought was 'Yes!' but none you will answer, "No thanks, the memory will come back in its own time," and even as she said it, Jan knew that it was only a hope, and may not be a reality. Without another word the doctor went to the door and called the nurse in as he left.

The nurse came in with the wheelchair and with Rob's help they got Jan into the chair, "Are you following me there as well?" Jan didn't want to admit that she had gotten used to Rob's company, or even looked forward to it. It was definitely better than any of the newspapers she had received while she was here. Most of them had half the articles cut out and only old romantic fiction books to read she felt out of the loop. There didn't even seem to be any radio or TV to be had within miles of the place. She felt CNN deprived.

"No, I'll wait here for you," and again Rob took his place in the straight back chair, pulling out a cell phone and looking out the window as the nurse rolled Jan out of the room.

It was the first time she had left the room and a feeling of freedom breathed through her like the first whiff of spring. It was intoxicating. The hospital wasn't different than any other she had been in. And the fact that she could even remember being in a hospital before just led to more questions. Carefully, she pushed those questions to the back of her mind, and concentrated on the moment. The walls were an institutional gray white color that appeared in most hospitals. The tile floor was older but well cared for, and as clean as you would expect in any hospital. On the floor were lines of red, blue and yellow. It was obvious that these lines would lead you to different areas of the hospital. Jan paid closer attention as she watched the nurse take the red line to the black circle and then follow the blue line to the right and past one another black circle to enter an elevator. So far Jan had seen no doors leading to the outside, two nurses' stations with three people in them each, but this would be normal for almost any hospital as well. The other thing she didn't see was any other patients around, or lots of windows. Jan knew her room was not going to be on the first floor, but now was the first time she could figure out just what floor she was on. As the doors closed the nurse pressed the button for basement. As Jan concentrated on the elevator LCD, a strange thought crossed her mind. She wasn't even sure why she would be worried about taking a break, a break from what? She let the thought drift out as easily as it had drifted in. It had confused her and didn't seem like her own thought. Four, three, two, ground, and then they were in the basement. Jan now knew how to access the elevator and what floor her room was on. If she could get around the security, soon she would be able to explore the hospital more on her own.

The doors opened to the darker basement hallway. The light here was not natural, all flickering florescent. The journey had been quiet, and after the nurse passed the first two doors on the left, she entered through the third, backing Jan through it. Jan was introduced to the physical therapist in charge, and told what was about to happen, and the processes she would go through. After the initial assessment by the physical therapist, and the required reading of the chart, Jan was informed that her case would be turned over to a competent colleague in the field. Jan acknowledged this and the therapist in charge helped Jan get from the wheelchair onto the worktable. He gently worked her neck and took measurements with no talking, only slight almost inaudible sounds. After he was done he came back into her line of sight.

"Today we will start with only a couple of simple exercises. If you feel comfortable enough with these, you may do them back in your room twice a day, but don't over do it. Jake will take you through it and be assigned to your case. Each session will include exercises, heat therapy, massage, and a cold pack." There was nothing special about the instructions, or the therapist, "Jake will see you back here every other day while you're in the hospital and later we will discuss the other options you have. Depending on your progress he may need to adjust your schedule, and increase your exercise load as you progress out of the cast and the wheelchair."

Jake wandered into Jan's view and much to her credit, he mused, she didn't let on that she recognized him at all. It was the same six foot frame, except now she was sure of the height, but the hair was slightly different, and the glasses didn't do much to enhance his facial features. The hospital greens hid most of the rest of his shape from her as they had the other day. Jake, or Ward's, hands lay by his side relaxed and the smile only tipped one side of his face, but danced at the corners of his eyes. He clapped his hands, "Ready for a work out?" and he placed her back in the wheelchair and pushed her to the back of the room. Jan chose to remain quiet, letting whatever thoughts drift through her mind, as this seemed to bring about a new sense of surrounding. Her thoughts drifted toward feelings of pride and protection, both of these thoughts confused her, as again they didn't feel like thoughts that belonged to her.

"Not a great disguise," Jan said after the therapist had left, "Some how I would have expected more."

"I have a ton, but any more than this and you might not recognize me," he sat down above Jan's head and placed his hands on each side of her head. His hands felt warm and comforting, "and they aren't going to look for me here. Right now they are watching your room because they are afraid I am going to come into your room and try to whisk you away," at that he smiled completely allowing his eyes to join in without restraint. It seemed only a smile that she would have seen, one not shared with many, "That's why Rob has been there most of the time, to protect you from me. If he's not been by your door, it's been Sally." He placed a heating pad on her neck, and sat waiting for her muscles to loosen.

"Do you know what you're doing here?" the thought had crossed her mind as he removed the heat and began to gently move her head toward her right shoulder. It also concerned her that he knew who was watching her, when she didn't even know.

"Not to worry, I do have a medical degree among other things I'm certified to do," he paused and gently moved Jan's head back to center, "Yes, it's real, and," the thought had crossed Jan's mind, but she had never spoken it out loud. There was a pause to add emphasis to the next part, and his voice deepened, "I would be the last one to hurt you," as that thought bounced around in Jan's head he moved her head toward the left shoulder. "You need to tell me if you are feeling any sharp pains, pretty much I'll stop when I feel you tense up, now, for more important business Babs. We only have a short time every other day, and you have lots of questions that aren't going to get answered any other way, at least Rob won't give you the answers right now. Shoot."

"How do I know you're going to tell me the truth?" the thought crossed her mind.

"You don't. But you aren't going to get any answers from them until they know if you have any of your memory back, and maybe not even then if they still suspect you," he gently continued to rock Jan's head back and forth. Jan felt the muscles tense, but he always seemed to stop just before there would have been pain, "Now, try it once yourself."

"Not easy," as Jan slowly moved her head to her right shoulder, "Where was I born?"

"Interesting place to start. New Mexico."

"And you?"

"Now that's more like the Jan I know, Wisconsin."

"Do I have any family?"

"No, not that you keep in contact with anymore anyway, and neither do I."

"Do we work, ouch, together?" Jan had tried to move her head just a little too far. He placed his hands on each side of her head and gently moved it back to center for her.

"Slow the movement down a bit and you'll be able to stretch your muscles out more. We used to work together on occasion, that's how we first met and got to know each other, but not anymore."

"Why?"

"Long answer," he stopped her head, "Enough of that for now, you're doing a bit too much. Let me help you roll over," And as she did she noticed that the table she was on was also a massage table, and the way he had placed her on the table originally made it just perfect for the placement of her face as she turned over for the massage part of the routine. "The short answer is that I don't work for them anymore. Let's just say it started with a difference of philosophy for right now, and leave it at that."

Jan let that sink in as Ward undid the ties on the back of the grown, exposing her back. He felt her tense, "How well do I know you?"

"Well enough," and he sounded sure of himself, "Now relax as I go and get the heating pack, otherwise it won't do you any good." Jan heard him leave, solid steps, not one bit hesitant of where he was going or what he was doing. Jan let the bits of information seep into her brain while he was gone. He didn't seem to hesitate on giving her the answers she needed or wanted to know, but he wasn't volunteering anything more either. In itself, that may not be such a bad thing. Too much information could just muddle up what pieces she had. The best thing was that he didn't seem to be going anywhere. Jan was lost in thought and didn't hear him return. Surprised, Jan jumped a bit when she felt his hand on her back.

"Not like you," he rested his free hand on her shoulder to calm her, "I didn't mean to scare you," his hand moved back to the heating pack, "Tell me if this is too hot. I have some other work to do, but I'll be back in about fifteen minutes."

"So you really do work here?" There was amusement in her voice.

"For now," and he left. She let the quiet minutes be just that, quiet. Although she could hear other things going on in the room, most of the room was out of her sight. The table she was laying on was in the back of the room, in the corner, away from everyone else. This brought a new thought to her mind. It was important to start putting the questions in order of what she needed to know first, and he seemed to know all there was about her and her nothing of him. That would come later, she was quite sure. Could she sort out what might be true and what wasn't? For now she decided that any information she could get would be useful no matter what the amount of truthfulness was. As it was, he had turned out not to be a figment of her imagination, and he seemed to care. Two steps in the right direction. Ward had moved to the other side of the room and although he looked as if he was filling in paperwork, his face kept turning to look at Jan.

He didn't want to let his eyes off of her. Her condition was much better and there would barely be any scars. She needed the time to think, and he was the only one that could help her find herself. In the past he would have thought that anyone saying that was pretty full of himself, but experience had led him to believe that it was true. As he stood doodling with his pencil on paper, he wondered just how safe she would be with the department. He hadn't been. Rob would keep her as safe as he could, he always did, but then again he was a by the book man most of the time. Ward was also very certain now that he had had a chance to assess her condition that Jan was in no shape to protect herself. He lost his thoughts and just openly stared at Jan for a few minutes wishing things had been different a month ago. If they had, neither one of them would be here now. Sensing that he was beginning to draw attention to himself he put the charts down.

She heard the steady footsteps Ward made as he returned to her table, and for some reason she didn't feel so alone any more, "What should I call you?"

"Call me Jake here. Later we might discuss something else," she couldn't see the smile, but she could feel the warmth of it and hear the twinkle in his voice.

"You called me Babs, why?"

"You hated it when I called you babe," he took the heating pack from her back, "Do you mind?"

"Not really, but it might be better if you stick to Jan, at least until I know you better," Jan felt his finger trace her spine, quickly, and then it was gone, almost as if it never had happened. All the short answers started to annoy her she wanted something more.

"First rule is never give away too much information in our business," Ward didn't wait for her to voice her question. She wasn't sure of how he knew, but he had known that her next question had to do with all the short answers she was getting. It seemed unusual that he had now done that twice with her. The thought ran through her mind, 'Do we really know each other that well?' Jan felt his hands splayed across her back, and although it wasn't a feeling she should have been used to, his hands felt normal and natural covering the width of her back.

"Have you done this before?" Glad he couldn't see her face as she asked this question.

"Lots," and he let his voice pause before he went on with a chuckle. "Just gave away three back rubs today to other patients besides you," but they both knew that wasn't what she was talking about.

"You know what I meant," Jan voice sounded more accusing, and annoyed, than she meant it to. She wanted to know just how well he knew her and he wasn't giving her anything.

"Yah, I do." He continued massaging the back of her neck and then let his hands slip down to check out the tape on the ribs. The absence of the warmth of his hands when they were on the taped area disturbed her, even though his hands were still on her. As if he sensed this, he moved one hand off the tape, and back up to her shoulder where Jan could feel the warmth of his touch again. Jan felt the tensions ease from her body, along with her muscles, "Your ribs are feeling pretty good. Should be up and around pretty soon without all this tape and hardware."

"Who was Kevin?" Ward's hands never missed a beat; it was if nothing she could ask would surprise him.

"Worked in the drug world and pretty high up. Decided to turn in his bosses once the agency got onto him," it was now time to put a cold pack on her shoulders, "Not a healthy thing to do as you may have figured out. That's why you're here and he's dead," he adjusted the ice pack and placed a towel over the top of it, "I'll be back in about ten minutes, and then we will be finished for the day."

Jan had time to think now. If Ward was telling her the truth, then she was from New Mexico and he was from Wisconsin. This would mean that they were not related, and knew each other another way. Running through the rest of the information she had gotten, both verbal and nonverbal, he seemed to know what she did for a living, and had done the same type of work at one time himself. But for some reason, he didn't work with her or them anymore. Jan was letting the information that she had gained and memories she had merge together. From what she knew now she had figured out that she was supposed to provide some kind of protection for Kevin, and in some way she had failed in her duties toward him. What she was still unsure of was why she had been there and why was she unable to protect him. In one of her dreams she had had a vivid recollection of talking and arguing, with a nameless person. Jan had to now assume that this person's name was Kevin. What she couldn't remember is what had started the argument. She wondered if it had been the topic of travel, and where they were going, or should go?

"Not bad," Ward had returned, but somehow, she didn't think he was referring to the ice pack or her injuries. There was something else going on here. She couldn't put her finger on it and he seemed to have a good handle on it.

"I have so many more questions that I need answers to. Is there anyway I can see you sooner? Two days will feel like an eternity," Jan rolled over with his help. She hated the feeling of needing anyone's help.

"I will be here as long as you are here, but I think you need to have some time to think, and process the answers you do have for now, before you get anymore from me. I only have one reason to be here," Ward looked straight into her eyes, "I am here for you." He took a shallow breath and continued, "It won't last forever." There it was again, his uncanny sense to understand what was bothering her.

"What if I tell Rob about you?" Their eyes riveted to each other, never unlocking. His gaze seemed to hold hers and she couldn't look away. It was a bluff, and maybe not even a good one. And once said, she wanted to take it back.

"You won't." Slowly a smile crept up on him and softened his face. He could see the old Jan beginning to surface, and felt hope.

"How can you be so sure?" Jan watched as Ward turned to get the wheelchair.

"Let me think," pretending to really concentrate. "If you do, I disappear; you don't get anymore of the answers you want. By the way, if you are ready next time, I'll give you some special exercises," and that was the end of that. Of course he was right, it was an empty threat to see what he would do, how sure of himself he was. He had called the bluff and he was very sure of himself. As Jan got into the chair, she thought of one last question for the day.

"If you called me Babs, what did I call you?" Defeated she changed the topic. Ward pushed her toward the door and her nurse that was waiting for her there.

"Remember, only do the exercises we showed you today when you feel comfortable, rested, and relaxed this will help you recover even faster," Ward leaned over and placed his lips close enough to brush her ear and she could feel the warmth of his breath tickling her ear, "You always called me

Trouble." It was said in a lowered voice that rumbled up from the depths of his being and solely for her ears. It should have made her worry, it would have made any other woman worry, but an inner voice, and gut feeling, reassured her that she was truly safe with him.

The nurse didn't speak on the way back up in the elevator, and as Jan got farther from the basement, she began to feel an empty spot grow within her. She knew that in a couple of days she would again see Ward, but she couldn't shake the feeling that the sooner she saw him the better she would be. There had been a connection there that she hadn't felt with anyone else that she had met so far. She made a note that she needed to cross check the answers she had gotten with Rob, if he would answer any of them.

Jan took notice of the route back up to her floor. As they left the elevator on the fifth floor, she looked for any other ways off of the floor, other elevators, stairs, or any way people could move from one floor to another. What she did see shook her to the core. There seemed to be no other way on, or off the fifth floor. There were other hallways, but all dead-ended without any other way to go down. There were no other people around in the halls except the staff and, no one smiled.

To other people, that may not have seemed important, but to Jan who could feel and sense the unhappiness or emptiness that surrounded her, it sent a cold chill down her spine. How could she know what they were feeling? It must have been something she was picking up from their faces. Was she picking up the emotions from their actions, or was it something else she wondered? As she was pushed down the hall she began to think. Even if her condition bettered, she wondered if any of these people working on the fifth floor would allow her to leave. Was she a prisoner of the people that she had worked with, as Ward had alluded too? Just as they got to her room she could over hear Rob on the cell phone completing a conversation with someone that must have more influence over him and what he was to be doing.

"... it just may take more time, ... no..... the doctor says she may or may not remember," it seemed he had more information on her condition than she did, but this time he wasn't trying to hide it as much as before. In fact, it seemed like he wanted her to hear his side of the conversation. When she entered the room he continued the conversation with his attention half on her, "...couple more days, that's all I want....Thanks."

Jan started to sense something as he gazed at her. It seemed as if his thoughts were drifting through her mind, and something he was thinking, or feeling, wasn't right. She wasn't sure that they were his thoughts, but she knew one thing, they weren't her thoughts either. What he was about to say, Jan sensed, was not the complete truth, there was something else to it. There was something that he didn't want to share. Jan stared at her lap for a moment, letting her neck stretch a bit. Just how could she be sure of the information Rob would give her, and even before that question, she had to have the answer to who she could trust? Thinking back, as unreal as it seemed, she thought she had picked up on some of Ward's thoughts during the therapy session. There was an easy familiarity she had felt with him. And at the time, even though it hadn't seemed too strange, he had answered questions before she had time to ask them. Letting the thoughts pass from her mind for now, she listened to what Rob had to say.

"I know this has been hard on you, and the department really wants to give you all the time you need to recover, but they have been hoping that you might be ready to share some information," his expression looked slightly pained as he moved so that she could see his face better. The creases between his eyes and around his mouth seemed to have grown deeper, making him look tired. Everything suggested that this path was not the one he wanted.

"Who are they?" her voice lay heavy in silence that followed from Rob. "This hasn't been easy for you Rob; I know that you care about me.

And right now, even as I begin to remember some things, it is only in bits and pieces, of little use to you and even less to me. If I thought it would do you any good, you would be the first I would tell," okay, that was a small lie, "Tell me, is the surveillance equipment in here to protect me, or just to collect information?" Rob's face didn't give anything away. Silence lingered for a while. Then he smiled.

"O.K. Jan. We both know that you have some of your memory back, and that neither one of us wants to be the first to share information, so let's call a truce," he stood up from the chair he had seemed to have inhabited for days. Walked over to the wheelchair and squatted down to look Jan straight in the eye. It was a completely different feeling than when Ward had done it, "I've worked with you and I know that even if you do or don't remember who you are, you won't give anything away unless you feel that it won't compromise anyone. It also seems that some of your skills may be returning even if you have no idea what to do with them, or more importantly, even what they are. So let's say I give you a piece of information and you try and give me one. O.K.?"

"Alright," it sounded to be a fair trade, and this way, maybe, she could at least check out a couple of facts, "I can remember some faces, Kevin's for one I believe, and I remember an argument with him just before the accident, not what the argument had been. It took place away from the attacked, I think, I'm not sure, but for now that is all I can remember." She heard the sigh escape his lips and the frown lines seemed a little less pronounced. His whole body seemed to relax just a little, and he stood and walked toward the window. He turned and looked out for only a second before he turned back to face her and spoke.

"It's a start and it will keep them off your back for a while longer. Now what would you like to know?"

"Where am I from?" it seemed repetitive, but a necessity to check out just who she could trust.

"As far as I know, somewhere in the southwest. Never knew much more than that, nor did I ask," simple, but enough to confirm what Ward had said.

"Let's try for where are we now?" this may be pushing it, but she had to try.

"They won't let me tell you. They feel you will be safer if you don't know. Won't let anything slip then," he was still looking out the window.

"Who would I let it slip to? You have complete control over all my comings and goings," Jan knew she wouldn't get a response to this, and even as she asked the question Rob just smiled.

"My turn. What else do you have for me?" that me actually meant us, and Jan knew that to give just a touch more information might just get her a bit more freedom.

"The attack is still very fuzzy, but there were at least three people that I was aware of," Jan waited just a few minutes, and then looking Rob straight in the eyes she asked, "Who is all the surveillance for, me, or others?"

"Both." Rob stood and walked back to the door, "Just in case someone wanted to come in and finish what they started, and just in case you talked in your sleep."

"Well, do I?" Rob was halfway out the door.

"What?" Rob turned back to look at her, a quizzical expression on his face.

"Do I talk in my sleep?" it was just a second before Rob let out a small laugh. The smile touched both his mouth and his eyes. Her personality was peeking through.

"Not yet, but I keep hoping" Rob leaned against the door frame, "We are only monitoring by sound, as you may already have guessed or know, so you don't have to worry about anything else," there was a pause, "just yet." Jan wasn't sure if that was a threat or a promise.

"Well let me know if I start," Rob smiled and stepped out.

It wasn't until later that day, after she reread the censored papers and flipped through the old books one more time to help her occupy the empty spots in her day, that Jan allowed herself to drift into a deep sleep. At first, as she lay quietly in the hospital bed, her eyes closed and her thoughts cleared from everything that had transpired during the day.

When her mind seemed as white as the starched sheets on the bed, she began to focus in on just herself, and her breathing. At first Jan took stock of every muscle in her body, tightening it and then relaxing it, letting the stress and fatigue of the day drift away. Next, Jan concentrated on just one image, and that was of herself since this was the information she was wanted most. This always seemed to bring on more focused dreams; she had discovered this a couple of days ago. Jan knew it was a meditation trick she had learned years ago, but was unsure of when she had learned it, or why. The dreams had changed over the three weeks that she had been in the hospital as her meditation pattern had improved. At first the dreams had been disorganized, a barrage of colors and images that had made no sense at all. Now, when the dreams came to her, they were clear and had a purpose. Sometimes the dreams didn't come, and sometimes she couldn't make any sense out of them, but this time the dream did come to her.

It was late in the day when she stepped out of the car. She had been driving and Kevin had been in the passenger seat. It had been warm; yes she could see the sweat on his forehead and her hair was tied back. The trip up until then had been very quiet. Kevin had been worried about something, but his thoughts weren't clear, and his confusion bounced off Jan's mind keeping her from getting a clear idea of what was going on. The car was old, not one she had driven before, or could remember owning. Then she swung the car into an empty parking lot and parked. She had seen this place before but couldn't identify it. It was a nondescript building with a gray facade.

Small rectangular windows lined the upper levels of the building. The parking lot was spacious, concrete in need of too many repairs, and empty. Low trees and unkempt landscaping surrounded it. Jan noticed herself looking around for something, or someone. Yes, she was checking the area, it was standard procedure, but what she was looking for she couldn't remember. Someone else, a friend, yes, that was who Kevin was looking for. He pointed to the building and Jan saw herself shake her head no. The argument continued in her dream without sounds, and then they went into the building, Jan running after Kevin as he, in a fit of rage, left and headed toward the building, this time his thoughts focused and readable. Once inside of the building, Jan was aware of how open and ugly the space seemed to be. Scarred from years of use as a factory, it seemed to have lost all ambition for life or character, and now sat lifeless and rundown. Kevin was standing in a large open spot. What was he going to do? Jan saw herself start for him, trying to stop him, pull him away, and then he yelled. This time the dream carried a clear sound to her waiting ears. She heard him yell a name, Sandra. Then all went black as the dream fell away, leaving her with more unanswered questions than when the dream started again her situation had changed. Staying in complete control of her thoughts, she watched.

    She could feel the warmth of the sun on her back and face, and as she opened her mind's eye to the dream, the soft golden sand became clear. She felt the pressure of hands on her back, a good feeling, massaging, exploring, tempting, and tracing the curves of her body. Jan felt lazy and relaxed in this dream. There wasn't any sound here either, and more important no one who was unfamiliar. Watching the dream unfold like a television show, Jan decided that it was time to try and discover her companion. Trying to take control of the dream, Jan willed herself to turn over slowly and easily to see the face of her companion. As she began to turn she was suddenly awakened by the sound of her hospital door and reality. She lost the dream as the nurse entered with the tray of rubbery, tasteless food that was supposed to be her supper.

Jan lay there quietly, unmoving; with eyes closed, hoping to get the dream back as the tray was placed before her. The nurse only turned and left the room, making no announcement to the fact that the meal was present, or that Jan should eat it. Not caring if Jan was awake or asleep as she left. For Jan it was too late to reclaim the dream, it was gone, and so was the identity of the companion with it. Part of the dream was familiar, the argument. She had seen that part before, in the midst of the muddled images that had plagued her many times at rest. From what she had sensed, the argument must have taken place outside of the factory. But this time the dream had been different. It had gone into more detail and had been placed in an order for her to be able to decipher it more clearly, but then it had changed. Jan attributed this to the meditation techniques she used, and had gotten so much better at using.

Jan felt puzzled though as to why the two dreams had come together. Why had the one dream placed her at a beach with another person? What was the link, the information she was supposed to connect? No matter how hard she tried she couldn't see a connection. She decided to attempt the plate of food placed before her, and to spend more time later on analyzing the second dream she had just had. As Jan placed the fork through the crusted top layer of mashed potatoes, she wondered what Ward's take on the second dream would be? She made a mental note that she may want to discuss this with him in the days to come.

Chapter 3

It had been two days since she had seen or talked to Ward, but the time hadn't been wasted. The nurse came to pick Jan up for physical therapy, and by working together with the nurse Jan was able to get herself into the wheelchair. Jan had been practicing getting out of bed when no one was around. One of those times she thought that she would need to call for help as she slid off the bed and almost fell to the floor, but she had managed to right herself. All these experiences had made her stronger, even if she tried not to let her slow progress depress her. It had been almost two days since she had seen Rob as well, or anyone else besides the hospital staff. It had been strange to be on her own and alone for so long of a period. Jan had come to expect the continuous questions, and even the uneasy company that Rob had provided. He had known Jan long before this, and the more time she spent with Rob, the more she had begun to learn about who she was even when he didn't tell her anything. It was the realization of what type of work she may have done before, that made her feel uneasy. Jan had sensed that he had been around but he hadn't come in to go through his regular questioning routine. She wondered if it was as simple as the fact that he had been happy with the little tidbits of information she had given him, or was there something else. As they left the room Jan tried to look around to see if he was there, but saw no one, and nothing unusual. Curiosity peaked and she initiated a conversation with the nurse, "I haven't seen my friend around recently. Do you happen to know where he is?"

"He's been in and out the last two days," the nurse commented in a flat tone and then continued along the floor lines past the dot giving no indication that she in any way wanted to or would be involved in a conversation.

"Does that mean he isn't worried about me any longer?" Jan knew this was not the case at all. Something had happened and she just didn't know all the details, and not knowing was worse.

"No." the answer was simple for the nurse, and she never missed a step.

"Where are we?" If she couldn't find out anything about Rob then why not try for other information Jan thought.

"In a hospital," they entered the stainless steal elevator.

"I mean ..." Jan tried to turn to look at the nurse.

"I know what you mean, but that is all I am allowed to tell you," the doors slid closed and the rest of the journey to therapy was quiet.

As Jan entered the therapy room this time she was met by Ward's smile and taken to the back table in quiet. Ward noticed the frustration on her face and in her mind. She noticed that Ward took the wheelchair without effort relieving the nurse of her duty, and moved it along as if Jan and the chair were no more than the weight of a feather. Jan felt that Ward had an attitude of possession of the occupant of the wheelchair and control of his surroundings. There was also a hint of lightheartedness to his step as if she had amused him. Jan was glad to see a face that she had begun to trust, and relaxed as he ushered her to the back of the room. She wasn't sure how she felt about being his entertainment. The corner of the large white room was the same corner that Ward put her in before. It was away from most of the other tables, quieter, so that with a lowered tone, they couldn't be over heard. Ward wheeled the chair around easily and now smiled a warm and generous smile, the kind that included the corners of his eyes, right at Jan, and said in a low deep voice with just a hint of mischief, "D' ya miss me?"

"Well," Jan returned his smile as she pretended to contemplate her answer. If she was going to be entertainment then she was going to do it right, "I'm not sure. Are you the one who brought me a rubbery, tasteless supper last night, or the one that cleaned the room this morning?"

"Could be, but probably not, seeing that I am here doing therapy right now and not emptying the bed pans upstairs," he lifted her effortlessly onto the table without even waiting for her to help this time. "Plus, I would bring you nothing but the best fish dinners you have ever tasted and your room would be filled with orchids and calla lilies of every color if it wouldn't draw undesired attention to you," Jan lifted the corner of her eyebrow. Somewhere deep inside her she knew that those references meant something, but she still couldn't put a finger on it. "Guess I'm going to have to make you pay for those meal and maid comments today, let's say twice the workout then."

"Sounds quite unfair to me," Jan laid back and relaxed, pretending to be put out as the routine started, "I have really had a hard time waiting to see and talk with you," the corner of his eyebrow lifted, and his smile slipped sideways, "to ask more questions. Is there any way we could get a bit more time today?" The warmth of the heating pad felt good.

"Ten minutes, probably not any more. Let's get started," his voice was more businesslike. Ward moved Jan's head to the left and then to the right. The feel of his hands on the side of her head calmed her and yet she was anxious because they made her feel as if she were missing something that should be so clear.

"Where are we?" It was simple, yet Jan was at a disadvantage not being able to see Ward's face. Somehow though, she knew that didn't matter anymore, knowing she would be able to tell what he was thinking before he said it. It was becoming familiar to know most people's feelings lately although she still just wasn't sure why or how she was able to do that.

"Tucson," Ward continued to move her head back and forth.

"It isn't the same town the factory is in, is it?" she felt his surprise, "I'm beginning to remember bits and pieces, nothing that makes any sense though."

"I see. No," with care he continued, "that was about 500 miles from here on the Pacific Coast."

"Who do we work for?" Jan had asked this especially to get more information out of and about Ward. Information Rob wouldn't give her. Ward continued with the exercises, being careful not to move her head too far to the left or right.

"We don't work for the same people anymore remember," Jan watched the ceiling lights move in the semi circular manner feeling only amusement from Ward. "You still work for a little known governmental department or agency. Paranormal Enforcement Department, or 'PED' for short, that creates and then takes advantage of people like us, and not always for the good of others, as they would lead you to believe. I used to think that I was truly being of service when I worked for them just like you did or do, but I don't believe that to be true anymore, at least for myself."

"I guess that I must still believe that I am being helpful," Jan wasn't sure what she thought. Things were getting weirder by the minute.

"That has been a source of discussion with us before," Ward moved around the table. She could feel that the discussion had not always been calm.

"Did we ever reach any agreement?" Jan tried to watch Ward's body language.

"Do you think we'd be here if we did?" his muscles had stiffened for only a moment before he again focused on the job at hand.

Jan chose to let the last comments go, time was too short to get into a discussion of who was right or wrong, and she had the feeling that they had never settled it anyway. He seemed to know a lot about her and she had very little memory of him right now. This seemed to please him in some way and irritate them both in others. Then there was this PED department that she had to know more about.

"What did you say the department was, PED? I find that really hard to believe," Jan was skeptical, and Ward was glad to see the Jan he knew was still there. She couldn't see his smile but it beamed across his face.

"Believe it or not Babs, but it does exist. No matter how bad you think the name is," he went on with his assessment, "Let's move on to a different topic for now. How's the meditation going?"

"I have been having dreams," for now she would let him steer the conversation, "but they have only given me bits and pieces of information. As I meditate more, different parts seem to become clearer, but I never get the whole picture and it is frustrating me to no end," she thought for a moment on what she had just learned before continuing. How did he know she was meditating? Maybe it was a standard physical training for them, "I'm even able to control the dreams at times but just not enough."

"I'm glad your meditations and dreams are becoming helpful to regain your memory. It will take some time so don't try and rush things. That's why I'm here, and by the way, the job is where we differed as of late, whether it is better to work for them, or hide from them. On other points we were always in perfect harmony," Jan tensed for a minute and let what he said soak in. It had been as if her thoughts were out loud. Ward saw this, and realized that she had tensed up again. Ward hadn't meant to say it. It had just slipped out. He had let himself get too comfortable with her too fast. He would have to control himself better or risk losing her. She had always been the one who he could open up to; be himself. Slowly he closed down his mind just a little.

"I didn't ask that question out loud, did I?" Jan was now very concerned about the way he so casually, so easily, seemed to know what she thought.

"No, now turn over," Jan did as she was told, and tried to sneak a peek at Ward. The tone in her voice seemed to confirm his suspicions. She was unable to see his face, but his body was just as relaxed as it had been when they started. What had he said, people like us. A whole new set of questions entered her mind at one time, but she refused to deal with them right away, other things had to be answered first.

"Since you seem to know where I work, do you know what I was working on?" Jan tried to steer the conversation back into clear waters. Ward continued with the topic knowing that Jan would want the information on what she had been working on first. Years of training would dictate that, and he tried very hard not to get ahead of her again.

"I had a chance to investigate a bit on what you were working on, and found out that your basic mission was to keep Kevin Mason safe from the drug cartel that he had given evidence on. In general, it would be a routine mission for most of us. Something went wrong, as you know, and you ended up in the factory in worse shape than you have ever been before. I'm not sure of much beyond that; no one is sure why you were there at the factory. There have been theories, some not so complementary, seeing that you should have seen an attack coming, and the drop off place was not anywhere near there. Most, like Rob and I, believe there must have been a good reason for you to be there."

"That's all you have for me?" it seemed to have too many missing pieces yet. It also struck her funny that Ward had referred to Rob in a friendly tone.

"In a nutshell, yes," Ward placed the heating pad on her shoulders again, and bent over to see her face as she gently tilted her head to see him,

"There is more to it, but that's mostly hearsay, and not reliable at that. I don't deal in hearsay, and neither should you. In the department your job is to provide protection, detection, and deception. It was the last one that gave me the most problems when they began to practice it on me. Now, relax as I go help Mr. Green with his new hip. Try to meditate a bit more; it may help to answer some of your questions as well as organize what information you now have to put with it." He walked away knowing that he should have told her more about herself, and the special skills she had. 'Time,' he thought, 'give it time.'

Again, Ward seemed to know more about her than she knew about him, Jan mused as she watched him walk away in his green hospital outfit. That was fair considering she was still trying to regain her memory she guessed, but for him to know what was going on in her mind, both now and the last time, seemed to be far beyond normal, or was it. When Ward returned she would ask him more about the PED. Jan felt the heat sink into the upper levels of her muscles and began to relax. Maybe meditation was an answer to this moment since she was already relaxed. The last time she meditated her thoughts had organized into groups. Jan was able to start to sort out the information and bring memories safely to the surface. What she really did want to know was who was on the beach with her. She started to relax all of her muscles and then to empty her mind of all her questions and even the answers from earlier, she focused on her breathing. This time she did not sleep, but allowed her mind to bring up the images, thoughts, and feelings that lingered amongst the darkest corners.

Within moments she was back on the beach, the warmth of the soft golden sand all around her, and the gentle pressure of strong, warm hands on her back and moving lower. Jan heard the lapping of the ocean in the farthest reaches of her mind. Wherever this was it was a good place. Jan relaxed as the memory of the hands slowly smoothed away the concerns of the day, week, and month. She enjoyed the moment for a minute and was glad that these were the first thoughts to drift through her mind. The beach memory had come from a particularly busy time of her life, she could tell by the tension she felt in the dream, and how good the back rub felt. It was a comfortable silence that surrounded her on the beach, as the sounds of the ocean filtered through her mind, the seals, the seagulls, and the breeze on the beach. Jan realized that it was the first time sound had clearly come through. There was no talking between her and the stranger, just the relaxed company they shared. Enjoying the dream, but wanting more, she again decided to try and discover the identity of her companion on the beach. Taking control of her dream, Jan imagined herself turning over on the beach. The sand in between her fingers as she pushed herself up, and as she opened her eyes she could see Ward.

"Wait a minute there," Ward appeared in her line of sight, the white of the hospital behind him, the green hospital garb confusing her, and the blue sky and salted sea air mixing eerily with reality. Jan began to wonder if he was part of the dream, or had the dream ended when he came back over. She wondered, with a frown beginning to form on her face, if she would ever discover the identity of the person with her on that beach. Was it a trick of her subconscious? Ward had been the only one to truly show her compassion and caring, and this made Jan wonder if her mind was trying to have him be the one in the beach picture. "It's not time to turn back over," there was a pause as their eyes met, "I'm not done with you," and somehow Jan knew as a lopsided smile appeared to soften his face, that he didn't only mean the therapy, "This is my favorite part," and his voice barely contained his wicked delight. Jan blushed and quickly changed the topic.

"What happened to Rob," Jan thought it was best to steer the conversation back to something safe, business maybe. "I haven't seen him since we last saw each other two days ago," Ward started to massage her shoulders and work the kinks out.

"There's been a break in the case from what I hear, and he's off to try and discover the guys who did this to you and killed Kevin. He's a good guy, and takes care of you like you were his own daughter. That may cause him some trouble higher up very soon. He's never been married, or had kids. You were it," Ward let his hands gently massage the area of the rib cage that was taped. Jan tensed suddenly. She recognized these hands that were on her now. They were the same hands that had been in both of the beach dreams. Ward pretended not to notice the reason for the tension, but Jan knew that somehow he knew. There was that awareness that she had had some recognition of him. The words were unspoken, but the feeling still existed, and she knew it pleased him, "Is that sore?" It was back to the safe conversation, but the tone of his voice was more intimate now.

"No, it's O.K." They chose to spend the next few minutes in silence. Ward had enjoyed the feeling that Jan recognized him in one way; he smiled and let the moment last for as long as it could. Jan on the other hand, was letting this new knowledge settle in. Again more questions that would have to wait came to mind. She wondered, 'Were they more than friends?' If so, what kind of more were they if he felt the need to hide from Rob? And lastly, 'Did she have the same type of insight as he did?'

"Relax, time will take care of some of the questions Babs," his voice was soothing and Jan, relying solely on instinct now, did just that. The massage seemed to go on forever; to Jan, nothing but the feeling of them being together mattered for the next few minutes. Ward felt her muscles relax under his hands and he began to work the muscles in ways that seemed to make them feel stronger, and with what seemed intimate knowledge of what to do just for her. Jan felt the energy of her muscles increase, and a new bond between them began to be forged.

"Have you been up to my room in the last couple of days?" Her voice was just as relaxed as her muscles. To her ears it sounded lazy.

"Not easy to do, so I try just to stay down here out of their way. I do keep up with your progress though. I know that in a couple of days, before I see you again, they will have the casts removed. This information is easy to get for any patient I would work with." His hands drifted lazily down the center of her back, and his voice lowered, deepened into something else, "It's been hard not to come up to see you though."

"I have noticed," teasingly she paused. She had also noticed the emotion in his voice but chose to ignore it, "that the room and floor I'm on is sparse, and there seems to be no other people around except for staff. Am I on a secured floor?" Jan had wondered this since the last visit. With no other patients around she had wondered if the staff as well as Rob were involved in her protection, or incarceration.

"Secured?" amusement again filled his voice, "You're in lock up, otherwise known as jail. This means that the staff are all up there to watch you."

"I thought I wasn't the one in trouble, that it was just hearsay?" Jan felt a rush of concern. There was a familiar old feeling churning in her stomach. One she knew had helped her out many other times.

"You're not; not yet. It was the safest place to keep you, and to keep your identity a secret from those who would want to harm you. As far as anyone else knows, you're dead," Ward was almost finished with the massage. The last sentence didn't take Jan by surprise. It was a relief to know that her assailants thought that they had done their job and were now out of the picture. But she could tell that Ward didn't think this was true, "Happily Rob didn't let me think you were dead."

"You said earlier 'people like us', what did you mean?" Jan's thoughts drifted off to Rob and the fact that he must have somehow let Ward know she was alive, and injured. It put a new twist on things. The massage ended and Jan waited for both the answer and the cold pack. Instead his hands rested gently on her back, as if trying to decide how much would be prudent to tell her. He had waited a long time for this question.

"Part of that answer you already know. You're beginning to sense the feelings and thoughts of people around you again; it feels as if their thoughts just drift right into your head, later you will become more focused again, and in control. As strange as it may sound right now, but that's why I have been able to answer some of your questions before you've had a chance to ask them. Some people you'll meet are easier to read," Ward placed the ice pack on her shoulders and could feel her trying to enter his thoughts. It was rudimentary the way she tried, but it was all he could do not to smile and laugh as he helped her through it. She could feel, and even see with her minds eye, the smile on his face, "others will be harder to read, or feel. We are part of a grand experiment, discovered through bogus psychology experiments in colleges. Then we were drafted into a lifetime of service for the department. There are at least ten of us that worked in the Southwest division plus our partners, but otherwise they really don't want you to know much about all of the others. I worked out of the Atlanta office for a while and there were about sixteen of us there. Once in, you're partnered with a person that has been transferred from one of the other agencies to help guide you, complete your training in many other areas, and to keep you in line.

"We were an accident, working together on a couple of assignments, and then later we became," he paused for only a split second, but Jan noticed, "friends. For a while it suited their needs, and then it sent waves of concern through the department. And when I left, you were questioned for hours. The dreams you are having now are a way for you to remember, and reconnect slowly. They will tell you more about your assignment and the connections that you have made as you are ready for it. Meditate as much as possible. It will help focus your thoughts and energies, and bring back those that have been hidden," the cold pack began to do its job. "I am pretty sure by now that most of your memory will return; when it will I can't tell, but from what I can read from you, you are on the way to figuring it all out yourself. The more you use the meditation techniques you know, the faster it'll most likely be, but don't push it or rush it," it was a warning. "I'll be back in a few minutes," and he felt an air of sadness settle around her and hang in the air. Jan could see that there were advantages and disadvantages to being able to see into someone's thoughts.

The time went by quickly and Jan had little to no time to think in depth about all that she had learned. She silently put the information in order. She was in the jail ward in a hospital in Tucson, 500 miles away from the attack in the factory. Although not in jail, they, the government, felt the safest place for her right now was in jail. She had also learned that Rob had had a break in the case and was off dealing with the leads that the information had brought him. She also knew something else; whoever attacked her thought she was dead, and Rob knew how to contact Ward. Rob had also contacted Ward and she wondered for whose benefit.

Knowing that Ward had been on a beach with her at one time or another fairly recently set off an array of emotions inside Jan, most of them good, some of them unknown. Lastly, as Jan had started to understand, she was able to sense people's moods and thoughts. This was how she was linked to the PED department. Jan could see why these skills would be an asset in all sorts of areas and how they could be useful. It was also an area where secrecy was of utmost importance and keeping control over their agents a priority. The word deceive came to her mind. A chill ran down her back and it wasn't completely from the ice pack on top of it. Ward walked up disturbing her thoughts, and spoke in a low, gentle tone.

"It's O.K. You don't have to have it all figured out in the next few minutes, just give it time," Jan felt the ice pack being removed and the ties of her gown being knotted back together. "As for those special exercises, take a look at that man over there," Jan followed his directions. "All thoughts are energy, electrical impulses. As the neurons fire, they leave a signature, look closely, and clear your thoughts." As Jan did this, she got a clear impression in her head. He was thinking about the next set of exercises he was supposed to do, he didn't want to do them at all. She turned to look at Ward and saw him smiling, obviously he knew that she had read that man's thoughts, "That's enough for now, we will work on types of focusing later, and yes even various ways of reading people who don't want to be read."

It was time for her to go; the nurse was waiting at the door. Jan looked at Ward and let her mind clear. Jan couldn't sense anything from Ward at this moment. It was not the fact that he wasn't feeling anything; she could see that, it was that he was keeping it from her. This she was sure of. This was a new development, and somehow she knew he hadn't ever kept his thoughts shielded from her before. Since the realization of being able to read other's thoughts and feelings was still new to Jan, she was unsure how to deal with his concealed thoughts, or the fact that he was concealing them from her. It was the first time she felt walled away from everything.

"Too much too soon is not good," Ward let his thoughts linger on all the memories he had with Jan as he tied her gown back together. There were years of history, some good, some so-so. All played through his mind. He lost himself in the thoughts as he knotted the gown being careful not to share any with her. He was pretty sure that her memories would return, but it was hard for him to wait for them, especially when he was so close to her in all senses. Pretty sure was not conclusive though. From what he had seen and what he suspected had happened, her memories could all be gone and there would be nothing he or anyone else could do about it. All his training over the years, and the experiences with others, let Ward deal with these emotions and put them aside, away from the reach of others, and sometimes even him. Jan's beach dream in the therapy room today had been initiated by her and directed by him. A weak moment he knew. To play with another's thoughts is unethical, usually immoral, and had never been mastered by anyone still in the department, but in this case he thought it might be better for him to play with her emotions than the PED's officer that would be sent soon. No one had shown up yet, but it was early, and Rob would allow her all the time he could officially manage. This emotional manipulation had now made Ward feel just a bit guilty. How could he be better than what he had seen and experienced if he himself succumbed to making that memory surface, and maybe the memory of it was too soon? It had just been too tempting when he sensed their hideaway at the front of her thoughts, and he too wanted to relive the moment, even live in the moment with her. She had dreamed of it herself already. Plus, being inside her mind again had provided him information about why her absence of memory may not be a result of the accident. Tonight when he connected with the databases he had a lot of work to do.

His thoughts drifted to another disturbing moment. He had felt the recognition inside her as he had massaged her muscles, and had lingered in that moment with her. They had had a lifetime of work and memories together. Yes the memories, they were lost or stolen from her now, not the trust they had in each other. That had returned even without all the memories. At least that hadn't been taken from her. Ward just wondered what would happen when the memories returned, and the sooner she remembered the better, maybe.

It was the next thought that entered his head that bothered him. What would happen if Jan never remembered everything? It could be better for him, maybe easier for her to leave the department, or would she be trapped in it? They had discussed that in Mexico. The last night they had argued loudly about which way their lives would be better, and how they were going to continue on from here. She was in constant danger decided on by others, and he was constantly running, or hiding from what he had been. She had made a valid point, he was still in danger as he continued the same style of work, but she had totally missed the point. He chose the danger, not them. He chose which cause to fight for, which wrong to right.

She had also pointed out that the danger he lived in was now from two sources. It was then that he had made the final blow that could have endangered everything he held dear. If she just left the PED then there would be one less group to endanger him every time he wanted to see her. She neither stormed out nor fell into his arms; she stood there with a semi-shocked look on her face. The storm had calmed shortly after that, with nothing more to say by either of them. Finally, they had agreed not to discuss it anymore, and moved on to better activities that night. Those activities had been a fresh fish dinner with the ocean as their backdrop, wine, and a long, hot, intense evening. It was now that Ward really had wished they had agreed on the work part, and what their future should have been. It would have made his decisions easier now, and they might not have even have gotten to this point.

The relationship now could go in either direction, resulting in the ending of what had been a long and lovely association, or the start of an even better one. The department would never let it be the same. Rob would never let them be the same, he was sure of this. If Rob knew where Ward was right now he would have to have him hauled in on suspicion even though Ward knew he silently hoped he was near. If Jan never remembered the complete past would this be better? Could he, in all good consciousness, remove her from here and care for her himself without her consent? Removing her from their grip is what he had wanted from the start when Rob had phoned him. It was what he had promised Rob he wouldn't do. Then again, Rob didn't tell him where she was so that he couldn't find her. His thoughts were interrupted by the distant sound of Jan's voice.

"One last question for today, and then I'll go," he helped her into the wheelchair, letting his hand rest on the nape of her neck just a little too long. The spot warmed quickly to his touch, "Are you a good guy, or a bad guy?" The question had come from her heart, and he could see the curious look on her face as her head tilted back to look him straight in the eyes. He could also tell there was fear attached to the question, because of his concealed thoughts. She must have sensed them and that had scared her. Ward looked straight into the eyes of a woman he had known for at least the last four years. In her eyes he could see the friends they had been early on in their careers, then the lovers they became later, and finally the partners in a rendezvous hidden away from the world. He saw the woman he would love to spend the rest of his life with, and spend forever getting to know anything he didn't already know about her. His eyes held hers, and she didn't flinch as she awaited his answer, only looked a little puzzled as she saw some of his thoughts play out in his eyes. Ward knew from that look that the woman he had fallen in love with was still in there, hidden, hurt, and confused, but still there. He had a world of memories he would love to impress upon her mind at this moment and give it all back to her in a matter of seconds. He had also learned the hard way this was not the moral route to go, no matter what the cost to the future might be. It would also not bring about the results he wanted. Patience was the only word that could fit this situation, and it was something he had yet to learn. He brought his face closer to hers, and his hand played with the loose strand of hair on her forehead.

"The good guy" and he brushed the hair from her face before he took her to the door in silence. He watched her as the nurse wheeled her out and the door closed behind her. He ventured thoughts now that he knew Jan could have read if she were still in the room, as transparent as they were he would never have been able to hide them from her, no matter what her condition. He wanted to hold her, to kiss her, and to smell the sweet fragrance of her hair again. He wanted both their minds and bodies merged together as one. And more than before, he knew he wanted to wrap her up and protect her and carry her away. Before now, he was unsure, and even now, even if Jan remembered all they had been, would she be willing to give up what she knew for what she saw as an unsure future?

Now he had circled back to the argument from the beach, and could go no further. He moved on to more pressing thoughts. Ward was unsure just how much longer he would be able to stay around without being identified by any number of people that were here, or could show up at any moment. He walked over to his next patient and took off the heating pad. Many people from the department knew him by sight, and some had already been in and out of the hospital. He had ducked their glances for now, but the fact of the matter was; it wouldn't be long before they would start to look for him here.

'That was always the problem with being on the outside,' he mused, 'Never being able to stay long enough with someone you are close to on the inside.' He turned and went back to work, readying his plans in his mind.

Chapter 4

Her eyes were open, she knew that, but the room was dark so she closed them again. No light filtered into the room from the small window. It was the night of the new moon, and even the stars seemed to be taking a break, or maybe it was just cloudy. Her hospital room was located on the dark side of the building anyway as no street lights existed below on this side of the building. There were no parking lots, sidewalks, or streets that needed to be lit. Jan had spent many nights in this hospital now and as she awoke from her deep sleep she could sense something was wrong. Something was wrong. She didn't know what had woken her up to begin with, but that funny feeling was back. She had heard all the normal noises to be found in the hospital, all that she had heard too many times before, but now she heard another noise. The noise was out of place. A small scraping sound came from the same area around the door. Opening her eyes would be a waste as there was no light in the room to see by. Jan stayed still and let her senses take over. She listened for a sound again, and it wasn't long until she only just heard the sounds of footsteps. There was no mistake; whoever was in the room was getting closer to her bed.

The feelings in the room that Jan picked up on were as dark as the night, evil and heavy. Jan began to worry. It was pure instinct that she didn't start to tense her muscles and her heartbeat stayed constant. The listening equipment, or eavesdropping mike as Jan called it, in the room was on and working when they had checked on it just yesterday. That gave her some sense of comfort now knowing that she was being monitored and if she needed help someone would be there quickly. Whoever was in the room had no clue where to look for the device, she hoped. She began to wonder who her intruder could be; the thoughts she was picking up were sinister and centered on fear, her fear. Jan searched again to see if she could sense something else that would allow her to identify her guest, and realized that he was feeding the fear in her own head. The more she had tried to read him the more he was able to get into her head. Not being as skilled she knew she had been was only aiding her intruder. Suddenly she felt the need to get out of the room, but knew this man as well as her injuries trapped her.

"Don't say a word," a large hand clenched around her throat unexpectedly, making the thought of talking and breathing nearly impossible. The voice was deep, raspy, low and barely audible. It made her wonder if the microphone would even pick it up, "I want it. And I want to know where you are hiding it now," Jan felt the warmth of his breath against her ear, and the silky brush of his black ski mask on the side of her face. His voice carried a clear threat, and she had no doubt that he would kill her to get the information he wanted. He was being careful not to be heard, or seen as if he knew they would be monitoring her.

Opening her eyes slowly, she could just see the outline of the man's head beside hers. Jan's eyes studied the ski mask that kept his identity from her, but the voice would be all she needed to be able to identify him, that and the eyes. It was the eyes that bothered her the most. She knew them somehow. How had he managed to get past the others outside her room? The hand loosened on her throat, just enough for her to speak.

"What are we talking about?" Jan was careful to keep her voice low, not because she was scared of the intruder, that in itself was a given in some sense or another, but there was something to be learned from him, and the longer she could keep him talking the more she would learn. He had also not given her any choice as to how loud her voice would be as he restricted the airflow quite effectively. Jan was at a huge disadvantage. Although she no longer was in a cast, they had been removed earlier today; she was still fairly unable to defend herself in this type of a situation. Somewhere in the back of her subconscious she knew she could have at one time, but not now, there were way too many holes yet. The thought of Ward crossed her mind and she looked into and past the dark eyes that seemed to grip her from inside the mask. Ward had been the only one to skirt his way around the security before, and she had to be sure that this was the attacker from the factory not Ward. Then the eyes behind the mask hardened, in a heartbeat she knew without a doubt that the intruder was the same person that had been responsible for her current condition, not Ward, and it appeared that no one had seen him come in. She was on her own for now.

"My patience with you is about to end sweetheart. You know what I want, and you have kept it a secret from me long enough. Really, I should have made sure you were dead before I set the factory on fire, but I didn't want to waste the time, or. . . ," he took a raspy breath, and stifled a cough. His free hand started to trail down her body slowly, "I'll figure out how to get its whereabouts out of you if it's the last thing you do."

"If you kill me, then you still won't have what you want. If we have met before you will need to remind me of it. I still don't remember anything about the last three weeks, and if you think you're scaring me, well, you're not," her voice stayed low and even. Her mind warned her that events were to turn even darker, and she braced herself.

"Bitch!" Emotion got the better of him as his voice raised above the level of a whisper. That was it. The noise had been too much as they both noticed the light start to blink from the corner. "You are a miserable liar.

Too bad he couldn't teach you how to do that better, he seemed to keep me from reading you. If I had time I would remind you of what could happen to you," and with that said he slapped her across the face without warning and hard enough to make her head snap back to the right, pain searing through her brain and her face. Jan could hear heavy footsteps coming down the hall at a running pace as she bounced between realization and the nothingness he seemed to leave in his wake. "Next time I won't be so nice," and she could feel the sneer and menace that lay behind the mask in the dark room as he moved toward the window. Focusing for only a minute, she knew that there was no way they would catch him. He had planned his escape carefully and then, as if on command, her mind unfocused as if out of her control.

The door to the hospital room flew open and the lights blinked on in the room blinding Jan for a moment, breaking the grip on her mind. The sound of breaking glass came next, and a gasp. Jan could see the figure at the door move swiftly to the window but didn't hear what he had to say. Jan didn't need too, as they were only a string of explicatives anyway. Jan refocused her thoughts as the figure by the window turned and she recognized Rob's familiar features. A wave of nausea hit and just as quickly cleared. She remembered, all of her life in that instant, but as quickly as it came, it disappeared. Some of the vague impressions remained, but not enough. She remembered working in the dull graying rooms of the department somewhere in Arizona, and she remembered whom she was arguing with Kevin about in the dreams that had caused his death in the end.

Now she knew who Kevin had been looking for, and who she should be looking for, but not what. Holding tight to that thought, so that it wouldn't slip away, she let her mind continue with its deductions. She had been doing her job, protecting Kevin, and they had been on their way to the airport to send him off to who knows where, the airport was where her duties were to end. This also kept the information safe. They were to meet with another agent from another department, and then she would turn Kevin over to him. She was to keep him from running off scared before, during, and just after the trial. Who would be better than a mind reader to predict and protect his every move. Pieces were now falling into place. When they changed cars, that's when she sensed the surging uncertainty within him. When he started to talk to her she knew he wanted to pick up a special lady to travel with him, and it was then when she could read why. It wasn't an argument about getting his girlfriend out, but the fact that the place he had wanted to make contact with her was unsafe, and unsecured. Almost everything buzzed through her head at once, but there was still a missing piece to the puzzle. She wanted to know what her assailant was looking for. There would not have been a good reason for her to leave the prearranged plan unless she had gotten good information from Kevin. That was the missing part, the item the man was looking for. Nothing more was clearing up, nothing more had managed to break through the wall that had been erected in her mind. Then she turned and looked at Rob.

Rob seemed tired and drawn, as if he had been working for days without sleep. His shoulders drooped and he leaned on the window frame, unaware of what was going on in her mind. He seemed to have aged another ten years since she last saw him. The clothes were casual, clean, and creased from sleeping or sitting in them too much. The lines on his forehead were deep and his brow was knitted together. He took his hand and rubbed the lines away on his forehead. Jan looked closely at him and began to pick up the sense of loss, and something that seemed an unusual feeling for him, hopelessness.

"Had his escape pre-planned. Repelled right out of here. He's gone," Rob moved closer to Jan's face, he held the hook the man had used for his escape in his hand, "You're hurt," it was a statement, and a thought crossed his mind and bounced off hers, to call for the nurse. But there was another thought that Jan picked up on as well. Picking up on thoughts had become much easier since Ward had shown her a simple way to do it. It was the casual thought that had passed through his mind so quickly that Jan would soon focus on.

"I'll get the nurse in a minute. Who was that?" Jan kept her voice comforting even as she felt for the nurses' call button. She could feel a definite swelling starting on her left cheek, and the area throbbed.

"Did you recognize him?" the question was again straightforward and delivered with a flat tone. He wasn't going to tell her anything yet. Rob had no way of knowing for sure that her skills had returned, and more importantly, that Jan was able to access them with more ease. Jan noted that Rob must not possess any of the mind reading skills so desired by the department. He was, in essence, a baby-sitter to keep people like her, and Ward, from escaping the life of the department, as she had been told. Some how Ward had escaped and she now needed to decide how she was going to live from now on. Jan suddenly realized that was the continuing discussion, or argument, she had with Ward. It had caused so much tension between the two of them in the past, but she couldn't remember anything more, it just wouldn't come. He gently inspected the bruise that was quickly forming on her face with his hand and then moved away letting his hand drop to his side.

"Rob, somehow we have been through a lot together, most of which I am still piecing together. But on some level I trust you," at this point it was unwise to let him know any more of her thoughts, or skills, "I can tell you that whatever has happened here tonight wasn't just an accident. He thought I knew where 'it' was and he was willing to stop at nothing to get that information. But you already knew that, you heard the whole thing," Jan pressed the nurses' call button, beginning to feel the need for some ice. "You expected this, or at least something like this, but it got out of control just a moment ago I suspect from the look on your face. You didn't expected him to be so bold, or for me to get hurt, but you did expect him to come looking for me when the information got out that I might still be alive." Jan's eyes never left Rob's face, and she could see by the increasing frown on his lips, and the furrow of his brow, that she had hit home. It felt good to be getting back to some sense of normal, being on the attack, under control. She had carefully worded it so that he would still be questioning how much of her skills had returned. "What you did expect was that they would come in here and either let something spill, or I might 'remember' something more with the shock of the experience," the nurse came in and checked Jan's face. Jan let her examine it and then she left to get a cool pack without saying a word. Evidently they had all been in on it. "It would also prove to you and whoever else, once and for all, if I was involved. You may be sure I'm not involved at all, but I suspect it's the department you have to convince right now. Just who are they looking for?" Jan had no clue who, and hoped that this test of Rob's loyalty would prove that he was back on her side completely, and ready to work with her. Rob's expression changed slightly, and Jan thought she could detect a small smile.

"You are getting better. Either that, or you are a damn lucky guesser," Rob said this with a note of sarcasm, not once stating that she might be picking his brain, but all the while suspecting it. Once it was said out loud there would be no way of keeping them from knowing what was going on, but the thought was clear in his mind. "But we still needed to figure out why you were at that factory. The boss thinks it was a set up gone bad. That you somehow let other factors," a small pause as he decided if this information was worth imparting, "or people," and at this point Rob raised one eyebrow and didn't even try to hide his thoughts, "influence you, and that you may be the one responsible for Kevin's murder," Rob waited for some kind of acknowledgement but got nothing from Jan. He was sure now that he was making the right choices. Her actions had confirmed it. From now on out it would get tricky. "Even by just seeing other people outside the PED, the department would find it disagreeable, even if their actions seemed to be honorable. Now, you don't need to be told just how serious that can be to all involved, even if you don't remember everything.

It could implicate you in a conspiracy even if you are not involved," conversation stopped as the nurse entered with the ice pack, she turned to look at Rob. Rob's expression would have stilled a raging bull at that moment, and if the nurse had chanced a thought about asking him to leave, she thought better of it then. Leaving the ice pack by Jan, she went scurrying out, "Because I didn't believe that you had been influenced by any particular factors, I started to work the case by myself. This, the department is aware of, and unhappy with. I was trying to push the issue tonight. Solve things too fast. I also didn't believe that factor was capable of going that far. What I found out tonight confirmed only the one theory I was working on. You're not directly involved."

"I'm not involved at all," was Jan's stern response. Rob just nodded his head in agreement.

Rob sat down, "Just quickly; Kevin had a significant other, that information he kept to himself, and we somehow knew nothing of her. It's my guess that Kevin thought he could protect her enough without our help, pick her up later with the 'it'. You never picked up on her existence, probably he never gave her a thought when we were in the room, or there wasn't any reason for you to think she was important. Maybe he didn't think she was important until it was time for him to disappear forever, and he needed her for some reason. Not sure which it was. Up until that time most of it ran smoothly. That's until you were assigned to get him to the airport fifty miles away from the courthouse, and to be relocated before the cartel found him. You never made it, but most of this you know," Jan adjusted the ice pack on her cheek. This she knew to be true, because it wasn't until Kevin knew that they were shipping him off that the thoughts of his girlfriend had become important, but the 'it' still remained a mystery to her. Jan fought back the impatience of not being able to remember it all right now, and sighed.

"Are you telling me that I might have been stopping to pick up his

S.O. when we were attacked at the factory?" Jan made the reference to his significant other with a bit of anger.

"Not sure, at least trying to make a contact. The best part is that it doesn't sound like they have her either after what I heard tonight," Jan looked at Rob, and Rob's expression softened. "Sorry you got hurt, not in the plan," Rob stretched, walked over to the bed and moved the ice pack a bit to see how bad it really was. "You will have a nice bruise there," his touch was protective, gentle, and caring. "Don't let him get too mad at me," they sat in silence staring at each other. Rob winked, and gave a half-hearted smile. No other words were needed. Jan read his mind although she didn't need to, and Rob made his thoughts clear. He stood and walked out of the room, turning out the light, and not looking back. He paused in the doorframe silhouetted by the hall light.

"Don't do anything silly," was all he said. Jan wasn't sure what her next move should be, could be. They now knew she was alive; she had been attacked; Rob knew of Ward and how they were meeting from his thoughts. The morning seemed far away, and even farther was the next therapy appointment she had with Ward. At that moment she didn't know if Ward knew that his cover had been blown. As Jan drifted back into a disturbed sleep, she wondered if Ward would be there to meet with her tomorrow. The fresh air coming in from the broken window stirred her senses and lulled her back to sleep.

The dusty haze of morning drifted through the window and across the desk. The mirror reflected the pinks and purples just beginning to color the sky. The morning rays gently reached the bed, and as Jan entered the weightless time just before waking, the breeze again reached into her hazy mind to seduce her back to conscious thought. The broken window and her stiff jaw brought back the events of the night to the forefront of her mind. The smell of fresh cut grass mixed with the gas fumes from passing cars, already on their way to work, drifted in through the window on the breeze.

Jan remembered how nice it was to wake in the morning and take an early morning walk. A walk, it was now something that she must accomplish soon in order to maintain her safety. Since a walk in a park was out of the question, she began the only process that seemed to help at all. She started to meditate on the events that had transpired in the last twenty-four hours hoping to bring more answers than questions.

Breathing slowly in and out she calmed her mind and body to allow the thoughts just to drift through. The first thought to enter into her consciousness was again of Mexico, but this time there was more. The hands that had massaged her back were definitely Ward's, but this time after the massage they were walking down the beach, hand in hand. There had been an argument, and it was a whopper. Jan mused that the past month seemed to have been filled with many fights, and disagreements. But this fight was different. It seemed that it had been a long discussion. Jan was unable to ascertain what the argument was, or had always been, but she was beginning to have a guess.

Jan relaxed and allowed the meditation to proceed to its natural end, down the beach and then to fade into the background as her eyes opened to the upcoming day. Lying on the bed with eyes fixed to the ceiling, the day before her, her life in danger, she began to plan out what she was going to do. It had been almost four weeks in the hospital, boring and without current news; she had been kept from the world. And until last night, the world had been kept from her. It was time for her to break out of her bubble. Glancing at the time on the bedside clock, it was still at least two hours before therapy, and she had time. Slowly, allowing one foot to drop toward the floor, she sat up. The muscles were stiff and tender, the pain in her face and legs, very real. Allowing the other foot to drop toward the floor she decided she was ready. Taking a breath, she began to slide off the side of the bed, being careful not to make too much noise. The thought or threat, of Rob being outside and listening, made Jan stifle the small gasp that wanted to escape as she began to place weight on her legs. To the best of her ability she had locked her leg muscles in place and the legs seemed to hold. The pain slowly decreased. Without the cast and bandages, it was more painful to try and walk. A smile grew; the last time she had tried to stand the casts had supported some of her weight. Using the bed as a make shift cane, she hazarded a first step, and then another. It felt painful, yet yielded a satisfaction that could not be compared to anything else as it became easier and easier to move around the bed. She couldn't win any races, even walking ones, but at least now she was under her own power, sort of. It didn't matter that she wouldn't be able to get away from anyone by walking, but she was progressing.

Jan now knew she was close to leaving this place. Just where, when, and how she would choose was yet to be decided. That thought played through her mind as she completed moving to the other side of the bed and then easing herself back into the bed before anyone came into the room. Rob had said not to do anything stupid. What she had to decide was whom it was more stupid for her to stay with. Who had the means to protect her best from the people who now wanted her and would probably make sure she was dead? The information they wanted, she could only retrieve in bits and pieces. As the morning continued, and she paged through magazines that she had read a thousand times before, but not looking at what was inside them at all. Something about her attacker bothered her at a deeper level and she couldn't put a finger on it. All of a sudden it dawned on her. She realized what the first question she needed to know the answer to was, and it didn't matter who told her.

Later in the morning, she watched the maintenance workers fix the window. Rob had not shown his face today. Jan was not sure where he was. It had been nearly two hours since she awoke and no one but the workers had ventured into the room. One of the workers picked up some of the tools and it seemed to be fairly routine work. At least she was pretty sure, as she focused on their thoughts and practiced her rediscovered skills, that they were not dangerous to her in any way.

Jan had looked at herself as she walked around the bed earlier that morning and decided that there would be no way of hiding what had happened last night. Hopefully she would avoid any awkward moments and questions. As she rode silently down the elevator with her guard, or nurse, she decided that Ward would need to have complete access to her thoughts from last night as she came into the therapy room, that way the story would be short, even if not very sweet. A second thought passed through her mind, one that she had not thought of since last night. Would he still be there? That panicked her for a moment. Ward had found her before, but the thought of losing the one sure link she had to herself, even if she wasn't completely sure of the relationship, scared her. It would be like losing herself all over again. Rob knew her, but Ward seemed to know about her. Plus he was a large key to the plan that was now developing in her mind to get out of here. Jan put her thoughts in order as they entered the therapy room, not wanting him to detect her plan just yet, and fairly sure the bruise would distract him away from it.

She relaxed when she saw that Ward was there and as he turned to look at her, Jan could tell even with the unflattering hospital garb, that every muscle in his body went tense. Jan noticed that his jaw muscles tightened and never loosened into his easy smile, and she thought she could actually feel her head throb with his anger. Jan felt her thoughts intermingle with his. She wanted to ease his stress, to say it was all going to be okay, but she could feel that they had been down that road before. Ward was too upset to hide his thoughts, or shield Jan from them, and for the first time she began to concentrate and see his thoughts clearly.

At first, what Jan could feel was only raw emotion. A primal knee jerk reaction, deep, dark, and as she explored his feelings more, the anger that surfaced was both at the department and at her. This surprised her on one level, but on another level, Jan had expected this type of emotional reaction from him. No words were spoken as she was moved to her usual therapy table. The routine began as Jan and Ward continued with only each other's thoughts as communication.

The question of why meandered into her mind, and another unfamiliar thought crossed his conscious. Jan was unsure if Ward had really wanted her to know the second thought, his anger had made him a bit careless with his thoughts today, and she was getting much better at reading him. Jan was fairly sure that he had wanted to take her away from the hospital the first moment he saw her. For some reason he thought that he would be better able to protect her. Although the thoughts brought both calming and loving emotions to her, it wasn't what she was looking for. She dared to let that thought cross her mind. Right now what she needed was not only protection, but to find this other person she had seen in her dream before the bad guys found her. If they were willing to approach her in guarded custody, how could this Sandy, the person in her dreams, possibly survive without it? Ward's hands pressed harder on her back as he picked up on her thoughts and worked out his tension on her muscles. Neither had commented on the previous night's happenings yet, she was sure that they wouldn't, as their thoughts locked together as one. Jan let the strange sense of having someone else's thoughts be hers and hers belong to another wash over her. It wasn't until that moment that she understood how powerful this tool could be, especially between two mind readers.

"Come with me Babs," was all he said, and the trance was broken. There was a pleading in his voice as he spoke in a low ragged voice.

"Where do I live?" Jan blasted back as quietly as she could. She felt this unnerving need to leave and be free, but not to lose control of the situation or her freedom.

"No good. They're watching your place, been there a couple of times and couldn't even get in," Ward turned her over and looked straight into her eyes. Their faces barely inches apart.

"What do you suggest?" it came out in a hoarse whisper. Jan could hardly breathe with their faces that close, afraid of his answer, afraid to look into his mind. She was afraid that if she allowed their thoughts to mingle again she would lose herself in him, to him, if she weren't careful. Had this always been her fear with him? Was this what had held her back and distant from him in some way?

"Come with me, we can continue your rehab somewhere safe," there was a small pause and his voice dropped another octave, "and maybe," there was no guessing at what that meant.

"Rob knows you're here," the tension had begun to slacken until then. It now filled the room, and felt as if it had saturated the air she breathed.

"You have to decide Babs. Rob's a good guy, one of the best they have working there, but even he can't let me stick around if he thinks I might influence you away from the department. He's a career man. He has probably known I've been here for the last week and hoped that with me here you might remember more," Ward stood up and Jan watched his body move toward the wheelchair effortlessly. Ward had gotten a strange message from Rob earlier that week, and now he was sure that he understood what it had meant. In her mind she had no doubt that he would be able to protect her, but that wasn't how she had lived up until now. Of that, she was pretty sure. She was used to taking care of herself, "Until you start walking, you are a sitting duck," he countered, reading her mind. As of yet she wasn't sure just how to keep him out of her mind.

Jan let Ward continue to move from the table to get the wheelchair. He seemed to have again distanced himself from her; this had chilled their mood a bit. With that in mind she let herself slide from the table and land carefully on her feet. From previous experience she knew that there would be the initial pain and then most would be gone, at least enough to prove to

Ward that maybe his 'knight in shining armor' bit wasn't exactly what she wanted or needed. He turned just in time to see her slide off the table. He was just out of reach to catch her, but that didn't stop him from trying. He watched her feet hit the ground and noticed the flash of pain cross her face, and then Jan was able to stand. His hands reached her waist after the initial moment, and lingered there.

"Been holding out on me. I should tell you that you are not ready for this. That you should wait one more week and do other exercises first, but in view of what has happened I'm assuming you are giving me an answer," there was a mixture of both pride and fear, and she could feel him holding back, "that still doesn't answer the question. I can't stay here any longer. I have to leave. Will you come with me?" The nurse entered the room, and Jan knew the question needed an answered.

"We need to talk, and I need to know just how," Jan let Ward help lower her into the chair, his hands still burning a spot on her waist. She wanted to tell him yes, but held back. That didn't stop Ward from seeing the answer though. He tried not to shout for joy as the smile on his face widened.

"I'll bring you the list of exercises later today that you asked for," the nurse was too close and although his words said one thing, his thoughts said another to her. Jan knew that she would see him later, how and when was still unclear, but he would be there. The nurse wheeled Jan out of the therapy room as silently as she had wheeled her in, and back to her prison on the fifth floor.

Chapter 5

Ward walked over to the phone and started to dial as he watched Jan wheeled toward the door and out of the room. Jan turned just in time to catch a glimpse of this as she left the room. She thought nothing of it until she reached the fifth floor and the door to her room. She stopped the nurse short just before they went into the room by grabbing the wheels. At the end of the hall she just could see the waiting room and who was in it. Rob was talking on a cell phone with his back to her room, voice too low for her to hear and thoughts protected. All she had to do was look at him and she could tell something was wrong. It occurred to her that this might just be a routine phone call for him, but from reading his body language, he seemed a bit tense. He stood straight up, elbow out, fist clenched, and muscles at the ready. At this point she was aware that the conversation dealt with her. Trying as best as she could; she looked for more of his thoughts. He was hard to read, almost as if he knew someone around him could read his thoughts. Quietly she pointed toward the waiting room, hoping the nurse would wheel her toward it. The nurse shook her head no and pushed Jan through her door, not letting her get close enough to easily read any more of Rob's thoughts or overhear anything. The hospital room was feeling more and more like a jail cell, and this time when the nurse left, she heard just the slightest click. It was the sound of the door being secured from the outside, something that had never happened before. Jan smiled. At least they were now treating her like she was some kind of threat to them.

The nurse had not volunteered to help her into the bed, so Jan wheeled the chair back to the door and gently pushed on it. As she had anticipated, it was locked from the outside. Anger started to build, and Jan knew that any route out of here and away from these people would be better for her, and Sandra, wherever she may be. Who was on that phone? The thought raced through her mind as she managed to get back into bed. Suddenly, a strange thought occurred to her. Ward had been about to make a phone call, Rob was irritated with the caller on the other end of his phone, and now her door was locked from the outside. She wondered if somehow the two were linked. She had just completed the last thought when she heard the lock move on the door to her room, and it opened.

It was no surprise to see Rob walk in. Even the expression on his face she had expected, hard, with frown lines growing across his forehead. She knew, by the way he came into the room this was a no-nonsense visit, and his thoughts were focused, controlled. She even felt a little sorry for him. Jan waited for him to start the conversation, "I hear you're walking, or standing now. That'll change things you know. Since you are obviously feeling better, they will be calling in Pat to help with your recovery. Best agent to address your need to rediscover your skills now," there was a pause. There was something he wasn't telling her. The frown deepened, and then he went on, "We will move you from here tomorrow; security has been breached in more ways than they will let me get away with anymore. I will be removed from this case as of this afternoon and you will be assigned another agent. They will be here tomorrow, although they won't tell me who it is yet," Rob walked over to the newly fixed window and looked out. It had been a stance Jan had seen so many times, yet this time there was more he wanted to tell her, she knew that, but he was also afraid too. She could sense the conflict in him but she couldn't quite read it. They stayed like that for what seemed forever. No one talking, what could she say that he didn't already hear, and that she didn't want to let anyone else know?

Jan tried to read his mind again and got nothing of consequence, just as he had planned it. Rob walked over to the mirror and put his hand behind it. Carefully he removed the small listening device that had been put there. Jan had known where the device had been, but until now had no reason to mess with it. It had mildly surprised her that he had taken it out. Rob flipped the tiny switch, and tossed it at her. Jan caught it and checked to see that he had indeed turned it off.

"Won't you get in trouble for this?" Jan sat up straight. He smiled. It was the first easy smile she had seen from him during her time in the hospital, and it was a smile she recognized deep within.

"Can't get into much more than I'm in now. Have to change the batteries at some time or other now don't I. I'll just tell them that you had a nice long nap after therapy today. And anyway, after the calls I've gotten today, I think I need to talk to you," Rob stressed the last I. Rob sat down in the chair and his shoulders slightly slumped, "You can't do anything stupid, or maybe I should say you shouldn't. I think you're planning something, I'm not sure what, but I know you remember more than you have told me. With all the changes that are going to happen, you need to know that I may not always be around to help out, protect you, from both sides.

"They still suspect you. Not for planning the murder, but of working with someone else who is pulling the strings. They think they know who it is, but I have already proven it to myself that it isn't. They are afraid of mind control now. Pat is supposed to put you back on the right track, and with a new partner that will," his smiled widened, "keep you under control, and out of the field. They've told me that I have given you too much room and that is why we have a problem now. I got a good dressing down. I really didn't think it would come to this. I knew you had to be seeing Ward here, not how you two were meeting right away, but from the progress you were making in other areas. Well, it couldn't be all on your own, there had to be someone else and I figured I knew who it was. I started to do some investigating and found out there were a couple of new hires, only one sounded likely. I checked it out and found Ward. As far I know he doesn't know that I have found him, but soon the rest of the team will. He's probably not too worried about me."

"How long have you known?" Jan had watched as the slump to his shoulders increased, and he leaned his elbows on his knees.

"Just a week, but you knew that didn't you? Hell, he probably did too," he rubbed his head, "Tomorrow they will take you back to headquarters and you will finish recuperating there," he wasn't telling her everything, but he kept his thoughts closely guarded. She was unable to tell what the rest of the information he had gotten from the department was, "Then you will be put back to work, and maybe we will get a chance to work together again someday, but not as partners."

"There's something else," Jan leaned back, half pretending to be tired, and knowing there was plenty more.

"Yah. Remember when I said don't do anything silly. I meant it. You won't be any better off with him than with the department. I know he cares greatly for you, but I'm old enough to be your father, well almost, and if I had a daughter I wouldn't want her running around with him. What type of life does Ward lead; living in the shadows, hiding from everyone who once knew him. You may remember, or not yet, that he has never stayed around very long. The last time you saw him," Rob looked her straight in the eye, "Yes, I knew that the last trip you went on was to see him, and about most of the others. Don't worry no one else knows, I didn't tell them. I was hoping that you were going to break it off. This relationship all started after you two worked on a couple of assignments together, there was a mutual attraction growing. As time went on, it got more involved, and you spent more time together. The department wasn't pleased with him and that's when the trouble began; soon after Ward left the department. I'm surprised he hasn't told you all of this, but I suppose he has his reasons," there it was again. It was just a feeling, but she could tell there was more to it. "There were other reasons which I won't go into, but let's say they really don't like him back in the office, he's on the wanted list. After he left the department you two started seeing each other secretly even though he was wanted. You trusted him, and as of yet I'm not completely sure why. I didn't find out for a while. Even though policy is not to take separate trips for long periods of time, I trusted you. I don't know how much you two saw of each other, but I thought you would follow policy better than this," at this he sneered, "I allowed you leeway, not wanting to lose you too. We'd already lost two good agents, one died. I never believed what the department said about Ward though, and I never thought it would come to this."

"What happens to you?" Jan was shocked at the forthrightness of his words; the conflict coming to the surface now.

"I get reassigned. Start with a new partner in about six weeks, maybe," he stood up and walked over to the bed, "I have to go through their training again as well," he sat on the edge of the bed this time, "So I never let something like this happen again. Then they decide if they trust me. If not then I will ask for reassignment back to the CIA."

"What if it's not what I want?" Jan folded her arms across her chest and looked over at Rob who was waiting for an answer. He smiled wildly, and then stifled a laugh with his hand.

"Don't remember it all yet do you?" and he relaxed back into his easy smile again. She wanted to be mad at him, but just couldn't. Jan smiled back at him.

"I've been using daily meditation, and it has been helpful. I am remembering more bits and pieces each day, but," she was sure that wasn't what he meant as the smile didn't seem to disappear from his face as he starred directly into her eyes somehow knowing she was unable to get a good read on his thoughts.

"Just take care of yourself, for me okay. I don't want to see you hurt," Rob half stood up and leaned over to kiss the top of her head, "by anyone."

"I won't get hurt," she had a feeling that she wasn't used to being fussed over, "Ward's not done anything to influence me one way or the other, so you don't have him to worry about. In fact, it's almost been downright frustrating. No one seems to want to give me the whole picture. So without all the information I have choices to make. Whatever I do, it will be what's right," she left off, 'for her,' knowing that what was best for her may not be what was best for the department anymore. Rob picked up the transmitter and went to turn it on, then stopped.

"No good-byes. We will see each other again," and he flipped on the transmitter not giving her time to respond to his comment, and placed it behind the mirror just before he left the room, not looking back once. He had given her all the information that he knew from the department, and it sounded fairly ominous. He'd also given her a brief history of her relationship, or what he knew of it, with Ward. It had felt strange for Jan to speak Ward's name aloud after keeping it to herself for so long. It had now been confirmed that Jan's feelings toward Ward had come from something other than the fact that he could save her. There seemed to be some kind of history between them. She smiled at Rob's back and the door closed.

Rob let the door close behind him. He knew she wouldn't be there in the morning. In some ways he hoped it would be true, in other ways he knew that he would miss her. If he allowed them to take her back to the department, she would never be let out again from what they had told him. That was the only thing he had kept from her. She was now what was considered damaged goods, and would be put to work in a 'safe way'. Pat was okay, for a trainer. Pat's job, after she left the field, had been to welcome in the new people and condition them to be part of the department. In other words, give up their life, friends, and loved ones for the department, just a bit of brainwashing. It had been an ugly affair with the department when Ward and Jan had gotten together; it was good that Jan didn't remember it yet. They had allowed Jan and Ward to work together, even get close, and they had even hoped that with a little encouragement they could start other things. It had been a grand experiment to them. This was no different than what they always did, play with people's lives and manipulate them to get the outcome needed. The information had been passed on to the geneticist, and they agreed that it was a possibility that the offspring of two well-trained readers would produce a stronger and better mind reader. It wasn't until Ward had gotten hold of the information, after his accident that all hell exploded. It was one thing for the government to control his working life, but the thought that they would want to control and even manipulate his love life, as well as, whatever else happened was way too much. Ward soon left the department, on what would be called shaky ground. He was wanted for trumpeted up charges, Rob was sure of that. As it was, it was already too late to break off their relationship, they were in love, or at least the closest either one could get to it. Rob had wondered if Ward could ever really be close to someone again after what he had told the department. They hadn't believed him, but somewhere in the back of Rob's mind something said Ward just might be right.

      Ward had had some interesting jobs, and been in some ways mentally scarred by many of these experiences that most mind readers would never have lived through. This had given him a very different view of the department and of life. How much of this view he had shared with her was always in debate, but for the most part Rob had known that Jan knew little of this. Rob never knew whether or not Ward had even wanted to share this with Jan. Up until today, they had never discussed Ward and her relationship; it had been a taboo topic. If he had known officially he would have had to do something about it. This way it had been easier to ignore. Since he was no longer her partner it didn't matter. Rob had known Ward was at the hospital, even tried to talk with him. Now it was important that he did some talking. Rob opened the cell phone up and began his text message. It read, "Urgent. Call me back. It concerns someone we both care for," Rob hoped that would do it. He gave a quick glance at Jan's door and then walked to the waiting room to wait.

Jan lay on the bed staring at the door. She knew that with Rob, there must have been some breathing room, but as she listened to the lock slide into place, she knew that something more was up, and the little bit of freedom she had was about to come to an end and it might be forever. The muscles in her arms and chest tightened. The future seemed out of her hands at the moment and that was unacceptable to her. She knew that if she tried to wait until tomorrow, leaving this bunch of people who had control over her now would be difficult thanks to Rob. For a moment she wondered if it would it be so bad to have them protect her? Whoever had attacked her the other night was still out there. Then another thought occurred to her; she was also supposed to protect Kevin and look how that turned out. With this thought in mind she made her decision, slid off the bed and onto the floor locking her legs just before her feet hit. Now more than ever she needed to be able to walk more than just a couple of feet. She couldn't let herself be imprisoned by these people or by Ward. Jan did laps around the bed until she thought her legs would fall off, and she would be just a pile of mush on the ground writhing in pain. She welcomed the pain because it was the only thing she knew was real.

She had made progress; she was able to walk, not well, not without using the bed for total support, and as she slipped back into bed for a necessary rest, she was well aware of her limits, unsure of what to do.

Taking a deep breath she allowed herself a small smile. No matter what happened now, she had at least gained some control over her life again.

Rob was in the waiting room barely seeing the stained Formica side table that he looked at. The cell phone chirped in his pocket, not more than fifteen minutes from when he sent the text message. He didn't have to look at the number, he knew who it was. Taking a deep breath he pressed the button on the phone and put it up to his ear, "Thanks for calling back."

"What's up?" Ward's voice was guarded, waiting for the next brick to fall.

"I know you've been seeing her," Rob wasn't sure just what he wanted to happen, and Ward picked up on the hesitation in his voice.

"Something's happened," Ward tensed on the other end of the phone. He had just seen her; nothing could have happened to her, could it?

"She's fine, stop worrying, but they did get the girlfriend. Didn't find what they were looking for though," Rob took a breath.

"How do you know?" Ward wasn't sure he wanted to know, but if they hadn't found what they wanted, that meant that Jan was still a target, only this time a bigger one, and probably the only one.

"Let's just say they left a message for us. She doesn't know yet," Rob paused, thankful that Ward never asked whose idea it was to release the information that she was still alive, and knowing that he was too far away to read him. If Ward knew who had let out the information he didn't think any amount of protection would have been good enough to keep Ward from him. When Ward didn't say anything he continued, "Pat's coming in tomorrow, and so is another agent to be her partner for now. They've recalled me. You have to leave her alone so that they can protect her," only half believing that he would, and half hoping that he wouldn't listen at all. He had to say it though.

"Well," Ward let all the information seep in. Rob wanted him out of the picture. Nothing new. It was nice that he was giving him a heads up to let him get out of here before the changing of the guards. He looked at his watch before continuing the conversation, "We've never been friends, nor will we ever be, but what makes you and yours think they can protect her better?"

"She'll be kept at the department from now on. They'll be back after her. Don't you get it? She doesn't know what they want, unless she told you?" It was a question as well as an accusation.

"Unless you want to tell me something else, I think this conversation is over," Ward disconnected. Both men slid the phones into their pockets, stared into space as if the answers were floating out there somewhere, except Ward was pretty sure what his answers were, and the plans were ready. Rob had said a lot without saying anything. He all but told him that if he was going to make a move, to do it tonight. What he didn't know was that it was already planned. Others would have wondered if there was a set up, not him. Rob had been nothing but honest with him, and with any luck, maybe one day he would call him a friend.

Jan had drifted into a dreamless and welcome sleep. The therapy session had made her tired even though she hated to admit it. Unaware of what had transpired after Rob left, she didn't give it another thought until she heard the movement of the metal lock. Listening carefully, now fully awake, she heard it again and knew it had not been imaginary. It jarred Jan back into the present. The door did not open right away. This caused Jan to tense her muscles. The last thing she wanted was a repeat of the other night, this time she would not be caught unaware. Jan slipped off the bed and moved carefully, and as silently as she could half crawling, half walking to the chair. The evening was just beginning and the lights had not been turned on in the room. The shadows hid more than just the finer details of the room; they were able to hide Jan. The chair was positioned behind the door and as the door started to move, Jan moved as silently. As the door opened she waited. What took only seconds seemed like hours.

At first glance she was only able to identify the figure coming through the door as a tall male, and he was dressed in hospital garb. As the figure reached over to turn on the light, Jan caught a thought. It drifted through her mind easily, as if it were a feather on the wind. Jan took a deep breath, for in that moment she knew the identity of the man, and what he was there for. Jan realized that she must have slept longer than she had thought and this must be the time that Rob went for dinner, and someone else took over. This was the moment in which her room had easier access. It was a relief to see Ward and as he turned on the light, he looked toward the bed. Jan waited, guarding her thoughts, hoping to hide hers, and wanting to know what his thoughts would be. She needed to get a better definition of their relationship and this was the first opportunity she had to be on the attack. At first there was a small panic, then she could see the corner of his eye, and the muscles in his neck relax, as he turned toward her. She just smiled. Ward walked toward her; "Would you like another therapy session?" it was a question, but not about therapy. Jan pointed to the mirror to signal the listening device. Ward waved his hand in the air as if it didn't matter anymore and winked at her.

"Rob said I shouldn't do anything silly," Jan stood up carefully, and Ward went over to steady her, "Would that include going back to therapy so soon?"

"Probably, but now you have to make a choice," they stared at each other for only a moment, knowing what the next move had to be. Jan wondered what she was doing. She didn't know him any better than she knew Rob but there was something in his eyes that seemed to draw her to him. Something she trusted. For right now, she would have to trust someone and she decided it would be him, "Well then, I guess we have to get moving," and that was that. Ward lifted her over to the bed, "Put these on," he tossed a pile of clothes on the bed, "and then the gown back on over the top," there was what could only be called a wicked smile and a twinkle in his eye when he looked at her, "Do you need any help?"

"Turn around, if I need your help I'll tell you," Jan's cheeks turned two shades of red. One was embarrassment, and one was hopefulness. She didn't want to muddy up the relationship they had right now. There was plenty of psychological research to support the idea of her falling for the man that seemed to be saving her. Until she knew where they really stood she just didn't need those types of thoughts about him. Jan changed as quickly as she could, and he waited patiently with his back to her. His thoughts wandered in and out of her mind teasing her about the embarrassment; playing with half thoughts of what she could only place as what they felt, or might have been to each other. He was having a hard time hiding the excitement he felt at being able to take her away, "Okay, turn around."

"Not bad," Ward put her in the wheelchair and took her out of the room. His casual demeanor quickly disappeared as he walked out of the room and his expression again turned businesslike, "Don't worry," was all he said as Jan thought about how he was going to free her from this small jail. She didn't like not knowing the details, but there wasn't much she could do to be of any help. He waved at the person guarding her room right now from the waiting room. The nurse from the station moved out to meet them, and effectively block their way, as they approached.

"Where are you taking Ms. Hughs?" it wasn't a question, it was a challenge, and everything in her mannerisms said this. Her hands were placed on her hips and her feet were positioned just shoulder width apart. It was a good way to exhibit her authority.

"If you look at Ms. Hughs' chart she is scheduled for an extra therapy session today as she has started to try and walk," there was an exasperated pause, "on her own. Someone up here is not doing their job watching her. Without the proper attention, she will re-injure herself. I have stayed late tonight since we needed her to rest first. Her other session was just this morning," the nurse carefully looked over to the chart rack. She didn't believe any of this to be true, and Jan was amused that, in her thoughts, she was even angry at the fact that someone would accuse her of not doing her job. What surprised Jan even more was that her guard didn't seem to mind at all. Ward continued, "I'll wait, but not long. I have a family that is waiting for me to get home to go out to supper tonight and you try to keep a three year old waiting when you have promised to go to the PlayPalace," Ward took a relaxed stance, leaning on one side of the wheelchair as the nurse cautiously moved to the charts. Jan wondered about the family Ward had mentioned, but got nothing from him. Ward tapped his finger for added effect giving her very little of his attention. Jan was worried, she only felt calm from Ward. Ward said they had to get moving, but she had no idea where. A small sliver of panic crept into her head before she was able to push it away, what choice did she have?

If she stayed, by tomorrow she would have little chance to leave, and Ward would most likely have to disappear to stay clear of these people. If she left she would have to trust Ward, for the moment, with her future, and her health. She had told him the room was bugged, but did he understand? Whatever they said in there had just been recorded, had he known that? Looking up toward Ward, Jan reaffirmed her trust for him for now. He had made no demands of her, and only gave her most of the information she so desperately craved. Ward glanced down at her just quickly, and he gave her a quick reassuring grin. Then the thought in her mind was that somewhere there was a master plan. One she didn't know about, but it did exist, even if it wasn't hers. She watched as the nurse read the chart, and trusted her own decision. The nurse put down the chart and walked over to the phone.

"If you're going to make lots of calls, I'm just going to take Ms. Hughs back to her room and go home; you can be responsible for her progress then. I have better things to do with my time," the nurse hesitated as Ward began to spin the wheelchair around as if he was headed back to the room, and that was all Ward needed to do.

"Wait one minute," the nurse was not going to let anyone wreck her career, and they both felt that from her. Ward smiled before turning around.

"Okay. Let me get her down there and you go ahead and make all the calls you want. Will that satisfy you?"

"Fine, I'll be down to check on Ms. Hughs in five minutes," this was more of a threat than a promise. Ward wheeled Jan toward and then into the elevator. As the doors closed in front of her, Ward's mind became organized and unreadable behind her.

"You heard the fine lady, we only have five minutes," and Ward hit the ground floor button. The quiet lingered.

"So, where are we flying off to?" both Jan and Ward stared straight ahead at the elevator doors.

"Who said we were flying?" Jan could tell that Ward was just being difficult for the fun of it. The slight sarcastic tone in his voice and the smile on his face betrayed what fun he was having with her. She could also tell by his thoughts that he wouldn't tell her about any of the plans anyway. This was a bit unnerving, but what hadn't been in the last few weeks.

"The room was bugged, and the nurse is no friend of ours," it was a statement more than a question, "Won't it be easy for them to catch up with us?"

"Only if I told them, or you, where we were going," and by this time the elevator doors had started to open. Again he got serious. Instead of heading for the front entrance that was just ahead of them, Ward headed down a hallway. After going down a couple more halls at a moderate speed, just enough to be fast, but not fast enough to draw attention, he left by a side door. The outside light was fading, but the air was still fresh, and warm. Jan took a deep breath and leaned her head back. It seemed like years since she had been outside and she savored the seconds not sure how long she would be able to soak it in.

"You know they have us on the security cameras. They'll be able to tell where we left from, and probably the type of car as well," Jan closed her eyes and just enjoyed the breeze. If they were caught, which would probably be the case; she didn't know when she would be let outside again.

"Babs, I'm hoping they have us on camera," and he stopped by a silver car, not too old, yet not new. Quickly he stripped off his hospital garb, revealing jeans and a tight black tee shirt that showed every muscle. Jan decided to focus her thoughts on something else less powerful. She couldn't see the make of the car as he loaded her in the passenger side, and smiling quickly removed her hospital gown as well with one quick pull. Ward ran around the back with the wheelchair, popped it in the trunk, and got in the driver's seat. He tossed the hospital garb and ID over toward the dumpster by the door they had just left from. If he was trying to cover his tracks, he was doing a poor job of it, Jan thought. The car started, and they pulled out of the lot. If she had any reservations, it was too late now, and as she looked at her companion, she noticed that he was focused, mind only on the job at hand. He drove the streets without a word, and without hesitation. Jan watched the signs and noticed that they were on their way to the airport. She was going to ask again where they were flying off to, but knew that would be useless. Instead, she began to reposition herself to lessen the pain in her neck and right leg.

"You doing okay?" his voice just held a small note of concern. Ward had noticed her wiggle in the seat, and had continued glancing in her direction when he could as he drove quickly down the road. No one was following them yet, but soon they would be, and he was betting on not too long. In fact he was counting on it. It was a good thing he had changed the plates on the car two days ago.

"Just finding a comfortable position," Jan answered after seeing his concern and they continued to drive in silence for the next few minutes. She was finding it hard to find any position in which it would be comfortable and she hoped that they wouldn't be in this car for much longer, "You said you hoped they caught us on camera. Why?"

"Deception. How else will I throw them off the track?" Ward turned into the airport, "I can't make it easy for them, otherwise they will know it's all a decoy, but I have played with them before so they will expect some tormenting from me. Don't want to disappoint," he pulled the car into the long-term parking and just near enough to a camera that they would be noticeable, but not overly obvious. Jan noticed all of this, and was amazed that this had been arranged so easily by Ward, and she also knew they were not even near their final destination if he still wanted to be seen on camera. She had tried to pick up on his thoughts as he got her out of the car. All she got was half a smile.

"Not yet," putting her in the chair he quickly brushed the side of her face with his fingertips.

Jan let Ward push her to the entrance. Ward left her only about three feet away as he did the e-tickets. Watching him, she noticed that he wasn't trying to get noticed anymore, but wasn't trying to hide just yet. Things were beginning to change. He was beginning to change. He was less noticeable in the crowd; his shoulders had dropped a bit making him seem a couple inches smaller. The bag on his shoulder, he had also somehow managed to pack a small bag for travel, which he now carried only helped him blend in even more. Jan was feeling helpless, she had no money, no car, no way of knowing what was coming next or controlling her destiny. How long had he had this planned? Was this really what she wanted or just some idea planted in her head? The fingers of panic started to grab at Jan again and she fidgeted in her chair. Ward had looked as if he was concentrating on the tickets, but had kept part of his mind locked on her. As soon as she started to panic again he looked her way. As he walked back over, he unzipped a small pocket on the end of the bag and pulled out a small purse. He smiled as he handed it to her, "Watch your thoughts, you never know who is around," Jan was amazed how well he read her. "Here. Knew you would want this," handing her a small purse, "Got it this afternoon. It's the purse you keep at my place."

"Are you always this far ahead of me?" Ward took hold of the chair and started down the hallway toward the gates for the planes.

"No, but it sure feels nice sometimes," Ward and Jan didn't notice the people as they busily passed on their way to other places. Ward had checked out his surroundings and was a bit more relaxed when he talked.

"I just knew that you would want your own stuff after this long. I don't want to put you too far out of your comfort zone. That's not what I want to do. I want you to be comfortable with me, to feel safe. By the way, the cards and ID are in your name, but in a name unknown to the PED. You know the name, or at least you will remember it sometime, and where we are going, they only know us by that name," there it was, a small hint of the plan, but that was it. The thought that passed through her mind was of something green, a lush plant green, and a lot of it. Nothing more was forth coming.

They stopped at security and waited to be searched. It took forever to get to the front of the line, and it seemed that even Ward was getting impatient. Obviously this wasn't part of the plan, but his thoughts had grown more guarded than ever. When they finally made it to the front of the line Ward let her and the wheelchair pass through one way so they could security wand the chair and her. As he passed through the magical security doorway, he never took his eyes off of her, and waited for the security officer to finish the security check on Jan. Without a word he picked up the bag, slung it over his shoulder, handed the purse back to Jan and began to quickly push her down the long line of gates. She noticed that he hurried, but still not enough to draw attention to them. Not that any of these travelers would notice anyway. There was no talking, or smiling now, only his full concentration on the task at hand. This was it.

He stopped at gate 16, and Jan noticed the plane was due to take off for New York in about twenty minutes. Boarding had begun already, and Ward presented the tickets for their seats to the attendant. The attendant asked all the regular questions, along with asking if they would need any special assistance. Ward assured her that he was capable of taking care of Jan, and after waiting only a couple minutes he was issued boarding passes. They were now on their way down the jet way.

"So we're off to New York," even as Jan said it, she knew she was wrong.

"I don't think so," he said. When they got to the end of the jet way a flight attendant was there to meet them. She was tall for an attendant, and she had her blond hair pulled up into a stylish bun. She leaned over to Ward.

"You're almost too late, I've had a hard time keeping them down there," Ward leaned over to her and kissed her cheek.

"Security was a bit tough today. Here are the passes," as he handed the passes to her, she handed something to him, "Thanks. Now remember, we were on this flight if anyone asks, and she was difficult," Ward pointed at Jan and gave her a crooked smile. Then Ward turned the chair toward the exit door of the jet way, and looked at Jan. "Okay, time for you to stand Babs," he helped her up and through the workers' exit of the jet way door. Jan looked at the steps and sighed, "I know you can't do this; there is a chair at our destination. Sage will take your chair, so no one finds it here. It will be loaded on the plane and unloaded in New York, far away from where we will be." Ward swept her up in his arms. Jan felt the strength in his arms, and the warmth of them funneled new life into her. She was going to get free. Ward carried her down the stairs as if she weighed nothing. Jan was careful to guard her thoughts. They bounced back and forth between wanting to stay in his arms, and wanting to find out who Sage was to him. After all, she still really didn't know who she was, or Ward. She wondered if Sage was part of the family he had talked about earlier.

As they got to the bottom of the steps, Ward walked easily over to the luggage cart, placed her in the passenger seat, and slipped on the spare jumpsuit that lay on the seat. Placing the ear protectors on his ears he then handed her the other pair. He got behind the wheel of the cart and drove over to the baggage department without hesitation. Jan just watched as she now had an idea of how he had thrown off the department, for a while at least. They would start looking at the airport, find out that the destination had been New York, and find the wheelchair there. For all they knew, from New York they could be anywhere in the world, and a search would take forever. She waited in silence. Well, not silence. She was deafened by the noise of the planes and unable to even hear herself talk or think, so she waited. It was amazing. As he drove into the basement of the building, he stopped the cart. The noise level was slightly less, but still impossible to hear. Relying only on her ability to read his thoughts she was able to tell what he needed her to do in the next step of the plan. She started to get off the seat and was ready when he got to the other side. Again he lifted her, not even allowing her to try to walk and took her straight through the employee exit and out to the employee shuttle van, dropping the protective ear gear on the side of the building and into the large tub where there were many others waiting to be cleaned. They saw others, but no one seemed to take notice of them at all. She wondered if they all knew him, or was he able to some how manipulate their thoughts so as to appear invisible. That would be another question for later. Jan looked around and noticed that there were no security cameras to be seen. Right now, they seemed to have escaped the hospital, the town, the cameras, and the department. They were in essence invisible to the world.

"Nice," was all she had to say to no one in particular. Ward smiled at her.

"We are the best they have," he leaned over and whispered in her ear. A few minutes later they pulled into the employee parking lot and got out. Ward helped her off the van, and then as if the driver knew, he brought a wheelchair around the side of the van for her. Jan made a mental note that she would need to get out of the wheelchair as soon as possible. It was cramping her style.

"All in a day's work," Ward wheeled her to the corner where a white Ford Explorer was parked, "Our chariot awaits madam," and he exaggeratedly bowed for her.

"Is this your car, or the stewardess'?" Jan tried to keep the other question out of her voice, and out of his mind. The effort was lost.

"You already rode in her car Babs," he smiled mischievously, keeping his thoughts to himself as he loaded both her and the wheelchair into the vehicle. Jan had to admit the leather seats and the padded armrest were far more comfortable. Jan sank into the seat, and as Ward got into the driver's seat, he powered up the car and reclined Jan's seat until he heard the slightest of sighs of relief escape from her lips. At which point he stopped and put the car in gear, taking off for points unknown. Jan felt the seat begin to warm, and knew that Ward had turned on the heated seats to relax her even more, so she complied. Jan let the day drift off, the sun was now fully gone and night had claimed their world. It was too early for stars, and too late for beautiful sunsets. She could change nothing now. She had made her bed so to speak, so Jan decided it was time for a nap.

"Wake me when it's time for supper," she had decided that it was too late to turn back, Ward could tell. It was too late to leave a trail. It was too late for her to worry. And, it was too late for her right now as she was tired and in need of a rest. As she drifted off, she heard the CD player start. The music was eerily beautiful. Ward put on the only CD that seemed to completely calm her right now. It drifted around the SUV effortlessly and filtered through her thoughts. As the Native American flute music continued it gently carried her with it and into a deep restful sleep.

Chapter 6

The SUV came to a stop outside a small diner on a forgotten road somewhere in the desert. Jan didn't stir. Ward was unsure whether or not to wake her. He sat there for a minute just looking at her as the parking lot dust settled. It was such a peaceful moment; it was almost a shame to disturb it. He watched as she breathed peacefully and remembered the first time he had watched her sleep. It had been their first official date. Not that they hadn't been out many other times for coffee, lunch, and the occasional breakfast, but never a real date. When he had finally convinced her, he had insisted on a specific day.

"I still don't understand why we had to go out today on our date," she got on the boat and watched as Ward untied the small yet comfortable boat. Jan had noticed the steps to a small room below, probably a bedroom. He pushed the boat out of the dock and hopped in.

"Just wait," and he started the engine and steered the boat out into the middle of Saguaro Lake. Jan looked around and noticed the setting sun in the west. The colors complimented the red rocky canyon walls. She sat back and relaxed. She had no idea why he had decided to bring her out here for a date, but she did love being out on the water.

"So is this where you live when you're not at the office?" He tossed a can of juice toward her and she caught it. Looking at it she was mildly surprised he had remembered that mango was her favorite. She wondered just how much more he had found out about her.

"Sometimes; most of the time I have an apartment in the city like you, but I know how much you love the water and I spent my summers out in the Dells in Wisconsin. That's where I learned to boat, rock climb and freefall. Not all in that order though, and not all intentionally. My dad was happy to be rid of me each summer," he steered directly toward a small ribbon of water that led off of the main part of the lake. Few other boaters would have chanced taking their boat between the two rather large boulders that flanked the entrance, but Ward didn't hesitate. He looked as if he had done this a thousand times.

"Fell off a number of times I guess," she got her answer as Ward nodded an affirmative and continued to concentrate on the task at hand. "Most people would say you shouldn't try to get through there. Not enough room. Don't know the depths of the water, and just what may be lying just under the surface of the water," she said as he maneuvered the boat into the small space. She noticed that the sunset was even more intense as it reflected and bounced off the rocky walls that surrounded them. Ward hadn't missed the double meaning laced into the words she had just spoken.

"Good thing we're not most people," he cut the engine and let the boat float for a moment.

"Why this place?" She stared at the beauty before her and the brilliant reds and oranges that painted the sky, beginning to understand just why he had brought her here, "Lovely." It was his private little oasis. He flicked a switch and soft blues music began to play. He had done his research well. Not many people knew she liked blues, especially with a touch of jazz to it. She smiled and leaned back on the seat, placing her feet on the edge of the boat and watched the sunset as the music played on.

"Don't like crowds," he sat down beside her to enjoy both the sunset and her. Mostly he had looked at her. Later that evening he had pulled the boat further into the canyon to catch the rising full moon. It was the only night that the moon would come up between the rock walls they had just passed through and do a dance upon the small pond in which they floated. A friend had told him of this spot and he had spent many times here himself, just himself. Now he couldn't be happy without sharing it with her and tonight was the most magical of all of them. They sat quietly enjoying the sway of the boat and the way the light had changed, creating subtle soft patterns in the canyon itself, and the soft gentle hum of the music.

"Have you guessed why it had to be tonight?" and Jan responded by just shaking her head yes. Once the magic was finished, he pulled the boat up to the shore. When they had docked against the small bank he pulled out a picnic basket filled with all sorts of goodies and they sat in candlelight enjoying their feast. They talked a little, and enjoyed each other's company completely.

"How did you find this place?" Jan lay back on the blanket and watched the stars in the sky.

"I followed an eagle one day," and he smiled down at her as she caught the reference to his code name. A new song started and he held his hand out to her, "Dance with me." It wasn't a command, but it wasn't a question either. Taking his hand they stood and began to dance to the song 'Blue Moon' and that was when he knew he had fallen completely for her and could never live his life without her again. He also knew that was when she had fallen in love with him just as completely. The words of the song only added to the mood. He had known this feeling before but it hadn't belonged to him. When their lips touched he opened up his mind and she opened hers. The connection was more intimate and intoxicating than either could have imagined.

They made love for the first time that night and awoke in each other's arms with the sunrise. Things from that day on had only gotten more complicated and intense, but he had never regretted anything about becoming involved with her except the time they weren't together.

He tried to think about the last time when he had been able just to sit and watch her. It was the first time he had had this chance since they had last been in Mexico. Ward had driven through the early evening and into the night, wanting to put a little distance between them, Rob, and the PED. It had only taken about three hours to get near the border on the other side of Yuma, Arizona and into California. Another thirty minutes and they would be across. Ward worried that Rob may have thought about the border, but Ward knew the border patrol agent on duty right now, and he was sure there would be no problems crossing. Plus, if they had taken the bait, they would be looking for them in New York by now, not here, and he didn't think they would be listening to Rob right now. Sage was good, and would be able to convince them that they had really been on the plane, and probably convince most of the flight crew as well. At another time he might have looked upon her as a recruit, but that was another lifetime.

Jan had been asleep the whole ride and in many ways he had wished that they had talked for at least part of the journey. There was so much he just wanted to tell her. Knowing that telling her wasn't the way she should discover it, but more than anything he wanted to give her all her memories back and make her whole again. That was one thing he couldn't do and patience was what he needed to practice here as well. He was pretty sure of what had happened to those memories, and he hated the idea. If she had time she could have locked them away from him in a way that she could have retrieved them easily. But had she had the knowledge, time or strength, he just didn't know. She had placed her trust in him, a big step, and he wondered if that was wise?

He could take care of her physical concerns, even brush her up on her training, but was he doing the right thing knowing how they had felt when they last parted. Ward gave himself a mental shake. Now was not the time to doubt what had just transpired, but it was the time to wonder just what he expected of himself and of her now that they sat here, just minutes from the border, and their whole other life. A life she didn't even remember yet. Jan stirred in the seat next to him. Ward gently brushed the hair off her face and smiled, "Hungry yet sleepy head?"

"Mmmm...," Jan tried to move and found her muscles a bit stiff. Ward moved toward her ready to help, "Just wait. I want to do it myself. Are we going in?"

"Yah, it's a place I usually stop. I know the area well. No one will bother us here," Ward started to open his door, "Let me get your chair and we'll be on our way. They make the best chili here, but don't try the fish unless you have a death wish," Ward was out of the car and around the back quickly. Jan picked up the purse off the seat, and opened her door. Having rested and her mind clearer, she knew she needed to look in the purse to gain a glimpse of who she really was, maybe. He said it was hers, and she guessed she would trust that for now. Gently she slid out and let her feet hit the ground. As she hit she felt pain and her right leg collapsed. She fell and Ward's hands grabbed at her, catching her as she fell against his chest and lifting her up.

"Go a bit slower next time and you should be able to stand. Or just give it a minute and I'll be there," a thought drifted through Jan's mind that he would always be there, no matter what she decided to do. Funny, Jan thought, this was not a new thought to either one of them. His thoughts were less guarded at the moment, but no less mysterious. She could still not see any clue as to where they were headed; only that he was starved and that was what his priority was at the moment. As he wheeled her in through the small double wooden doors into the diner Jan noticed that the light didn't get much better inside the place. The entrance hall was small and cramped, the yellow lighting filtered down from some fixture that was at least as old as she was. Once past the entrance, the dinning room was a maze of tables and three quarter walls. They eased their way to the back of the empty diner. Just as Jan was about to say something, Ward wheeled her toward small doors marked 'Cowboys' and 'Cowgirls'. Ward was about to say something, and Jan quickly held up her hand. It wouldn't have taken a mind reader to know what he was going to ask.

"Just hold the door open please. I'll handle the rest," Jan wanted the time to herself as well as to use the facilities. Once inside she closed the door and tried closing her mind, she hoped. Opening the purse, she pulled out all the items and placed them in her lap. Most of the items she saw were the usual ones she would find in a purse, bits and pieces of used makeup, pencils, pens, paper, tissues, some cash, and then what she was looking for. Jan pulled out the driver's license and the credit card. The picture on the license was of her. She let her eyes drift over to the name, Janet Lowe. She figured the address on the card wasn't correct so she didn't bother to read that. She checked the name on the credit card, Janet Lowe.

Jan quickly put all the items back into the purse, used the restroom and headed back out to the dinning room. As she made her way to the door, she watched it open and found Ward on the other side. She wondered how closed her mind had really been.

"Beginning to wonder, thought you might not have found all you needed in the purse," Ward looked at her turning his head sideways. "No, I didn't need to see your thoughts on that one. If it had been anybody else, the first thing they would have done was look in the purse to find clues to who they were, but I knew you would wait for a private moment," he pushed her to a table.

"So are you my warden now?" the question was genuine. Jan was unsure if he would allow her any more freedom than she had had before. They got to the table and she found that the sodas were already there.

"My dear," he said as he walked to the other side of the table, "you are free to leave my side at anytime," Ward sat down, a serious, dark look on his face, "even if I didn't wish it or want it. Your happiness is my greatest desire. I am nobody's jailer."

"I don't even know your last name," Jan realized that she had embarked on this adventure with very little knowledge of who she was traveling with, not that it would make much difference. He had been her way out.

"That's right," there was a pause, a bit longer than normal as if he were weighing just how much to tell her, "you don't."

The rest of the meal was quiet. Jan took Ward's advice and ordered the chili. It was the best food she had tasted in a long time. Hospital food had nearly made her taste buds go dead, but the spice in the chili awoke each one. Jan savored each bite, along with the cornbread that had been served with it. Ward sat and enjoyed watching her eat almost as much as he enjoyed his own food. She took notice of this and decided to ignore it and him for the moment, the food was too good. Jan noticed that the silence between them was not uncomfortable; in fact, it was a warm and welcoming silence, even without them reading each other's thoughts. It was the type of silence old friends shared. They had shared a few moments like this before in the hospital, but Jan hadn't known that this was the norm between them. She now suspected that they had shared many comfortable silences, as well as other things. Ward glanced at his watch, as well as doing a visual sweep of the diner.

"Are we needing to be somewhere?" Jan finished the last of her chili.

"Border closes in an hour. We can stay around here tonight, or go across."

"Border, huh," Jan was unsure what to think. She was unsure of where they were, and for that matter, which border they were going to cross, although she had an idea and was pretty sure she hadn't been asleep that long.

"Want to push on, or do you need to be out of the car?" Ward looked at her as if he had no cares in the world. It was a look and a face she could get used to. She wondered what lay beneath that look, and tried not to go past it for the moment. It would be nice to think that they really didn't have any cares, but she knew that wasn't true. Crossing the border was probably the best idea; at least it might give them some cover for a while.

"I'm ready to go if you are," Jan smiled. At best, she was only feeling half-ready for the next part of the journey. Jan was sure that where ever he was taking her was meant to bring up memories of the past. Some she may want to deal with, and others, well, maybe not. He had thought this out well. Planned for her recovery, and had been there to help her when she needed. The trip ahead of her also scared her, what if none of the memories came back like he planned; what next? Would he want her in her damaged state? They pushed away from the table and Ward threw a ten and a five-dollar note down on the table. And before Jan could say wait up, they were in the Explorer and on their way. She noticed that when he started the Explorer the music he played had changed from the original flute music she had fallen asleep to. As the first song started she recognized the music. It was a song by the Eagles. Ward let it continue to play on, and it drifted throughout the SUV hauntingly, as if it were trying to tell her something. Ward quietly hummed the tunes as they drove in silence. Both were aware of her fears, and if they had admitted it to each other, they both had the same fears. They didn't talk for the next half an hour as the music played and Jan took this time to study their surroundings.

The road they were on was sparsely wooded and hilly. It was hard to tell just what kind of trees they were, a juniper of sorts, but with the little moonlight they got, and the headlights, it would be impossible to tell more than that. It really wasn't her thing anyway, she knew, to be able to decipher plant life, it was more her thing to just sit and enjoy it. There were no hidden away memories of this road. No matter how hard Jan concentrated, nothing seemed familiar. This did more to frustrate her than anything else had. With each passing landmark she let the thought of it fill her mind. Trying to connect what little she had for pictures and images to what she was now seeing. After a while, Jan sighed and gave up.

"I was wondering how long it would take you to realize you have never been this way before," Ward casually stated this and then continued to hum along to the music.

"Thanks for telling me sooner," frustrated now, Jan folded her arms across her chest.

"Don't blame me if it was a good memory exercise for you to complete. Remember, I'm here to help you, not to hand feed it to you," but there was something else darker in his thoughts. "When we get home, I'll help you go through some more exercises that might bring up some other memories," there, he had said it, 'home'. It was out there, like an open sore, he hadn't wanted to say home, at least not yet, but what else could he say. As of yet he hadn't lied to her, and now was not the time to start, it was their home. Ward now could only hope she would remember something of it. There was a bit of a silence before Jan said anything.

"Home?" No more, no less, Jan was learning that sometimes what was said was just that. There was a lot to Ward she didn't know, and a lot he was not allowing her to see. There were also things to learn about Ward and their relationship, and this time the discomfort seemed to be on his shoulders. It was a nice change for her not to be feeling uncomfortable. She decided to leave the comment as it was and continue on with a different topic, "When will I be able to get out of the wheelchair for good?"

Ward was perplexed. He had felt her questions, and then felt her release them. It was as if she was content not to know for now. He had also sensed something else, satisfaction. She was actually pleased with his discomfort, or confusion. Jan may not remember everything, but her personality seemed to remain the same, "Babs, you will find the chair nearly impossible tonight when we get there. We can start intense therapy tomorrow and you should be out for good, pretty soon. It's up to you," he half looked at her and there was a question lingering on his raised eyebrow as if to say, are you sure there isn't something else you want to know. Not getting any reply, he continued, "You're in great shape, so it shouldn't take too long," he let the corner of his mouth that she couldn't see tip up. His mind lingered on the last night they had spent together.

"How do you... Oh, never mind. I don't want to know. I need to do some thinking. There are some things I want to try to figure out," Jan moved on to other thoughts being very careful to stay out of his.

She leaned back into the softness of the seat and closed her eyes, the memory of the other night entered her mind and she instantly tensed. That voice had been familiar, and the eyes, there was something about the eyes that she knew. Sandy, yes the name of the woman they had been after had been Sandy. She tried to remember if she ever knew what her face looked like. She couldn't and she couldn't remember what they were looking for. Jan felt Ward tense as well, but he didn't interrupt her thoughts. She wondered if he would have recognized the voice. Instead of interrupting her, he let her try to put the information together. Jan let her mind drift back even farther. She started her thought process at the fight before Kevin had been killed, and she had nearly lost her life. Sadness danced on the edge of her thoughts and Jan was sure of where those feelings had come from. There had been many times in the hospital that Jan had concentrated on this moment, and tried to live the moments that had happened right before it, and afterwards. In the hospital it had been hard; so many thoughts seemed to have crowded in on her in the hospital, without her even knowing it. Here was different. The night was clear, and the only thoughts around were Wards, and even his thoughts were being shielded to help her reach into her own mind more.

"We have to stop," in her mind she had gone back to the car with Kevin. She was driving it but she wasn't sure where, the place was still unidentifiable to her.

"I'm supposed to take you to the airport and you will then be given a new life when we meet up with. . ." the name of the agent escaped her; Jan concentrated more on the conversation, it was the first time she could remember any of the conversation, "What's your problem? Up to now you've been happy to just let me take the lead and all the risk."

"I'm not leaving Sandy."

"Who's Sandy?" even with the question out Jan was starting to read his mind and dive deeper into his thoughts. An untrained mind was not able to keep a mind reader out, and if the other person didn't know he was being read, well it made it easy to gain access to most of their thoughts. Jan started to see numbers, but they weren't clear, and the images were beginning to fade and the sounds in the Explorer started to intrude again.

Jan concentrated even harder, focusing on her breathing, anything that would bring the lost conversation from the past back into focus. As the images began to fade, Jan tightly closed her eyes. The more she tried, the more it faded. The movement of the SUV and the sway of the music were coming back into focus. With frustration building, she allowed the muscles in her body to tense. Totally aware of her surroundings now, she worked even harder trying to bring up the last moments she was able to remember, the tension growing. A hand, gently placed on her thigh, startled her and released her from the stress and at the same time created its own.

"The harder you try, the more it will elude you. It's not all your fault you can't remember," there had been more to that statement that hadn't been said. He left his hand lay there for a while, and reluctantly with a pat, removed it as they drove up to a small official building that barely resembled a border crossing. The large lights around the building illuminated the building, the area, and the sign, which officially stated that it was the immigrations and customs office, as well as the entrance into Mexico. It was tan to match the surrounding scrub desert that Jan had not seen creep up on her during the last half an hour in the vehicle. Ward drove straight up to the gate, and with a few simple questions, and no ID exchanged, he was across. To Jan, this seemed too easy and she decided to question it.

"Another favor?"

"No, he's just seen me come through here a lot. I always cross here. No reason for him to stop me," Ward changed the CD again, "Remember, I can read what you're thinking, and no he doesn't know you," Ward had definitely left a piece of information off, and Jan was about to question it when Ward changed the subject, "Just about forty five minutes more, and then we are there. I'll have to carry you in, but the place should be ready."

Jan took the information for what it was. Ward wasn't ready to share what was on her mind; he had seen it coming and avoided it. Jan turned and watched out the window as they drove out of the small border town they had entered. She decided that the song playing, another Eagles tune, was very correct, 'you can't hide your lying eyes,' but what it didn't say was that maybe you could avoid the subject altogether which Ward seemed very good at. Something about the memories, she sensed, had disturbed him. Jan was pretty sure that it wasn't the fact of her getting hurt, not this time, but maybe it was the possibility of it. Not sure how to approach this with someone who might as well be a stranger to her, she let the thoughts go. This time, Jan hummed to the music, and they both rode in silence.

The road they were on intersected with another road not more than about twenty minutes away. The road they turned onto was far more interesting. It ran through the middle of Tijuana and then down the coast of the Baja peninsula. Jan opened the window a touch to hear the ocean after they had left the city behind. As the waves broke on the banks of the cliffs that lined the seaside, Jan could remember and begin to feel the importance of these sounds and the feelings that surrounded these memories. They played at the edges of her mind. Even though she had no memory of it yet she had the feelings that it stirred in her, like she belonged to the water. She belonged here. She tilted her head back and let the salty breeze fill her. The more she relaxed, the more she could feel the warm, happy feelings associated with this area. Since it was night the birds were quiet, and the road empty. A relaxed smile stretched across her face. Jan noticed the sign for 'las playas' and turned toward Ward. She wanted to read his thoughts, hoping that he was thinking the same as her, but afraid it just might not be so, she relied on a direct verbal assault instead.

"Can we stop for a minute?" Jan's eyes held a ray of hope that Ward couldn't see. She felt like a little kid asking for permission half hating it and half loving it.

"Are you okay?" in his voice a hint of worry betrayed him. He had been lost deep in thought, not concentrating on the moment, or her thoughts. Jan became aware of this and quickly made her wishes better known.

"Just fine. But I feel like I really just need to go to the beach for a moment and put my feet in the water. It sounds and smells so wonderful," again she waited, as another sign for the beaches was barely visible in the distance.

"Always the water baby. If you had your choice you would have lived in the ocean, not just by it," a smiled betrayed his sarcasm. "These beaches aren't the safest, but after the next sign, we can stop for a minute. I think you'll find where we are going much more to your liking though." Jan reached over to the radio and switched it off. She closed her eyes and just enjoyed the sound of the ocean in her ears.

"It was one of my first returning memories. The beach, I mean. I don't know why I feel so connected to it," Jan purposefully left off the part of Ward being there.

"Any other memories that went with that?" Ward probed; he knew that he had been a part of those memories in someway. That is how they had connected in the therapy room the other day. He had brought it to the surface. He hadn't controlled it so he had very little knowledge of the memories himself. He had worked very hard at not pushing things along. She did connect the beach to him, but just how much more could she remember? Impatience tugged at his self-restraint.

Jan saw Ward take a controlled breath, the first she had ever seen. He was truly hoping for something she didn't remember, but she didn't have the heart to tell him that what memories there were of him were truly limited to just the beach, and only that one day. Somehow she knew that she couldn't hide that fact from Ward, but she didn't want to hurt him. The silence dragged on and Jan knew she had to say something, as he had probably already read her mind, "I'm sorry," was all she could offer him. The word patience rang through her brain as if he were reminding himself of that lesson and the fall out from it bounced through her brain.

They pulled off the road and down the tiny lane to the beach. The closer Jan got to the beach the sooner she wanted to be on it. As soon as Ward stopped the Explorer, Jan opened the door and swung her feet out. Ignoring his warnings coming from the other side of the car as well as her body, she slipped off the seat and let her feet hit the sand. Ward took only seconds to move around the car and catch her. Then he helped her down to the ocean's edge. Although the night was dark, the light from the distant moon a silver glimmer, the sound of the waves and water whipped up pleasant feelings that Jan never thought she would know again. Not able to identify any of them in particular, but able to identify with all of them she stood there dazed and confused just letting it all hit her.

Ward stood and watched her breath in the atmosphere. Even in the dark he enjoyed what he could see and feel from her. Jan stood with her eyes closed, and Ward's hands supporting her, on her waist. As his arms slowly slid around her, he pulled her into him, and it felt so right. She rested her back against him. Her thoughts started to dart, images flew into and out of her head, overwhelming her. The warmth of his body, the input of images from her mind, and the smell of the ocean started to cloud her thoughts, and she began to get dizzy. Jan was well aware of the effect Ward and the ocean was having on her and she went to move his hands. She placed her hands on Ward's arms and started to push them away. She now wanted room to remember and not have all the thoughts and emotions assault her all at once. This was not letting anything become clear and clouding her judgment as to what was real and what was only in the moment. She heard a low, hushed voice.

"Not yet," it was a plea, a moan, and a wish. He had waited to hold her and knew that the next time this may happen, may be a long time from now. It left Jan unsure of what to do until she heard the cell phone in his pocket ring.

"Damn." He pulled the phone from his pocket as he pulled slightly away from her, but still stayed near enough to steady her. Parts of her body regretted the absence of his body heat but her mind cleared a little. Before he answered it he looked at the number calling him, "Hey Sage." Suddenly Jan had no problem now with him pulling away, "Really," there was a pause, "Well, thanks. Let me know if you need anything. Bye," and he dropped the phone back into his pocket.

"Just checking up on you?" she was unsure why she felt cheated, or even why she should care at all about the phone call. She also hated the jealous tone she heard in her own voice and felt inside.

"They found the chair and the boarding passes in the airport at New York. Sage planted the chair for us as soon as they landed. They have interviewed all the flight crew. Sage was able to convince them that we were on the plane. It helped that the cameras showed us going down the jet way. It will keep them guessing for a while," he was interrupted by the chirp of the cell phone again, only this time it was the signal for a text message coming in. Ward looked at it, read the message, and put the phone back in his pocket, "Ready?"

"Anything important?" Jan leaned back into his arms as she allowed him to pick her up.

"No, just work," he helped Jan back and into the Explorer.

"By the way, what do you do?" Jan sat on the edge of the seat, looking at Ward.

"This and that, mostly that," he closed the door and walked to the other side. He really wished that she had asked about the house before now, or him. Hopefully this wasn't too much too soon. What other choice did he have? She needed out of the hospital and away from all of those who would hurt, or cage her. He had to take her to a safe place. He had wanted to wait, but Rob didn't give him that chance. Rob had made a few mistakes, ones that had made their lives what they were before this point, and ones that had developed what this moment would be. Ward thought of the message again. All it had said was, "Where!" He had known it was from Rob even before he looked at the number. It was a message not worth answering yet. There was no going back. He had done what Rob had expected. Ward got into the Explorer, feeling a bit bold as he looked over at Jan and said, "Let's go home," letting her mind see a bit more of what was in his.

"Ready as ever," Jan felt the need to grab on to something, to prepare for the next onslaught of emotions, but instead she just looked forward. The SUV rolled backwards and turned around headed further down into the Baja. Just how much farther to 'home' Jan wondered as they passed through the next small town. So many questions, but more and more, there became only one focus to her thoughts. If he did a little of this and a little of that, maybe he could help her find this Sandy person, and put the rest of this little gang away, removing her from danger. He seemed well trained, and if all he had said was true then he was. It all seemed so simple.

Now all she had to do was talk to Ward about it. Turning to look at him, she noticed that his grip on the wheel had tightened again, and the muscles in his arms and shoulders were rigid. Jan wondered if he had picked her thoughts, and figured he had. One day, maybe he would show her just how to have such easy access to wander through minds, or filtering out the unwelcome intrusions, that he was so good at.

It wasn't too many more minutes into the drive when Ward pulled through the gates into a little development. He drove to the street closest to the beach, farthest from the main road. It didn't look like much, and in fact, there were only three complete houses, and about five that were in various stages of repair, and disrepair from the last five to ten years. As they pulled up to the last house, tucked into the corner of the cliff amongst the greenery, Jan saw a small Hispanic man come out of the house. It was as if he had been waiting for their arrival the entire time. Ward smiled and he waved when he saw him. The little man waved back, he turned and hollered something back toward the house as the Explorer came to a stop in the drive.

Chapter 7

Ward hopped out of the Explorer and walked up to the older man who Jan could now tell was in his early sixties. A younger man, mid-twenties, came out of the house while they were talking, and waved at the SUV. Jan watched as Ward threw the keys to him and he tossed a set of keys back at Ward. Jan looked past the men and into the windows of the house. The curtains were just sheers that covered the windows. She could see other activity going on behind the sheers, but wasn't sure who was in the house, or what was going on.

Looking at the house there was nothing to set it apart from any other house that they had seen driving down the road. This house though was a bit more secluded and seemed to be just a bit better cared for than the rest. The light from the lanterns lit by the younger man let her see the house and surrounding yard in more detail. The house front was painted a lively burnt orange with green on the trim. The rest of the house was the color of adobe brick. The side of the cliff seemed to be covered with various forms of plant life; in fact, it seemed to have come off the cliff to take over parts of the house as well. To the right of the house there was a walled garden, not unusual for a Spanish hacienda, but not well taken care of from the looks of it. The plants had entangled themselves and overtaken the only entrance to the patio along with a couple of cars, at least twenty years old, parked in front of it as well. The cars reminded Jan of large pots where plants were growing.

Jan could see the conversation coming to an end and the elderly man look at her. There was an expression of sadness on his face, and his thoughts betrayed his concern for the both of them. Jan smiled as she thought that mind reading must be multilingual. Ward walked back to the Explorer. Jan watched him stop as he looked at his cell phone again. He dropped it back in his pocket without answering it, and Jan suspected she knew who was sending all those messages.

"Ready?" it was more of a question directed at him than at her, as Ward opened her door.

"I take it they know us," Jan slid out of the car and as she touched the ground she began to be overcome with a sense of familiarity that the place brought to her. She swayed, and almost fell having no control over her muscles or actions. If it hadn't been for Ward catching her, Jan would have fallen to the ground.

"Slow down, no hurries here. No one knows where we are. The Garcia's here know us and have been waiting for us to arrive since I called earlier today, but..." Ward stopped and looked at her and saw how pale she was. He picked up on her thoughts, not giving her time to explain, or even to hide them as he wrapped his arms tighter around her, "Is this too much?" he stared straight into her eyes.

"Probably, but no time like the present, especially when you are looking for your past. And I'm beginning to think I will find it here," feeling and sounding less assured than her words, she went on, "Are we just going to stand here, or are you taking me into your home." Jan felt a stab of pain from Ward's thoughts on top of all the other emotions that she was feeling, and she looked at him quizzically. He picked her up and started to walk toward the overgrown gate, all the while he was thinking patience, patience, patience, explaining nothing to her.

All of the sights, sounds, and smells started to trigger memories without substance in her mind. All of the images were disconnected and unclear, but familiar in some ways. If she hadn't been in Ward's arms, she would have collapsed into a useless pile by now. She felt weak and vulnerable. Ward's arms were warm and secure, but did nothing to stop the onslaught of emotions; in fact they were magnifying them, as she got images from his mind as well. Jan hadn't been this confused since awakening at the hospital. She wanted to stop, to run away. Ward stopped, and hesitated, Jan signaled weekly with her hand for him to continue on, so hesitantly he did. This time more slowly.

She barely saw the courtyard as they entered through the door. It was beautiful, lush with green plants hanging from the rafters, and the vines climbing the walls. Very different than what she had expected from the look of it outside. Somewhere in the back of her mind it registered that this was the green she had seen in Ward's mind earlier. It was well trimmed and had a table and chairs in the middle. She heard the engine of the Explorer in the background and looked, panicked, toward Ward. Their faces were close, and the word darted on the edge of her conscious mind as the feeling between them seemed to dominate the moment.

"Manuel is moving it so that it's not easily seen," something about Ward's voice was strained, and not from carrying her. No it seemed to Jan that he had carried her like this in this very garden before, "You're not looking too good, I better get you into bed," Jan couldn't have agreed more. With everything she was experiencing right now talking was difficult. She was unable to voice her concerns at this point, and she allowed Ward to carry her down a flight of steps that were hidden off to the left of the garden. The door was unlocked, and they went in. He took her across a dark room, and without turning on a signal light, he avoided all the obstacles with a simple ease and grace one could only have if they knew the place well. They entered another room and he gently placed her on the bed. The softness of the bed and pillows seemed to cradle her, and the warmth of the comforter he placed on her only added to the drowning effect she felt from the bed, the emotions, and the events of the day. Giving in to the waves of clouded images, the onslaught of emotions, and the welcome comfort of the bed, she passed into a wild and disturbed sleep.

Ward sat with her for the next two hours, just watching her sleep. He had worried that this would all be too soon, and now he was afraid he had been right. Her reaction to this place seemed to put her emotionally over the edge. He watched as she twisted and turned in the bed, and listened to the occasional moan. She seemed to get no rest at all. He sat quietly in the dark, in the corner, not wanting to awaken any more memories in either one of them, afraid of just what might happen. Wishing he could turn off his memories at this moment, he just sat there. His heart felt heavy in his chest. He had seen agents go mad from experiences only half as mentally grueling as this. He had been close to it himself once, and it was only by sheer dumb luck that he hadn't gone mad. It had been one of his worst memories, and had happened just before he had left the department for good.

His only hope was that since these were all good memories here, maybe they would stimulate the rest of her mind to awaken and balance the effect. In the morning he would be able to tell more, but he was afraid to leave her here, alone, with nothing but unclear memories and clouded thoughts to torment her. Again his phone beeped, and he looked at it. This time there was more to the message, "Please, just let me know you're both OK. Phone. Rob," Ward had known Rob for a long time. He had been an agent for a long time even before joining their department, but in the past years, he had broken a few rules for them. Whether it had been because he hadn't known at first, a notion Ward knew wasn't completely true but liked to entertain it anyway. Or was it just the fact that he had missed this in his life and in some strange way hoped for better for Jan. Ward knew that he was not the person most liked by Rob, or anyone from the department for that matter. Rob would have been happy to see her with just about anyone else. No matter what Ward thought of Rob, Rob truly cared for Jan and wanted the best for her and he could not leave him to worry. The Jan he knew wouldn't have allowed that.

Ward sat for a moment and then started to enter the number to the secure line that he always used with Rob. It was a number they had set up after Jan had started to disappear with him. It was fine so long as he was able to get a hold of her, and since Rob had bent some of the rules they had decided on a neutral way to contact each other, so the department as well as Jan, would not discover that Rob was in contact with Ward. He thought for a moment before he typed in his message, "All fine. Keep me informed," he pressed send, and hoped that what he had typed was the truth. Shortly after, as he stared at her again he gave into the strain of the day, and fell asleep.

She started to move, feeling like she had been asleep for years, yet only resting for minutes. In between the two drapes Jan could see a glimmer of light. Something was different, changed from what she remembered as normal. As she began to look around, she realized that this wasn't the hospital room she was so used to waking up in. The sheets smelled of roses, and the bed was soft and comfortable with feather pillows, not hard and compact from many years of use. She moved so she could look around, and saw Ward in the corner, in a chair, fast asleep. The memory of the night before started to trickle in. They had left the hospital and in a round about way ended up somewhere in Mexico. She had assumed that this was his place, not knowing anything more about it, and remembering his familiarity with the elderly man. She moved, and her head began to swirl. It felt as if she had the mother, and father, of all hangovers. Her head threatened to explode with each beat of her heart. Her stomach churned, and it was all she could do not to vomit. All she could do was to lie in bed, eyes closed, hoping this would not last long as a little moan escaped her lips.

Ward jumped to his feet and was quickly by her side, as if he had never been asleep at all. She could feel his hand take hold of hers. He waited for her to open her eyes again, and he smiled. Jan, for the first time since she had been with him, noticed that she couldn't tell what he was thinking. She tried, and then relaxed as her head began to beat and throb again. It worried her, and she closed her eyes again letting the wave of nausea pass.

"I can't see your thoughts," her eyes remained closed and Ward frowned, it had been too much, but at least she still remembered the last month or so, for the most part he was pretty sure.

"Just an overload right now. Let yourself adjust. Are you wanting breakfast yet?" Ward watched her turn two shades of green, and barely held back a booming laugh, "Okay, later. Would a cool pack sound better?"

"Much," Jan flexed her muscles and found that they were still responsive, sore after yesterday, but responsive. When he left the room, Jan carefully, slowly, sat up, and looked at the room in more detail. The bed was large, and there was a dresser as well as an overstuffed chair in the corner that Ward had used as his bed last night. The thought that Ward had watched her sleep made her a touch uncomfortable. She decided to work on those feelings later. Right now when she let feelings enter into her mind it felt like thundering herds of elephants trooping around up there. Probably too much too soon, it was a hope. This room was certainly not just a place to stay, a hotel room of sorts, it contained personal touches, ones that were not made by a man. Of that she was pretty sure. She was also sure that it was his home, but who was the other occupant? There were pictures on the dresser of places and people. The pictures were too far away yet to tell just who they were, something to do later when she felt like crawling out of her warm, soft, comfortable spot. Looking back at the windows she noticed the curtains were solid in color, light green, with a small color block print in pastel shades of red, and blue. Not what she would have expected out of him, but maybe the people who lived upstairs had decorated this place, not a thought worth entertaining right now either. The bedspread matched the curtains and the cushions in the chair and on the bed were varying shades of the colors found in the room. Overall, she liked the look of the room, it made her feel comfortable, relaxed. Her eyes kept lingering on the drawn curtains, as if some secret hid behind them. Ward walked back into the room in time to see this. Without a word he handed her the cool pack with a small smile on his lips, and walked over to the curtains. He pulled them back slowly to ease the strain on the eyes from the light that filled the room. Jan gasped as she saw the view that awaited her behind the curtains.

"It's beautiful," she gasped. The ocean danced in front of her eyes as she looked at it from the cliffs above, the bed perfectly placed to make the view the central feature of the room. The vines that had looked so wild the night before framed the picture window, and if she looked hard, she could see hints of the deserted sand on the beach below. She looked out the window for what seemed an eternity, "Thank you."

"For what," Ward looked a touch confused.

"For sharing this with me, it must be hard," she didn't want to finish the sentence; she didn't want to know if it belonged to someone else besides Ward.

"I'll let you enjoy the ocean for now. I've got a couple of things to do. If you need me, just yell. I won't be far," his voice was soft. He left the room moving silently without a word, and without looking back at her. Jan watched him leave and then slid carefully off the bed. He was giving her some space and she decided to take it.

Carefully she used the support of the bed and then the dresser to make it over to the window. The view was even more breathtaking here. She watched the birds dance on top of the waves and the wispy clouds move carelessly over the sky. Off to the side she noticed the balcony that must have led off the living room. Ward had walked out onto the balcony, standing quietly and looking out onto the ocean. He stood facing the ocean, and began taking in deep breaths. She watched as he removed his shirt, and without knowing he was being watched, started a Tai Chi routine. Jan realized that he was keeping his thoughts to himself and being careful not to touch her thoughts this morning. With that realization, the pounding began to diminish in her head, as the ocean and Ward's concern wiped away the haze of last night. Jan found her eyes moving back toward Ward as she watched his muscles move through a routine that seemed to be one fluid motion, imprinted on his muscles. Jan's muscles seemed to want to respond to what he was doing, to follow the pattern as if they knew them.

Jan knew she was watching something very private, but for some reason could not take her eyes away from him. His muscles showed their hidden power, and his control over them. Her concentration became focused on what Ward was doing, and who Ward was. Her mind began to awaken, and small bits of emotion, and memory, trickled in without any pain. All of a sudden, Ward stopped, turned, and looked straight back at her. Their gazes held, and Jan felt guilty that she had imposed upon a very private moment. She turned quickly and grabbed for the dresser. Before she could move more than two steps, Ward was back into the room.

"Wait!" He yelled as he hurried into the room, "It's okay you just shocked me. I wasn't sure you were ready to stand and walk yet today," he moved toward her and helped with his gentle hands guiding her toward the chair, "I can see that you are, wait here while I get something for you." When Ward left the room Jan took the opportunity to look at the six picture frames on the dresser that were mixed in with the shells and rocks from below. Most of the pictures were of either Ward, or Jan. A few of the pictures included people she did not know with them. There was even one of Sage, another man, and Ward. Then there was one combination picture frame in particular that was interesting because the center picture in it was missing. The frame itself could hold three pictures. There was one of Jan relaxing on a beach somewhere; she thought it might be here, one of Ward rock climbing, and an empty spot in-between.

Jan's hand reached out to the empty spot and touched the glass. It seemed as if there should be something there, it almost felt warm to her. Earlier, both in the hospital and here, she had felt they had a history together, at least a friendship. Rob had confirmed that in his round about way, even hinted at something more. Looking at the pictures, she was now pretty sure of it, but just what kind of a relationship was it? It was the missing picture that held her attention, the secret, and distracted her as Ward silently entered the room.

He quickly came to a stop and stood there for a moment just looking at her. Her hand was on the glass where the missing picture should be, the one he had removed last night after they got in. He had placed it in his desk in the other room. He took the picture frame from her and placed it face down on the dresser.

"What was there?" Her voice soft, gentle, so much so that it took him off guard making him want to tell her.

"Us," then he suddenly realized what he had said and that the information might be too much, "when we were on one of our . . . adventures," the last word didn't come out evenly, and Jan hearing his discomfort, let the subject drop.

"What have you got there?" it was a simple redirection, but effective, and Ward accepted it, he had also put his shirt on she noticed. Ward took the European crutches out from behind his back.

"Simple to use, not hard on the arm pits; notice the sleek wrist grips and hand holds, and this type will work better here for as long as you need them. Would you like to take them for a spin and see the rest of the place?" Doing a quick comical routine to model them she laughed. Ward wanted to ask if she was feeling more normal. Could she read his thoughts? Could she remember anything more? With shocks like this, he knew from experience, that the brain may shut down all of its emotional responses for a while just to cope with all the input it was getting. He tried not to overload his thoughts, or to turn them loose, as that would only make the recovery process longer.

"Well, let's give them a spin. How hard could they be," and Jan stood up letting Ward adjust and fit the new crutches. Jan smiled as she thought about the wheelchair, and how it would be history from now on. Just as he got the last bit adjusted his phone rang. Pulling it out of his pocket, he looked at the number.

"I'll be right back," was all he said as he left the room. Jan carefully made her way across the room to the door. It wasn't easy, it wasn't graceful, and it wasn't completely silent, but it would have to do. She was able to hear Ward's side of the conversation from the other side of the door.

"You got five minutes," there was silence as Ward listened, "Nothing unexpected, better than if you would have taken her," another pause, "No haven't told her, she's not ready," she could hear Ward move, "If you can't find us, neither can they," a pause, "No, it's not for her own safety that you want her there, and I don't care what you tell the department. Tell them I overpowered you for all I care. I'll let you know her progress, but right now let me take care of her. I'm the only one that really knows how to," she could hear the anger in his voice, "I'm not her jailer, and if it had been different earlier we wouldn't have had this problem," Jan figured he must have clicked off because she could hear him turn and walk back to the bedroom. Jan had just enough time to get out of the way of the door before he came in.

"Should have known, how much did you hear?" he didn't seem overly angry or shocked, but he didn't smile.

"Enough to be confused and to be able to guess who you were

talking to." Jan moved a little, "What about the tour you promised me?" A little surprised she didn't ask for more, Ward moved from the ocean side bedroom to an even larger living room with another breath taking view, and a balcony that started the small tour. Ward became more relaxed as he showed her around the place. The room contained comfortable furniture, as well as some distant memories she could feel, scattered about the room. In one corner there sat a computer set up on a small wooden desk. The kitchen was small, but adequate with a microwave, stove, and fridge. There was another bedroom, small but nicely decorated in shades of green, with a small window off to the side. There were two bathrooms, one definitely a guest bath. The larger one in the main bedroom where she had slept seemed to have all the essentials in it for two people, with a large shower, and even larger tub off to the side. As she walked through the rooms she got the sense that she had been here before, although most of her feelings had been guarded from her, or just plainly turned off, she was unsure of which it was that her mind had chosen. This worried her, she had been able to pick up more information from things and people around her in the hospital, and now it seemed as if she had lost one of her senses, the one that could connect her to her past, what she wanted most.

The relaxed feelings that lived in the apartment seemed to have the same effect on Ward as they had on Jan. Together they finished going through the apartment. She looked over at Ward again as they went back into the living room. She had a slightly confused look on her face.

"I can pick up on some things, mostly what one could normally observe. It's like someone has switched off a part of my brain. It's like losing my sight, or hearing. I'm even having trouble reading you, but you may be blocking me. I know you've done that before," Jan sat down on the sofa that faced the ocean. Everything here seemed to focus on the ocean and the sky, and its sense of calm.

"I may have brought you here too soon; too many memories trying to crowd in. I just didn't know where else you would be safe, and I knew you would be here. The mind will switch off in self-defense, but the fact that you can pick up on some things is very positive. We will work with that," Ward sat beside her, just far enough away to keep from making physical contact, "In a couple of days, your head will start to clear, and I'm sure you will pick up on many other things."

"The people upstairs know we are here," Jan knew that most things were truly never a secret, and this was a factor she needed to have cleared up for her. If even one other person knew, then there would always be the possibility of others finding out. Even though she had recognized the masked voice in the hospital, she didn't want to be reintroduced to him anytime soon.

"I did him a favor. He had been in some very big trouble, or his son was in trouble to be more specific. I took care of it for him. That's what I do," there was something more he wanted to say, but stopped there.

"It must have been something very important for him to keep this place quiet," Jan dared not look at Ward, he was too close.

"He gets to live here free, and all he needs to do is take care of the place right now. Son's got a good job in a town not far from here, and Mama Garcia is cooking and cleaning and singing most of the time, happy now. When you are ready, I will reintroduce you to them," they sat in silence for a while.

"You were doing Tai Chi out on the balcony a bit ago, will you teach me?" Jan looked toward him.

"I plan to, it will be an important part of your recovery amongst other things we will do, but not on the balcony, that's not where I, or you for that matter, enjoy practicing Tai Chi. I will take you down to the beach," Ward could tell that there was something there as he looked back into her eyes, but he guarded his hope, patience he reminded himself. They stared at each other until Ward broke the silence, "Would you like to go to the beach now?"

"Please," Ward got up and started to help Jan, "Wait," and she pushed away his hands. If she was going to recover, she wanted it to be sooner, not later. Somewhere in the back of her mind she got the impression that she had always been this impatient and impossible. She made it up and adjusting the crutches, she walked toward the door with Ward close to her, watching over her like a hawk. When they got to the door, they walked out and Jan looked up the steps and then at Ward, "Okay, you win," and Ward picked her up letting the crutches dangle by his side, and a smile tipped the corners of his mouth.

"Somehow I thought I might," once up the steps she expected to be put down, but he didn't. He walked through the courtyard and over to a set of steps as overgrown as the courtyard had looked from the outside.

"When we get to the beach, I'll put you down," carefully Ward made his way down the stone steps, ducking when the branches got too low, placing his feet carefully on the uneven and damp surfaces. The vines and leaves obscured the view of the ocean until they broke through the last bunch and out onto the beach. The sand was warm and inviting, the ocean called to her with every wave that hit the rocks off to each side. The rocks off to each side were what made the beach so private, secluded, and hard to reach. The birds played off to the side running away from the waves as they inched up the shore. In the distance she could see a pair of dolphins playing in the waves. It was paradise, simply paradise. Ward watched her and enjoyed the feelings that he saw dart across her face as he saw her repeatedly take in deep breaths and be emotionally fed by the nature around her. Her eyes glistened and her hair danced in the breeze. He didn't dare eavesdrop on her thoughts for fear of upsetting what healing was occurring right in front of him.

"So do you like it?" it was less of a question, less of an interruption, and more of an observation. Ward helped her sit down on the sand.

"More than I could have hoped for. Now, I think I will begin to feel whole again," her hands started to play in the sand grabbing handfuls and letting the grains fall through her fingers back to the beach. Ward watched her for a moment and then walked away a bit, removing his shirt; he started into his routine again, this time, not concerned if she was watching or not. As hard as she tried not to watch him, the more he moved, the more she watched. Not only did watching him please her, it began to jog her memories. She thought back to the beach in her mind, and the warm hands. Suddenly Jan took a sharp breath, but it didn't disturb Ward at all, he continued totally focused in the moment, lost in the routine, secure with the thought she was safe. She realized that this was what had been happening in the visions she remembered from the hospital. It was of him, and it was of here. She continued to watch him, and began to feel more comfortable with a relationship she knew very little about, but felt very connected to. She felt the sand in her hand, and let it trickle back to the beach. All of a sudden she felt an uncontrollable need to be wicked and playfully throw a handful of sand at his back. As it hit, it stuck to the sweat. Breaking his concentration, he turned, smiled and then ran back at her.

"Feeling better are we?" he grabbed her and lifted her up like a feather, "Now, let's just see how much better," and with a playful smile that seemed to encompass his entire mood, ran toward the water.

"No! No! I'm not dressed for swimming!" She was half-fighting, half-laughing, and completely relaxed and happy.

"Too late now," and into the water they went. It was cold at first and all her muscles tightened. But as the waves washed over them, she felt new, and refreshed. Still in Ward's arms, but this time face to face, body to body, she could feel the warming connection between them. All of a sudden they stopped moving, both their faces so close they could feel the other's breathe over the breeze of the ocean. Ward started to lean into her, and then backed away as the memories of what had happened last night replaced his needs and feelings of the moment. Jan on the other hand almost wished he had continued with his actions, even though she was afraid of what emotions it would awaken. She confronted the idea, as Ward moved back, that there were too many unknowns yet to deal with, "We should go and get dried off," his voice was deep, and rough. He changed her position in his arms into a regular cradle hold and walked out of the water. Once they were back at the top of the steps he decided to chance a conversation again, "Tomorrow we start the therapy again for both the mind and the body," he glanced a little too long at her wet clothes, and Jan warmed from the inside out. The rest of the day was even less eventful, and they mostly avoided each other, until supper. Jan couldn't help but think about what she really owed this man and what she couldn't give to him right now and maybe never again. Could he ever tell her what they were without feeling the pain of the lost memories and shared times? The memories seemed to be coming back, but not fast enough for her, or for him.

The smells of supper cooking wafted into the bedroom as Ward fixed the meal. He had busied himself in the kitchen for the last hour. Some of the time he was in the kitchen he didn't need to be. Jan knew he was just using cooking as another way to avoid her. She could smell the aroma of cooking fish and wild, spiced rice as it wafted out of the small kitchen. He had set the table with all they needed, and when she made her way to the kitchen to help, he had only sent her away. This time she hung around at the door. "When the phone rang earlier today, who was it?"

"Rob," he let the answer out in a flat voice as if it had no meaning, continuing to slice vegetables. It surprised Jan that he answered without reserve, and not trying to keep it from her. Jan leaned into the kitchen and grabbed a piece of cucumber to eat. It was the first time she had felt like eating all day.

"He wanted me, didn't he," she leaned on the doorframe.

"Yes, but unless you wish it, he can't have you," he tossed the veggies into the pan with the rice, "and they have no idea where you are."

"They may need help looking for the woman that had a connection to Kevin. I remember her first name, it's Sandy, not sure it will be any use just yet," Jan looked longingly at the chair at the table, but remained standing, she felt as if she could push herself now, it was safe to do so.

"That won't be necessary, they found her," he left off the details about how for now, and continued to cook the meal. No need to let her know that Sandy would never be able to help them find what Kevin had hidden, that much they had found out. The fact that no one knew what it was, seemed irrelevant for right now. Even if Jan had known what it was, Ward was sure that she had no memory of it now.

"Something's wrong," Jan looked at Ward with a bit of worry. Ward's phone rang. It lay on the counter closer to Jan than to Ward.

"Would you look to see who's calling?" he stirred the rice and vegetables.

"Okay," Jan looked at the phone's display, "Sage."

"Pick it up will you?" Ward stirred the rice and veggies in the frying pan, busying himself with the food.

"Hello," Jan felt very unsure about this as she answered the phone, still wanting to know more about Ward and Sage's connections as well as her connection to Ward.

"Hi, how are you feeling?" She sounded as if she was concerned.

"Better."

"You're in wonderful hands there. Ward handy?" she looked at his busy hands, and then smiled.

"He's right here," just then he walked over and took the phone, whispering thanks to Jan. This time he didn't leave the room.

"What's up," he smiled an easy smile as he talked with her, "Who questioned you?" Ward smiled, "No, they should leave you alone now. Don't worry about it; they don't know you have a connection to me. Just go about your life. Love ya, and thanks again," and he rang off, putting the phone back on the counter, "Ready to eat?" and he walked the filled plates to the table.

As they sat in silence at the table, Jan looked at Ward and tried to decide if she should ask what was working its way around her mind. The food was delicious and just spicy enough for her, but she stirred it around on her plate trying to think, to remember anything. Ward looked up and noticed that she wasn't eating.

"Too spicy?" he waited for the answer.

"No, it's wonderful, but," and again she paused, Ward waited patiently, "who is Sage?"

"Oh, is that all that's bothering you," he took another bite before he continued, savoring both the bite and the moment, "A year ago, her husband disappeared, I won't go into the details, they're not important. I happened to help find out what happened to him. He had been involved in some pretty nasty stuff. She wasn't happy to get all the details, but in the end, at least she knew what happened to him. That's why she was happy to do us a small favor, and why I was able to get around the airport so easily. Most of them have seen me there before," he forked another spoonful in and looked down at his plate.

"Was he alive or dead?" Curiosity tweaked her interest.

"Dead."

"So is that how you earn your living now, after leaving the department?"

"Sometimes," he stopped and looked at her, "The people I help sometimes pay me something, and sometimes not. I'm not a mercenary. That doesn't mean I don't help them or accept pay if they want me to take it. There are other things I do to make a living," he paused, "legal things."

"Am I another one of your projects?" Jan fidgeted in her seat, and looked back at her dinner, not sure she wanted the answer to that question.

"No," his finger touched her chin and moved her face so that he could look her deep in the eyes, burning a hole through to her soul, "you are different."

Jan wasn't sure if that was all, but knew that was all he was willing to give. Happy with that she dropped her chin when he removed his finger. She ate her food without another word, not remembering when she enjoyed a meal more. The rest of the evening was quiet, and soon she went off to bed. After being in the bedroom a couple of minutes, she turned around and walked back out, about to ask a question, but she was stopped before she could.

"I'll be in the guest room if you need me," Ward was already on the computer in the corner, and most of the lights were out, he didn't turn around as he worked on whatever had his attention. Jan thought to herself, probably righting another wrong in the world, and she went back in the bedroom and to bed.

Jan couldn't have been more right. Ward had taken on the job of discovering who was after her, and what they wanted. He had hacked into the department's mainframe to discover what he could about the circumstances of Sandy's murder. Since Sandy was now of no help to anyone, whatever these people wanted, whoever they may be, they would assume that Jan had it. Yet Jan still had no memory of what they might be looking for, which put her at a great risk. He was needed to protect Jan, and Ward took this job very seriously. He stayed on the computer for about two hours before giving up and going to bed.

The rest he so badly wanted was not going to be easily attained. He lay quietly on the spare bed for another hour just thinking, memories of Jan, the department, and of the past year drifted through his mind. Something he had read on the department's mainframe confused him. Something was wrong with it, but he couldn't put his finger on it yet. Ward found cases far easier to deal with when he could deal directly with people, not paperwork.

It was there that his skills as a mind reader made the difference; otherwise he was just like any other good agent. When sleep finally came, it was a fitful one.

Two weeks passed quickly in a calm, routine manner. It was clinical in the sense that Ward was very concerned about how her recovery was progressing, but there were those times that they both reached beyond the bounds of doctor and patient. Ward had been very careful not to push too far. A casual caress or a peck on the forehead was all that he had attempted. Every morning they would go to the beach to do Tai Chi. Jan had been a quick study on the lessons of this ancient art. It was very natural for her, and Ward never let on that she was actually the one who taught it to him. After the lesson Jan would settle on the beach for a meditation session and Ward would take an hour run, preferring to do his meditation sometime in the afternoon. They would return to the apartment and have a quick salad for lunch, a rest and then a discussion on what memories the meditation had brought up, as well as a few mental exercises that honed her skills greatly as a mind reader, more than Ward had picked up on. Phone calls were almost nonexistent by the end of week two, and Jan had discovered more of her skills than she thought she would. She picked up quickly the lessons he gave her to strengthen her mind reading, and to focus her thoughts. It was becoming second nature again.

Through all this discovery process she had learned very little of her past, but got glimpses by deja vue. She was sure that she had known Ward for sometime. Although the memories associated with him were still very disconnected, they were still the clearest memories she had. She could remember them on various outings, rock climbing, skiing, at which she was terrible, and on long quiet walks. When her meditations had drifted off toward Ward she was content to leave herself there in that time and space; all were very tender memories. Very little of this she had discussed with

Ward. Somehow he knew that there were bits and pieces slowly coming back, but with each passing day, there seemed to be more feelings of frustration that surrounded Ward, all having to do with the amount of time it was taking her to remember. In the afternoons they practiced focusing techniques used for mind reading, and it was during this time her thoughts were most vulnerable. He had picked up on the bits and pieces she was getting about them, and she had picked up on the one word he reminded himself of often, patience. One of the first lessons he had taught her was how to close her mind, but it was useless when doing the other activities to strengthen her skills. She was amazed at how easy it seemed to him, and how reliable it was becoming for her. From the time in the hospital to now, it seemed as if she had changed. The skills she had become aware of at the hospital were so primitive to what she was able to do now, and it was a well-developed skill that was still increasing. In this, Ward seemed pleased with her, and her progress, at least what he knew of her progress.

There had been other memories as well; ones that could only be associated with what had been her job. Most of those memories led to violent images, faces without names, and dark places she could only imagine going to because it was part of her job. These things she discussed with Ward without much detail, only to clarify the associations, and to try and put names to these faces. Most of which he didn't know either, except for the faces of people who worked at the department with them. They worked on connecting these images with the past incidents, but without any luck.

Jan knew there was something there, just out of her reach, and she would try to reach past it. Each time her frustration would start Ward would stop the exercise.

"When you get frustrated, the mind works in a different way and will not allow itself to remember what has caused the trauma," Ward walked around to the back of the kitchen chair and began massaging her shoulders.

"It's just that I am trying so hard to remember what happened so that we can find this Sandy before it is too late," she felt Ward's thoughts stop, "We're too late aren't we. That's what you're keeping from me," she turned to face him. Defying him to tell her she was wrong.

"You're right. I've known since we left the hospital that they found her. I know more of the details because I slipped into their computers, nothing that I think you would find helpful, or pleasant. They tore her place apart looking for something. No one is sure what it is they are looking for," he paused. "Right now, you may be the only one holding the information. Even if it is trapped in your head, and that makes you very valuable, and vulnerable," Ward was interrupted by the beep on his cell phone signaling an incoming text message. He had not received a text message for quite a few days. They both looked at the phone. Ward walked over to it and read the message silently. Jan practiced her newfound skills to pick up on some of his thoughts, she knew the message had to do with her, but that didn't seem like it was hard information to come up with.

"What is it?" she looked at Ward.

"It's from Rob. It says, 'Don't come back. Something's wrong here. Jan's things trashed. Keep her safe. Rob.' He must be serious if he's giving up control to me," Ward was still looking at the phone. Jan felt a shiver go up her spine. Ward put the phone down and walked out of the room.

Chapter 8

Ward had spent hours on the computer that night. Jan could hear him clicking away long after she had gone to into the bedroom. They hadn't spoken, just settled into a silence that was neither comfortable, nor uncomfortable after the message. He hadn't been that focused since she had first gotten there. She was about to fall asleep when she heard something hit the wall with force and shatter. She immediately sat up and got quietly out of bed. She was able to use one crutch now to move around the apartment and this made the journey to the bedroom door far quieter. First, reverting back to her training and instinct, she reached out with her mind to see if there were any thoughts, other than hers and Wards, in the apartment. She couldn't feel or see anything, not even Ward's mind, and this worried her. There had been many times when she couldn't read Ward's mind, but there had never been a time when she couldn't tell it was there.

Quickly her mind retraced the events of that evening. After they had received the message on the phone, Ward had gone right to work. He had decided that it was time to figure out just how to get these people out of their lives. He had spent his all his time this evening, making connections with whomever he could reach on the computer, and ignoring her. Mostly it had turned up dead ends. Going after the information he needed in a different way, he went back into the news reports prior to, and during the time that Kevin had turned himself over. Most of the information he was getting was stale and useless. Not wanting to look over his shoulder all the time, Jan had gone to bed, and neither one of them had said anything to each other.

As soon as Jan disappeared into the bedroom Ward stopped for a moment to stare at the door. He didn't move, just stared. Every night after she had gone to bed, he had removed a picture from the desk drawer. He held it so that he could see both the picture and the door. Pain and patience tore at him from the inside out and in opposite directions. They had achieved an easy friendship over the last few weeks, and even made inroads to the past, and what they had once been. But it had never gone too deep. He had felt her desire at times, and she his. There was recognition on some level of the past, but they were unable to get there just yet. He blamed himself for not readying her for this earlier. The computer beeped and interrupted his thoughts; he turned to see the e-mail that had just come in. After reading it and digesting the information, he knew he would sell his soul to the devil to keep her safe, and he wasn't going to be far from it. Ward looked at the picture he held in his hand again. He hit the reply on the e-mail menu and typed his message. Ward now had all his fears confirmed concerning Jan. He knew why she was having trouble with her memory. With reluctance he completed the message and hit the send button. Anger and frustration over took his control, and he picked up his glass to get a drink. Slowly his hand began to tighten around the glass as every thing soaked in. The past the present, the future all endangered by one person. Instead of drinking what was in the glass he allowed his emotions to take over, and he flung the glass across the room and watched it shatter like his life against the wall. Emotionally spent, patience exhausted, he then collapsed on his folded arms at the desk.

Slowly she opened the door just a crack. From the opening she could see Ward slumped over the computer, unmoving. Jan visually scanned as much of the room from the opening of the crack as she could. Nothing was out of place. She was unable to see what had hit the wall and where it had broken. Ward had still not moved. 'He could be asleep, he could be...' and the thought left Jan's head as fast as it had entered. From across the room she heard a strained and weary voice that she barely recognized.

"I'm not dead, just frustrated; sorry if I woke you," Jan opened the door as Ward lifted himself from the computer desk. His face looked tired and drawn. The strain showed in his shoulders and arms. There was no emotion left in his eyes. Jan felt her heart leap in her chest, "You're safe here, I have to go out," and with that said, he got up and grabbed his jacket by the door. Without looking back at her he walked out leaving anger in his wake. He closed and locked the door. His footsteps were light on the steps, and were gone within seconds. The silence overtook Jan. It was the first time she had been alone since the hospital, and she didn't like it one bit.

Jan walked over to the desk, drawn to something about it, wanting to know more. She sat down and looked at the computer. Somehow, she knew it was time to find out as much as she could. He had logged off of the machine. Jan started the machine up again and spent some time looking through the files on the desktop, and then the rest of the hard drive. Most of these files had nothing to do with her. Respecting his privacy, she chose not to read those that didn't deal directly with her, or the job she had been on. Most of what she found involving her were news reports of the incident that were sensational, and the dry reports written by Rob, copied from the department's mainframe. These reports from Rob were from her time in the hospital, and her recovery, or lack there of. Jan lastly read the reports written by Rob about Sandy's murder.

Details of how and where Sandy had been found were in the report that she read. Nothing had been left out. It also discussed the condition of the room in which she had been found. The room, a hotel room, had been left in disarray. They hadn't discovered many personal effects. Jan had expected to find herself disgusted by the details of Sandy's death. On one level she was, but she was also amazed at the fact that somewhere in her mind she knew she had read similar reports before, and even written them from time to time. Jan knew something was happening, and was unsure of just what it might be. Work seemed to be making a connection for her.

She had been resting her head on her hand, and now as she lifted her head up she let her hand drop to the desk. A piece of paper fell from the desk. She bent over carefully to pick it up. As she touched it she realized it wasn't a piece of paper at all, it was a picture, and as she turned it over to place it back on the desk she felt her mind connect to it. She knew instinctively that it was the picture that belonged in the frame in the bedroom where she slept. She had somehow known before she turned it over, and was sure of it now as she saw the picture.

Jan let her eyes focus on the picture where there were two very happy people. They were locked in an embrace, and they were focused on no one else but each other. Jan let her fingers trace the outlines of the people in the picture. She recognized the people. She let her fingers trace the image of Ward, and then she let her finger trace the image of herself. Her hands began to shake as her mind exploded with the realization of what the picture was. Images that had only floated on the edges of her mind, now were connected, whole, and had meaning. Clouds that she had never known were there, cleared and allowed everything to start pouring in. As Jan sat in the chair she now remembered picking out the furniture for the apartment. Shaking, she slowly let the information soak in. As the memories turned into a flood, Jan just sat there overwhelmed letting it wash over her. Jan tried to connect everything she now knew. Most of the holes in her memory that she had lived with for the last month were filled in now, both work and play, with startling clarity.

She held her head and was surprised when she realized that there were tears coming from her eyes. Ward had been working with her for over a month, nearly two, and had learned of her accident two weeks prior to that. It had been two months before that, when she had seen him last. When they had last left each other's company, his words rang through her mind, "Remember, if you're ever in trouble, come here. Whatever you choose remember, no one knows of this place, it's ours, and will always be only ours. If you come here, I will be here soon after you," and they had kissed, deep and long. Other tears escaped. He had gone through so much pain in the last couple of months, all caused by her. And Jan now knew the hell he had been going through. She even remembered the last argument now, "Leave the department, and come with me Babs. Don't go back there; they don't care about you or the people they say they help. All they are interested in is the power, and the control. You're a possession to them, a tool, nothing more."

The shaking finally stopped. Jan picked up the picture and cradled it in her hand as she made her way slowly back to the bedroom. She picked up the frame that the picture belonged in, and placed it back into the spot it truly deserved to be. As she set the frame down she smiled. She sat down in the chair and stared at the picture. Something so small had made such a big difference. A week ago, a month ago, she wouldn't have been able to take the onslaught of emotions this picture had brought on. She smiled, as she knew how strong she had become; how strong he had allowed her to grow without complicating the matter. While marveling at the difference and the growth she had made, especially in the last week with Ward's help; she heard the door open and close.

Jan made her way over to the bedroom door in time to see Ward throw his jacket on the couch and turn away from their bedroom, deliberately not looking in that direction. His shoulders were hunched, and she was afraid to read his thoughts. She had not discovered where he had gone to that night, but knew it had to do with her, and with the job she had been on. He began to walk toward the small guestroom, not aware that Jan was watching him, keeping his mind from searching her out. He thought she was asleep, and he looked utterly defeated. She reached out only enough to sense that his mind was in turmoil, not completely closed, and not wanting to look for her mind, for her. She looked directly at his back as she spoke.

"Aren't you going to the wrong room?" Ward stopped and stood motionless, stiff, and afraid to turn around. Jan just waited, letting her thoughts drift over to him. As her thoughts drifted into his mind, his back straightened up. His muscles tensed tighter than she could have ever imagined they could.

"Do you remember?" hope tugged at his voice. He turned slowly to meet her gaze. His mind started bursting with images, uncontrolled. He wasn't even sure which mind the images were coming from, and for once, he didn't care.

"Come here," she said as he walked over slowly, stiffly, not wanting to believe this was happening. This could only be a dream; it couldn't be real. He must have fallen asleep at the computer and at any moment he would awaken and find himself alone, again. He had dreamt of her before. He stopped walking for a moment not wanting to awaken from what might only be a reoccurring dream, afraid it would never come back. Jan just beckoned him to her with a small wiggle of her finger, and a smile on her lips. He followed her into the room and over to the dresser.

It only took him seconds to see that the picture was back in the frame. He looked at it as if it were a lifetime away. He reached out to touch the glass as Jan spoke, "I remember this day, the day we were married. Almost a year and a half ago," that was all she got out. Ward grabbed her, and whether it was joy that some of her memory had returned, or whether it was pure desire, he held her tightly to him and kissed her. At first the kiss was gentle, and then it deepened. Jan welcomed the kiss, getting lost in the moment of rediscovering Ward, the Ward she really knew. Jan was sure of what was coming next, and she leaned into Ward even though it seemed impossible, letting the crutch drop to the ground. Ward stopped only for a minute. He smiled. She had done that on purpose so he would have to support her.

"Oh Babs," whispering, with his mouth close to her ear, his arms almost too tight around her, afraid she would vanish again into the cloud she had been living in, "You don't know how much I wanted to tell you everything, but you had to remember it yourself. I couldn't force it on you, not even if it was what I wanted. We've never lived like that," he let his lips play with her ear, "Are you sure you want me in here tonight?" He had to know.

"Tonight," Jan melted further into him letting him support her completely, "and every night," and with that, they became lost in each other's thoughts, and each other as he carried her over to the bed.

Jan awoke happy and content in Ward's arms, in the bed they had shared many times before now, and that they would share many more times. Afraid that last night had only been a dream, she snuggled deeper into his arms letting the warmth of his body surround her, reassure her. In his half-awake state, he stirred and kissed the top of her head.

"That was much better than any dream I've ever had," they laid together way past the time they would have normally been up and gone down to the beach for their exercises. Letting their minds mix as they lay there in the easy way they always had. The silence they shared spoke volumes. Ward was amazed; she was back, she was right here, and she was his again. It wasn't until the phone beeped in the other room that one of them spoke.

"Who could that be?" Jan was the first to speak both of their thoughts.

"Some one with very bad timing," Ward rolled toward Jan and neither one of them thought of the text message on the phone for the next two hours.

Jan rolled out of bed and left Ward asleep on the other side. Wrapping the robe around her she looked back at Ward and smiled. She couldn't remember a time that she had been happier. Grabbing the one crutch she could find, Jan walked to the kitchen and got out a glass and juice from the fridge. The phone caught her eye. Picking it up, she decided that she should read the text message that had come in earlier. She read it in silence, "Rob says Hi. If you want to see him alive, you'll let me know where it is."

That was all it said. The joy Jan had just found had been stolen away so quickly. The image of her faceless intruder appeared before her. No matter what joy she now knew with Ward, she couldn't let Rob die out of pure selfishness. He had done so much for her, for them. At that moment, she knew what she had to do. Ward appeared at the bedroom door, looking toward her. Their eyes met, pain showed in both faces.

"You can't go."

"I have to."

Chapter 9

Ward was leaning on the doorframe with nothing but a towel wrapped around his waist arms folded tightly in front of his chest. He wasn't smiling, and he seemed to be in need of something to do to help him keep control of his emotions. Ward walked over and grabbed the broom and dustpan from behind her. He silently cleaned up the broken glass and threw away the pieces while Jan watched. Jan knew it was all he could do to keep calm, and yet there was some other turmoil going on in him, that she was unable to read. Ward had taught her not to eavesdrop on people's thoughts, and to control the random images, but with him it was different. Here in the middle of this silent discussion, she didn't think a look would be considered eavesdropping, not with all she now knew about their relationship now, plus he didn't seem to mind the company in there.

"The department will take care of Rob," he moved to the big picture window and door that led out to the balcony. Ward now stood with his back to her looking out at the ocean. Jan looked at him. She could see every muscle in his back, tense and tight, his arms again folded in front of him, the tan that had developed over the last two weeks showed, and he looked healthy, fit, but not happy.

"Both you and I know that's not true, we are living proof. What about all those people that we don't know about? Rob never left me for dead on any assignment as the department would have had him do a couple of times, especially this last time, and," she paused waiting to see if Ward would turn around, "if it wasn't for him we wouldn't be together right now. He allowed you to get away with all of this, not easily, and not outright, but he did and you and I both know it."

Jan put the phone down, and walked over to him. His body did not yield to hers as she leaned up against him, so she straightened up again and leaned back on the crutch, and not him.

"You're in no shape to go yet. How much do you remember of what happened? Do you know what they are looking for? Do you know who is looking for you?" There was a small hint of an accusatory tone in his voice, "Do you remember what it was like for any of us at the department? Do you remember all of it?" pain tinged every word.

"Yes and no, but I'll be okay thanks to you, without you I may never have gotten this far. This place, our life here has been healing. It allowed me to reach back in and find myself. I couldn't imagine how I could have done this without you. And I can't imagine being without you now," she looked directly at him, mind open and willing to allow him to see into her mind, "As for my memory, most of it is back after last night. After I saw the picture, it all came flooding back, and now it is the sorting and piecing together that I have to do; no one can do that for me. I am still struggling with what happened around the time of the beating, and Kevin's death. Those memories don't seem to want to come back. Those memories seem lost, almost like they were hidden, locked away from me," Jan felt his mind close tight. He felt a million miles away.

"It won't do you any good to try to help Rob if you don't know what they are looking for, and can't remember," Ward didn't move.

"The department must have some leads on it, I'll start there," Jan watched a pair of dolphins in the distance playing in the waves.

"They don't know. I've been through all their files. That's one reason why you were so important to them. They wanted to use you to find the missing piece to the puzzle. The other theory is that you, and I, were a part of it, in either case you would know. Nothing you or Kevin had with you seemed to lead them anywhere. Nothing found at the hotel Sandy was at was of any use. Now that Rob has been kidnapped, these people hope to get to you before the department does, and find their missing item. They know how important Rob is to you. With that information they are hoping to ferret you out first," Ward focused on the dolphins as well. It was the one place he could let himself connect with her for now, any deeper, and she would know it all.

"I can't tell them what it is, I just don't know yet," Jan walked back over toward Ward, and touched Ward's arm, "But I can tell you, I can't leave Rob to die. I know you can't either. They have killed everyone they could find so far except me. I need to know why that is, and it's not right just to leave Rob, you know that," Jan turned and walked to the couch to sit down. She hoped she had struck a nerve in him. Ward turned to look at her and her eyes were looking directly into his. His eyes were dark, angry. Jan never backed down from his visual assault. The silence grew, and although she didn't mind the view, the silence grew uncomfortable. He turned back to look out the window.

"I know what they are looking for," Ward stayed still, stock still, letting what he said hang in the air. The ugliness of it weighted the air down in the room. It was out now and there was no way he could take it back.

"What?" it was a mixture of shock and disbelief, and she tried very hard not to shout it out. "How long have you known?"

"Last week I started looking for these people to rid you," he paused, "us, of them. I want you safe. As you know now, I have a vested interest in your future," he half laughed, "After looking through the files at the department and slipping into every computer they have, and not finding anything I decided to make a few other contacts. Finding nothing of use there, I chose to go see a man last night about some information. That's where I went last night," Ward turned. His face set in stone, "It was useful," Jan felt the conflict in his mind. He was careful not to show any more emotion than was necessary, but his thoughts were having a hard time staying closed. His mind was not at all calm even though his body language tried to display that. Jan backed off, not wanting to intrude in his thoughts, not sure she would survive if she did. Whoever this contact was, it had cost Ward something for the information, something important, but she may never know what the price had been.

"What did Kevin have? Should I know where it is?" Jan's voice was low, small in the room. Ward looked back into the expanse of the ocean and composed his thoughts before he continued.

"It seems that Kevin hid a payment for a drug shipment into New York, never turned it over to his higher ups before turning them in. It was a large shipment of cocaine. This made for quite a tidy sum, no one wants to say how much, but around five million might be underestimating it," Ward never turned to look at Jan, "Seems he had a retirement plan. These people don't take kindly to things like that, and they want their money back, as you have now discovered. And they will stop at nothing to get it using any means they have at hand," Ward turned to look at Jan, his eyes dark and face set in stone. There was more, but he wasn't going to share it. How could he tell her all of it, "They made an example out of him and anyone having anything to do with him. They hired professionals to do both jobs." He paused, "I don't know if you have any clue where it is. I do know you're not involved."

"So even if I don't help Rob, they will still be after me," a pause, "and now you," it was a statement, nothing more, nothing less. The quiet dominated the room, as neither one spoke. Their eyes locked again but this time there was an understanding that passed between them. Their history went back more than the two years they had secretly seen each other. In fact, they had known each other for about four or more years. At least they had known of each other. They had worked together at the department. They had loved together outside of it. And now they were about to take the next step, to work together outside the department.

"If we do this," it was Ward who broke the silence, "you have to make me one promise," Jan waited, knowing what it was going to be before he even spoke it. It was what he had always wanted, what he had hoped for since before the day they had married in secret. It had been their last argument before she had so nearly lost her life, "You have to leave the department, forever. I can't go through this again with them in control of your life and not you," he paused for emphasis, "I won't," Ward's gaze was intense. "We'll be free and clear of all of this and can start again doing anything we want." As she looked into his green eyes she realized that this time he was serious. This was something he had never done before, issued an ultimatum, and by the look on his face, he was serious. This long argument, one they had had ever since he had left the department, would be over here and now. She just had to make a decision.

Jan thought through all she knew. Ward never shared the circumstance of his last departmental job with her, she still wasn't completely sure of what had happened. She had read all the reports she could get to, but something had been erased, or classified. His last assignment had gone terribly wrong, that was all she knew. He didn't share it, or even think about it, at least not with her around. It was something never to be discussed, not even to be used to convince her to leave the department. Jan looked around the room and then back out to where the dolphins were playing in the ocean, trying to decide what she wanted. It was tempting, it had always been tempting, but the fear of the unknown and the sense of obligation had always won out with her.

"I'm supposed to make that decision now?" her eyes pleaded with his back.

"Yes." He turned and waited for the answer.

"What if I can't?" Jan looked away, refusing to look directly at him. She knew the answer before she had asked the question. He had made it clear without saying a word. She could feel his eyes burning into her. Was she willing to take that risk, to lose him again, this time forever? Would she really lose him if she chose the department? The two dolphins were jumping and playing. They were truly free devoted solely to each other; forever together to enjoy each other's company. Ward didn't speak. He didn't need to. She could read it in his eyes, the tightness of the muscle in her jaw, the way he held his arms, and the thoughts he tried so hard to keep from her. She knew what would happen if she chose the department again, this time he would be gone. The pain that had been caused by the department, by her, this time had been too much for him. Jan took a breath, and upon releasing her breath made a decision, "I'm yours, but only after I find Rob. Then I won't go back, I'll leave and this time it will be for good. We can stay together and enjoy each other, forever."

"No, we will belong to each other after we find Rob," he emphasized the word 'we'. Ward walked over to her stiffly, but letting his face soften a bit, "I'm not letting you do this alone. It is too dangerous for you alone in the condition you are in. You have to remember I know your medical condition better than anyone," he stopped in front of her, "This time though, before we get started, I intend to hold you to your promises," he left the room, heading for the guestroom, and quickly returned. He sat down so close beside Jan that she could see his face and feel his breath. His hand opened and Jan steeled herself to look into it, "This time when we put these on, we don't ever take them off because of the department. No more secrets from the world," and he placed the thick gold band on her finger, and instinctively, she picked up the other gold band and placed it on his finger.

"Together," she said not sure of what the future would be with him, but she knew for certain what it would be like without him.

"Together," and they both turned to watch the dolphins play in the surf, leaning into each other's arms on the couch, hoping that they would both return to this happiness after the mission they would soon embark on.

It was later that night that things started to get moving. Ward had spent the afternoon on the computer downloading all the information they may need onto two portable units. Each unit looked and acted like a cell phone, but they also worked like a high-powered PDA. As of yet they had not responded to the message they had received earlier on Ward's phone, being careful not to seem as if they were too easy, or eager, to be reached. In this aspect they might be able to buy Rob some more time if he wasn't already dead. A thought that neither of them wanted to entertain, but it had crossed both of their minds already. Both realized that the group of people they were dealing with didn't like to leave loose ends, and right now Rob was the bargaining chip, and later, well, that was best left until then. Jan knew they would have to deal with that aspect and so did Ward. Jan spent the time in exercise and meditation, preparing herself for what was to come. They had not talked after putting on the rings, they knew what they had to do, they were well trained, and they were focused. They had made their commitment to each other public again and now it was time to switch back into work mode.

This time during meditation she focused on the time period before the attack. The clue had to be there. She focused on the time when they stopped in front of the factory. Her mind was allowing her to see the place, the argument, but none of the conversation was coming through. This time as they entered the factory and Kevin yelled, she heard an answering yell. The voice sent a chill through her. It was the voice from the hospital, a voice that she recognized. In her meditation she focused on the voice, trying to turn and see who owned it. Her focus was on the sound of the voice as the words were not coming through clearly. It was as if the volume was too low, and muffled. There seemed to be some surprise on her part connected to the identity of the voice, but still she could not put a name to it. The verbal exchange had to do with where the package was. Jan understood the package contained the money. The Jan that existed in the dream seemed to know where it was stashed and what Kevin's plans were, even if she didn't agree with what she had learned. As she tried to get Kevin to leave, their pathway was blocked, it was at this time they had become out numbered, and she counted the people in her vision. At first she had thought that the number of people to overpower them had been three, but she noticed now there were four. She remembered pulling her gun, and then losing it as the pipe connected with her side. She couldn't actually remember if she got a shot off. She was unsure and it didn't matter anyway. The others had started to beat Kevin as soon as they had knocked her over. They had been well trained, and warned that she carried a knife which she was quickly relieved of. They were also armed with guns, but they definitely preferred beating to try and get the information out of Kevin. As she rolled to avoid a blow, she saw the original speaker come out from the shadows. He was the fifth person in the building. He had not been involved in the original attack. He had stayed in the shadows. But he was the one that came after her personally as she lay stunned on the ground. She couldn't find a face; she refocused her meditation removing the pain of the beating from her mind to try and identify the leader. The face became a bit clearer, but still not enough to put a name to it. One thing was for sure; she knew beyond all doubt, she had known him from somewhere else. She just couldn't figure out where yet.

"I know him," the words broke the silence in the room. Ward stopped and turned. He moved toward her as Jan opened her eyes. Leaning on one knee in front of her he waited for more information. He was almost scared at what he would hear next, "That voice from the hospital is also from the factory, and I know it. I just can't place who it is," but Ward was almost positive that he would know who it was, in fact he was sure of it after his meeting last night. The work that he had done earlier on the computer was leading only to one place. "It's the face that just won't come through. If I had the face I think I could be sure of who it was."

"Don't force it, it will come," but he could tell Jan wasn't willing to wait for it. It wasn't safe for her to know yet, she would know soon enough. She had been strong enough to resist him and to keep herself intact. The fact that those memories were even returning to her was amazing to him. It had taken much longer when he had experimented on Ward. Ward knew what he was dealing with, and just how capable of a mad man he was. He decided to change the topic, "I'm going to have Manuel get the car ready. I'm not sure when we will need to leave, but it probably should be tonight. You may want to take a look at the new phone I programmed for you. It's a phone to everyone else until you put in the code, our wedding date, and then you will have access to the web as well as all the information and security codes I downloaded into it. Press menu to prompt it for the code. You do remember our wedding date?"

"Yes, and when you get back down, we need to call and see what they want us to do," Jan fell into the couch holding the phone, and waved Ward to go. She watched Ward leave, and let out a sigh. She began going through the phone. She noticed that there were codes to all the high security fields including computers and doors. Jan began to wonder just who she was dealing with again. Then she smiled; she knew how good Ward had been in the department and now knew that they had divorced themselves from a very valuable asset.

She had known Ward was working and following his own moral code, helping out who he could. But never once had Jan ever wondered where the money he needed to live on was coming from, 'Could he have made enough on odd jobs to afford this?' The toy she held in her hand was easily worth a couple of hundred and he had two, the place by the beach, the apartment across the border, the car, and what else? Could she really join him in what he did? He had said he had ways to make money legally; maybe it was time to ask.

Ward was back too quickly. In his hand he held a warm oven dish. He smiled as he came in and let the smell drift across the room. Setting it in the kitchen he yelled out, "Mama G. wanted us to eat right. Says it will be the best thing for you, and it will help if you put some meat on your skinny bones. Her words not mine. Personally, I like your bones just as they are," he smiled at her, "I let them know that we will be leaving soon, but to expect us back here sooner than normal," Jan came into the kitchen and they both looked at the cell phone on the counter. Putting the PDA phone aside, she handed the other cell to Ward. They had decided that he would be the one to make contact for now, no need to let them know her recovery was going well, and ahead of schedule. As Ward dialed the number to return the call, she felt her emotions slip away from her, and her training took over, instinctively.

"I hear you have a friend of mine," were the first words he spoke, no other greeting, "I may know where she is, but she can't help you," his words were composed, and straight forward. He listened to the words from the other side, "Whoever beat her made sure that the memories wouldn't return. You should have told your buddies to be more careful, she hardly knows who she is let alone where whatever you want is. By the way, what is it that you're looking for?" a long pause, "Fine, fine, I'll be there," and he hung up. He looked at Jan. From his eyes she could tell that the news was not something either one of them would like, or wouldn't have expected. He leaned against the counter, and pulled out some plates for the food that sat beside the phone.

"We have five days to find the money, otherwise the department will get Rob back, in pieces, in the mail," not what he would have expected from him, he usually didn't go for gruesome, cruel and mean maybe, even sadistic, "We leave in the morning," he shrugged his shoulders, "Nothing more to do till morning. Enchilada?" and he looked back at Jan.

"Not very original is he, and yes to the enchilada part. We need to go over the layout of the department and designate contact numbers as well as times," Ward dished out the food.

"Top draw of the desk, already printed it out. As for the contact numbers and times, the phones will only vibrate, so if I call you at a bad time, you can ignore it, and vice versa," he walked the plates to the table, and Jan carried a couple of sodas over to the table without using her crutches.

"What are you going to be doing?" Jan set the sodas down.

"I have a few people to contact, and they will help me pick up some information, maybe a lead or two," he leaned on the edge of the table, "These are people who don't want to be known by the department, so I keep a low profile with them. They're good contacts, but let's just say that some of them aren't always doing what they should be. I also need to meet with someone who is part of the problem. They want to go over the details in person," he had to meet with the devil ahead of time, and with any luck it wouldn't cost him his soul.

"Wait a minute," the hand that held the soda stopped halfway to the table.

"By the way you need to use your crutches," he glanced her way, "At least keep them with you. And no I won't be alone," he was still keeping something from her, but Jan decided that this was best left alone for now.

"Any other therapy tips," Jan looked at him with one eyebrow raised.

"Yah, plenty of exercise and good food. Eat up, there is no better cooking than Mama G.'s," she pulled out the plans from the drawer and joined him at the table. As they ate, they went over the plans in detail. Ward let her know which rooms needed codes that were contained in the phone, and why she may want to have access to them. They went over the location of the evidence room and the organization of it. This was the best place to start, as it would have all the items they had found in the car and around them at the factory. Jan studied the plans carefully. Most of the place she remembered with a casual ease, but it was reassuring to review the floor plans. This time she would be on the other side of things. Feeling confident that she would be able to get around and find what she needed, she finished off the food on her plate. She stood and held her crutch.

"Be careful," Ward looked up at Jan, "any item in there could be a trigger to the event for your memories, just like our picture was, and may cause you some mental overload. Go slow; only handle one item at a time. This way you might be able to localize, and control the flood of memories if it starts," Jan didn't want to think about the memories of that day coming back. He was right; she wouldn't want to deal with all those memories. But if they were going to help Rob, she may have too. No use in trying to push any more information in for now. Jan smiled at Ward in a way he had not seen in a long time. The look on her face drew his eyes to her eyes, and he could see the depths of passion in them.

"Are you coming?" Jan turned and dropped her crutch, then started to walk slowly toward the room. Ward let the corners of his mouth turn up, and a questioning look played at the corners of his eyes, as he swallowed, "You did say I needed regular exercise," Ward stood slowly, following her into the bedroom. She let herself tip over a little and Ward was there in seconds to catch her and carry her the rest of the way. It was a shameless trick they both knew, but neither seemed to care. They never turned on a light and they never said a word. It was an unspoken fear between them that this would be their last night together. Letting their clothes fall to the ground, they spent the night locked in each other's arms, hoping the morning would never come.

Chapter 10

The morning did come. The sun came through the open window and crept silently across the floor. When the rays finally touched the bottom of the bed they had already been up for an hour packing and getting the place ready to leave. The job now controlled them. They had put their own personal relationship on hold, and neatly packed away the feelings. As they closed up the windows and the curtains, neither one spoke. Jan took one last look at the ocean through the bedroom window and then with a sigh drew the curtains. They were not looking at each other's thoughts, they didn't need to, and both were focused on the job to come. 'So this is how it would be,' she mused. It would feel good to work with him again, to know every thought and action.

Jan switched thoughts as she placed that last item in her bag, and began to wonder on the best way to approach entering the department again. After leaving, would they really take her back in and allow her to work, or would she be caged again? They would cage her. Both of their thoughts were the same. She wanted to broach this topic with Ward, but he had finished with his bag. He turned away and now he seemed preoccupied with something else. Again, Jan wondered what he had given up for the information he got. She watched him for a moment. When he had left that night he was despondent. He knew who was behind the attacks on her, and he also had spoken with someone else. Whatever deal he had made during that conversation, it had seemed to suck the life right out of him.

She watched him move his bag toward the far side of the dresser. He had packed a small bag, no more than a couple of shirts, and a pair of jeans. He opened another drawer and took out a small metal box. In all her time here she had never seen the box, and he placed it deep in the bag. Jan watched his thoughts, but saw nothing, his face was drawn, and his shoulders drooped. It was a private moment; she left the room and went to make breakfast. Ward came out ten minutes later, and they both ate in silence. Jan stared at her food. Ward looked up at her, and then finished his food, cleared and cleaned the dishes. He now looked back at her.

"You ready?" she wanted to say no, yell no, but Rob's life was in their hands and for all she knew, Ward's and hers as well. Jan stood and quickly turned away from Ward.

"Let's go," she said as she walked out of the apartment and up the stairs, not once looking back at any of it. They each threw their small bags into the Explorer and were off.

The trip was quiet as they started down the road. Jan stared out the window, and Ward let the silence hang in the air. On the way here he had played CD's, and been in a general good mood and less focused during most of the trip, relaxed, after leaving the airport. Now he was focused, and the mood was somber. As they left the beaches and passed the cacti, Jan decided it was time to start the conversation.

"How do you think I get back in without becoming a prisoner? You made a point of letting them see us leave, and I wasn't exactly fighting it," Jan focused on the road.

"Tell them the truth of that time. You left with me because you were scared after the attack. I had promised to keep you safe and make you better, but after regaining some of your memory you decided it was in your best interest to go back," Ward continued on, focused on the road. Jan could see every line on his face; she noticed the set of his chin, and the dark green color of his eyes. She was sure he thought he would lose her to the department again. Looking closer she noticed the small scare just above his left eyebrow. She didn't remember this; it could simply be the fact that this was one of the memories that hadn't surfaced yet, or something she didn't see before. Was it something that had happened since the last time they were together?

"And you think they will believe this?" she focused on the scar, her hand reached out to touch it.

"Don't," he intercepted her hand and held it in mid air for a second. "They believe I'm dangerous, so why wouldn't they believe that you got tired of being controlled by me, and decided to let them rescue you. Rescued from me," a tiny sarcastic smile played on his lips, "In any case, we'll discuss this more in a bit, if you want, or wait until we get back to my apartment," he let the sentence hang in the air.

"Well," she looked at him and memories came floating back in. All of his files had been classified after he left. She had tried a couple of times to access them, but to no avail. The talk around the department had been that he had lost his memory, and then lost his sanity. She had known that the last part was not true. He had contacted her shortly after he left the department. It was during the time period that they had not been in touch with each other that Jan was unsure of what had happened to him. He never talked about those times in his life. It was too painful of a memory to him, but she knew he wasn't crazy, dangerous, or immoral. Far from it. He had never done anything that would, in her eyes substantiate those rumors in all the time she had known him. Of that there was no question in her mind, "They will reassign a partner to me, probably one that will keep me under tighter surveillance. I won't be able to do much."

"Babs, your only job is to figure out where Kevin hid the dough so that we can get Rob back, get rid of the bad guys, and then get our lives back. And the only place that information could be right now is in your head. Believe me, everyone has tried everywhere else," he paused. "We have to find the key to unlock the last pieces and I'm afraid it is probably in the evidence locker. They just don't know what it is, but you will." The conversation was over as fast as it had begun.

They crossed the border in silence, and drove up to the diner they had stopped at on the way down. This time she could see the diner and the surrounding area. It was on the outskirts of a very small town, with a dirt parking lot, and an old neon sign that only had the first three letters of diner lit up. She was sure that she had never seen the place before the other night. She studied the area, and knew that it was out of the way, and nondescript. There were six old cars in the parking lot. She assumed that there were only three people actually in the place eating, and the other cars belonged to the cook, owner, and waitress. Ward pulled into the lot and parked. He turned and looked at her.

"You hungry?" his face had very little emotion, just a small smile, which was a cover for what he truly felt.

"Must be a favorite place of yours?"

"Definitely," he slid out of his side of the SUV and walked around to Jan's. They walked in and sat in the same place they had sat before. They placed the same order as before, and Ward looked at her. In his eyes there were the emotions of a worried man, and one who was trying to hide it. Although Jan couldn't see his thoughts, he was hiding them; she had become accustomed to again being able to read his body language. Every muscle again was tense, and his jaw line was set. Jan decided that at this point it would be better to switch into work mode and finish discussing the finer details.

"Standard procedure will be that as soon as I am back they will hold at least one debriefing, and then I will have a thorough assessment, both physical and mental. I will be on probation, and they won't allow me any weapons, even though my life is still in danger. Not a pleasant thought. They will also probably not put me on Rob's case, so the codes you have given me will come in handy. I'll keep the phone out of sight, or they will take it. Lastly, I also realize they can't protect me. They weren't able to at the hospital, and even if it is safer at the department, I know I can't let my guard down," Jan placed her hands folded on the table. Ward allowed himself to give her a more genuine smile at her assessment of the situation, but Jan could tell there was something he was hiding in that smile.

"You will be a bit better protected in the office, but not much. The people who are after you may have contacts there as well, but it will be harder for them to reach you in there. They will put you in one of the apartments. It will be fairly safe. There is only one apartment that someone on crutches can stay in with any comfort, so that will narrow it down for me where they place you in case you need me. And by the way, for the others as well," the conversation stopped as the food was placed in front of them. They both gave the waitress a smile, but she left as quickly as possible knowing that she had interrupted an important conversation. The last thing she needed was to hear information that wasn't any of her business and may get her into trouble. The food was just as good as Jan remembered from the other night. As she began eating her food, the idea that whoever was after her also had ways into the department made her shiver. From what she remembered, she could now put two and two together and was getting a very unpleasant four. Not only did the department think that Ward was in on it, she now believed he knew who was. Rob had told them not to return, but never given them a solid reason why. Time for a little straight talk, but before she could start, he cut her off and continued, "As for any equipment you may want, you need to take a closer look at your crutches." He gave her half a smile as he started to eat.

Jan stopped eating and focused on the crutches. They were unusual for temporary crutches, more like the ones people used when they had a permanent disability. They had the wrist guard, and the palm support, but nothing unusual. Picking one up, she inspected it more closely. Finally, putting the stick down, she looked back at Ward, "I don't see anything special."

"Good. If you missed it, so might they. Friend of mine made these for you. They will go through any airport security without a bit of trouble, but don't make any mistakes, they are made of the hardest alloy around, and if you turn the palm grips in opposite directions, they unhook and can be made into numb chucks. The stick itself can be used for self-defense as well as offensive maneuvers because of its strength. A secret compartment is located in the bottom of the right cane. Last but not least, if necessary, there is a knife that can be taken out of the center of the left cane by turning the bottom pad right three times. Then pull it out three inches. Then turn again three times in the opposite direction. It will come loose after that and I know it is complicated, but it hides it well," Ward was matter of fact about all the information that he had given her. At the department they had some pretty fancy toys, but this was quite the item for a civilian to get a hold of. It had been one way of keeping her from questioning him about her concerns of what he knew, but those questions were still there and he knew that no matter how long he stalled she would soon ask them. They finished the chili and their drinks. Ward threw the same amount of money on the table as before and walked away, Jan followed.

"I'm not positive," was all he said as he helped her into the SUV. Jan knew he was answering her question as to who was after her, and was pretty sure he was lying to her. She saw a glimpse of his thoughts, of faces she didn't know and one she thought she might. She wanted more information. This was no way to start out their partnership, even if it had been developing for over a year and a half. This was different, she had now promised to start working with him, and leave the shelter of what she had known for the last ten years. It was time to face up to the battle that lay ahead.

"How about some more information, since we are working together? Who do you think is involved?" Jan waited as he started up the SUV and pulled out of the lot. When he didn't answer, she continued, "Well? Shouldn't we be sharing information if we are partnering together?" The one thing Jan knew was that when you closed off your mind to others, it made it harder to read anyone else's thoughts. This gave her the advantage, as he was keeping his thoughts very closed. The Explorer continued to go across the desert in a different direction than before, and Jan knew where they were headed, back to home base, back to Phoenix.

"I won't be positive that I am right until I meet with him. Yes I'm pretty sure I know who did this to you. As for sharing information, when we are through here and you meet me back in Mexico, then I will tell you anything you want to know, as for now, I just need to know that you will come back," his look was hard, "this time," and Jan was taken aback. She stared at him ignoring the scenery outside; trying to remember what could be the cause of this outbreak.

Then it came to her. It was the day they had gotten married, for some reason he had believed that she was going back to the department to do just one last job and leave. She had believed that as well after the two weeks they had spent together. Once back there, she got comfortable with what she had always known and the clandestine meetings with Ward. It had left their relationship in a virtual time warp, and left her intentions always in question. He had a right to be worried. This had happened before, although it had been very different circumstances, but he was preparing himself for it to happen again. Jan was unsure that anything she could say would be helpful, or convincing, so instead she laid her hand on his thigh, and watched him in silence.

"Where are you going to be staying? Will it be your apartment?"

"No, the people I need to deal with won't be anywhere near there, and I thought it might be time to get rid of the place," he let his glance wander in her direction. "If you call from there and say that's where I have been keeping you, they are going to watch the place like hawks anyway. At least that will keep them away from me and out of my hair for a while," he now began to smile again. "And just for the record, no I am not involved, even though that is what they suspect right now and would have you believe. I have a vested interest in only one aspect of this case. And that would be you and our future, together." The last word was emphasized.

The rest of the ride was uneventful, quiet, and when they reached the outskirts of Phoenix, the air conditioning in the car seemed to heave a sigh and work twice as hard, even though it was September. Jan watched as she entered a town she knew by instinct and yet it all seemed new to her again. She made mental notes, and connected images and memories to what she had seen and was seeing. Now and then she would make a connection to what she remembered and what was around her. Mostly she spent the time watching the road and the signs as they came into the downtown area.

Jan couldn't help but compare the two worlds, the one she had just left, and the life that seemed to hum all around her here. There were people all over, flying past in cars, on the bridges over the freeways, and even the hum she could feel from people she couldn't see. She focused her thoughts, and tuning out all the rest except the ones that she could see from Ward, she looked to see the tall buildings of the downtown. Nature had surrounded them in Mexico, and the gentle hum of nature had nurtured her healing. Now more than ever she knew if they had brought her here she never would have recovered. She would have lost her mind and her sanity with all the other images and feelings that would have forced themselves into her head. The disconnected feeling she had with the earth, with nature, would never have allowed her to progress as far as she had. Looking back over at Ward, she realized that he had been watching her thoughts, and he was smiling. It was good to see. He hadn't really smiled at her like that since she had decided to come back. In the background, behind his profile she caught sight of a tall building that seemed to reflect the heat, and instinctively knew it was the place that housed the department and Ward's easy smile she so enjoyed vanished.

Ward exited the freeway at Seventh Avenue. After going down a couple of major city streets, and then onto a small residential road, Ward finally turned off into an alley. This was the way she remembered getting to Ward's place. It was a granny flat built at the back of a lot with an old ranch style house built in what must have been the early fifties in front of the lot. The apartment itself had a separate access to it from the alley and in general, it was clean and well taken care of, the same as the main house. The people who owned it built the flat in back to make a little extra money. It was in need of a little tender loving care, but it was not a place where anyone would look for Ward, or would care if he were there. Jan had only been there once, and when she walked in for the second time, she noticed that things had not changed much. It was very basic, with a couch, chair and a small room to the side that served as a bedroom. There was only one door in and out, and a small kitchenette finished off the main room. But, she knew it suited his needs when he was in town.

Looking around Jan also noticed that most personal items had been removed. Pictures were gone from the walls, and looking around again, she noticed that nothing had been left here that couldn't be lost. There was also nothing here that would connect the two of them in any way other than the working relationship they had had.

"You weren't coming back were you," she stated simply as he was going through his bag and pulling out the small box he had brought.

"I was hoping I would never have to," he said matter-of-factly. He never looked at her.

"No, you weren't coming back. You never had any plans to bring me back," Jan stood and stared at him. It was almost an accusatory tone she used. She could see in his mind where he had planned to just take her away from the very first time he talked with her in the hospital. It hadn't worked like that though and Jan was confused more than angry. Instead he had been patient, and even allowed himself to be placed in danger because of her. Ward finished what he was doing, never opening the box in front of her, zipped the bag, and turned to look at her. His face was hard, emotionless.

"No, I said I wasn't coming back, I have never held you against your will or controlled you. I have only given you my protection, promise, and love," his voice rumbled low out of his chest as if he were trying to control a beast. "You are, and have always been free," he walked toward her. Jan never moved, not wanting to lose ground, afraid that if she moved, she would. It was an age-old problem between them. The closer he got to her, the more emotion she felt from him. It was a churning feeling between love, passion, and anger. He kissed her. His body never yielded to hers as it had before. As the kiss deepened, she felt the passion swell between them. As he pulled away from her lips he spoke, "We only have four days left to help Rob. They mean business. I'm leaving, do what you need to do," and he turned and left, her lips not even cold yet when the door closed.

Jan stood there for many minutes; she really wasn't sure how many. Did he mean what she thought he meant, what she had seen in his mind? Could she? They had met in secret many times over the last two years, but this was different, she was planning on going back with him, she thought. Jan knew what she needed to do. When she dialed the emergency number, there would be someone here in minutes to get her. She was only about ten minutes from the building. But it would mean one thing. It would mean that there was no turning back. Ward would be left homeless here, and the fact that he could not return would be the first step to their life together or their separation forever. He was serious, but so was she. Whatever the outcome, Rob needed her now, and she needed back in. Making the call from her cell, she gave her location and told them to hurry as he would be coming back to move her to a different location soon. She ended the call, and placed the phone back in her pocket. Walking over to the chest of drawers that served as a catchall, a dresser, and a coffee table, she leaned on it and looked out the window. Looking down at her hand she noticed the wide gold band that held them together. She began to wonder just how this piece of jewelry would go over in the department. Whatever she told them, she would have to believe it herself, if only for the time she was with them. Jan's eyes looked toward the end of the chest of draws. There lay a note, and an intricately crafted gold chain. She picked up the note and read it. As the words left the paper, they took on the feel and tone of his voice in her head.

"Babs, just in case you need this. Remember always keep your crutches with you. They may save your life. Always Yours," and that is how the note ended. She had time to read it just one more time, and then to quickly hide it in the bottom of the crutch. She looked at the chain and studied it. It was interlocking loops, and she smiled at the importance. Looking again at her hand, she gently slid her ring off and looped it onto the chain. Placing the chain around her neck, she could feel the heat from the ring on her chest as she slid the chain and ring inside her shirt. No turning back, that was their motto for now, no matter what happened.

Just then she heard the metal of the dead bolt slide from the frame, and with caution the door slowly opened. Jan made sure her hands were on both of the crutches, and she was using them for support. It was no surprise who was at the door. It was Pat. She waved at Jan to move toward the door, and Jan made her way across the small room. Pat helped her into the black car with the tinted windows. How ironic, all this time she had hid from them out in the open, and here they were using a black car to clandestinely pick her up, and hide her away again. No wonder she never had a chance on the last assignment.

As the car pulled away from the apartment, she noticed the two other surveillance people left to catch Ward when he supposedly returned. A bit of sadness played at the corners of her mind, and Jan quickly pushed it away. It was an emotion better left for a private time, not now. Pat was the best of the best at the department. Retired from active service three years ago now, her only job was to train new individuals, and to keep an eye on those who might be willing to falter. Jan assumed that she was here to pick her up for the second reason, although, she had still not said a word. Jan could feel the intrusion of Pat's mind in hers and she pushed it out. This left Pat no other choice but to talk with her as they sped back to the tall office building in which they hid from the public, and the world.

"I see you have been practicing your skills," flat tone.

"I'm not sure you would have appreciated me letting Ward just wander through my thoughts," Jan stared straight ahead, working harder than she planned to keep the panic of the possibility of never seeing him again, at bay. The void inside of Jan only deepened as she could almost feel Ward getting farther and farther away from her and their lives again separating. She felt as if she was drowning and her only comfort was the warmth of the band that hung around her neck. Jan wondered if they were really getting farther apart, or maybe starting a new venture. She didn't let the thoughts enter fully into her mind for fear of them being picked up, but she kept them safely tucked behind barriers in her head, and surrounded by other thoughts of her recovery process.

"Probably wise, do you remember much?" Pat was a plain person and nothing about her would make her stand out in a crowd. Her style of dress was plain and so was her style of hair. Jan had never seen her blond hair with its streaks of gray pulled back into a tight bun styled any other way. She wasted no time getting to the point, a point that Jan chose to ignore right now.

"Most of it is back, not all. A couple of nights ago it was if the cloud was lifted. Let's wait till I get settled in so that we can do the whole report in one go," and with that, the conversation stopped. In moments, Pat was at the underground park, and Jan took a deep breath as she pulled into what had once been her haven from the world, to what might now became her prison. The downward slant of the drive only emphasized this fact for her. It looked and felt for all intense purposes that she was slipping into a dark canyon with little hope of escape. And for what might be the first time in Pat's life, she tried to comfort Jan with her next statement.

"It's almost over," but she was wrong. It was only beginning for Jan.

Chapter 11

Jan wondered what she was doing back here as they got out of the car in the dark parking garage and walked over to the elevator. Jan knew the stainless steel elevator they stepped into was dedicated for the department's use only. The doors slid closed. Trapped came to mind, caged, and imprisoned were all words that loomed in the corners of her brain. Knowing that Pat would be trying to pick up on any thoughts of the last few weeks, she focused her thoughts on Rob. She wondered where he was right now, and how he was doing. By focusing on these thoughts, she knew she would keep Pat quiet. Since she had just been recovered by the department Pat would not be allowed to discuss these matters with her until the results of the debriefing were in. With that information they would decide if she was tainted material now. She watched as Pat placed the key in the elevator slot, turned, and they were now on their way to the thirteenth floor. Jan closed her eyes, took a breath, and tried to read Pat's thoughts. Nothing. But then what did she expect, Pat would not have given anything away, at least not this easily. Jan wondered when they would tell her anything at all or just put her in a little room. Debriefings sometimes took days, weeks, or in the worst-case scenario, she may never be allowed to have clearance again. The elevator stopped, and the doors opened. There sat the security guard behind the desk in front of the door that led into the departmental abyss that would be hard to escape once she was back on the inside.

The guard handed Pat her ID and smiled at Jan. Jan knew what that meant. Without any ID, she was not allowed to move at all in the building without an agent right by her side; she was marked. The door opened, and the hum of the department that loomed behind those doors was ready to swallow her up in one gulp if she wasn't careful. But for now, she steeled herself to walk through the doors, pretending to rely deeply on the crutches she used, and the small bag slung over her shoulder, that contained all she would need for a lifetime. It was how she had learned to pack when she had joined the department. It was how all agents had learned to pack. Pat walked slightly ahead of her, clearing the way of both people and of chairs that blocked her path.

They had entered the large expansive office area with three-quarter walls, desks, and most of the agents that weren't out on assignments at the present time. The sound of typing and people talking on phones filled the air. Thoughts filled Jan's mind, and she pushed them all aside with skills that were now retrained and even refined beyond what they had been. Small offices lined the outer walls, and when Pat stopped, and turned toward another person, she gave them a small nod. They jumped out of their seat and grabbed the wheelchair that was close by, ready and waiting for Jan.

"No thanks, I really want to try and get back into shape. I want back into things, and to get a new partner as soon as possible. Before I left the hospital Rob told me that he had been reassigned. I figured that was because of how long it would take me to recover," Jan had decided earlier that she had wanted to wait to discuss Rob, but it was a split second decision. It didn't seem right not to talk about it at this moment. Not something that Ward had discussed with her, but then again, some things just didn't feel right. If she let them know that she knew about Rob, how could she convince them of Ward's innocence in the whole matter? This way she could also assess just what they would tell her about Rob, if anything. But instead, all she got was silence. She hadn't really expected anything else, and at least she hadn't been disappointed. Pat waved the chair away and motioned for her to follow. They continued the trek through the maze of half offices until they reached the door that lead to the private quarters. Pat led Jan to the room that both she and Ward figured she would get. Pat then chose to speak.

"Get settled in, shower, eat something if you want. At five, I will be back for you. Your debriefing will be with Gregg and with me, in the inner office. We will discuss your reassignment more after the debriefing," she said routinely as she turned to leave. She then stopped in the doorway and looked back over her shoulder. "And by the way, welcome back," and Pat left. As the door closed, Jan moved closer to listen. That's when she heard it, the sound of metal sliding into place, from the outside. Again the prisoner, not where she wanted to be, not able to do what she wanted to or needed to do without breaking the rules. With no other choices available to her at the moment, Jan decided it was now time to assess her surroundings looking for what modifications may have been made in the room. Since she had an hour of uninterrupted time, wasting it was not on the list.

The apartment she was locked in was just about the same size as Ward's granny flat they had just left. There was a very utilitarian gray green couch, as well as a chair that matched. There were no frills to these rooms. The vertical blinds on the windows had been cleaned recently, as well as the rest of the place to get it ready for someone to stay. It had probably been readied for her a few weeks ago. A small kitchenette was off to the right, with two upper cupboards, and one cupboard under the small sink. There was a small fridge, and microwave in the kitchen as well. Off to the left was an open door that led to what she knew would be the small bedroom, and the bathroom area off of that.

Jan now started to visually search the walls and cracks for any surveillance items. She knew they had to exist somewhere, but finding out where they were could be an asset for her. It was also about the only productive thing to do in the apartment at the moment. Like the hospital room, it was sterile of anything that would help to keep her informed, or up to date. Most of the rooms were not like this. These rooms were to be a place where they could stay and work in-between assignments if they didn't maintain a place in town, and weren't normally stationed here. They were also rooms that any agent could bed down in and work in or from at anytime of the day or night. The only time apartments were emptied of computer equipment and telecommunication hardware was when an agent, like her, was in question. Jan guessed that there were no surprises here. She, and her mission, had been in question for longer than most, and if she had been the assigned investigator, she would be keeping a careful eye on the person in here. In fact, she had done just that, one other time. It was easier being on the outside though, than on the inside of the fishbowl, she mused.

She let her eyes concentrate on the valence, just above the only window in the living area. It was an easy place to hide things, and she noticed a small wire loop that just brushed the top of the valence. A less trained eye would have missed it. A better-trained person would have hidden it. It was a device that was placed in an area that could see most of the room, if it contained a video camera. If it were just voice, which was an unlikely choice right now as they would want to make sure not to lose her again, it would also be in the right place. Jan realized that when she left for the debriefing, a team would be in here searching her things. Good thing she got to keep the crutches with her, if given time, they would figure them out as well, but the phone wasn't a good thing to just leave around, nor could she take it with her. The problem she had right now was where to place it that wouldn't be discovered, or seen as she did it. Quickly, and without looking, she palmed the phone, and placed in it in the loop of the crutches that surrounded her wrist.

At one time she had spent many hours learning how to hide things from people who were looking for them, and find those things that nobody wanted her to find. Now she had to hide it from the people who had taught her how to hide and find any number of things. The obvious places, like the bedroom and the living area, would be searched with a fine tooth comb if she moved toward any of it. She knew where she had to hide the phone, and with any luck, no one would be the wiser. Carefully, pretending to use both crutches, she made her way to the kitchen. First she opened the fridge, and began looking for something. There were prepared meals in the small freezer, and a selection of drinks. Jan looked at the drinks, moving the cans and bottles around, and finally taking out a can of cola. She opened the cupboard above the sink, and as she reached into the cupboard to get a glass, she slipped the phone into a drinking glass at the back of the cupboard, out of view of any camera, and out of suspicion of anyone watching. The exchange was so quick that even a professional watching her would not have picked up on the drop.

Jan poured the cola into the glass, sipped about half of it down, and then left the glass with the rest of the cola to set on the counter for later. Then she went over to the couch, and pretended to lean back and fall asleep. Instead she began to meditate, looking for answers, and a respite from the pressure she felt all around her. She felt strained and drawn here, very unlike the feelings she had gotten in Mexico. Nature was a powerful source of healing and of replenishment. She had felt comfortable there. They had picked it as the place to live, even if it was secretly. She could feel the pull of minds here, and even when she walked through the large office area earlier, she could feel the eyes, and minds on her always trying to pick up one more piece of information. She had once been one of these people, but there had been a definite change in her since the accident, and now more than ever she knew she could never come back and be one of them here.

She wondered how Ward could ever think that she would choose this. Then she thought about all of the good reasons she had given over the last year.

Jan got up and walked over to the window. She could see the Bank One Ballpark from here, and the few people that milled around outside at the end of the day, going home. People everywhere, thoughts pouring in, and the only thing that kept it from being overwhelming, was the training that Ward had done with her. Jan tuned it all out and sat down to think again. She needed to keep in mind a timeline in which to work, and Jan began to list the things that she wanted to do in her mind, and the order that they needed to be done. At the top of her list, was to check for other minds that would be trying to read hers right now. She got no feeling that she was being intruded on so she continued to make the list. First she had to get to the evidence room and retrieve her stuff. Find the missing item that would unlock what was still locked in her head. Get to Rob and get him the help he deserved. She also needed to clear Ward and herself if there was time. If she couldn't convince them of Ward's honesty, and her innocence, then an escape was going to be needed, and a cover necessary. There was a lot to do in just four days.

Jan's thoughts switched to something closer at hand. Pat was obviously assigned to read her right now, and in some ways that was an honor. Pat had been a top agent in her time. Mind readers were usually only in the field for about fifteen to twenty years before being pulled out, or worn out. Once removed from active duty, agents were put on the training grounds for the new recruits, and with each year you spent training, as a consequence, your skills improved. It was rare to be put back on the active list, but it had been done before when skills were of the utmost importance. Pat had been a trainer for three years now. As a top agent her skills were about the best of the best, and this was not just Jan's opinion. Now she was the agent sent to read her. It would be a test of Jan's mind against Pat's.

It was especially important for Jan to keep Pat from the thoughts that would let her into the world Jan wanted protected the most. Also, to keep Pat from suspecting her of any collusion, which the department already felt existed. If she refused any access to her thoughts, she would be suspected, and maybe even accused which would mean a much longer time within these four walls. Jail was never an option with this line of work. There had never been an agent that had ever been convicted, except maybe for Ward. Jan made a mental note to look up Ward's confidential file, since he had given her all the codes into the main computers. If she let Pat read too deep into her thoughts, she would give away Ward, Mexico, and a life she so wanted to return to. Ward had faith she could do it, but did she? A sigh escaped Jan's lips as the meditation failed to relieve the stress of all the minds around her and the thoughts that beat in her head. It had only created more stress and a list of things to do that continued to increase. Jan opened her eyes and looked back around the room.

"Damn," was the only word escaping her lips. Without the computer in the room she would have to rely on the phone that Ward provided for hacking into the computers. Not that she couldn't handle that, it was only that now she was going to have to find a spot that was private to do this. This place was going to be nowhere near private.

Jan stood up and walked unsteadily on the crutches to the bedroom, only enhancing the picture that she was still in great need of the crutches to get around. She was not surprised to find the small bed in a small room with a small dresser to match. No agent needed more than a couple of changes of clothes and a single bed, at least no agent until her. In her mind she mused at the thought that she was an agent, even if they didn't believe she was, she was still very much on the case. Walking around the room and into the bath, she made mental notes of the area, and decided that under the covers of the bed would be the only place that would be unseen in this room. Mentally giggling at the irony.

She heard the knock, and then the door open. Pat must have entered the living room as Jan could feel another trained mind focus in on hers. The one thing they hadn't counted on was Ward's retraining of her mind, as well as her body. Her mind was better than they had expected, or could have done. Her thoughts switched back to items that were noncommittal and she let the boundaries go up.

"It's five, Gregg's waiting," Pat walked right into the bedroom.

"Debriefing time," Jan turned with a smile and followed Pat out. When she stopped to close the door, Jan noticed that it was an electronic lock, and would probably take a remote signal if she needed to get out. She walked behind Pat, and with her at the same time as Pat's mind tried to get glimpses of what had happened. Jan did want to oblige, some, so she threw her a couple of thoughts inconspicuously. Jan concentrated, and began to think of a plane trip, and how painfully uncomfortable it was. She let the picture of Sage pass through her mind, so that there would be no doubt of the time and place. Pat picked up on the random thought, and never missed a step, and neither did Jan. It was the carrot she had wanted.

They passed back through the door into the outside room and went off to the right this time. After passing all the three-quarter walls again they quickly reached the secretary's office of the local director, Gregg. The secretary looked up and nodded that it was okay to enter. Jan's thoughts slipped back to her room, thinking that at the same time they were entering this office, someone was entering her room to search her things, and maybe even Ward's apartment as well at the moment. They must know by now by now that he wasn't coming back. Jan didn't try to hide these thoughts as Pat would be expecting them, and it would lend a sense of sincerity to her for Pat.

"Jan, good to have you back, take a seat," Gregg never got up, never smiled. His voice was insincere at best, "I'm sure you're familiar with the routine. We will try to be as short as possible tonight as you look very tired, and with your cooperation we should be done quickly. We hope your quarters are well prepared and comfortable. You have been through quite a lot," and she could tell that he wasn't just referring to her injuries, "Now, we have a few questions that we need answers to as quickly as possible and it seems that you may be the only one with the answers," he motioned her to a chair. Jan sat down, but never leaned back. Gregg was the type of director that never made anyone feel comfortable. The previous director, Ted, was the type of guy you sat down with, had a cup of coffee or tea, discussed the weather or sports scores, and then got down to business. Gregg on the other hand, had spent ten years in the FBI, and then moved over to the CIA. Not an easy move. Later he transferred into this department, and soon became director. The years had not been easy on him. His face worn and the rest of him slowly losing the shape he had spent many years acquiring. The paunch in the front tugged at the button on his suit jacket, "Pat is here to help support you," but Pat never sat in the other chair, she only stood off to the side and a half step behind the chair Jan was in.

"I'll be happy to tell you what I know, but most memories I am still struggling with myself. Items before the attack are fairly clear, and I have some memory of the attack, but still no faces, I am unable to identify who was involved, or why," Jan knew that some of the truth would be helpful here. In their strange and twisted way, she knew they were only trying to help. She watched as Gregg switched on a small tape recorder.

"Okay, let's start at what happened after you left the court room with Kevin," Gregg looked straight at her and Pat was beating in at her brain. Jan took a calming breath, and closed her eyes.

"If I remember the assignment correctly I was to take him to the airport via the back roads. During the trip I became aware that it was a route he was not familiar with. He seemed to be getting irritated, and that is when I discovered that we had missed or dismissed his girlfriend. That's a fact that I am still unsure of. He had something for her though. I can't remember if he had it with him, but he was planning on giving her something. Have you found her?" Jan waited for the response.

"Yes." Not as much information as she wanted, or hoped for.

"Was she any help?" Jan kept her thoughts focused, eyes open and straight-ahead.

"No," his eyes never met hers.

"We argued about something, I still haven't remembered what it was. No matter how hard I try, the closer my mind gets to the attack, the less the memories seem to come together. Then we ended up at the factory. After that I have vague images of people, no clear faces, and then of being outnumbered. The rest of my memories belong to what Rob had told me in the hospital. Rob was returning to the airport via a different route when he heard the call come over the scanner. For some reason he didn't tell me, he knew that I was in trouble and came after me," not everything was a lie. "By the way, who is Rob's partner now?" This time she wanted more of an answer, and she left the question open as to what may be going on with Rob. She was testing just how much they were going to trust her.

"Rob doesn't have a partner right now," Gregg's face betrayed no emotion. Well trained and well defined, he gave nothing away, but this time that wasn't good enough. With all her efforts focused on Pat and her intrusions into her thoughts, Jan was unable to try to read Gregg's. She didn't linger on the thoughts of Rob as she didn't want to get Pat too suspicious.

"I know the people who attacked us were after that something. My attacker at the hospital made that fairly clear. He was the same man that attacked us at the factory, the voice was familiar, but the last time he came after me, he covered his face. He didn't cover his face at the factory though because he didn't expect me to survive, and if given enough time I am sure I will be able to place it. He was the leader. But right now I am worried about Rob. If I am still in danger, then so is Rob," Jan let the silence hang in the room. No faces moved. No expressions changed. Rob's whereabouts seemed to be only a slight annoyance to them.

"Rob's gone missing. It happened just a couple of days ago," Gregg spoke first as his eye's focused down on the papers on his desk.

"What?" She made a good show of surprise and disbelief. "Do you have any leads?" Jan knew to ask this was totally out of line, but she had only limited time and patience, and any other reaction wouldn't have looked right.

"I don't believe that pertains to you right now," Gregg's voice held a note of finality. Jan gave Gregg a look, and Pat a thought to express her feelings on just how could it not affect her in any way, "During the time you were kidnapped, did you give any information to Ward?"

"Wait a minute. Back it up here. You don't know where Rob is and you don't think that is any of my concern. How could that be? We were partners for ten years. If he needs my help, shouldn't I be there to help him?" Jan let her tone of voice reflect her frustration with everything she had been told, and not told as she ignored the other question.

"We are trying to get to the bottom of this, and any help you can give us right now may make the difference. How much have you told Ward?" Gregg's voice was demanding.

"Nothing. And to set the record straight, you may want to know that it wasn't a kidnapping. I had just been attacked at the hospital. I had no memory of who I was, and I was still very confused. The urge to runaway was great, even from the moment that I became aware of where I was. When he asked me if I wanted to leave, I told him yes. I saw it as a way out," but she knew that they didn't believe her.

"Are you sure?"

"Yes," she would have a hard time believing it as well if she were on the other side of the desk.

"Did he read your mind?" He kept the questions coming.

"No, he never invaded my privacy like that," Jan didn't look away.

She knew the fine art of deception as well.

"Could you have told if he did?" that question came from Pat. The tone was almost accusatory.

"I can tell you are trying to read me right now, so yes," but that wasn't enough for her.

"Even in the beginning?" Pat's tone didn't change, but her thoughts did. Jan was sure she was referring to the hospital.

"Yes," Jan turned and looked at her.

"You were able to keep him out?" Gregg again. Jan turned back to face him.

"I didn't have to. He never tried to invade my thoughts. He did though allow me in his thoughts for practice," and with this she looked back at Pat. There was a small amount of surprise on her face that quickly vanished.

"What was he trying to accomplish by taking you away?" this was Gregg's way of trying to connect Ward to the murder and attacks. Jan chose this time to lean back and take a deep breath.

"I don't know, maybe trying to help me in a way he never got," Jan could see that her words had hit their intended mark.

"Did he ever ask you what Kevin was hiding?" Gregg had the tenacity and temperament of a bulldog, and refused to give in.

"No nothing like that at all. I guess you know the whole story now. A while back we worked together on a couple of assignments," she took another breath as if she was revealing a large secret. "On our last assignment, we sort of got involved. It ended when he left, and since then there's been no contact. I guess that maybe in some odd way, when he helped me out he might have been trying to do a good deed. But he never pushed for anything. Not information, not even for physical contact."

"You knew the policy," Gregg drew her attention back to him.

"Yes, and I am back here where I belong aren't I?" Jan only

projected work related thoughts.

"Good. Was there any physical contact between you two?" Gregg put the only question in the air that she really didn't want to answer and had tried to ward off. It was a logical question to determine what they saw as the kidnapper's hold on his victim.

"Nothing more than friends. How long until I'm cleared to go back to work?" she changed the subject. Jan needed to know just how long they were going to keep her under surveillance.

"You are not ready to be out in the field physically, and this is not the time to discuss anything else. You still have a lot of recovering to do," he jotted down a couple notes.

"Who will be my partner? We can at least start to get to know each other," Jan forced the conversation not wanting to get up and leave when it had appeared that Gregg had already dismissed her. The look on Gregg's face did not lead her to believe that the conversation was in any way appropriate in its timing.

"Let's get back to what happened after the attack in the hospital," Gregg looked at Pat and she took a step toward Jan.

"Let's not. When I get a partner and a chance to look at my things, I might jog a few memories loose, at least enough to help find Rob. Which is my only goal right now. If they found me in the hospital, most likely they have him and are trying to get to me. You also have all the records of the attack," Gregg's expression changed from uninviting and hard to unwelcoming.

"You are not going to be put back in the field. And as for Rob, if we had any leads to follow we would have already. He let the information out that you were still alive to try and catch them, but that backfired. As for Rob, he's probably dead by now. We aren't going to spend too much time looking for him. They have killed everyone else they've had contact with," he paused for emphasis, "except you. Maybe you should have discussed more about Rob's disappearance with Ward. By the way," he now chose to smile, a heinous smile, "you don't know anything about Rob's disappearance do you?" and with that look and his tone, it implied all that they had hinted at the moment before. Jan's blood boiled. It was bad enough to be accused of something she didn't do, but to her partner, that was unacceptable, unthinkable. The shock of knowing that they would never allow her back in the field again only added to the anger. She looked at Pat, and decided right then and there that this was not who she would be in five years, it wasn't her speed, or her calling in life. If she had ever doubted it before, she didn't now.

"I think we are done for now," she closed off her mind tightly, the only thing they didn't know was how done she really was with them. "I don't have anything more than you do, in fact, even less. I thought my help would be appreciated, but I can see that we still haven't made it past the facts that Rob pointed out to me in the hospital. You think I am involved for some reason, and you won't be happy until you have solid proof," Jan stood and turned to look at Pat. "Now Pat if you will take me to my cell, you can then come back and tell Gregg all the wonderful things you saw as you picked at my brain."

"Take her back," Jan heard Gregg's voice behind her, rough and hard as he dismissed her. Pat looked at Jan and then took her to the door. After leaving the room they walked in silence back to the apartment. Once inside the apartment, Pat closed the door and then spoke.

"You know, we are here to support you," it was the first words Pat spoke since they had left the office. Jan didn't turn around. She knew this was part of the debriefing, the drill. Now it was make nice time so that she would talk. Jan thought about all that she knew about department policy, and couldn't imagine that any of these people had really thought she could have possibly forgotten all that she knew. Pat stood and waited. Jan's back was facing Pat and she slowly turned to look into her eyes; time to play along, for a while.

"I know, it's just that Rob has been so helpful over the years as a friend, and as a partner, I couldn't have asked for better. I just don't want to see him hurt, too many people have been hurt on this one," Jan made her way to the couch and sat down, letting her shoulders slump as if the effort that she had put out had worn her out. Jan had glanced around the apartment and noticed that the glass of cola still sat exactly where she had left it on the counter.

"There are people working on it, they just don't know where to start. Kevin's girlfriend was a dead end," Jan felt the bile rise in her mouth at Pat's choice of words. "If you could just give them a bit more information, then maybe," Pat was good, she just let the sentence hang, dangling the hook in front of her. Jan leaned her head back and planned her next step as she closed her eyes. Her thoughts drifted off to the ache in her muscles, and she focused on the pain, trying to make it seem more than it was. The pain would help to keep Pat out of her mind for now.

"Both you and I know how much an object, or smell, can help trigger a memory," Jan lifted her head and opened her eyes. Looking over at Pat she continued, "Maybe if I could just see or handle the items that were left in the car, I might be able to figure out what they are looking for."

"Did you recognize any of your attackers?" Pat sat down trying to look relaxed.

"The funny part is that I recognized the voice in the hospital as one of the men involved in the assault, but . . ." now it was her turn to let the sentence hang.

"Yes," a patient quiet voice, yet it was tinged at the edges with the hint of hopefulness.

"I may have heard it somewhere in my past. The one thing I do know, I would certainly remember that voice if I heard it again. It is burned into my brain. And no, it wasn't Ward's voice like you are thinking. Do you still have the tape from my hospital room?" Jan hoped the question would not go unanswered.

"Let me talk to Gregg. I'm sure that we can do something about letting you see the evidence and maybe even starting in on the tape," Jan knew that she wouldn't be going into the tape files any time soon. Even if they let her hear the tapes they had, she knew which voice she would hear first even after stating that it wasn't Ward's voice in the hospital. They would change it and try it anyway. All their avenues here pointed one way, and Jan never felt more lost.

"I think I need to rest, it's been a very busy day," Pat stood up and walked over to the door.

"If you need anything, just ring the buzzer, and someone will be here to help you out," Pat left and the door closed. The lock slid into place. Jan leaned her head back and waited for Pat to walk away from the other side of the door. She could still feel her mind, waiting, just waiting.

About a half an hour later, when Jan was sure she was alone, in all ways, she let her thoughts wander a bit. She pitied Pat in some ways, how she had chosen to live out her life. Maybe in another life or time she could have chosen to stay with the department, but the rift was just about as insurmountable as it could get right now. Jan got up off the couch. She went into the bath and took a nice long hot shower.

The shower stall was small but adequate. Jan stood there and let the warmth of the water ease her aches and pains that she could now easily dismiss. Except for her surveillance team, she was alone until morning. Jan's fingers felt the chain around her neck and fingered the gold ring. The warmth of the ring lingered on her fingers. Tonight she would talk with him. She could feel it. She thought about their last meal together and decided that all the food found in here, the type that would be reheated and re-hydrated, would only be a disappointment compared to what she had been eating. She decided that skipping the evening meal was the better choice.

The water rushed over her head. It was now late Monday evening, and most likely Pat and Gregg were still discussing and comparing notes. Good for them she thought. Soon it would be Tuesday morning, one more day gone, and one less day in which to find it all. By Friday afternoon it would all be over, good or bad. She could leave, and with any luck, Rob and Ward would be back where they belonged as well. Jan took her head out from under the shower and shook off the water, "Fool," she said out loud to no one. Once out of the shower she wrapped the robe around her and tied the belt. It was now time for her to go to work, and see just how well she could still do her job with or without the department's backing.

Using the crutches, which were beginning to become a nuisance to her, she walked back out to the kitchen where she had left the half-finished cola on the counter. She picked up the now warm cola, and finished it off in one gulp. Paying attention to every detail, and making sure that if the surveillance was visual in here they could see everything she did. Carefully she looked in the refrigerator. Taking out one prepared meal, she looked at it, and pretended to read what it was. Putting that one back, she went through the ritual three more times before she finally closed the door of the refrigerator with nothing in her hand. Jan planned to look as normal as possible, so as not to draw any suspicion to her. Finally, she washed the glass she had used, and put it back in the cupboard. With great care she turned and made her way back into the bedroom, and then turned down the comforter on the small bed. Jan smiled as she noticed it was a down comforter, she couldn't have asked for more. Jan turned off all the lights, leaving the lights from the city outside to light the room. Laying the crutches by the bedside, she unbelted the robe, and crawled under the covers. Fluffing the comforter up, she then quickly slipped out of the robe and draped it across the bottom of the bed. Anyone watching would have known that she had gone to bed sans clothes, and surely without anything else.

Anyone that knew Jan would have known that she had pocketed the phone in the robe when she was in the kitchen, and had now taken it out placing it under the bed covers just before she threw off the robe. Jan slipped down deep into the bed and pulled the covers over her head. At first she twisted and turned, as if trying to find the most comfortable position. Finally, she lay still for five or so minutes, so that anyone watching would think she had gone to sleep. With one last check for mind readers near her, and only being able to sense the presence of an untrained mind, or what they called an unskilled mind, as the guard outside her door for the night. She then switched on the phone to find out exactly what it and she could do. As the light of the phone filled the space under the cover of the bedspread, Jan smiled. She knew she was completely ready for this step.

Chapter 12

After pressing a few buttons the phone began to hum. A low hum, that wasn't noticeable over the noise of the air handler that blew the air-conditioning throughout the room. Jan dialed the phone, entered the code, and connected with the department's computers. She knew that by not having a direct connection, the time it would take to get the information she needed would take a little longer. She waited for the computers to connect and then went directly to the files that contained the information of who would be outside her room, guarding the door. By getting this information she would have a better chance of knowing when the best time would be to move about with a bit more freedom. She could break out of the room, of that she was sure, but she wouldn't get as far, or as much information as if she were allowed out. There was a beep and the information came across the small screen of the phone in a stream. Jan paged through the information, and stopped when she found Tony's name.

Tony had been in the department for a long time working security within the building. Of all the people sent to watch her, he would be her best bet for a little freedom. They had been friends for a while, and Jan knew his wife. Jan knew exactly how she would get past him, and get out of this small prison. Tony came on duty only at three in the morning, so she had some time to collect and interpret some information. Jan turned her attention to other matters at hand.

She went on to the computers to see if a report of the debriefing had been filed yet, and found Pat's preliminary report stored on Pat's computer. Jan wondered for only a second about where Ward had gotten all the codes, who knew, but it was making Jan's work far easier. It took a full five minutes to download it to her phone, and then she read it. Reading through the report, Jan was glad to find that Pat had been unable to go past the spots in her mind where she had set up the barriers. Once more, Pat had not seen the barriers Jan had put up, and seemed pleased with the information she was able to see. The only part of the report that concerned Jan was when Pat had written, "Jan's mind is currently unstable, and unsure. To pursue any type of retraining at this time may result in the types of psychological problems we have experienced in the past." Jan knew that her mind was sound, and not one bit unstable, it had only been what she had allowed Pat to see that had influenced her interpretation. It wasn't that assumption that bothered her. In fact, that was what she wanted them to think. She didn't want retraining to start anytime soon, she had other things she wanted to do with her time.

What did bother her was that there had been another incident before hers, and in that case the person involved had not recovered, or at least not according to what she had just read. Jan read the report one more time looking for information that might give her a clue as to the other person's identity, and then put the phone down for a minute. Was it three years or four years now that Ward had been gone from the department? The thought passed through her mind and she tried to remember. Looking back at the phone, Jan started to access the confidential files of all agents. Ward's file was locked, like she expected. She started trying all the pass codes, one after another that Ward had loaded on the phone.

It was after the sixth try that Jan found the code that opened his sealed file. She only hesitated a moment. 'Would this change things if she knew what had happened?' Jan thought about Ward and what she did know about him. She knew that he was quite sane and trustworthy to a fault. They had wondered through each other's minds a number of times, and in each case she could only remember one thing that was taboo for her to read, and that was his final assignment in the department. Those memories hurt him, and he never spent time with those memories himself. He had once been a top agent, and had a promising career. He had worked for the department three years before she had joined. On the jobs they had worked together, he was always professional and intuitive. His mind reading skills were only second to Pat's, and even that had been in dispute at times in the department. Jan and Ward had worked together on about five assignments, all of which Jan had learned one or two new things about being an agent from him. Their friendship had deepened from the moment they met as well as the draw they felt for each other. The department had backhandedly encouraged their growing relationship, even if relationships were in general discouraged. Rob had spoken against it, said that there were other motives and that it wasn't a healthy relationship. Always keeping both the department and Jan in mind, he was afraid it would backfire on everyone. It had. On Ward's last mission, something had gone wrong, and although he never shared it, the department started to discourage their relationship. They discouraged her from knowing where he was, and contacting him. They even made sure that their paths never crossed when he was back at the office. Once that mission was done, he had left for another, and never returned. It was these jobs that he never talked about. The only thing that Jan had never known was that the department had never sent him on his last mission. He had just taken the assignment, on his own, without Gregg's approval. Very unlike Ward at that time in his life, and career. Jan had never known if he had returned from this job. She had been questioned for hours, but at that time really knew nothing. It had all been in the guise of helping him. She now wondered if he had put up the same walls and decoys as she had just done to protect someone else.

It was months before she heard from him again, and by that time, it was clear that he had left the department without clearing the proper channels, as if the channels even existed. Jan knew that once in the department, a mind reader never left, so knowing that Ward was gone had been alluring to her when he first tried to reach her. Wanting to know more, she made contact to try and find out what had happened, but he had never allowed her to see it.

It was these files that Jan started to download. She knew in the pit of her stomach that these files held a clue as to the person trying to kill her. That funny feeling was back. 'That was the strange part,' she thought, 'If he had wanted to kill her, she should have been dead. He had had two chances.' With any luck Ward's files would allow her to find her attacker's identity. As she watched the screen, she saw the slow advance of the download bar and knew it would take some time. Watching the bar slowly move across the screen was hypnotic. Her eyes grew tired and finally, the stress of the day took control, and before the download finished, she had fallen asleep.

The night was still bright even at one thirty in the morning. The city never went dark. The streetlights were all working on the side street, in a good neighborhood, in a subdivision, in a satellite city in the Phoenix area. The good people of this neighborhood would never know what happened when the morning crept in, but he would. Each time they met it was different. Surprise was never a good thing when they met, and so he had parked the car on the street an hour ago, and waited. There was nothing special about the car he waited in. He waited in a four door white car that could have been found in this neighborhood on any given day. In fact, in the Phoenix area, it could have been found anywhere on any given day. It was a car that he had borrowed in order to meet with his nemesis. He let out a quirky smile as he realized how superheroish it all sounded, but as he knew, the rules of the relationship had been set up long ago, and not by him.

There was no fear that he would show up early. He had no fear of Ward anymore. The occupants in the car, relaxed, and waited. Just waited. It was a meeting that had been arranged before he had even left Mexico. It was a meeting that he wasn't looking forward to at all. The last time he had encountered him was a memorable experience, in a lasting sort of way. Allowing his fingers to brush the scar on his eyebrow, he let the memory fade back into the depths of his mind.

He had been sitting in the car for the last half an hour and was looking for something to get his mind off things as he waited for the next half-hour to pass. Looking at the sky he saw the dotting of stars, the crescent moon, and the clear endless space that was sky here in the southwest. A stray dog wandered down the street exploring each post he passed, and leaving his mark on most. In the distance he could hear the sound of cats fighting and the cars on the main road, far away from here. He had counted every car on the street three times and the number had never changed. There were exactly five lampposts on the south side of the street and one speed limit sign. The phone in his hand felt warm, as he looked down at it, he stared at the lifeless number pad. It hadn't even been a full day and he felt the emptiness that existed without her. It was a feeling that he had lived with before, but wasn't prepared to live with again. In the beginning letting her go back to the department had been easy. As the day went by it had become harder and harder. This time, he was afraid of losing her completely. Letting the tips of his fingers brush over the numbers of the phone, he decided that it was late enough to make a call. His fingers punched the buttons on the phone as is if they had their own memory. The man that sat next to him barely glanced at what Ward was doing as he continued to watch the street. Placing the phone to his ear, he waited for the answering voice that would sooth his nerves.

It had been a deep dreamless sleep, and as she felt the vibrations next to her leg, she began to wake. Jan realized that it was the phone vibrating against her leg and quickly awoke. She smiled, knowing it was Ward on the other end of it. While waiting for the information to download, she had remembered getting tired, and then she must have fallen asleep. Excitement tugged at her composure once she realized that she would again hear his voice. She wondered what time it was. Sliding under the covers she brought the phone to her ear and pressed the button to answer as she made a quick mind sweep of the area, "Hey you."

"Hey," silence warmed the night, and the distance between them disappeared for a minute before they continued to talk, "How you holding up?"

"Not bad, but I can hardly wait to leave," Jan was careful to keep her voice low. Letting her fingers play with the band on the chain around her neck, she thought about Ward.

"Found my gift?" it was both a question and a statement.

"Yes, it was very thoughtful. I have it on right now," Jan's hand continued to play with the ring.

"What else do you have on?" there was silence on the other end of the phone for a moment.

"Nothing," and she thought she could just barely hear him catch his breath before he spoke again.

"Too bad I'm not there," he took a deep breath before he continued, "Better get back to business. Have they treated you okay?"

"I'm locked in, had the first debriefing, and the first argument. All in all nothing unexpected," again she made sure her voice would not carry past the bedclothes, "You've already read the report right?"

"Yes, Pat has never had a gift for writing. It was pretty boring, and if the debriefing had been that boring you would have been asleep on Gregg's desk after five minutes. Any reason you didn't tell them you were kidnapped?" Ward had wondered that after reading the report. Her decision had almost set her path out of the department in stone. He didn't give himself the luxury to hope though.

"Something's wrong, not only here, but with you as well. Ever since we got the call you have seemed distant, as if you knew more than you wanted to, and wanted me to. That's the way it feels here, except I know who they suspect, you. Now," and here she took a planned breath, "I know you didn't have anything to do with this, but you do know something I don't."

"Yes," and that was it. Jan had expected him to defend not telling her his secret, or at the least deny it, but nothing happened.

"Okay, I'll ask, why?" Jan felt just a bit exasperated, and sighed.

"If I told you, it could cause problems right now. It's not a coincidence that you were targeted after Kevin was killed, or that he left you alive. You just have to trust me on this one for right now," and now it was his time to sigh. Hoping against all hope he would not lose her to the department again, "if you can."

"Okay." although it wasn't, she hoped every job they did together didn't go like this.

"What are your plans for getting into the evidence room? From what I read, my guess is that you aren't going to get invited there anytime soon," Jan had to remember to check the confidential files they now had on her, Ward seemed to be one step ahead in this game. He had been on the outside for longer, so his skills were more refined.

"Tony comes on at three, so I will feign muscle spasms and ask to go to the gym. I'm sure he'll let me. From there I will be able to sneak out without much trouble and retrieve the stuff. It can't be much, and then get back here," she heard him start to speak, "before I look at any of it. That way, at least I'll be in a fairly safe environment."

"Good." Ward wished he could be there with her. He wished he could make this all go away, and in many senses it would when they were finished on Friday, he just hoped she wouldn't go away as well.

"Something wrong?" Jan thought she heard something in his voice, it was rough and tired, but she couldn't place the problem.

"No," Ward closed his eyes, and let his guard down as he pictured her in his mind, on the beach in Mexico.

"I'm missing you as well," Jan knew that they had spent nearly two months together, but most of the time she had no idea who she was, or who Ward was. It had been a waste of time in some respects, and the waiting had worn on Ward. In other respects, they had gotten to know each other on a new level, and it had created a deeper commitment to each other. And just when they thought they would have time to reacquaint themselves as husband and wife, work and duty called again. Jan wanted to change the subject, "What are you doing?"

Ward knew it was a simple question. He also knew that she would know if he lied to her. Not because she could read his mind right now, that was impossible with the distance, but because she knew him so well. He waited just a moment too long and Jan continued.

"You're meeting with him aren't you," Jan's tone was flat. It was the only way she would be able to control herself. The man had already killed twice, and was now holding one person she respected hostage. She didn't want Ward to fall into the same trap.

"Yes, we need to arrange some things. And I need to make sure that Rob is still alive if we are going to continue this venture," Ward took a breath, not revealing everything. He heard Jan's silence, and knew from experience that the secrets would not help. Right now, he didn't have a choice, knowing who attempted to kill her twice, would only complicate her healing, soon she would know. He was sure that she would figure it out; she had to make the connection he couldn't. No one at the department would believe him back then; no one would believe her now even if she could remember him, and she would.

"I'm not comfortable with you doing this," Jan was far from comfortable with this. It had been different before when she hadn't been in on his jobs outside the department, but now, things were changing, and so were they.

"Comfortable or not, I've got to do this. Don't worry, I'll be fine. He won't try anything with me this time, remember he still wants you. I also have a friend with me. I'll call you in the morning," Ward could see a car turn onto the street. He could feel his mood change, and the thoughts around him become dark and dangerous, "Still going to run away with me?"

"Who's going to stop me," and with that, he hung up. Jan knew that whoever this person was, he was dangerous, and now he was there. She had heard the change in his voice. Jan couldn't sleep. Nervous tension seeped into every pore of her body. Without turning on a light, she climbed out of bed and put the robe on. Looking at the clock, it read two in the morning. Jan turned up the covers of the bed, and hid the phone in the pocket of her robe. It was an item she was sure to need when she left in an hour.

Walking with a slight limp into the living area and over to the window, she just stood and looked out. Looking down at the street she could see the nightlife of the city. It was an odd mixture here. People leaving the theaters, hookers waiting and walking, and even the gangs all mixed together. Somewhere out there Ward was meeting with a man who had proven he had no regard for human life. Suddenly she realized that she had left the crutches by the bedside, it was a mistake she might regret if someone was watching on the cameras. Slowly she made her way back to the crutches, and picked them up. Looking at her watch it was now two-forty. She decided to get dressed in a black leotard. On top of that she put on an oversized tank, shorts, and then her robe. She placed the phone into the top of the leotard, and hid it under her breast. The tank covered all signs of the phone. Taking one last look out the window, and a moment to wonder what was happening with Ward, she then turned and went over to the door phone. Picking it up she could hear the chirp of its call outside the room, and then the familiar voice of Tony answered.

"What are you doing up so late?" it wasn't an accusation, just a genuine question, and that was the one thing she liked about Tony, he was genuine. In a world of half lies, and deceptions, he had always been true. Too bad he was the one she would have to slip out on. Jan really didn't want to see him in trouble, but he was her only hope, and more to the point, Rob's. Hopefully he would understand one day.

"Hey Tony, is that you?" Acting surprised.

"Yah, is there some kind of problem in there?" he was still waiting for his answer.

"Yah, I've been up for an hour or so. Seems my muscles need some work after today. I've done too much and I am having all sorts of spasms. I just can't sleep. I know my therapy routine, but I need the gym equipment. Is there any way you can take me into the gym tonight, so that maybe I can get just a bit of sleep later after I work the kinks out?" Jan waited with baited breath.

"Sure hon. I'll be right in to get you," and with that the door slipped open and in walked the very reliable Tony, "Nice to see you again, wish it was under better conditions." He was a head taller than Jan and had the same type of training, and his muscles showed it.

"Yah so do I," Tony reached out to help her, and she allowed the help. The less he thought she could do, the less he would watch her once in the gym. It could also become an asset later on to make him feel as if she were depending on him. Together they walked out of the living quarter's area and into the great hall of offices again, only this time most of the area was dark and quiet. The gym was close to the evidence room; at least it was down the same corridor, unlike the living quarters. Once in the gym Tony looked at her as Jan made her way to the first machine, "It's okay if you want to just wait outside, as you can see I'm just such a major threat security."

"You know the routine, I'll have to stay here with you," that was exactly what she wanted. If Tony were here when she went into the ladies she would be able to slide out the rear exit door and head for the evidence room. All the while, Tony would be watching the front door, not knowing she was gone. Easy but there was one flaw. The hallway that came from the rear exit went past and within eyesight of the chair he now sat in. This time, she would have to leave the crutches. She didn't want anything that could accidentally make noise. Jan worked through her routine, slowly, and making it look painful, grimacing when appropriate. She also worked through her plan. As she finished up, a half-hour later, she felt better and a bit more limber, but acted as if her muscles were now really sore, and painful. Tony looked concerned, "You okay? Did you do too much?"

"Just a bit. Would you help me over to the locker room door? I think I should jump in the Jacuzzi just to loosen up a bit before I head back to bed. I think I'll feel a hundred percent better after twenty minutes in there," Tony headed over to her and helped her to her feet. He got her to the door and then sat right at the entrance to the locker room, which put him at the wrong angle to see her leave, but he still would be able to hear her if she wasn't careful. Jan entered the room and filled the Jacuzzi.

"Tony," she called from inside the room. The door slightly opened and his voice came floating in.

"Yah," he sounded half afraid.

"I'm still dressed, but I could use some help running the tub," Jan smiled at the thought of Tony being uncomfortable.

"Oh sure hon," and he sounded relieved. "Should have been more thoughtful," and he brought in a chair for her to use as well as lean on when she needed to get in and out of the tub. "If you need anything else just yell," and he left.

Dropping the robe and the oversized tank top to the ground, she pulled the phone out of its place of concealment. Once she started the Jacuzzi, she slipped over to the exit door, looked up the code information on the phone, entered the code that would keep the emergency exit alarm from sounding, and gently pushed the door open. Jan held her breath waiting for an alarm to sound, but none did. Ward was as good as his word, and the codes were all valid. Slipping the edge of the robe tie into the door so that it wouldn't close, she was on her way. She felt unstable without the crutches, in some ways she still needed one for balance, but knew that if she had brought one along, it would only be a liability, not an asset.

Jan carefully slid along the wall and out of sight of Tony. She noticed that Tony was reading a magazine as she moved along. When twenty minutes were up, she knew that Tony would enter the locker room, no matter who was in there. It was his job to make sure he knew where she was. With a little wish, and a prayer, she slipped out of the gym and down the hall. Quietly Jan moved down the hallway, using the wall as support, and well aware of the minutes moving along. She made it to the evidence room door, and entered the code. It was here that she knew, no matter what, a camera, was always on, and the camera was always visible. As she entered the room, she looked at the camera, and noticed that it wasn't aimed at the door at the moment she had entered. What luck! As it panned the room, she was able to stay out of its path, and lower to the ground, which was helpful to her. Using her arm muscles more than her legs, she was able to negotiate the room. She knew the case number by heart, and went toward the lockers labeled with those numbers. Once over there, she stayed down to be less visible as she located the one and only locker she needed in. Looking at her watch, she knew she only had about ten minutes left to get back. Waiting for the camera to pan away, she noticed that the lockers themselves were not individually locked. This would save her time. As she opened the door with only a small click escaping, she noticed that only two small bags were in the locker. One was her old purse, and the other one a mostly empty duffel that would have belonged to Kevin.

Jan grabbed it all and closed the door while she ducked back down behind the shelves as the camera panned its way back over again. Just holding the items made her feel a bit woozy, and she took a deep breath before heading out the door and into the hall again. She had begun to remember the last moments again, and it was only now she began to wonder why Kevin had only carried a few items, and not more, like others she had babysat in the past. Carefully she put her purse into the duffel and hung it over her shoulder. Blocking out all thought except the ones of getting back to the gym she made her way down the hall and silently back through the gym doors. It had been easy. She was tired, and limping just a bit more, but it was that moment she realized; it had all been too easy. It was then she noticed that Tony had moved. Tony's face was in full view of the hall. One wrong step or sound and he would see her. Why he had moved was a mystery, and the thought that he may know that she was not in the locker room crossed her mind. She watched as he leaned back against the wall, and glanced at his watch. Time, it was a commodity which she had very little of at this moment as she needed to be back in the locker room in about two minutes.

Jan reached out with her mind. It was a reflex reaction, training. He was not thinking of Jan at all, and the thoughts that were in his head were, let's say unflattering about his current job. She skipped those and looked farther. He was wishing he was in his bed, alongside his wife right now, and wondering how he had gotten this rotten assignment to watch someone he considered a friend. For the minute, her secret journey was safe. Jan looked at the duffel she carried, and put it on her back. She squatted as low as her legs would allow with the support of the wall and the floor. She slowly started to move toward the rear door of the locker room. Three feet, three feet was all she needed to get past Tony, and as she neared the clear area, she knew it would be impossible to go past without him seeing her. Jan looked at the treadmill she was hidden behind. The safety key hung loosely on the cord. Gracefully with her fingers Jan loosened the key noiselessly, and pitched it across the room ready to move when Tony glanced at the noise. It was an old trick, but always one worth repeating. Jan watched as the noise of the key reached Tony's ear, and he turned, not to look at the sound, but to look right at the locker room door. It wasn't quite the natural reaction she was looking for.

'Come on Tony,' Jan thought, 'just go and check it out, it'll be fine. Where could I go?' and with that last thought, Tony moved toward the key. Jan didn't stop to wonder at all if she had influenced his actions. She just moved using hands and legs, and with less grace than she wanted, but quick enough to make it back into the locker room. Jan threw the duffel to the ground and secured it in her robe. Stripping down, she got into the tub and waited. Taking a deep, relaxing breath, her muscles eased in the warmth of the water. It was less than two minutes later that the door opened, and Tony walked in, eyes shielded, trying to keep from embarrassing him more than her.

"Jan," he waited for her reply, fingers nervously playing at his eyes.

"Yah Tony, what's up?" Jan sunk deeper into the tub making the most of her two minutes.

"Good, you're in here. I think I should get you back to your room. You ready?" He shifted his weight from one foot to the other.

"Where else would I be Tony? You're right though about time to leave, my time is up. Let me get out and get dressed, preferably with you out of here. Give me two minutes would you. And by the way," Jan let the moment hang, enjoying his discomfort, "I forgot to ask earlier, how's

Julie?" Tony left, but not without Jan being able to feel just the slightest hint of embarrassment coming from him with the mention of his wife.

Jan got out of the tub, dried and dressed quickly. This time she didn't put the robe on; she draped it around her neck, with the duffel hiding inside the fabric. As she walked out of the locker room, she looked at Tony, "Okay, ready when you are."

"Need any help?" this time Tony was right by her side quickly, and as she let him help support her weight on the one side only, they quietly went back to the room in which she was imprisoned.

Chapter 13

Jan leaned against Tony while he keyed in the code to open the door. A smile tugged at her lips as she waited to get back into her room and go through the bags she had hidden in the folds of her robe. She was able to push off the feelings from the bag, that had made her weak earlier, and she was feeling on top of the world now. She had done it. Feeling like her old self, she knew she had gotten into the evidence room and out without being caught, and now with any luck the secrets that were in the bags would save Rob. The door slid open and she walked in. She sensed more than saw a figure sitting in the dark. There on the couch sat a man, the light coming in from the windows silhouetted him, making it hard to see his face. The figure on the couch was unmoving and being unable to see the face of her intruder caused a split second of fear, even though she never showed it, and her stomach did a flip. Leaning into Tony and taking a quick read of his feelings, she realized that he had no fear in his mind. He knew the identity of the man in her room. She looked closer at the intruder and confirmed who was in her room with her mind. She had faced off tougher adversaries in her life, it had been a part of her job, her training, but Gregg had years of experience and training on her. What was worse was he was supposed to be a friend.

Jan's first thought was that she might have been seen on one of the cameras. She was pretty sure she had avoided all the cameras. She knew where all the cameras were, even the ones that had been installed recently thanks to Ward and his computers. Searching her memory she remembered there were no cameras in the hall, she had known that for years, and the only one that could have seen her she avoided. Quickly she retraced the steps in her head and realized that the only way anyone would know is if Tony had come into the locker room when she wasn't there. Tony switched on the lights, and Gregg's face came into full view. Jan chose to, had to, read all of Tony's thoughts now. Jan was sure that Tony had moved to answer the phone in the gym, now she had to be sure why. She looked at Gregg, but focused her mind on Tony's to unlock the secrets that were in there. The phone in the gym had rung while she was supposed to be in the locker room. It had been Gregg on the phone, and he was unhappy. He had gone to see Jan in her room and found neither one of them there. Tony didn't know why, but knew he was to return Jan to her room, immediately. Tony stuck to his guns and refused to bring Jan back before she came out of the whirlpool, which she had seven more minutes to go. He told Gregg that he would wait until she was finished in the tub because she had overworked herself on the equipment. That would have been only about five minutes before she came in the room. Jan couldn't get any more information, so she left the rest of his thoughts alone and focused on her boss, or former boss. He was more practiced at keeping mind readers out, even though he was not one himself, his mind was very focused, locked down, and he knew the tricks. No one had talked yet, and Jan wasn't going to be the first. Tony stood by her side, as they all seemed to be in the middle of a face off.

"Did you get what you needed?" Gregg broke the silence, his voice low and menacing, but only fishing for information. She could tell by how he spoke that he had had no clue that she had been to the lockers.

"If you mean did I complete my therapy routine so I could continue to heal, yes, thank you. It would have been good if someone had asked me about it earlier today and taken me to the gym, I may have avoided this late night trip. I am now very tired and want to rest. Could you leave?" Jan knew that wasn't going to happen. She glanced at the valence the wire was gone.

"Wire's gone. Tony, did she leave the locker room, or the gym without you?" Gregg looked at Tony, and if Tony had had a weak character, he would have cracked with the look now on Gregg's face. It was a hard look, no smile, and his eyes seemed to pierce through Tony's exterior. That's what had made him good early on in his career, and why he had been picked for this department.

"No. I even went in and checked like you asked. Everything according to the book," Tony felt unsure as to what was happening. Jan picked up on the vibes, as well as his embarrassment. Jan felt a twinge of guilt for making him feel guilty in the locker room.

"It's okay Tony; they just want to know that I was where I was supposed to be. I shouldn't get any freedom until they are sure that I haven't been brainwashed," even though she talked to Tony, Jan never took her eyes off Gregg. "If it's okay with you Gregg, I'll go get changed," Jan turned to go into the small area called the bedroom then turned back, "unless you think you need to watch to make sure I'm not going to run off, or that I'm not hiding something sinister under these sweaty clothes."

"Don't take long," but his thoughts screamed profanities all aimed at her. At least she got to him, and satisfaction set in, as Jan understood that this was now a battle of minds, wit, and experience. With his hackles up he would be a bit more careless. "Tony, wait outside," Gregg dismissed Tony with a wave of his hand, and Tony left as he had been told to. Now the battle began, and Jan was determined to win, losing was not an option here.

Jan walked into the bedroom area and laid the robe on the bed; she quickly grabbed her clothes out of the drawer, and didn't bother to take the phone out of her bra. He probably wouldn't do a body search so she would leave the phone where it was safe, but she wouldn't put it past him to search the room again while she was in it. She would have to trust that he wouldn't find the bags. Jan was out of the bedroom in two minutes flat and walking with her crutches over to the chair. Running her fingers through her hair, she looked at Gregg. He had stood up and was looking out the window. Jan didn't push, she had learned long ago in situations like this that she needed to be on the defensive, not the offensive, at first. She knew the rules of the game, and so did he. Every ounce of training would be needed to keep him at bay, and even some tricks she had learned out in the field.

"Sorry, but I was sure you would have tried to get out. My mistake," he turned, but Jan was sure he wasn't sorry by just reading his body language. It had only been words, not feelings, "Level with me, Ward had control over you for almost a month before we found out, and then he kidnapped you. I worry about him at times. As you know we were once partners. What happened?" Gregg turned looking straight at Jan. It was the next ploy in his arsenal of games. Jan looked back at Gregg, wondering just how she wanted to handle the next step.

"Nothing, we just did therapy routines when he was around. I'm not sure why, but he thought he could get me to recover faster than it would happen, could happen here. Maybe it was his experiences that led him to that decision. I don't know anything about that though," she saw him grimace slightly, and knew that she had hit some nerve. "Other times he left and I didn't know where he was, or what he was up to," Jan leaned back in the chair.

"What did you talk about?" his voice began to betray his cavalier attitude. He wasn't prepared to work this hard for information he didn't want to hear.

"The weather mostly, therapy for recovery, my progress," Jan let her eyes drift off as if she was thinking, "news when I asked for it."

"That's all," he truly didn't believe her, it was obvious.

"Really, yes."

"You started up your affair again," he didn't know for sure but was willing to risk the statement.

"Affairs, as you put it, are not allowed in this business. I did my job sir," Jan was not going to give him anything.

"So he tried," a smile of satisfaction crossed his face.

"No," Jan looked away wistfully, "At first, when I still had no memory of the past, I'd be lying to say I wish he hadn't, but he never did."

"Did he meet with anyone else when you were with him?" Gregg's patience was beginning to thin. He wasn't getting what he wanted out of her by trying to be the nice guy.

"No."

"Are you sure?" he leaned toward Jan trying to push an answer out of her.

"We've already covered this in the debriefing sir. Shall we stop playing games?" Jan stayed calm, deadly calm, "You didn't come here at four in the morning just to go over what you already know. You want to know if I'm working with Ward, and whom else, if anyone, he is working with. Every question since I got here has had to do with what he was doing, and if he has influenced me. Well you know, I don't know how many times or ways I have to say it, he hasn't done any of that. I stayed loyal to the job and department. What more can I say?" Jan decided to force the issue, and force reading his mind, there was one way around the blocks people put up. Ward had showed her, and it may or may not work, it was not a technique taught in the department. If not, it may leave her open, in less control of her thoughts and emotionally vulnerable and explosive for a time. "You didn't come in here and remove the security devices to be Mr. Nice," Jan started into the meditative sequence of breathing quietly. She started to intensely focus on the thoughts that Gregg had put up as his mental block "You want to let me know what's really happening here?"

"No," Gregg's voice was unyielding. Jan focused harder, and started to get a glimpse of his thoughts, losing control of the direction of the conversation for a minute. As she started to tear away at his mental wall and glimpse what lay behind it a shiver ran up her spine. What she saw scared her. The images were vivid. Not only did he think that they were working together, he thought that somehow they were responsible for Kevin's death, trafficking of drugs and other items, and Rob's disappearance. "Let's get one thing straight. There is no way I will believe you aren't involved in this somewhere. I've read the records; you and Ward had a relationship prior to his disappearance. From what I can guess it was pretty hot and heavy and for all I know it never ended. I've turned off the cameras so that we can work a deal," there was a pause, "maybe for the both of you," Gregg leaned against the window as if this would be a welcome invitation for her to open up to him. Liar! Jan had not recovered from the reading yet and her emotions were raw and exposed as she pulled away from his mind.

"You ass!" Jan was now mad, and she had lost all emotional control she had at the beginning, "You are such a stupid asshole and always have been." Gregg walked over from the window and placed his hand on either side of the chair arms she was sitting in, effectively trapping her in the chair. He leaned in toward her.

"Now that I know what you think of me and I have your attention," he smiled but it never reached his eyes, "you want to tell me just what is so tempting as to set both you and Ward on the wrong side of us, or is he just that good," Jan worked hard and had regained some composure. It had been a stupid outburst, and she took in deep breaths to recover. Gregg must have thought that he was the cause of her discomfort. She may regret what she had just said, but most likely not. Gregg's face moved closer until it was just inches from hers, "I think I could work a deal for you," and his eyes dropped down to stare at her chest.

"Gregg," Jan let her breath out slowly. She was now in complete control of her emotions again, "if you don't move, I'll make sure you'll have nothing left to make any deals with."

"Too bad," Gregg pushed off the chair, "Maybe I can make you another deal. What do you have that they want?"

"Gregg," Jan continued to regain control of the conversation and the meeting, "I told you, if I knew I would tell you. I don't know. Ward doesn't know. I'm not involved. And even more surprising to you is that he isn't either. All he was ever interested in was my recovery. Maybe it was friendship, guilt, or something I just can't put a finger on. Something you know nothing about like compassion. Instead of hounding me, shouldn't you really be looking for the people you let attack me in the hospital?"

"The cameras are all off, the tapes are stopped. You can tell me," if it wasn't such a pathetic attempt to get information, she would have laughed. "It could be a long time in this room if you don't. If you turn Ward over to us, I might be able to get you out sooner. If it's truly over, then you won't mind. It would prove your loyalty to the department. Trust me, trips like you took tonight will look like a three week vacation if you don't."

"I think it's time for you to leave. The sooner the better," Jan stood and walked toward the door. She knew she couldn't open it, but hopefully it would give him enough of a hint.

"Just what I thought, he's corrupted you as well. I can make your life miserable you know. You should never have even tried to come back," that she knew, "Sure you want me to leave like this? You may never get another chance to get out," he walked up close to her, trying to intimidate her.

"Just leave," and Jan turned and headed toward the bedroom. There was a dead spot inside her now. In some ways she felt sad. It was a chapter in her life that was now over. A place she had once felt safe was now a place that imprisoned her. 'Was this how Ward had once felt?' was the thought that passed through her mind.

"I know you're involved, you and Ward, and I will prove it," the door slid open and Gregg walked through letting the door close behind him. Jan looked at her watch and noticed it was now almost six, and the sun was just thinking about waking up. Time was short, and no sense in wallowing in the past. She got into the duffel and pulled out her purse first. Knowing that she should only take out one item at a time, but realizing time to be the one item she had very little of, she dumped the items on the floor looking them all over at the same time.

She was looking at all the bits and pieces, and nothing really stood out. There were no weapons in her bag like she always carried, and she didn't care who had taken them. Deflated emotionally, she thought, she had expected to find something that just jumped out at her. She started to put the items back in the bag. A lipstick and some other general makeup, a set of keys, a pen, some tissues, and then she saw it. A key that lay unattached from her key ring. Picking it up she got the distinct impression that it was not hers, and this was what she was looking for. She fingered it and turned it over in her hand, looking at the writing on the other side. It said USPS.

Suddenly her mind flashed back. She was in the car with Kevin. She could see his face, his thoughts, a post office, a box, a bag, and a partial number, 675. Jan caught her breath. She saw the money. Somehow she had buried the memories so deep. The money was in a post office. She had lifted the key when he wasn't looking as they got out of the car. It had been mailed to a post office box somewhere, and now as the memory faded, it was time for her to find out where the post office was located. One thought remained, why had she buried the memory so deep?

Concentrating, Jan tried to think, to complete the memory as it faded in her mind. Jan knew that the memory wasn't whole yet as she sat motionless on the floor. Suddenly she realized she didn't remember sitting down on the floor in the apartment. Frustration tugged at her reserve. Taking in a calming breath she then continued. Grabbing at the duffel she looked for something that would complete the memory. She knew she had seen it all back then when she was with Kevin and all she had to do was remember it. Jan's pulse started to race, and her breaths became shorter. She knew that soon she would reach an overload, and then who knew what would happen. Carefully she touched the items without looking at any, just waiting for something to stop her, and it did. Jan had gone through about half of the bag, a couple shirts, socks, and a few toiletries. When she touched the letter, she stopped breathing. Slowly she brought the letter into view. Looking at the envelope she saw the name on it, Sandy, and the address on it was in Florence, a town about an hours drive from here.

Suddenly her thoughts were back in the car, just outside the factory. Jan could now hear Kevin's voice clearly. She was standing on the driver's side of the car, he was on the passenger side, and the car doors were open. She even remembered that they never did close the car doors. The argument they had had was about going inside the factory, "I need go in, she said to meet her here."

"You really should have told us about her sooner. You can't meet with her now we need to get you to the airport. You're not safe yet, not anywhere near here, and my job is to keep you safe. I'll call and have a team sent out here to get her. I have a bad feeling about this. And isn't there something else you should have told us?" He had no idea that Jan could read minds and that she was definitely getting bad vibes from the building as well as him. Jan had started to walk around the car, but it was too late, he was on his way into the building.

"I got plans, don't think I was so stupid as to leave my future up to all of you. Try to stop me from going in," he made it into the factory before she could stop him. She had been right on his heals, and had forgotten to grab her purse from the car. It had been a stupid move, a rookie move. Now that she remembered going into the building she also remembered coming face to face with her attacker, only this time, she could almost make out his face. It was familiar, fuzzy, but somewhere she knew she had seen that face before. She saw the bat coming at her from another person and tried to block it. As it connected with her chest she could hear the other attacker say, "Hi from the boys on the outside!" Jan remembered feeling a tug at her thoughts and pain. His face was very important; she knew it was a key to what had happened to her, and with that realization Jan felt the room begin to spin. Colorful dots began to fill her field of vision, and she passed out on the apartment floor.

When she awoke, she didn't know how long she had been on the floor. The flashback had stopped when she passed out, and her breathing began to slow. It was still far too fast to be considered normal as she was jarred into a semiconscious state, and when she felt the phone vibrate again she tried to refocus, but couldn't. She knew who was on the other end, and she knew what would happen if she didn't answer. Slowly she pulled out the phone and put it to her ear, rolling over to the bedside to hide what she was doing. She would have had no way of knowing if Gregg had restarted the cameras.

"Hey," even her voice didn't sound normal to her. It was strained, and barely audible.

"Jan," he waited, and then the his voice became more insistent, "Jan!" there was still no answer, "I'm coming to get you now," it wasn't what he was going to say, but from the sound of her voice and the silence on her end of the phone, Ward knew she was in trouble.

"Wait," with all the other thoughts crowding in on her brain, one thing she did know was that he couldn't come near here, ever. That was what Gregg had wanted, maybe even orchestrated. They wanted him and she was the bait.

"Jan, are you alone?" Ward's voice was deep and quick. She could also hear a bit of panic.

"I think so, I can't be sure," she was beginning to feel more normal, even if she wasn't ready to sit up.

"I'll come get you," Ward wanted to keep her from the hell he had experienced.

"They will be waiting for you. Gregg was here, and I read him. They think you are involved in this and are using me," Jan took a breath, "Not that they aren't using me as bait right now."

"Tonight I'll," he never had a chance to finish.

"I don't need a knight on a white horse riding in to save me. Just listen," Ward was afraid of losing her, she knew that. And in some ways, she was afraid of losing herself right now, but she wouldn't let him know that. Right now he couldn't read her, "I know where it is. Meet me tonight at the usual place and time. I'll get out, don't worry," there was silence, he understood where to meet and when, it was a long standing arrangement they had, "We are Rob's only hope. They aren't looking for him, just you. They believe I'm involved in whatever you are doing, or not doing," she hoped that would give Ward a bit of relief from his fears.

"He's still okay, but not for much longer," Ward's voice hardened and Jan didn't miss that.

"I saw my attacker in a flashback just now. It was fuzzy, but I know that I know his face. Was he a friend?" just a little information, that was all she wanted.

"At one time he was like a brother," Ward's voice held no emotion, "If you are just an hour late, I don't care who wants me, I will come and get you," and it was more than a promise.

"I won't be late, I have a plan," and they rang off. Jan tucked the phone back into the spot where she had it safely hidden. She lay on the floor for a couple more minutes, and then it hit her. She had downloaded

Ward's files. Looking at the clock, she knew she had about three hours before she could leave. It was now or never. She knew if she waited until she met up with Ward, she would never look at it, and he would never allow it. Erasing all possibility of her discovering what had happened to him forever. Sitting up slowly, and putting things back into the duffel, she placed it under the bed. She didn't care if they found it later, she would be gone, and soon she wouldn't care what they knew or didn't know. Once they had the money, they could arrange the exchange with the department as back up. This way all parties concerned would be safe, the department would think they could get Ward, when in reality they would catch the true problem, while saving Rob. Everything would end happily ever after, she hoped. Ward didn't have to be involved in the switch, and then all would be clear. Or, at least most people would be clear. She was pretty sure Ward's name could never be cleared the way that Gregg reacted. She was sure there was something personal between them that she didn't know. She pulled the phone out and started to open the files.

Ward put the phone down and leaned his head back on to the seat. It had almost been too much. It was one thing working a job; it was another thing working a job that he had so much at stake with. It had been a long time since he had been in a position in which he could lose himself and everything that mattered. It had only been one other time that he nearly lost himself, and he had lost his friend. Ward had argued with Jan for the last year about leaving the department. Although he couldn't see the future, he knew that the future would be filled with pain if she stayed. Letting his thoughts drift, they went back to when he discovered she had been hurt. Rob had called him. Ward had felt dead inside when he heard the news. There were things in his life that he had given up, but she would never be one of them.

Good old Rob. For as much as he didn't want to allow them to be together, he had known it was only a matter of time before they would be. He'd seen it. Rob had bent the rules for them. Even after Ward disappeared, he had believed in Ward's innocence, even if no one else believed him after the accident. Rob had just believed that there were better ways to go about it than leaving. He would have made a good best man at their wedding, no matter what they had thought of each other. Maybe one day they would let him know, if they all survived.

Looking at his watch he realized that he hadn't slept in the last twenty-four hours, and sleep seemed to be the last thing he wanted, or could indulge in. The meeting had gone well, if you could say meeting with the devil ever went well. Ward still owned his soul. He wondered what had gone wrong. At one time they had been so close, like brothers, that it never would have crossed his mind that he could have turned bad. What had happened to him to change his character so much? Had he always been that way, and they had missed it? Had he fooled Ward for all those years? That was the one thing he still couldn't piece together even now. The best thing Ward could do was to stay out of his way, and his life. After all, no one else knew he was still alive, and Ward was only one man, the only man who knew he was alive. Ward would never be able to take him and his allies on. His skills were just as refined as Ward's.

At one time, just after Ward had left the department, he had asked Ward to join him. The thought still sickened him. When he refused, he tried a bit of coercion. That is when he got the scar, but it was much deeper than just the cut on his eyebrow. All he knew was that the sooner Jan was with him, the better he would feel. It was the one person that Ward knew could be used to get to him right now, and Ward was sure he wasn't the only one who knew it.

"What's next," the deep, rich voice in the car brought Ward back to reality.

"We wait. She's got it, but has to get out. Won't meet with her until tonight though," his head still rested on the seat, eyes closed.

"You need some rest," the voice continued, "Let me go spring her, and you go back to my place and grab twenty minutes or so. It's goin' to be a long night."

"Don't try and spring her. You can't get in anyway. She said she didn't want a knight on a white horse riding in to save her," Ward sounded frustrated as the other voice rolled out a barreling laugh.

"Sounds like her from what you've told me. Can hardly wait to meet her. How 'bout a horse though?" Ward turned and looked questioningly at him. You couldn't get any farther away from the knight image than his companion was. Ward just wasn't sure about what he meant by the horse, until he saw him point at the car, "I'll just wait outside and hand over the reigns to the horse when she walks out," now it was Ward's turn to laugh.

"Okay, with you watching over things, I think I'll be able to get a cat nap in," Ward started up the Explorer and pulled into early morning traffic.

Chapter 14

Jan sat crossed legged on the floor, the cell phone in her hands as she stared at it like it had taken on a life of its own. Once she read his file, there would be no return. Taking a relaxing breath, she finished accessing the files. The case file, Ward's file, was written by Gregg. That explained the reason why Gregg had such a vendetta against Ward. Gregg and Ward had been partners at one time. The report started out normally, stating the general information about a case he had been on, and relating it to the current happenings.

'Agent Lowery and Agent Malone reported in two days prior to said date to both of their partners. No new information on the case was given. Have not been able to contact said agents since. Contact has tried to be reestablished without success,' the report went on with information about how they had tried to contact both Ward and Malone. Jan found this part uninteresting as sometimes contact was lost for days. She needed more information than what she had learned from these files. What she knew now was that he had been working with another agent, a mind reader, at the time of the incident. The next report continued three days later with more information, 'Agents Lowery and Malone were located, yet not able to explain their disappearance, or what exactly had happened to them during this time. They were brought back into the Phoenix department for debriefing separately. Both Agents Lowery and Malone stated that the gunrunners discovered their identities and they were kept separately in a drug-induced state for an undetermined amount of time. Neither of the said agents had an explanation as to why they were able to escape, or were released. They are now in separate rooms being watched and psychologically evaluated,' so far, except for the fact of confinement, there was nothing in it that would explain anything. Jan continued to skim down the report. They had been returned to active duty after one week of observation in which no one had seen anything that could cause any concern, and mentally they were in good condition. Three days after they were returned to duty the report became more interesting, 'Agent Robert Malone has disappeared from the Phoenix department. This has caused Agent Ward Lowery some mental duress and he seems to be spending an inordinate amount of time trying to locate Malone.' Jan wondered who Agent Malone's partner had been. Jan tried to remember Malone without much success. She couldn't place his face. This was mildly strange. The department was based in about six cities, but all the mind readers had working knowledge of the other mind readers that were assigned to their base. Jan closed her eyes and tried to remember his face. Nothing clear came to mind. Opening her eyes, she looked back at the report and continued to read. The overall tone seemed to be the growing concern over Ward's preoccupation to find Malone. The way it was written seemed to indicate that it had become an obsession for Ward, and a growing concern in the department as a whole. That was one of Ward's qualities she liked, the inability to leave anyone behind, or in harms way. She read on wondering why the records had been sealed until she got to the report on the automobile accident. She had never seen this report, or even heard of the accident before.

'Agent Ward Lowery was found outside the Phoenix area, off the Roosevelt Dam Road. The vehicle he was in had been involved in a roll over accident and was located halfway down the side of the cliff. Lowery was ejected from the vehicle and was found in an unconscious state about a quarter of the way down. Agent Lowery was air evacuated to the nearest medical facility for emergency treatment, and is still in a comma at the time of this report. Prognosis is guarded at this time. When he can be moved, Agent Lowery will be moved to a secure medical facility. The other passenger in the vehicle was never ejected and all remains were burned in the fire. Evidence found on the scene suggests the other occupant in the vehicle was Agent Malone. Agent Malone will be listed as deceased, according to all evidence including departmental identity documents, and remains, found at the scene. The DNA evidence was inconclusive because of the extreme heat of the fire. The remains indicate that the body in the vehicle was the same size and age of Agent Malone,' the report continued with the usual dry information supporting why they believed the other occupant to be Malone. No more information was given as to why the accident had happened. As Jan read through it she began to realize that the injuries Ward had sustained, or at least the recovery Ward had progressed through, had been similar to hers. This gave her the insight as to why he had been so patient, as well as his understanding of what she needed. She read through the rest of the report, and his recovery process, which had all been documented in both the reports and medical records that had been filed with them. He had memory loss at first, but it had returned quickly, and traumatically. The retraining program they had him on seemed complete, and when able, he was brought back to the Phoenix office. Jan checked the date on the report. It was interesting, she had been sent on assignment during this period of his recovery. They had purposely kept him from people he knew, and vice versa.

As she continued to read the reports, it was all fairly normal until the last two days. It was this report that caused her some concern. Statements like, 'psychological responses seem unstable' 'Insists that Agent Malone is not dead . . . today seems calmer and refused to discuss Agent Malone. Suspect he may be coming to terms with Malone's death.' It was at the end of the report that Jan started piecing things together, 'Agent Lowery has forcibly left the department, and is now suspected of crimes against the department, and state. . .' that was where it had been left. But something was eating at Jan. Something in the way he had acted had suggested other actions.

    She had known Ward both before and after the accident. There was a change in his behavior, but it had seemed that the change had been due to loss of faith in the department and their ability to positively affect people's lives, including the ones that they controlled. They had argued over this many times after he had left. Right now she had to agree with him. Gregg seemed focused only on bringing Ward in, not trying to save Rob, or even finding Kevin's killer and her attacker. Gregg thought they were one and the same, even though she had assured him they were not. That only seemed to implicate her, not clear Ward. Gregg could only see this as his best chance in a very long time to be able to bring Ward in, and it was by using her. What he didn't know for sure was that they had been meeting for years after Ward had left the department.

    Letting her thoughts drift back to Ward. Jan knew that she had wandered through his thoughts many times and was not even sure why she had never seen any of this. Funny what the mind can do when you lose a friend. Jan now understood why he was so protective of her right now. But still there was something in the report that bothered her. Being obsessed to find Malone was one thing, but not writing regular reports was another, and not typical of Ward. Why couldn't she remember who Agent Malone was? Closing the files on the phone and sliding it back into place, Jan leaned against the bed. She needed something. She needed to focus.

Jan stood up and not caring who saw her right now, she began to move slowly through the Tai Chi routine that she had done with Ward so many times. With her mind clearing and her body focused she felt centered, less out of control, in a time when she seemed to have little of it.

She was halfway through the routine, when she stumbled. She fell to the bed, and the flashbacks started again, only this time the face of her attacker was completely clear. The sounds of breaking bones, and a skull being crushed, pushed into her brain. Unable to control the images she lay helplessly as she watched the face come back after her, heard his voice, and this time, was sure of who he was. "I won't kill you this time. But don't get in my way again or all bets are off," and as Jan heard the words, she connected the name to the face, to the voice, and to the agent. It was the face and voice of the not so dead Agent Bobby Malone. Once a friend, an exceptional mind reader, and now it seemed, an enemy. Ward and Bobby had been friends, even closer, like brothers. They had trained together, competed together, and relied on each other. Ward had not recorded anything he had found out during his investigation into Bobby's disappearance, leaving nothing for anyone to work with. For him to do this, he must have suspected foul play on Bobby's part, and hoped to bring him back into the PED without incidence. It also left him with no credibility after the accident with his theories. Jan was now sure that he had believed Bobby was into some kind of trouble. And with the assumption of his death in the accident, they later did not believe him when he insisted that Bobby was still alive.

The flashbacks had paralyzed her for only moments, but it had seemed like years. Pushing the pain and images to the back of her mind, she was able to focus on the here and now. All the pieces of the puzzle were falling together. Ward may have left the department, but they would forever haunt him, and he would forever be haunted by the thought of them. Bobby, on the other hand, had not only left, but also covered it by faking his death, and implicating Ward in felonious behavior. That must be who Ward went to meet with last night. 'Didn't he say like a brother?' she thought. And that is why she had been spared once by him. Jan remembered what he said in the hospital. Bobby had said that he should have killed her. Would he keep from doing that? Was there still something left of the old Bobby? Jan decided that it would not be worth the gamble to find out. The stakes had just gotten high enough. Now, all Jan had to figure out was how to get out of here and over to the meeting place by seven tonight. Jan shook her head, she wished she could have accepted her knight in shining armor, but she knew if he came near, they would have him, her, and their lives would never be the same. Plus, before now, she had never needed anyone to come to her aide, and she wouldn't start now.

    Jan put the key to the post office box into her bra. She knew she would have to travel light on this trip, and carrying a bag was out of the question. The clock read eight ten. In one hour she would need to be on her way. Jan decided to worry about how to get out to the lake later, there was always a way. Looking through the dresser drawers she found a pair of causal slacks, and a pressed yellow shirt. Yellow would not be the color she chose, so she dug just a bit deeper and found the traditional white top used by most agents when in the office. Carefully Jan dressed as if she were about to re-enter the world of the PED. She combed and styled her hair and put on a simple layer of the make-up that she had found in her purse. Looking in the mirror, she could almost believe that she was ready to go back to work here herself. This was the part that needed to be beyond a doubt to anyone who saw her. Her plan was simple. Simple was what worked best. She picked up her purse and looked into a secret compartment that was located in the bottom of the purse. It was still there. Why wouldn't it be, they wouldn't be looking for that. As the plan formed in her mind, Jan pushed away the thought that only one slip, and she could be spending most of her life within these walls, or ones that were similar to them. That was one thing she couldn't afford.

She was about to put the purse under the bed again when something caught her eye. It was hers, she thought it might have been left or lost in the hospital. It was a gold chain bracelet that matched the necklace she wore around her neck. Ward had given it to her when they got married. She had never taken it off. A chill ran through her. Before he had left them for dead, Bobby must have taken it off of her, then, for some reason, left it in the car after going through all the items in the car. Maybe he had just dropped it by accident. Knowing this, she was amazed that the key had still been in her purse. It had been a good thing to secretly relieve Kevin of it before they went in, otherwise, Bobby and his bunch may have taken it. That must be how they found out where Sandy was going to be. They got the address to where she might be from the items in the car. They must not have found her right away as Jan remembered the visit Bobby had paid her at the hospital. He must have been thinking that the PED had already found and hidden her.

The phone started to vibrate, and Jan smiled as she took it out to answer it. Ward was concerned, he had already lost one person to the department, and he wasn't planning on losing two. The thought of talking with him again made her smile, and she relaxed. Playing with the bracelet she put the phone to her ear.

"Hey you," her mood was playful, and her voice was warm and inviting.

"Are you glad you're back?" The voice on the other end of the phone wasn't Ward's. It was deep, cold, and menacing. Jan froze. There was no feeling in this voice, no remorse. Although she knew the identity of the person, there was nothing she could recognize left of him. No other person but Ward had this number, she was sure of that. Concern for Ward left her speechless.

"Don't worry, your Wart," and he toyed with the last word, "is just fine. I stole the number from him last night and he never even knew it.

Wonderful gadgets they have now days. I figured why should he have all the fun talking to you."

"Bobby?" she still couldn't believe it. It was like talking to a ghost. In fact, the Bobby she had once known, was a ghost, this was a completely different Bobby.

"So, you have another piece to the puzzle. Is your memory finally coming back or did Wart tell you? Did he use what I taught him?" the coldness in his voice never changed. And she didn't much care for the way he referred to Ward as Wart, "Are you letting him make all the decisions now? He was looking a bit tired. Too much for the old man I guess. Hope he doesn't make a mistake," she could hear a small laugh, "He might just lose you again to someone else," the connotations were implied, "I could have killed him last night, want to thank me?"

"Did you call just to harass me?" Jan didn't know who this new Bobby was, but already knew that his character had changed drastically after leaving the department and not for the better like Ward's had.

"Not just to harass you, that's just been for fun. Just like when I first attacked you and took a trip through your thoughts. I've gotten better at scrambling thoughts don't you think? It took you a lot longer to recover than it took poor old Wart," he paused to let this sink in. "I called to tell you that I should have killed you at the hospital. That's twice now I saved your life. You owe me," it was meant to shock her as he spat the last words out, but Jan had been threatened before so she let the thought drift to the back of her mind and concentrated on the task at hand, staying calm. As much as she wanted to hang up the phone she didn't, and she continued with the disgusting banter. She needed all the information she could get.

"I owe you nothing. So, why didn't you kill me, getting soft?" Jan sat down. She had to keep focused to play word games with this mad man.

"Let's just say it was a favor for a friend," he paused and she heard him take a deep breath, "and you had too many good attributes once I got a good look at them," he chuckled. "Wart and I, you know, share," softly saying, "everything." Jan felt like throwing up, "It's been good talking to you. Make sure you're there on Friday. I'd like to have another chance at you, can't let Wart have all the fun now," laughing he hung up the phone. Jan put her head between her legs. In the past she had dealt with drug runners, gunrunners, white slavers, murderers, and even the occasional terrorist, but Bobby got under her skin in a very different way. He was once one of them. He knew the department as well as any of them, the training, and the rules that bound them. But for Bobby something had changed to make him different. Could it be that any one of them could be lured into this type of crime, and to finally sell out one's own soul?

Jan had to believe this wasn't true. It hadn't happened to Ward, it wouldn't happen to her. Something horrible happened to change him. Something only one other person could know about. They would need to talk.

Jan looked back at her watch. It was time to go.

Chapter 15

Jan went into the kitchenette. Taking out the milk, cereal and coffee she made herself a simple breakfast. Not her normal breakfast, but it was what would be expected of her to do, and that is what she was counting on. She sat at the counter and ate about half the bowl of cereal. She had never been a fan of cereal, but it would suit her needs until she could get out of here. The water boiled and as she poured the boiling water over the coffee she could hardly wait until it was ready. The smell of fresh coffee, even if it was just instant, did something to wake up her senses. Holding the cup under her nose, she breathed in the aroma deeply. She sipped at the coffee and then tore open the packet from her purse carefully. She wished she could finish the cup, but knew that wouldn't follow the plan. Jan always carried a small packet of rat poison in her purse. It was quick and painful, to rats as well. If one needed a fast escape, it was the best and cheapest choice. It was always handy, easily replaced, and easily detected if suspected. The last one was what she was in need of now. Carefully, keeping everything out of sight of any cameras that may again be running, she poured about half in the milk jug, and an eighth of the packet in the cereal bowl. She was taking great care not to touch the contents, as she really didn't want to poison herself or anyone else, at this time. With the right acting, and she had seen how the poison had affected people before, it would help make for a perfect escape. She thought through her plan and the next step as she closed the packet. Jan knew the one thing they wouldn't deny her was medical attention if she needed it in an emergency, and this would be an apparent emergency. Making sure the poison was mixed thoroughly throughout the milk jug and in the milk in the cereal bowl, she sipped at the coffee again until it was almost finished, making it look like she was midway through breakfast when it hit her. Tucking what was left in the package into her pants pocket, she was ready.

What Gregg hadn't figured on was that with him being in the room and turning off the cameras it would only help in her escape. Jan began to grab at her stomach, double over and look as if she was in great pain. It would be the typical reaction to this poison, and everything had to look right, and sound right. She began to hobble, stumble, and pull her way to the phone by the door, dragging along her crutches as she went. With each step looking as if it was even more painful than the one before, she began bending further and further over wrapping herself around the crutches. Grabbing at the phone she gasped for breath as she tried to speak into it. It hadn't been the first escape she had ever done, but it was the one with the most at stake. Jan took a long and dragging breath into the phone.

"Something's wrong," she gasped for breath again, "I need . . ." and she never finished the sentence. Instead, she fell to the floor letting the phone hit the wall. Jan laid there in the fetal position for almost a minute before the door came open this time. All the while she lay there and moaned softly. While she waited she loosened the right handle on the crutch, but not enough for it to come completely off. It would only take a half a turn and it would be free. All the while her mind searched for other minds outside the door and for what they might be thinking.

At first it was simply Tony's thoughts that she could pick up on, and he was very worried. She could also tell that he had gotten instructions from

Gregg earlier when he left, that he was not to go in or out of the room, or to let Jan go in or out. But this definitely tore at his conscious, and worked in her favor. Jan smiled inside as the thought of foul play entered his mind. Then it was cautiousness, as if Gregg had warned him to expect a trick. He wasn't sure who was, or if anyone was, being honest here. Jan moaned loudly to make sure that the phone picked it up. Tony, who heard Jan moan one more time, decided to phone to the inner office for assistance. Jan kept her fingers crossed that Gregg still took this time daily to leave and go to the local coffee shop to get a cheese danish and coffee. Pat answered the phone, and from his thoughts, Jan knew she was on the way. Pat would be easier to handle, but harder to keep out of her mind. She focused on the pain she had felt in the flashback so that Pat might pick up enough information to keep the questions few, and the intrusions into her mind to a minimum. Then the door slid open, and Tony came straight over to her kneeling down to talk.

"What's wrong," concern in his voice, Pat entered and quickly assessed the room. She did as Jan expected, what any trained agent would do, and went straight to the breakfast table inspecting the contents. After smelling the milk, and tasting a bit on her tongue she came in with the assessment Jan needed to get out of the building, and to, supposedly, the nearest hospital for emergency treatment. Tony continued to feel her head and check her pulse.

"Get her down to the car, someone has poisoned the milk," Tony lifted Jan up gently, but swiftly, "Has anyone been in here besides Jan?"

"Just Gregg. He was here when we got back from the gym earlier this morning. Before that the room was left empty and unguarded for about an hour and a half at around three this morning," she then came over to Jan.

"Did you do this?" her tone was harsh. Tony held her up easily in his arms and she was able to look Pat almost in the eye.

"If I were," and Jan moaned curling up even more in the fetal position making it hard for Tony to hold her, focusing on pain in her mind.

Jan wrapped her arms tightly around her middle and clutching the crutches to her chest even tighter, "going to kill," again she made a soft moaning sound, "myself, I think," and this time she let out a loud, agonizing moan and gasped again for air, "I'd choose something a little less painful."

"Tony, take her down. I'll follow in a minute," frustration in every syllable as she spoke, "I need to get a team into the room to search it, and get the tapes from when the room was empty." Before Tony could leave with her, Pat grabbed his arm, "Watch her," she commanded, and there was no guessing as to what she meant. If Pat was unsure of Jan, that meant only one thing, less time. She would do a quick preliminary search, and find nothing suspicious. She had accepted the pain for what it seemed to be, but if she let herself inspect the thoughts she had received more carefully, she would know them to be false. Most mind readers were taught to protect themselves against others' thoughts and feelings of pain, but if the need arose, they would assess those readings and Pat would be no exception. If they got to the elevator, she would most likely be free; there was only one way in, and one way out. If the elevator got to the garage before Pat could stop it that would be about all the time she would have. Her plan would have to be carefully orchestrated.

The next thing that happened was pure luck. They didn't try to take her crutches away; they just let her hold them. Jan just moaned softly and closed her eyes as Tony ran her to the elevator. She could feel the eyes on her as they went through the great hall of offices for her last time, and Jan heard the team rushing the other way. Tony stepped on the elevator and it started to descend. They must have notified security so that the elevator would be waiting. Jan took a small sigh of relief and hoped that it wasn't all for naught. She hated the thought of what she had to do next. He wasn't the bad guy, he wasn't even involved, but in the end he was the one she had to get away from. As the elevator started its decent, Jan started to count silently. She knew exactly how long it took for the elevator to reach bottom.

Halfway down, Jan went limp in his arms.

"Jan," he looked at her, shaking her a bit and trying to check her pulse, "Jan, just stay awake, don't fall asleep. I'll have you to the hospital in about five minutes now."

She felt the elevator stop and knew they had hit bottom. The phone on the elevator buzzed about ten seconds before they got to the basement, and Tony ignored it. The elevator doors opened into the parking garage. Jan waited for Tony to take that first step out of the elevator. She had freed the handle on the way down and now waited. When he was off balance is when she made her move. With her left hand, Jan brought the handle of the crutch up into Tony's face with such force, she knew she had to have broken Tony's nose. As the blood gushed from his nose and he stumbled from the blow dropping Jan. As she fell Jan rolled to land on her feet from his arms. She only had time for one more blow before he would get the upper hand, as her muscles would not hold her standing alone and in a conflict for long. Surprise was her only weapon right now.

"Sorry Tony, but I have to help Rob, I'm his only hope," and with that said, she landed the blow with the crutch handle that knocked him out. Even at half strength Jan was no match for the ordinary person. She was able to read what their next move would be and with the training she had received out match them. Everyone in the department got good training Tony included. Mind readers got better. They were people the department couldn't afford to lose. Jan looked toward the elevator and silently said, "Shit," the doors had closed and now she knew she only had about four minutes to get out of here and away. She had planned to wedge the crutch into the doors to give her a bit more time, but no sense in lingering on what could have been. There was only one way out of this parking garage, and it didn't matter if it was by car, or by foot. Looking at the cars in the garage she knew it would take too long to hot wire any of them and even then they would be able to trace and find them within minutes with the tracking systems that were installed on all the vehicles. She started to move to the driveway that led to the outside as quickly as possible hoping that once outside she could lose herself in the downtown shops long enough to get away. As she cleared the driveway gates she heard a catcall from a group of gang want-a-bes beside the garage entrance.

"Hey sweet thing, need a horse?" it was a question that threw her off. There was something in those words that caught her attention. As she turned to look at the man who had uttered these words she was shocked. There sat a two hundred and fifty pound black man with a diamond so large in his ear that one might truly call it a rock, a blue sports jersey with the number twenty-three on it, and a blue bandana tied around his head. Most of the weight was muscle, which didn't seem right, or in context. In all respects he had the look of a gang-banger, but there was something different about him, not the group that sat there, just him. She stopped and turned her attention on to him. Something about his looks and thoughts didn't match.

"I'm kind of in a hurry, what do you mean?" she moved out of the direct sight of the drive, figuring that her head start was about up, but something told her to stay. Eddy sat there. Ward had described her to a tee.

"King Arthur thought you might want the horse," and with that he threw a set of keys at her and pointed in the general direction of the parking meters. She turned and sure enough, the white Explorer sat there waiting, "It's open." Without saying another word she turned and went for the SUV. She quickly got in. Instead of taking off right away, she got in the back and covered herself up with the sheet that had been left in the car. She was close enough to feel the thoughts of Pat as she came running up the drive, and she was mad. Using a cell phone she called up to the offices as she canvassed the street with her eyes and her mind, hoping to pick up just a hint of Jan's thoughts. Jan knew that fear was a powerful thought, and one that was easy to pick up. She had been taught to guard against it ever since she had started in the department, so it was easy to place the emotion off to the side. Pat's eyes now focused on the supposed gang bangers, Pat tried to read their minds, not sure of what, if anything, they had seen, or even gave a second thought to. Eddy had changed the subject with them again so all Pat was able to get from them was thoughts of where their buddies might be, and all the conquests they thought they had had. Jan smiled, true to form, anyone Ward would work with would be trained to not allow their thoughts to betray them.

Jan was careful not to reach out too far with her mind for fear that Pat would sense her. So she shut down instead until she heard the foot search team leave the area. The heat in the vehicle began to be oppressive. Even in the fall in Phoenix temperatures inside a vehicle could easily get close to one hundred eighty degrees. Jan waited patiently, meditating to block out all thoughts as beads of sweat rolled down her face and across her back. She again heard the cat call, and knew that it was safe to take off with the Explorer. Without looking back, Jan climbed over the seat. She slowly pulled out into traffic, and she was off. She let out a sigh of relief, and wiped the sweat off her forehead as she enjoyed the blast of cold air coming out of the vents. She knew that the Explorer would not be recognized, or draw attention, as it had not been a vehicle they had seen before on the hospital security cameras.

It hit her like a brick. She was free. Jan took a long deep breath as she drove up the road and looked at the town and the people with a greater respect. Waves of heat came off of the street and sidewalks as she watched a businessman walk from one office building to another carrying his brief cases. A mother with a crying child in a stroller wandered down the street trying to stay in the shade of a tall building. A group of young kids played with an old soccer ball in the empty lot on the corner she was approaching. Little did they really know about what went on in the name of protecting them. With every passing minute Jan began to realize what it meant to be free. It had been a long time since no one had controlled what she was to do or to say in some way or another. It felt good, and she now began to understand just why Ward would never return, even if he had been on better terms with the PED. Freedom was intoxicating. But her freedom had come with a price. The thought of leaving Tony laying on the ground bleeding would stay with her a while. Inflicting pain may have been unavoidable, but she also knew that she would revisit the thought. She knew that he would be okay, and that he was already off to the hospital, but that did nothing to relieve the guilt. When she freed Rob, she would have to have him apologize to Tony for her.

Driving up the road, she realized that the heat in the car had made her thirsty. One problem with this whole plan, she had no money. She had not found any in her purse, and had to leave the purse anyway. Since Ward had thought of the escape car equipped with a sheet for cover and a tank of gas, she wondered if he had thought of anything else. At the next red light she opened the glove compartment and looked inside it. There, in a nice little bundle, was a driver's license, her license with the name Janice Lowe on it, and what looked like about a hundred dollars. She didn't take the time to count it, just smiled. She put the bundle in her lap, and as she got closer to the freeway on Seventh Street she noticed a small, run down Mexican carniceria, or grocery. By the looks of it, there would be no security cameras of any quality in this little ma and pa place to later identify her as passing this way. Pulling in she got out of the car and using the one crutch she still had together, she made her way in the shop. After looking around for a couple of minutes she decided on a bottle of cola and a bag of crackers to ease the hunger pangs. While she paid the lady at the counter she began to miss the little beachfront cottage in Mexico, their little beachfront place in Mexico. Jan also wondered just what her life was going to be like from now on. With that thought fresh in her mind, she thanked the cashier and got back into the Explorer heading onto the freeway toward the east, and a new life.

The freeway dipped below surface street level in hopes of containing the noise associated with it. She knew if she continued down this road that she would be able to get to Florence before noon. Looking at her watch she also knew that she could make it there and back before the assigned time at nightfall. One thing kept her from going. The memory of the phone call from Bobby was still fresh in her mind. He had discreetly picked up her phone number from Ward when they met earlier that night. Jan had a new worry, had he also listened in on the conversation? Ward didn't know of the phone call yet. As the freeway approached the small stack of roads that intersected here she wondered, would she tell him? Jan decided that unless it was needed, she wouldn't tell Ward about the phone call. Jan took the exit off one freeway onto another freeway that continued to head east. Checking the mirror she saw that the same white car had been following behind her, about five cars back. She had also known that it had been behind her for the last six miles. Instead of continuing to follow the freeway like she should have, Jan took the next exit ramp leading onto another freeway that headed to the south. She watched as the car followed her, and seemed to get a bit closer, so as not to lose her. It wasn't the department, but a thought crossed her mind, 'Could Bobby have been watching the building as well?' Jan changed speed. Moving through the traffic, and slowing, she forced the car to get closer. She saw a familiar black face in the white vehicle. Pulling off the freeway and onto the side of the road, she allowed the other car to pull up behind her. Getting out she slammed the door to the Explorer hard enough to shake the vehicle, and the man in the car winced. Jan approached his window.

"And just what do you think you're doing following me?" it was the big black man she had gotten the keys from earlier.

"Thought you might need some help, so didn't want to leave you empty handed," all the slang now gone from his vocabulary as well as the bandana. Watching her walk up and hearing the anger in her voice he had decided that some of the other missions that he had helped Ward on had been far safer. Jan noticed that the rock in his ear was still there, "Ward went to catch some shut eye ma'am. I didn't want him to worry, and we've been up most of the night. His directions were to give you the keys and then take off. I did that, but when I caught sight of the Explorer by the carniceria I decided to just hang around. By the way, name's Eddy, Eddy Darling," and with that said he watched as she choked back a laugh.

'What a name for a large, well muscled black man to have to live with,' she thought as she smiled instead, stifling the laugh.

"Go ahead, laugh, most everyone does the first time," and with a finger shake and voice a hair lower he emphasized the seriousness of the last bit, "and only the first time," Eddy was now more comfortable with the idea that she wouldn't break a few of his bones out of anger. "Now get in the car a moment will you, or do you want to advertise that you're out?"

"Sorry," she walked around and got into the white car, "Can't say I remember Ward talking about you. Have you worked with Ward long?"

"Only odd jobs, otherwise I do construction, and dabble in real-estate. Good steady work here in the valley," and he looked as if he had done lots of construction. The rock in the ear seemed to say he had done well in the real-estate market too.

"It's lunchtime and I need of some real food. Know of a good, out of the way place to eat around here?" Jan decided she should find out what had been happening in her absence, and Eddy seemed like the perfect source.

"Sure do. Want to follow me?" he pointed to the Explorer.

"With pleasure."

With that Jan walked back to the Explorer and started it up. They ended up in a little Middle Eastern place just down the road. For the next couple of hours they just sat and talked. Jan still preferred to find out about people by talking if she could, and she was able to find out a lot about Eddy. Jan found out that Eddy had worked more than just a couple of jobs with

Ward. In fact he was a steady contact in the Phoenix area, and maybe other places. The others waiting with him were real gang bangers he had once known, and called them in for a favor, they knew nothing as to what was happening, and they had been perfect stooges. He also knew very little about what the department was about, even if Ward had trained him well. For all he knew it was just another agency similar to the FBI, CIA, or any list of others. He didn't know that the department employed or even experimented and trained mind readers. Ward had only taught him how to focus his mind to allow the job to be completed better and faster, not that it was a way to get around a mind reader. He still was clueless to the idea of mind readers. Ward had also told him about her. Obviously Ward had discussed her a lot. Eddy knew how deep the feelings ran between the two of them. Jan could tell it by the way he talked about what Ward had said and how Eddy held himself. Jan moved the conversation back to business and asked Eddy about the meeting last night and if he was there. Eddy began to close up, and acknowledged he had been with Ward, but the conversation ended there. It was clear that the only thing Eddy was not prepared, or maybe permitted, to discuss was Bobby and the events of meeting with him last night. As they sat and talked, Jan worried very little about being spotted by anyone. They drew less attention as a couple then she did alone, so she felt justified in keeping Eddy around, and he didn't seem to mind hanging around and talking.

  At about two o'clock she bid a farewell to Eddy, and he assured her that she would see him again. She watched him drive away, and then she made her way to the gently used store across the street. Jan picked out some 'new' clothes to make her feel more like herself. Jan didn't take the time to change. She missed the quiet of nature, and by the time four o'clock hit she was ready to make her way out to the lake through rush hour traffic. Going north again on the freeway she checked her mirror a few times. This time no one was following her. It took an hour and a half to make it over to the

Bush Highway turn off. By six, she was in the parking lot at the end of Saguaro Lake Road, waiting and watching.

She watched the sun go down painting the sky brilliant colors of red, orange, and pink. The large brown rock cliffs loomed on the opposite side of the lake like watchful giants, and soaked up the colors of the sunset. The cliffs were raw and worn from the thousands of years that they had lined the valley. It had only been in the last few years that man had come in and filled the valley to make lakes and reservoirs to supply a growing need for water and recreation in an explosion of people looking for the perfect place to live. These rock guardians had seen many years in their lifetime, and people would only be a small memory in their history.

She had witnessed many a sunset here, and each was as different as individuals on the street. This sunset was somehow different, as she looked through eyes now free from what she once was. As the sunset stretched across the sky she noticed a figure step out from the bushes down by the docks right on time. Right away she could feel the warmth of his mind and recognize the shape of his body. Slowly she got out of the car, stretching. It was a meeting she had been wanting, but something stopped him. Suddenly she remembered that she may have picked up different clothes, but in her hurry to get out here, she hadn't changed. She wore the same outfit that they had all worn once.

Opening her mind to him, she raised up her left hand so that the fading light of the sunset bounced off the band and onto his face. His mind opened and his feelings of fear were released, he came up to her quickly. He took her in his arms, but before he had time to kiss her, she took hold of him and kissed him deeply. Joining together and letting their minds race, they forgot for a moment just what was at stake, and what was happening. There was no past, no future, only a present that was pleasant. After a couple of minutes they broke apart.

"So, how did you get out?" he smiled down at her. They turned and walked to the boat dock. She was quiet a moment, and he allowed her to be, feeling the remorse inside her. He untied the boat from the dock.

"Faked being poisoned, and punched out a friend with the help of the crutches," she followed him onto the boat, "I'm afraid I broke his nose though, as well as our friendship."

"Nice. Remind me not to become a friend," and he smiled back at her. Jan half smiled back, "Sorry, but we all do what we have to do," and she knew he was thinking of Bobby when his thoughts closed to her.

"How much time do we have?" Jan smiled as Ward piloted the boat out onto the increasingly darkening lake with the help of low running lights.

"All night Babs," Ward stopped the boat in an out of the way inlet that they often used, and led her to the bedroom on the boat, where they had secretly met many times before.

It was still dark outside, and inside, when they lay still, together in each other's arms. The world had gone away, if only for a couple of hours, and it was enough to put her mind back at ease. Ward had drifted off to sleep for a moment, and she lay peacefully waiting for him to wake up. Morning would bring back the world and work. They would again focus on the mission, not each other. As she waited she could feel the gentle sway of the boat, and hear the splash of the water on the side. She listened to the sound of the coyotes baying at the moon, and the chirping of the crickets far off on the bank. Again she felt strong surrounded by nature and Ward, replenished by all that surrounded her. They had been here many times before, but never as working partners. He had brought her here as a get away, to show her just what it was like not to have to always go into dangerous situations. To not always be on call to save the parts of the world the PED decided to save, not the ones she felt called to save. To be fed by and nurtured by nature. She could see it now. It was so clear, how had she missed it before? She rolled over and decided not to wait for Ward to wake. She gently kissed his cheek and then moved to his neck. She felt him stir, and she continued her exploration. She was smiling as she felt him stir until she heard the phone vibrate against the bedside table. It was her phone, the one Ward had removed from her bra and placed within arms reach earlier. He looked at the phone, and then looked at her. Sitting up, he grabbed the phone, and switched it on. Not saying a word, he only listened.

"Are you enjoying being out? Don't feel too bad, you only broke his nose, and he needed about six stitches. Is Wart really worth all that?" he could tell it was Bobby's voice, but he said nothing. He knew Bobby didn't know who he was taking to, "Did you forget what we talked about, I know Wart won't," and with a haunting laugh, Bobby hung up. Jan could feel every muscle tighten. She could feel his mind close around hers, trapping her mind within his. And she heard the questions both inside her head and his voice vibrate in her ears, loudly.

"When were you going to tell me he got this number?" it was an accusation, he was confused and in need of answers. Jan sat up and looked at him in what there was of the moonlight coming into the cabin. She opened her mind completely to him. He had to be sure that she wasn't lying.

"After we talked this morning, I went to the gym, got out and got the bags," she decided to start from the beginning and tell him about Gregg's little gamble, "Gregg was waiting for me in the room when I got back. He wanted it to look like he wanted to question me. In reality he wanted to make a deal to get you. After he left, I felt lost, like there was still a missing piece. I went through the bags, I felt very unsure about things. After the key, I knew I was getting some images, but I couldn't see them. I started in on the Tai Chi routine we do together, I guess I wanted somehow to feel more centered. Instead all the memories came flooding back in an uncontrollable stream. After the onslaught of memories ceased I lay on the floor until the phone rang, and instead of getting you on the other end like I expected, I got that," she pointed to the phone, "It was like hearing a ghost at first. You see in the stream, all the pieces came together, and now I recognized the voice, and I could place a face on my attacker, everything was there. As he verbally goaded me, I realized that the Bobby we knew was dead, and this one, well, had taken his place."

"What did he say to you?" his tone was softer, but he was still very tense. Not one muscle relaxing, or softening even to her. His jaw was tight.

"Not much I want to remember, or gave credit to. He told me he'd like to have another shot at me, and that he should have killed me already. Something we already know, but that he didn't kill me as a favor to a friend," and with that Ward got out of bed and began to dress. His emotions were confusing at best, and Jan could glimpse part of the past. She also knew that he had believed every word, but there was something else that was bothering him.

"The sooner he is out of our lives again, the better. I have dealt with him too many times and he will just keep hounding us until he gets what he wants," he pulled up his pants, and zipped them. "Get ready to go, we'll head for Florence tonight," he turned to look at her, all business in his eyes as he grabbed his shirt, "And by the way there are clothes in the closet, choose something else besides the standard uniform. It's not you anymore," and he walked back up to the deck of the boat. She heard the engine start, and they were headed back in to shore. She looked in the closet and found a pair of black jeans, and a black tank top which she quickly put on and then went topside.

Chapter 16

Before they left the boat Ward tucked a nine-millimeter into his waistband in the center of his back and put on a brown leather lightweight bomber jacket. In a small pouch in his jacket he had placed an array of tools as well as a set of handcuffs and a stun gun. He handed Jan a fully loaded nine-millimeter and a stun gun as well that she tucked away and then put on a lightweight black sweatshirt jacket over the top of hers. Being prepared was not only a Boy Scout motto. In less than half an hour they were on their way to Florence. Both of their minds had switched from being lovers to being partners on an assignment again.

The drive had been quiet so far, and the radio played arbitrary music from a local station, that neither of them was listening to. They didn't talk. They didn't have to. They ran over the plans in their minds over and over again. Each scenario and outcome carefully assessed. Both knew what was at stake here, and Jan knew better than anyone else what she stood to lose. Once they had been back in the Explorer for a while, Ward chose to break the silence.

"I didn't mean to. . ," and when he took the breath, Jan interrupted him.

"I know. When I realized just who was pulling the strings on this one, I knew how high the price had become," they sat again for a moment in silence. Jan unable to keep him from seeing everything she had learned. She knew that she would have to face the music sometime after reading his files; she had just hoped it wouldn't be here, or now. Quickly she changed the conversation back to business, knowing it would make both of them far more comfortable for the moment. Jan told him what she remembered of the post office box number and what had happened while she had looked through the items. She could hear the 'I told you so' in his mind, but he did have the decency not to say it out loud.

He thought that in a town the size of Florence, that might not be more than three numbers associated with the post office box number. Listing off the items she had found in the bag they both decided that there was nothing much of interest in the bag beside the key, and it was a good choice to leave it behind. They settled into silence again, but less comfortable this time. She hadn't told him about the bracelet, and why it wasn't on her wrist, and he had never asked. The thought of Bobby removing it from her arm, or even touching her at all, still sickened her. She decided to save that for another time, or maybe never. If he knew then it just might drive him off the edge, and Jan could tell that he was close enough as is. She finally broke the quiet.

"I didn't know that Gregg hated you so much," Jan waited.

"Made him look like a fool once, maybe twice. Never did get over it," shrugging his shoulders Ward kept his eyes on the road.

"He tried to get me to bring you in, to make a deal," Jan didn't say that she was propositioned by the jerk.

"Thinks he's hot stuff doesn't he, but really he's just another old agent looking for a place to spend his final years, not knowing anything else that he could do with his life. We were partnered together for a while, about two years I think. It was before I met you," Jan knew she was treading on thin ice, "It's okay, go ahead, ask," he read ahead in her thoughts, so she continued.

"Did Bobby set you up?" Jan let on to nothing else in her mind, closely guarding her thoughts.

"Babs, I know you read the file. Don't try and hide it. I would have done the same, if things were switched. I have read all of your files. It makes life easier now that I don't need to tell you about most of it, just what's not in the files, and it's a relief. I guess that's why I put that code in there for you, hoping you would take advantage of it so that as we really start our lives together we have no surprises. I know what you are thinking, but there was no easy way to tell you about him. No, they didn't believe me when I told them Bobby was still alive. You would have, but that would have only complicated your life with the PED. Before my accident, I thought I had a chance to bring him back into the department. You see our imprisonment was real enough for me. It was hell. I survived, but he sold out," things were quiet for a moment. Jan could tell that Ward was reliving the moments as he talked about them. She didn't dare enter his mind at this moment, "A small terrorist cell was holding us prisoner, and they used some different kind of mind tricks on us once they knew what they had captured. I made it through all the torture. Bobby didn't have the strength to, character flaw I guess. Bobby sold out early and made the reports in for a while before I was released. He got me released on the condition that he'd get me to join up like he had. That, I found out later. When we met by Roosevelt, I was trying to bring him in, convince him that he didn't want to spend his life that way. Find some part of him that still existed," these were the hardest memories, "When that didn't work, and it was clear that I wasn't going to see things his way, well," Ward had been open, but the memories hurt. Jan could feel the pain. It was the same feelings that she felt every time she went through a flashback. It had been more than a beating, now she knew; Bobby had mentally attacked her as well. The rest of Ward's story, she could figure out. Bobby had tried to kill him, or at least make it look convincing to the group to which he now answered. Once Jan had time to process the bits of information that Ward had just given her, he continued.

Quietly he said, "He's moved on now. Will work for anyone with money, do anything. The only thing he hasn't done yet is kill another mind reader," there was a small pause. Both knew he had come very close to it twice, "Yes the favor was for me," and neither Jan or Ward were sure if that would stop him a third time, "They tried to teach us how to manipulate minds, and that is what he did to both of us. No more secrets, hey Babs?"

"No more secrets," and Jan sat quietly for the rest of the ride with her hand resting on his thigh, eyes on the road. Their future lay ahead of them, the past, better left to the past, if they were to be allowed a chance at a future.

They pulled into Florence before the sun had a chance to overtake the dark. Ward set the GPS system to locate the post office, and when it beeped, signaling that it had found the directions for the post office, they were off. Neither one really knew what they would find in the mailbox, but both were sure that the money would be there.

"They knew she was here," Jan didn't need to say anything more. Jan was afraid that Bobby might have other people here, watching, and the last thing Jan wanted was to walk into an ambush.

"Bobby and I have an agreement, one which he will honor. As for his compatriots, I'm not sure about them. That's why we brought the equipment. Eddy's watching the road out here from Phoenix. Called him while you got dressed," he got out and walked around the Explorer opening her door, "if anything looks odd, he'll call. And if they had a clue it was here, the post office wouldn't have been able to stop them from getting it."

"When were you going to tell me that Eddy was covering us?" Jan really didn't expect an answer. Ward was still waiting for the end of the mission to make sure that she would not return to the department. It was understandable that not all of his tricks would be shared at first. Ward just shrugged as if it really didn't matter his face set in stone just like Jan's, "Anything else I should know?"

"Not yet. All in good time."

Once out of the Explorer, they both felt vulnerable. They did a quick scan of the area and then proceeded after noticing nothing unusual. Everything was quiet, nothing moved. Ward straightened his jacket, and causally checked the gun. Jan didn't need to check hers; she knew it was ready if she needed it. They walked up to the post office and checked the door that led to the mailbox area. It was, as they had expected, locked. Besides the door, there were no windows in which they could be seen through once they got inside. Ward turned and leaned against the wall by the door casually Jan continued to look inside the building. Although it may have looked very casual, both were checking out the area for any one who could be watching, or aware of their presence. When they were sure that no one was watching, or around, Jan slipped the lock pick out of Ward's jacket pocket, slipped on gloves, and unlocked the door. Both of them slid into the post office as if the door had been left open just so they could walk in. Walking over to the mailboxes, they started with only the large boxes first. These boxes had a combination of five numbers. Being able to read minds made the job very quiet, and quick. Both knew that with that amount of money involved, the box could not be small. Working at a unique pace, they quickly ran out of large boxes with the numbers that she had given him. None of the boxes with those numbers, or combinations there of, opened with the key.

Looking at each other in a puzzled way, their thoughts moved on to the midsize boxes, and they began looking at these boxes. It wasn't until they got to the smallest boxes that they found a box that the number was just as she had remembered it plus two more numbers on the end. Ward looked back at Jan, a questioning look on his face. He couldn't help but question her.

"Are you sure it's here? There's no way it could fit in a box this size," his voice broke the silence. Jan just shrugged.

"I'm pretty sure, try to open it. Maybe there are some missing numbers needed to be able to find the box. If it doesn't work we should we start trying the larger boxes again," Ward slid the key into the lock and turned. Jan immediately turned to cover Ward, eyes darting back and forth. Her mind watched through his mind, while he opened the door to the mailbox. As the door opened it became clear what had happened. There inside the box was a key to the package boxes. Ward took the key out and then locked up the box. Together they went over to the one marked B, the same as on the key. Ward handed the key to Jan and smiled. She was ready to do the honors, and as the door opened there it was. Wrapped in brown paper and the size of a small suitcase, sat a package addressed to the now late Kevin. Ward removed it from the box, and nodded. Jan closed the box, wiped the key, and they walked to the door. As they left, Jan relocked the door and wiped it down quickly to remove any stay prints. Although they had left no other clues to being there, she made sure that there would be no way to connect them. This was her life now. By this time Ward had the package in the back of the Explorer and they both got in the vehicle at the same time, and closed the doors. A collective sigh was released as they left the parking lot and the town with no one watching, and no one following them. It was done. They had the bargaining chip now. It was the next step Jan worried about as the sun peeked above the horizon.

Ward picked up on her thoughts of the sunrise and pulled off onto a dirt road into the desert. He pointed the front of the vehicle toward the sunrise, and together, in silence they enjoyed it. Their thoughts were together, focused on the colors, and the beauty of the nature around them. It was wonderful not only to see it through her eyes, but also to see it through his eyes. Jan had thought that their connections in Mexico were amazing, but now, with almost no secrets, there was no place that they couldn't go in each other's minds, except for one. When the colors had all vanished in the light of the day and the day's problems intruded into their thoughts again, they then looked at one another. Ward leaned over to Jan and reached into her bra. Spending a moment longer there than necessary, he took out the bracelet she had put there when she quickly got dressed. Quietly he put it back on her and smiled. Kissing her gently on the hand, and then on the cheek he whispered, "No secrets, no regrets, no turning back." Jan released her breath.

"Do we know where to meet up with him?" Jan waited for the reply.

"No, I have to call him to let him know that I have it. Then he'll give me the address where Rob is when I make the drop," he stressed the word I. Ward turned and looked back to where the sunrise had been.

"I will be with you, won't I?" Jan stared at him, she'd seen the thought, but didn't want to believe it.

"No, I won't risk you, not again," Ward wouldn't look at her, "and one of us will need to get to Rob quickly, as I am sure Bobby cares very little about whether he lives or dies after he's got the money. We are lucky that we are a day ahead, that might just give Rob a fighting chance," Jan knew it made sense, but if they reversed it she could ask for back up from the department, she wasn't in quite as deep as he was, "Don't call them. He'll know and then there is no way you or I will be able to meet with him. Rob will be dead, and most likely you as well, or worse. We have a better chance of him leaving me alive, but just remember he would kill you to get to me this time. He's already told us that in a roundabout way. He has always wanted me to join him. Watch your back, and don't get careless. Eddy will be with you, but he won't be armed, only you," Jan wanted to scream. Everything he said was right, but it all felt so wrong.

"We can't just let him get away with the money. The department will be able to pick him up, with our help. Clear your name, and maybe use it to save some other kids. This money is tainted with the blood of young kids, you can't just let him have it," with this Ward turned and looked right at her. His dark eyes burned through to her soul, his face stern, and unfeeling. This was the face of the job.

"This money will buy one thing, the only thing that matters to me now, your life. I have nearly sold my soul to this devil for us," and he paused, "and this time he has come too close to getting it." Jan sucked in a deep breath. He had hid this from her since Mexico, and it showed. That was the deal that had been made the night she had remembered who they were. Now more than ever she knew he wasn't going to lose her. From the beginning she had set up her side of the mission without regard to what it may lead to. Ward was ready to help her, but to do so he had to buy her freedom back. Ward was now honoring her desire to get Rob back to safety, and to free them from the department as well.

"Then take Eddy with you," it would be some conciliation to her, at least.

"No, he's with you. I already agreed to come alone. I need to keep my word. Besides, I'm pretty sure Rob is located in the desert somewhere around here, and you might need Eddy's help to get him out," Ward's mind was far away, and hard to reach. Even now he was distancing himself from her, before he made the call. Jan waited for him to make the next move. She realized the sacrifice he had made for her, and would never again doubt the dedication he had for her. One day she hoped she could return the favor. They were a day ahead of schedule thanks to one unfriendly call. In one way she wanted the day with Ward, but knew that the sooner they made the exchange, the sooner they would again be together with the pressures of the world behind them. And with any luck, Rob would be alive, and back in the hands of the department.

Finally, he pulled out his phone. Mentally she could tell he was ready, physically he was ready; he was focused and ready to move. She wasn't ready, and she would never be. As he dialed the phone, Jan felt her future slipping out of her control. She could feel the large dark hole that was draining her. Ward let his thoughts slip back for just a moment to Mexico, connecting his mind to hers, and then he placed his hand on her leg. Just as the future seemed to come close enough to catch, it ran away. Jan's head hit the back of the seat, and Ward ignored it. Ward had seen the future slip away too many times before, and this was no different to him. He placed the phone to his ear. Ward removed his hand, Jan focused on the mission at hand, and the world turned again the other way. Jan steeled herself for what was to come next.

"I've got it . . .. Yes, all of it. . . . How do you want to do this? . . . No, she isn't coming along. . . No this means you leave her alone, that's the deal I made with your bosses. . . Can't handle a day early. . . Okay, I'll be there," Ward closed the phone and dropped it on the seat. He started the Explorer without saying a word. Pulling back out onto the main road they drove in silence, staring only at the road, both afraid to read each other's minds, for fear of what they would find.

It wasn't until they got to Florence Junction half an hour later that Ward pulled off into the little area that could loosely be called roadside shops. As it was, there was just a small diner as well as a couple of places that one could buy gas, souvenirs, and auto parts. There in a darkened corner of the lot, in the shadows, sat Eddy in the white car he had followed her in yesterday. When he saw them pulling in, he got out of the car, and walked up to the Explorer. Ward nodded his head, and Eddy went right to the back of the Explorer for the package. She heard Eddy open the door and check the contents of the package quickly, letting out a low whistle. Ward turned and looked at her, and it was if they were alone in the world, and in some ways, they always were, and would be.

"I'll be fine. You need to finish what you started, get Rob, and get him back. If he knows who kidnapped him, it will help us. If not, it will still help you. I'm giving you the Explorer, and I will meet you back home when this is done. I have to finish what I started as well," and then he kissed her. It was deep, hard, and passionate. They leaned together for only seconds before he broke away and got out without saying a word. Eddy had transferred the package, and was waiting at the front of the vehicle, back turned to them. Ward said nothing to Eddy, and Eddy said nothing back, they just nodded to each other as they exchanged the keys to the vehicles with a small toss. Eddy stayed there, letting Jan have her space as Ward drove off. Neither Eddy nor Jan knew how long it would take, or if they would get a call. They both stayed in place for what seemed forever as the dust settled on the drive.

Only minutes after the dust had cleared, Jan got out of the Explorer. She had seen the owner of the shop open the curtains, unlock the door, and flip the closed sign to open. Using the one crutch, she leaned on it and spoke to Eddy, "If we are going out to the desert today, we have some work to do."

Jan checked to make sure the phone was hooked to her belt, and they both walked to the back of the Explorer. Jan opened it and pulled back the carpeting to look for the emergency kits that would be standard equipment in Ward's vehicle. Eddy stood beside her wondering what she was looking for. Then Jan saw it, two boxes tucked into the flooring. One box contained what she expected, weapons of various assortments, and sizes including the ammunition. It looked fairly complete. She looked back at Eddy, "Are you carrying?"

"What do you think?" he patted his side.

"Good, we may need it," she closed the one box and secured it back in the vehicle's flooring, relieved that he hadn't followed that order from Ward. Taking out the other box she opened it and took inventory of the contents. Inside of the other box were the standard medical supplies that anyone would carry, but because of Ward's medical background, he also had an array of medications, and syringes worthy of most emergency room kits. The types of bandages and medicines in the pack would astound most non-medical people, but only made Jan smile. When they found Rob, she hoped they would be ready for anything, as long as he was still alive she should be able to keep him that way with the items here. Off to the side she noticed a utility belt, rope, and gloves that would come in handy if they hiked through the desert. Pulling out the utility belt, she readied it with the basics she expected to need right away for Rob, bandages, syringes, and a couple bags of glucose. If he had been left in the desert, Rob was probably close to severe dehydration. The nights had been cool, so that would have been helpful, but there had been no indication that anyone had been taking care of him from Ward. She closed the kit back up, and after putting it all back in the Explorer's floor, Eddy closed the door, and she locked it up with the remote. He had shown no surprise as Jan had looked through the supplies; obviously he was familiar with the way Ward worked. She could probably look forward to working with Eddy again after today. Looking back at Eddy she gave him a wink and said, "If we are going to be out in the desert today, we may need some supplies that aren't here."

"Hiking?" it was a question that implied with her in the healing process yet she would not be able to do it. He looked down at the crutch and then back at her, "Do you think that will work?"

"I think it will have to. Just remember, I've worked with Ward a lot longer than you. If he thinks we can, then we can. And more importantly, I think I can," Jan had no doubts as she walked over to the store, "I don't fail easily." Her crutch that she still used was made of a strong metal alloy, and able to withstand most things. She remembered testing the theory on Tony. She also knew what her part of the job was; to retrieve Rob before he died. And she never did like failing an assignment.

With Eddy falling into step beside her, as if they had been partners before, they went into the store. Walking past the car parts, the candy bars, and the dusty case of chips in the old building cooled only by a swamp cooler, Jan found what she was looking for. She grabbed three gallons of water, handing two to Eddy. She also grabbed a dusty package of rags, and a couple of baseball caps. Paying at the register, they then left the store and went to sit in the Explorer to wait. No one said a word as they sat there with the windows down and Eddy in the driver's seat. Not until the phone rang, and then no words were needed.

Chapter 17

Ward pulled away from the roadside shops, and didn't look back in his rearview mirror. He couldn't, his part of the job was to drop off the money and pay this debt to Bobby, and with any luck it would be the last time he saw him. That's what they had agreed on. He drove in silence for the first half an hour. As he entered the outskirts of civilization, he turned on the radio to listen to the reports on traffic. Morning traffic could be horrid, and today he was in no mood. Looking down at the clock he noticed that it was now close to eight o'clock. He needed to be at the apartment complex by nine, it shouldn't be a problem he decided, as he listened to the latest traffic report. The money was safely in the back seat, and his gun was safely at his back.

The traffic began to get heavy and he had to pay closer attention to the road, he was more worried by what was about to happen. Bobby had arranged the meeting place, the time, and the advantages. He had only balked at the day early for Ward's benefit, not that it would really cause him any problems. Bobby had another agenda from the first time Ward had contacted him. He could feel it, not quite read it but feel it. It was the same old agenda he assumed, the one where Ward ended up under his control. Bobby's skills as a mind reader were pretty legendary. Not many had reached the same level, or accuracy, even Pat. Ward had just started to approach it, but Bobby didn't know this. Most of the mind readers they had had been identified in college, with very basic empathy skills. These people had always known they had a good sixth sense, but most had been unaware they were capable of reading minds. Mind readers had to be trained, focused, and skilled. But Bobby never had to be trained. Bobby had always known that he could read minds, and this made him different.

Ward's mind traveled back as he slowed to keep the same pace as the traffic. Bobby and Ward had trained together. They had done all their training together, and been in some pretty bad situations. In fact it was Bobby who had discovered Ward's talent and brought him into the department and out of his chosen field of medicine. Both of their talents were fine tuned by the people in the department, but Ward had discovered after their imprisonment that Bobby had somehow improved upon his skills, changed them. He was able to plant memories now, change and twist them. It was amazing what Bobby had done to him years ago. He had planted memories that weren't there, and tried to steal others. His skills were not fine tuned yet when he had experimented on Ward. When he used these skills on Jan, Ward had noticed that they were much improved. They had been experimenting with these ideas at the department, but hadn't found the right research for it, or process. The people, who had imprisoned them had it or something like it, but didn't have anyone who was trained nearly enough for attempting these skills. That's what had lured him away from the department Ward assumed, and away from the choice of a moral life that most people would have chosen to live. Ward had not wanted it that bad, not enough to give up his ideals and moral standards. Not to say it didn't tempt him, but he wasn't prepared to pay the price. The whole experience had also taught him that the department was not the answer to who he was, and what he wanted as well. They were little better controlling how he thought and felt, and if he was allowed to even have emotions.

At first he thought he would go into business on his own. As he took on jobs, had found it hard not to help anyone who asked him, whether or not they could pay. After being bankrupt and financially on the edge many times, he finally decided that the only way to live was to have another source of income that would provide him money to survive. It had taken a while, but he had slowly built up a network of rental units, both apartment buildings and single family homes. He was Eddy's silent partner. Not a very exciting way to earn a living, but it did allow him to do what he really loved, help others. Glancing at the road signs, he realized that it was now time to get off the freeway, and head for the apartment complex just off Southern and Mesa.

The area he pulled off in was an area you would find drugs, drug dealers and characters most people would find undesirable. It was an older area of town that over time had deteriorated. The apartment complex there would be a haven to most of these undesirables. Ward got the feeling he was walking into a nest of rattlesnakes, and he was their next meal. Taking a calming breath Ward pulled into the parking space he had been told to park in. Before he got out of the car, he checked the area. With no one in sight, he slowly got out of the vehicle and waited by the side of the car, leaning on the door, hands on the top of the car. Out of the corner of his eye he could see movement. Ward stayed still, letting his eyes do the work. Carefully reaching out with his mind, he could see the dark, cold, chilling thoughts of the person that approached, and he snapped his mind closed quickly.

"Either you're getting careless, or stupid," Bobby stayed about three feet away from him, but moved to face him, "No side kick. Where is Tonto?"

"You said come alone, I did. Let's stop playing games, where's Rob?" Ward didn't move.

"Now, now, now, is that how you treat an old friend? I think I need to at least see the package, don't you," as Ward began to move Bobby stopped him, "By the way, in case you think you are going to use that gun at your back, I'd think twice. I have two sharp shooters just watching for the wrong move on your part, and they won't miss." Ward understood the consequences of this and held his hands a bit farther away from his body, his fingers tighter on the remote for the car.

"I'm not even trying to bring you in, just helping a friend," with that Bobby laughed. It was an ugly laugh, and made Ward grimace.

"Neither one of us have any love lost for that department, so you must be doing this for something else," and a lurid look crossed his face, "Is she that good?"

"Get what you came for," Ward was having a hard time keeping his temper under control. His face tightened to the point where he thought his teeth would pop out. Bobby leaned into the car, looking at the package and the address, clearly enjoying Ward's discomfort. He opened the back door to the car, and looked closer at the package. After satisfying his need to know if it all was there, and it wasn't a trap, he turned to look back at Ward.

"I didn't think you'd do it, you of all people, selling out. Guess there is hope for you," Ward stood quietly, afraid if he moved he would kill him with his bare hands, "Here," and Bobby handed him a piece of paper, "Call her and Tonto. Tell her where to find him for all I care."

Ward slowly reached into his pocket for the phone, and dialed the number just as slowly. He tried to read Bobby's mind, but found that the clatter of everything in his head made no sense. It was an old trick, but effective enough to keep other mind readers out. Ward put the phone to his ear, and waited for Jan to pick up.

"Jan," his voice was flat, no emotion to let on to what was happening, no emotion to worry her, no emotion so that the job could be completed as it should. Emotion was not part of the job, that would come later and he could help Jan with those new feelings as well.

"Ward, you okay?" Jan kept her voice flat, pushing away emotions from her current thoughts.

"Yah, get a pencil, I have the place," he waited while she got a pencil ready. He didn't care if he had to wait a lifetime on the phone. It would be better to stay in this moment than what he was going to be dealing with in the next moment. It was his small connection to sanity, "Drive on out to Superior and then take highway 177 South to Sonora. Follow the signs to Ray, and then take the first dirt road outside of Ray to the right. Go about six miles, or until the road ends, and then it's all on foot from there. Follow the main path out about half a mile, then head up the hill to the abandoned mine located about a mile off the path to the South. A couple of Palo Verde trees hide the entrance located at the bottom of a small hill. When you get to the mine, you will have him," he listened to her repeat the directions, and confirmed them. When she finished he only had one thing more to say, "See you in Camelot Babs."

"I'll be there," and on that note Jan heard a small struggle as the phone was taken out of Ward's hands. She knew who to expect when the voice came over the line and she steeled herself for it.

"How nice. I'll let Wart know how much you miss him," and Bobby hung up the phone. He placed the phone in his pocket, and looked at Ward, "Now my old friend, hand over the gun," Ward hadn't seen it coming. He had expected some sort of trick. He unzipped the jacket, and lifting the jacket with one hand, he retrieved the gun with two fingers of the other hand.

"Here," Ward handed over the gun gently, "You have what you want, now get out of my sight."

"Not so fast, oh self-righteous one, I want you as well," Bobby opened the car door and pointed inside, as two other men, similar in size to Bobby, stepped over toward the car from the shadows of the complex wall. One reached inside and removed the suitcase, walking away and getting in a nearby car. The other man got into the car. Ward fingered the car keys while he held the remote in his hand, "I get a finders fee for you," a wicked smile came over Bobby's face, "And maybe I'll even get a finders fee for the pretty little thing you get off on. Or maybe I'll just keep her for myself."

Ward saw red.

The phone went dead, and so did what was left of Jan's feelings. She knew from experience that with no back up, Ward could be, and would be a sitting duck. Jan had never experienced this amount of feeling connected with a mission before. Jan couldn't let her feelings affect what they had both decided on now. Without a word, she handed the instructions to Eddy. Eddy took them quietly as he studied her face, not even glancing at the paper. She wasn't looking at him. She wasn't looking at anything, her face hard and steady as she looked through him. Eddy let her sit for another minute.

"What are you waiting for? Let's get moving," Jan's voice was all business. He had heard the same tone from Ward before.

"He's been in worse situations you know," Eddy tried to console her.

"Yes and no, and most of those times I haven't been his partner. Let's move, we have a job to do," Eddy just shook his head and started the Explorer. Jan looked in the direction of Phoenix, and looked in the direction of Superior. Both ways all she could see was endless desert. How could she find either person she cared about in something so desolate? How had she gotten herself in so deep without backup? She was trained better than this. Eddy pulled out onto the road, and headed for Superior. The vehicle was quiet. It gave her time to look back on what her life had been. For so many years she had done just this, except it had been without the feelings she was experiencing now. She had been trained to have no emotion that connected with the job. What had changed? Her eyes drifted off into the desert scenes that flew past her and the rock formations that jutted out of the ground, breaking the monotony of the small plant life, and it hit her.

Over all the years she had been connected with the department, there had not been any emotional ties. It hadn't been until this last year that major emotional commitments had come into her life, and grown. She had always realized that Rob treated her as if she were his own daughter. But it wasn't until she became involved with Ward outside the department that she had seen just how much she meant to Rob. Allowing her the freedom to even love, not being overly concerned by the rules set down by the department had been a big step for him.

And then there was Ward. From the beginning she had been intrigued by him, had loved him, married him, and then hidden away with him. It had been the last few months that had taught her how deep the commitment between them actually was. Feelings and emotions that were long suppressed had been awakened. There had been change, vast amounts of change that would affect her forever. Ward had known from the beginning that she could never return to the department after what had happened; it had just taken her a while to see it.

Eddy turned off onto route 177 and Jan refocused her thoughts back onto the mission. It wouldn't be long now, and they would be hiking through the desert. The future was not something she could read, and if Ward said he would be there, he would be there, barring a catastrophe. Only stupid people stuck their hands into coyote holes without a plan, and Ward was nowhere near stupid. Taking a deep breath, she let meditation take over while Eddy drove on. While meditating, she found the focus she needed to complete the job before her. Right or wrong, it was the principle they had always lived by, to serve others. Eddy was the first to speak.

"Shall we run down the drill," he looked to her for the lead.

"First we need to find the path he gave us. I have a feeling it will be easy at first, and get harder as we go along," watching the road she continued. "If he had been left alone in the mine for the last four days we will be looking at having to carry him out, and get immediate medical treatment. We will then have to have a story for the authorities that is plausible. Since the authorities out here will be less likely to check backgrounds as thoroughly and quickly, it will be easier. As soon as Rob is booked into the hospital or clinic, the red flags will go up in the department, and someone will be sent out immediately. We will only have a couple of hours after he is admitted to make our exit. There will be a couple of things we will have to answer to," Jan took a breath, "What we were doing here, and why we were able to give emergency treatment."

"Well," Eddy's accent changed from the smooth soothing voice to a broad east coast accent, "would this give us a bit more cover."

"Perfect," and she made her accent match his, "Is that accent natural, or are you putting it on?"

"Natural, moved out here when I was in my late twenties. Dropped it, and some bad memories as soon as I could," he turned the vehicle onto the road marked to go to Ray.

"Good, are we married or just friends?" Jan was matter of fact, the story had to hold water.

"Seeing by the ring; married. If they check, I did have a wife named Tessa Hill," Jan nodded her head, "and if they want to look they would find an address for her in New York."

"Tessa it is," Jan checked her watch, "We are out here on vacation from our jobs. You're a medic with the fire department, and I'm a resident at the county hospital. With a bit of creative lying and not volunteering any more information than they ask for, we should be able to cope," Eddy turned onto the nearly nonexistent dirt road that the directions had indicated.

"Time to rock and roll," the Explorer moved slowly down the dirt track. Jan and Eddy continuously scanned the area for the path they were meant to walk along. Both saw it at the same time and Eddy eased the Explorer to a stop.

Chapter 18

Once they found the path and parked both Jan and Eddy got out and walked around to the back of the vehicle. Picking up the supplies they had prepared, they took off. Jan had taken both her crutches with her when she started walking through the desert, although she was only using one. She kept the other one ready in case of snakes. She hated snakes. They had left the trail about half an hour ago, and even though it was only in the low eighties, both Eddy and Jan were sweating profusely under their hats in the Arizona sun. Jan was looking for any clue as to where they would find this mine they were in search of.

The way they had been told to go was difficult to say the least. The ground was covered with rocks. The scrub grass that came up in tufts made walking difficult for anyone with no injuries, but to Jan the small stones and tufts made it more and more strenuous on her legs, knees and ankles. They made the ground uneven and easy to twist an ankle. There were small trees that ranged from what some would call tall bushes to some that actually resembled trees raising ten to twenty feet from the ground with small little leaves. The mine itself would have to be located in some area that people would not tend to go, so they walked toward the ditches and rocky hills. Walking slowly, she looked for any sign among the brush, that anyone had been this way lately. The desert never hid its scars, so Jan looked carefully, and moved at a slow pace. They couldn't afford to miss any clue. Time was unforgiving in this case. Eddy was patient, but not observant. Tracking was not his strength, but he waited as Jan led the way. Jan stopped to take a drink of water after about an hour of slow hiking. Passing the jug to Eddy, Jan took time to look around while Eddy chugged back some water. All she could see was open space and it was disheartening. She saw Palo Verde trees, Mesquites, some Saguaros, but mostly she saw a lot of nothing. Then she saw something on the ground. It was a small scrap of tan cloth that was barely visible to the eye against the background of the scrub desert. Carefully she walked over to it and picked it up.

"Something?" Eddy stood with hands on his hips, resting as the sweat dripped down the side of his face.

"Yes," Jan smiled, "Looks like the type of clothing I would have been wearing before today."

"What are we waiting for?" Eddy smiled and they both started to walk in the direction that the fabric indicated someone might have been pulled along, down toward the next ditch. Jan suddenly stopped, and closed her eyes, "Something wrong?" Eddy's voice was low, wary.

"Yes," her voice was little more than a whisper, "We are being watched, one of Bobby's men. Could be more. We need to be careful. It could be a set up," Jan smiled and began to move again, "We must be on the right track," but he didn't smile as she started to move again. Eddy looked at her and then with a quizzical look followed on. He had always thought there was something strange about Ward, just figured it was Ward, but now he had just seen Jan do the same thing. After they had walked along in silence another twenty yards, Eddy spoke.

"You know he's okay," Eddy talked to Jan as she continued to move, and when she didn't say a word he continued, "Jan he had a plan. He didn't just walk in there to be a sitting duck." This time Jan stopped and turned.

With quiet and control, she looked into his mind as she asked the next question, hoping she would catch a glimpse of the answer he would never tell her.

"What plan?" and then it hit her. Her mouth dropped open for only a second before she recovered her composure.

"The car's got some extra's," he had been told not to say anything more, or even think about it, but somehow he felt as if he had to put her fears to rest. He thought about how the car was set up, "It's for an emergency only. He won't need it."

"Let's hope not," Jan turned and started to walk again. What she had seen in his mind didn't put her feelings at ease though. Watching the desert she thought about Ward's plan, and she didn't think blowing up the car would be one of his better ideas. She knew he wanted to stop Bobby, but that might be just a bit extreme and stop him as well. Jan began to move just a bit faster as she headed down the next ditch. And then, before she could even change what she was thinking she saw it, it was there. She stopped and pointed it out to Eddy without saying a word. There were two small Palo Verde trees that had grown very bushy around the entrance, effectively hiding it from the casual glance. Looking closely, you could tell that the trees had been trimmed recently from behind, and the shaft entrance cleared. Carefully they made their way toward it. Jan could still feel the awkward presence near, a grim darkness, but not by the entrance, or in the mineshaft. She was pretty sure that there was only one person now that had been sent to follow them. She guessed that Bobby's plan was not to leave too many loose ends. What really bothered her though was that she could feel nothing coming from the shaft. She hoped she wasn't already too late.

"Eddy, stay out here and watch for our friend. I'll go in and look for Rob," Jan only had to bend a little to get into the shaft, and as she did, Eddy grabbed her arm.

"Are you sure?" She felt his concern.

"I want you out here, and if anyone is going to find Rob, alive or dead, it will be me. Plus I'll fit through the entrance better," she turned and went into the mineshaft. Pulling out the flashlight, she could see that the shaft went back about forty, or fifty feet. Systematically Jan moved the light through the shaft, along the walls, ceiling, and floors to be able to navigate through the old mine. Carefully she checked out each and every support. The old logs used to hold up the ceiling were wide enough to hide a body, and the last thing she wanted was to make this her final resting spot with a cave in. She finally caught a glimpse of what looked like shoes sticking out from a support. Jan moved toward the shoes, being careful not to make any noise. The rest of the body was hidden behind a large support beam. Depending on how long he had been without water, if he was still alive, he could be delirious, or even paranoid. The body didn't move, and Jan could feel no thought, except for Eddy's outside the entrance. Unconsciousness sometimes felt that way. Coming up to the feet that lay behind the support beam, she could see that the body did, in fact, belong to Rob, as his face became clear in the beam of light. The support had an old rusted chain coming out from it, and Rob had been attached to the support by the chain. Jan walked up to Rob's side, and bent to feel for a carotid pulse. The pulse was there, fast, weak, but it was there. As she turned to call back down the shaft for Eddy, she felt it. There must have been another entrance to the mine that they didn't know about. Their stalker must have used that entrance to come in. Jan turned off the flashlight and listened.

Suddenly, Jan's instinct and training kicked in. There was someone else approaching her from the back of the shaft. From what she could see in his mind, she could tell he was armed and planned to finish off Rob and her if he needed too. He wore night vision goggles that enabled him to move about without a flashlight. What bothered her most was what else she could see in his mind. She wasn't to be killed if possible; she was to be taken back to Bobby.

What seemed like slow motion for Jan took her only seconds. Leaving all but one handle of her crutches lay on the ground, she turned toward the feeling, closed her eyes and reached deeper into the stalker's thoughts. They were dark and menacing, and she could see the mineshaft through his eyes. He was the only one here of that she was sure. This time, Bobby had made a mistake to send only one person, and she would take advantage of it. She looked deeper into his thoughts and learned that he had killed before, and then she found the information she was looking for. He knew, and had worked many times with Bobby. Her years of training, years of practice, years of using her skills made the movement to the gun, fluid and easy, as well as deadly quiet. Jan moved down the shaft quietly using his thoughts to navigate. Staying balanced and low she made no sound at all. In training she had been an excellent shot. In the field her aim was legendary, and against an adversary she was deadly. She didn't need the flashlight, or the sight on the gun to do what she had to do next. With a practiced skill, she used his mind as the target to aim her gun. Moving into a direct line of sight she tossed the handle of the crutch toward the opposite wall. When he turned to look she squeezed the trigger, only one shot. As the sound of the gun echoed through the mineshaft, she felt the explosion of the bullet through the thoughts of the man, and then a quiet nothing. It wasn't a feeling unknown to her, but each time she had used it the power shocked her. It left her feeling empty, this time more than most. Putting the gun away as fast as she had removed it, she yelled back out at Eddy.

"I'm fine, check the area now!" although she was sure that he had been alone; she didn't want any more surprises. Killing someone killed a part of her, and she didn't plan on having to do it again. Jan looked at Rob and saw him move, "Rob, its Jan, don't move I'll be back in a moment," she took the flashlight and went down the back part of the shaft, moving swiftly, and carefully using the wall as support. As the flashlight caught the edge of the body, Jan walked up and looked at what she could see of the dead man's face. It was one of the faces that had haunted her in the disjointed images she had from the factory. He had been the one to advance on Kevin first. Quickly she checked the pulse, knowing what she would find, nothing, but having the need to do it anyway. The bullet had entered the side of his head. Bending over the body, she gave it a quick search for keys, and found a set. Going over and picking up her crutch handle Jan left the body and returned to Rob.

"Jan, nothing out here. You okay, I heard gun fire," Eddy put his head into the entrance.

"Watch the entrance, I've got Rob, he's alive. I think the one that was following us came in another way. He's not going to give us any more trouble," Jan looked back at Rob. With a calm and soothing voice, "Hey partner, recognize me?"

"What?" his voice scratchy, strained, and barely audible. Jan assessed his condition and knew that she had very little time before the moderate signs of dehydration she was seeing now turned severe. He was already beginning to slip into it, and Ward was right, had they waited until tomorrow not much could have prevented him from dying in this remote location. It had been well planned, and thought out.

"Hang on while I try and unchain you here. When I get you out, then I'll treat you. We'll have you at a medical facility in just a bit. From there, they'll get you back to the department," Jan went to work on the chains that held him to the wall while she talked, all the time keeping her voice soothing. Finding the right key, she unlocked the chains, as he seemed to drift in and out of consciousness. Soon she had the rags out and tied together in a way that created a hammock of sorts so she could drag him from the shaft, sled style with the help of one crutch. She hadn't heard anything from Eddy, but the thoughts she kept receiving, were encouraging because she knew from them that he had seen no one else.

As she got close to the entrance she began to feel the strain in her legs and arms. It was not a feeling she was unused to, and knew that she was pushing the limits on her recovery as the pain grew. Pain was good and it was a warning for her as well. They had a long walk back to the car. She yelled and let Eddy come into the shaft the last ten feet to help bring Rob the rest of the way out. Rob had not said much, his mouth was too dry, but seemed to recognize her, as he glanced occasionally in her direction. His face registered some concern when Eddy came into view. Once out in the sun, Rob's arms went up unsteadily to cover his eyes from the sun. When he saw Eddy, his eyes grew wide, and his thoughts were filled with fear.

"Rob, this is Eddy. He's a friend of Ward's. He's going to help me. Once I get you bandaged, he can to get you back down to the car. Do you understand what's going to happen?" Rob shook his head a bit to acknowledge what she had said. Jan went to work on his arms where the chains had been and Eddy worked on checking for broken bones, as well as to give him small sips of water.

"Seems like everything is okay, just a bit battered and bruised. Not too severe. Looked more like torture was in mind for this game with Bobby," Jan worked on cleaning up his face and cuts along his forehead. Her hands were flying as fast as possible, and then she brought out the glucose bag and syringe she had brought along. Starting it was difficult in veins that were already constricting, but necessary to replace fluids fast enough to save him. "Eddy take some of the water on a rag and dab it at his eyes, nose and mouth again," when Eddy finished, he took the rag seat Jan had made and her crutches. He looked in her direction, and Jan confirmed his thoughts with a nod of her head. He began to fashion the crutches and rags into a sturdier sled to carry Rob on, back down the hill. Once finished he walked over to the rotting remains of a tall cactus. With the edge of his boot he kicked out a spine that had once made up the skeleton of a giant saguaro that populated this area. Making sure it was free of debris he brought it over for Jan to use. She looked up at him and smiled her thanks.

In a matter of minutes they were headed back through the desert, and back towards the path. Jan kept searching for other thoughts, but found none. Bobby must have thought that the one man would be enough. If she had not picked up on him before they found the mine, one man might have been. He had been careless though, and it had cost him his life. She looked into Rob's thoughts and discovered more than she ever hoped for. He was trying to communicate with her with his thoughts. Just like the good old days, she mused. As partners, he could make his thoughts known to her, but could not know hers. They had used this type of communication a number of times before, in situations where talking would be impossible, and unsafe. It was in those situations, he took the lead, directing her with his mind. This time, he wanted to let her know who had kidnapped him and what was going on. The thoughts went from faint and weak to strong and emotional, as he tried to tell her everything at once. Jan listened a while and then just nodded her head at him. Eddy still knew nothing about mind readers, and if Ward wasn't comfortable with him knowing, then she wasn't going to tell him. When Rob looked her way again, she spoke to him.

"It's going to be okay now. I remember what happened to me and the rest. I've been back to the department and we can discuss the details of that later," with that Rob relaxed and let himself drift back into a semi-consciousness state as he was taken the rest of the way to the Explorer. Together, Eddy and Jan put the seats of the Explorer down creating a makeshift bed to place Rob on. Jan got in the back and Eddy got in the driver's seat. As he made his way down the road, and back into Superior, he flipped on the GPS system to locate the nearest medical facility. They were in luck there was one in Superior. It was small clinic, but it would be adequate for their needs. Eddy went back in the same direction they had come, focused on the road. As Jan checked Rob's pulse and the glucose bag, he tried to talk.

"How long?" his thinking was definitely beginning to refocus, as

Jan was able to tell from the more controlled thoughts coming from him now. The bag was beginning to take effect.

"Not long, about a half hour I think," Jan's hand went up to check his pupils, and Rob caught her arm. Jan knew what he was going to ask, before he did.

"No," this time he fingered her ring, "How long?" speaking was still a chore.

"Oh this thing," Jan wasn't ready to tell him she was married to the man he wouldn't have chosen for her, and that she wasn't going back to the department. Right at this moment it was too much information for him to get. Deep down she knew that he had known she would never return from that moment in the hospital when they had gotten reacquainted, "I just have this on for cover, for when we take you in."

"No," he didn't want to give up the subject, and she didn't know how to make him, never did, "How long?" and this time he was as insistent as he could be both in voice and thought.

"A year and a half," Jan put his hand down and checked Rob's pupils. She then connected the last bag she had with her, placing the empty bag off to the side.

"It's Bobby," Rob croaked out the words. Jan shook her head in agreement, "They won't believe me."

"I know, and so does Ward. One of the guys who killed Kevin is back in the cave. He's dead. With any luck, they will take you a bit more seriously after they find him," Jan knew they were coming close to Superior now, "You also need to tell Tony sorry from me. I'm afraid he's not feeling too good right now, I had to leave in a hurry so I could find you," she felt Rob's amusement.

"The department," and Jan put her finger to his lips. She had known all along what he was going to ask. And she guessed that he had known all along what she would say. There was a mixture of feelings coming from

Rob. Jan knew he would miss her, and she would miss him. Sadness touched both of them. She decided to avoid it for now, as it was not the time to discuss this with Rob, and he allowed her that much.

"I'll see you there," and she smiled a sad smile. Rob smiled back in the same way, knowing that she was never going back there. They looked at each other for a moment and for that moment she didn't need to read his mind, and he didn't need to read hers.

When the vehicle stopped in front of the small clinic in Superior, Jan bent over and gave Rob a kiss on the cheek before they got out of the vehicle, "I'm going home now. They'll take care of you here." With that they took him in. As predicted, the nurse didn't ask many questions and the story that Eddy and Jan gave about hiking in the desert in their east cost accents satisfied all concerned. Before they went, Jan turned and gave Rob a wink; he smiled and silently wished her all the luck and happiness in the world. All went well with the local authorities as well, and Eddy and Jan were on their way down the road about half an hour later after giving the location of the mine. They didn't even take the license number of the vehicle. As they drove away from the clinic, both gave a small sigh, and relaxed.

Both rode along for about fifteen minutes without saying a word. Jan's relaxation only lasted a minute after leaving as she began to think about the next part of the job. With Rob back safely, her thoughts became focused on Ward, and what was happening with him. The more she thought, the more furious she became that he had not trusted her enough to let her in on all the plans. He had good reason not too, past experience had always led him to believe that she would soon be gone again, but it was different now. It had to be different now. Jan knew that after this assignment, there would be more trust, but it was waiting it out that was the problem. If they were given the chance, Jan would have a long discussion with him about working together. It didn't take long before she turned toward Eddy, as they drove through the small rocky pass and asked the question she had wanted to know ever since she had picked through his mind back in the desert.

"When were you going to tell me he planned on blowing up the car?"

Chapter 19

"Whoa!" Eddy hit the brakes, and pulled off the road at a scenic overlook that happened luckily to be right there, but they weren't stopping to look at the scenery. Jan grabbed the side of the Explorer to keep from being thrown forward. They were looking at each other intensely, "Who said he was going to blow up the car? I never told you that."

"Does it matter? I thought I knew Ward well enough. He isn't really planning on killing Bobby is he? I need to know. I need to know if he's changed," Eddy turned and stared off into the distance, looking at the various shades of rock facing, and tufts of green that highlighted it, and then at nothing. He sat like that for more than a few minutes. Jan's eyes were on him; his thoughts open to her scrutiny without his knowledge. Jan also knew that to look into his thoughts again would be wrong for her to do, it would be an intrusion. He needed time to organize what he wanted to say. If she read his thoughts, what they told her could be misinterpreted. It was always something to guard against, and knowing Eddy, she knew he would tell her what she needed. She gave him the time to think, but too much longer and she wouldn't be able to stop herself.

"You know, I've known Ward for a long time now. We have quite a history together. Worked with him on lots of jobs, or missions as you two like to call them," he never shifted his gaze, "He's real easy to work with. In fact, I've never ever doubted what he's doing. A straight shooter, I'd have him cover my back anytime. I've known him to read me like a book. Never thought I'd ever find anyone else who could do that but him. Working with you has been much of the same experiences, comfortable and easy, but you can also read me and I don't know what's up there. One thing I do know, this Bobby guy is scary. I've met him twice now, and the second time was much worse. Don't get me wrong, I know some pretty scary people, some which you have seen, some that don't crawl out until it's dark," he got quiet, and Jan just sat there. Eddy had a past. Most of the people Ward worked with did. That had been his specialty after leaving, finding the good in people and turning them around when possible. By the look on his face, she knew he was elsewhere, not here, not with the thoughts he had just shared, and she waited, "Ward only gets protective about one thing," he looked at her, "Understand?" Eddy wanted to tell her that the only person he had ever seen Ward lose control over was Jan, but he couldn't do that. Imply it yes, say it no.

Eddy knew that Jan would only worry more about Ward, and truly, what was done was done now. Ward had shared his feelings about wanting Bobby out of the picture, completely. Eddy also knew that Ward wouldn't kill Bobby in cold blood, only in self-defense, and that opportunity he would take at a moments notice, but did he get that chance?

The look in his face was all Jan needed to understand what he meant. Jan shook her head to acknowledge she understood what he was trying to tell her, "I've seen him kill only two people in all these years, both times, only in self-defense. So when you asked if I think he would kill Bobby," he paused again, this time longer. Jan didn't rush him. She wanted to, she needed to, but she couldn't if she was going to get the answer to her question, "No, not even Bobby. But if he has a reason, to protect someone, maybe," and he looked back at Jan with an expression Jan was not willing to investigate any further. She knew Eddy would blame her if anything happened to Ward. He didn't need to worry, Jan knew she would blame herself first, he didn't need to.

"He's fine. We are going to find him," it was a quiet and simple statement that Jan made as she turned and looked back to the road.

"No," and Eddy's voice filled the vehicle. He turned her to face him and with all two hundred and fifty pounds of him leaning in her direction to help punctuate his next phrase, he spoke quietly, and determinedly, "No, you have to go home. I will meet up with him at the prearranged spot, and see to it that his needs are taken care of before I send him home to you. Wherever home may be. If I don't find him there, then I'll deal with it, and let you know. I've done that before. Don't put me in the position of having to forcibly take you to the place you two call home, I will even if I have to drive half the world to find it. My last instruction from him this morning was to make sure you went home after this, and to assure you he would follow. He told me you'd do this," he stopped, letting the information sink in, "I have my job to do, and now so do you. If you plan to stay safe and keep him safe, then you need to go home. If Bobby is still out there he will use you as a bargaining chip, just as he planned to in the mineshaft. You have been the bait; even you can see that," there was a very tense pause, "With you safe, Ward will be able to take care of himself. I have your number and I will let you know as soon as I do where he is, and how he is. I expect you to do the same for me if you hear from him first. For all we know he's home by now. He did have a good lead on us. By the way, if you look my number is in your phone," Eddy began to pull onto the road again, and Jan began to protest. Before she could get a complete word out he stopped and looked her straight in the eyes, and there was no doubt to her that he meant what he said next, "I mean it. You go home and stay there. If he is all right, that is the first place he will head. I don't know where that is right now, and someone needs to check there. If I need you I will call and we will take it from there," he pulled out onto the road and the conversation ended.

They rode in an uncomfortable silence for the rest of the journey, Jan knowing enough to stay out of Eddy's mind. She was angry, angry at Eddy, angry with Ward, and most of all angry at Bobby. Whatever was in there, she was pretty sure she wouldn't like what she saw. After about sixteen miles she began to realize that the feeling wasn't healthy and she let it go. When he pulled off on the Priest Road exit, she turned to look at him.

"So this stop was also prearranged?" Jan waited for the answer.

"On this one, he make's the calls. Maybe next time you get to run the show, but for now, he told me to meet him here, and send you on," Eddy pulled into the doughnut shop and stopped, "Want anything before you go?"

"Yah, one old fashioned doughnut, one cup of coffee, one case transferred out of this car, and," she paused, "oh yes, one Ward," she forced a smiled as she looked at him walk toward the door to the doughnut shop. They didn't say anything. They didn't need to.

"You get the case, I'll get the doughnut," Eddy got out and went into the shop. Jan walked to the back to get the case, and thought about her last request. She really did want to be there for Ward, but knew if she stayed it presented a bigger target for too many people. The department would surely have Rob by now, and he would be getting the best medical care. Gregg would be fuming and soon have every agency he could think of looking for white Explorers even without a possible plate number. Both Ward and Eddy had set this part of the job up right. She needed to be on her way. Her way out of trouble and back to the secluded beach they called home. Right now, even Jan knew she could do more to help from there, than here. Eddy came back out and put the extra large coffee in the holder and the doughnut in the empty seat that would be beside her all the way to Mexico. He walked around to the back.

"King Arthur will be back you know. There's no way he'll lose you now. I'll take good care of him until he gets to you if I find him first," Eddy and Jan hugged. Eddy took the box and placed it in the old truck parked beside the Explorer that Eddy pointed to, "And you never know, he may be waiting there for you."

"Thanks Eddy. You know how to reach me," but she did know Ward wasn't there yet, as she walked over to the driver's seat and got in. Taking a sip of coffee, she started the car, waved bye to Eddy and pulled out following the signs for Interstate 10. As she got on the freeway, she sighed and placed the phone on the dash, turned on talk radio for any type of local news she could get, and merged into traffic. Without time, she couldn't access the web, and do a search of the news, or even check in with the department's computers. This time, time was not on her side. She had to get out of Dodge, before the local sheriff found her. Glancing at the phone while she inched along in traffic, she hoped. If Ward had gotten the phone back from Bobby he would phone. With any luck, the phone just might ring.

Two hours later she exited off the freeway, and headed down an old local road. The only thing that had been on talk radio was the annoying ranting of a far right conservative that only suited to anger her more by his misunderstandings of the government as she drove down the road. The station she was getting was beginning to break up and between the crackle of the interference, and the cackle of the host she had gotten a headache, and she turned the radio off. The local news had said nothing. 'That was a good thing, right?' she thought. The sound of the struggle lingered in her mind. She kept running through case scenarios and the only one where Ward would have been able to make things work after the struggle was where he blew up the car.

Pulling off to the side of the dusty deserted road, she just couldn't wait any longer. Picking up her phone, she dialed Ward's number. The answering service picked up right away, which meant the phone was either off, or worse, in pieces. In any case the phone was signaling it was off. Ending the call, she looked through the phone numbers he had loaded in her phone. There were only a few, most of which she didn't know. She found Eddy's. Sitting there for five more minutes, she tried to decide whether or not to call. Finally she put the phone down and pulled back onto the road leaving a cloud of dust behind her. It was time for the agent in her, not the lover in her, to do her job. Without letting herself think, she continued down the road the only goal in mind was Mexico.

It wasn't until she saw the lights of the diner enter her field of vision that she decided to stop the vehicle again. 'She needed to eat didn't she?' was her thought, 'and if she found out Ward had been by, more the better.' Walking in with her one cane and taking a seat, she thought about how things had changed since she was first brought in here. Looking around she saw the same waitress that had served them. 'Probably the owner, or relation of some kind,' Jan thought. Before she could even order, a bowl of chili and cola was brought to her. The waitress smiled at her.

"Where's your friend sweetie?" and pointed to the empty chair. It wasn't until now that Jan realized she had sat in the same chair all three times, and now Ward's chair was empty. Although the waitress didn't know it, she had answered a ton of questions that Jan had with just one of hers. Taking a breath, and not letting out the little sigh she felt, she answered.

"Couldn't get away," the waitress nodded, and left. Jan finished her bowl of chili and the cola. When she got ready to leave, she realized that she would only need to pay half the money to satisfy the bill this time. With a sad smile, she tossed the same amount on the table that Ward had left each time. As she got to the door, the waitress yelled over to her.

"Hon, you left too much," and held up the extra.

"Keep it in case he gets a chance to come through yet tonight. Just tell him it's already been settled up," and she left without turning around. At least if he came through, he would know that she had been there. She watched the sun sink into the horizon as she drove down the road. The shades of red, orange, pinks and purples were magnificent as they spun across the endless desert sky, but she didn't see any of that. What she saw was a night of emptiness, of fear, of not knowing what the future was for the first time, and actually caring about that. A night of loneliness, a night like many she had spent in the past. If they were to work together, Jan knew that times like this would come and go as the jobs did. A small bit of excitement tingled in her as she realized now that they would always be working together; taking on only the assignments they chose. Laughing out loud, she realized what arguments that could cause. Coming up to the border, she realized that she just might not get through this time. If Gregg had done his job right, they would be checking the borders for any Explorers crossing over which is why she had ditched the gun case. He may have even put her picture out, although that was pretty taboo even when you were trying to locate an agent. And there was no name he could give out, she had worked as so many different people, Gregg wouldn't know which name to use. As of yet, Ward's picture or names had never been circulated to any other agency. It had always been kept in house. Slowly she drove up to the gates, and waited her turn. She pulled up to the officer on duty. It was the same border guard she had seen before. Jan wondered if he always worked this shift. He smiled as he pulled her over to the side, recognizing the car and the driver inside.

"Hi, where's Ward," it was a casual question, but she knew that his orders were to check out all white Explorers as she had already looked through his thoughts.

"Had a meeting he couldn't miss and I was just needing to get away," she handed her driver's license to him. He looked at it and smiled.

"Well, well, Ward never told me he had a missus. When was the big day?" the border guard looked back at Jan smiling. It took Jan only seconds to look at his thoughts and she could see that it was a general question, one he would have asked of any person he had known. As an agent she had always been suspicious of motives, and learned that a quick peek was sometimes the way to avoid an ugly situation. As it was, he had become an acquaintance of Wards and was curious as to when he had gotten married.

"It's been about a year ago now, and it seems that our jobs always had us going in different directions and to different towns. Now we are, for the most part, on the same schedule," he handed her license back to her.

"I'll have to tell the ol' boy congratulations. Take care, and have a good one," she waved and drove on through. With that over, she was on her way. She smiled, borders had never been a problem, and seemed that they never would be.

It wasn't very long before she saw the ocean and heard the waves. The sound and smell of it was empty to her right now. The closer she got to home, the more it reminded her that she was alone. 'Is this how Ward had been feeling for the last year?' the thought shook her. It was one thing to feel alone amongst a group all pulling in the same direction, it was definitely a different thing to feel alone in a world where she pulled the strings. In fact, it was the first time she had ever felt that. She pulled off the road where they had pulled off when he first brought her to Mexico after the accident. She didn't get out; it was pointless without him, so she just looked toward the ocean without seeing it. Jan stared at the beach for a couple of minutes before she picked up the cell phone checking for service, and dialed Ward's phone again. Still nothing. Jan switched the cell phone to text. She began to enter in the following, "Assignment complete. All personnel with the exception of two accounted for. Rob retrieved and treated for moderate to severe dehydration and then returned to the agency. Unknowns at this point are as follows: Location of Ward Lowe and condition, location of Bobby Malone and condition, completion of monetary transaction between the two above agents. J. Lowe to contact personnel still located in the Phoenix area for the final report. Case complete. Status of agent Jan Tara, retired," closing the phone, she closed a chapter long needing to be closed in her life. Leaving as many unanswered questions about the past as she now had about the future.

She finished driving down the coast with the windows rolled up and her eyes fixed on the road. She approached the small development, and instinctively drove into the little housing complex that they had called home. There in the drive stood the older man waving 'Hi' at her. She couldn't remember a time that he hadn't been waiting to great them, and she smiled. This time she got out and in Spanish asked if Ward had arrived.

"No, no Senor Ward," He shook his head no as if to emphasis his words and called to his son as routine dictated. Jan exchanged keys with him and went through the gates into the hidden lush patio area. Jan stood there for a moment and let the day's work catch up with her. She was tired and sore, and yet she knew she couldn't ever sleep not knowing where he was. Carefully she made her way down the steps and to the front door. She checked for anyone that may be around. Just because they didn't see him come in didn't mean he wasn't there.

In general, no one knew of this place, not even Eddy. They had planned it that way. It was a haven for them both, and now she understood to the depth of her being, just why they would need it. Again the sounds of the struggle tugged at the edges of her brain. Bobby was pure evil, and both she and Ward had allowed Ward to be at his mercy. Just as she was about to put the key in the lock, the phone began to vibrate.

Chapter 20

Dropping the keys and grabbing the phone she answered it trying to keep the anxious tone out of her voice. She knew the phone number that appeared on the screen, it was Eddy's cell, "Ward?" Her voice filled with hope.

"Jan, it's Eddy," and he didn't sound happy, "Ward hasn't met up with me yet, and he was supposed to be here a while back. Is he there?"

"No, the caretaker here hasn't seen him," and as her hopes sunk, her calm, collected business like approach that had developed over the years as an agent, kicked back in, "Do you know anything about what happened this morning?"

"Yah," and there was a hesitation, "Jan I really don't. . ."

"Ward's not around and we need to find the answers, and him. I'm in the lead now, so tell me. All of it," it was a command. Not one to be ignored. She picked up the keys and opened the door as she talked.

"When he didn't show at the right time I did some digging for information. There was a reported explosion in a set of lower income apartment complexes just off Southern this morning. It happened about the same time we last talked with him. People report seeing three to four men talking, and then the car exploded. The funny thing is that only two of the four men were taken to the hospital, and the others were never found," Eddy stopped. Jan knew that any of the ones not found could be Ward, Bobby, or any number of combinations, as she had not been let in on these plans. Either one, or both, could have been destroyed by the bomb depending on its size and the intensity, but that would have hit the news big time. As if reading her thoughts, Eddy continued, "The man in the car at the time survived, we didn't make the charges especially hot. No report on the other one yet. Police are keeping this pretty hush-hush. They weren't meant to kill anyone unless they were too close, just to distract them. The other . . ."

"Have you had someone check out who was taken to the hospital?" Jan was walking over to the computer.

"No, didn't want to leave yet and it seemed like it could be a long shot up until now."

"Eddy, do you have someone who can get to the hospital before these guys might be released, or get released?" Jan was on a roll now; she had something to work on.

"Yah sure, but it might break our cover. I'm sure they are in a security lock up," Eddy sounded sure of himself.

"Do it. If it isn't Ward, call this number," and she gave him the emergency code for the department, "Tell them this has to do with Rob's kidnapping, and that it's a gift from Jan. Then get out of there fast, as the flies from downtown will start swarming any minute after that. Go yourself; we have to have a positive I.D. Try to keep a cover of some kind. Call me and give me the info once you, or your people are clear," they hung up and Jan's hopes rose just a bit, not much but some.

Walking into the empty apartment she noticed it was just the way they had left it. Clean, but nothing had been moved. The curtains were pulled and the windows were closed. The Garcias must have been in to clean the place because there was no dust, and there were no dishes that they had left by the sink when they had gone earlier this week. Jan realized just then that it hadn't even been a week that they had been gone, but to her, it had seemed more like years. She didn't bother to open the curtains or the windows.

She walked over to the computer and flipped it on. While she waited for the machine to boot up and hook up to the Internet, Jan took the time to walk around the place fingering all the items that they had purchased together. By taking the time to touch the items in the room, she was able to remember more of the life she had once had. There hadn't been much time to deal with all the memories that had returned to her just the other day. Soon it would be time for her to take stock of all that had happened, and who she was. Walking into their bedroom she was overwhelmed with the feelings of them together. Now she understood why Ward had never come into this room when she was recovering. She picked up the picture that had started it all, and going back into the living room, sat down on the couch with it in her hands. Jan began to meditate. She didn't know how long she had been there when she opened her eyes at the sound of a computer beep. Now ready to face what was next, she had taken the time to look around and allowed the sinking, helpless feeling to go away.

Somehow she had to get over the feeling that she had let Ward down. Pieces of the puzzle were coming together, but this time they were crystal clear. Ward had always wanted her to leave the department, for lots of reasons, some she could not have understood until now. He had known why, and now she understood. Ward had never tried to push her to leave. If she had gone back to the department this time, she would have been retired, retrained, and as she had learned by reading Ward's file, never, ever again trusted. Worst of all, she would have lost Ward. Her fingers flew over the keys on the keyboard and sites opened. She checked the news sights from the valley and the nation, and found nothing. This meant that whoever had received the money still had it. A find like that would have made the news surely. There were also no good eyewitness accounts of the event. Most of the ones coming over the news services contradicted each other. She then hacked into the computers at the department, as well as many other departments. Ward had set that up to be almost too easy. It had always been one of his specialties. He had used the remote access number they all had, and had even used codes from agents within the department to get back in there. Where he had gotten the other codes was still a mystery, but not one that she would need to solve, as given time, she would have done the same. The connection proved to be useful. She soon learned that the department had just received a tip from a local Phoenix hospital about the men from this morning's explosion. The tip could only have come from Eddy, so she knew that Ward was not at the hospital. This pleased her in one way, and made her wonder in another. Taking a quick look at Rob's medical report she discovered that he was doing okay, recovering, and now fairly lucid. Before she had a chance to check out the report Rob gave, her phone vibrated again, taking her attention away from the computer.

"Here," this time it was all business in her voice. She had checked the number coming in before answering the phone, and knew it was Eddy.

"Ward's not in the hospital, and the second person was released with mild injuries, long before I got there. The name given doesn't match anything I know for either Ward or Bobby, but the details of the accident matched the details of how the meeting was to take place. The description of the man released in general matches Bobby's description," Eddy took a breath, "I'm going to get a few old friends together and find out what happened from the streets' point of view. If he shows up there, let me know."

"First thing I'll do," and they hung up. Jan looked back at the computer and switched off the connection to the department's computers. Next she looked through the files left on the machine. Like all good agents, Ward had a record of the jobs, his jobs he had done after leaving the department. Most of the jobs he had taken on were of no importance to this case, and she left them unread. Then a case name caught her eyes. It said simply, 'My Brother.' Once they joined the department they had no family but the people in the department. My Brother could only refer to one person. She opened the file and began to read. Some of the details were disturbing. Ward had met up with Bobby after leaving the department, and within the details of the meetings there was a sense of loss written into the log. He had tried many ways to corrupt Ward, and as she knew, Ward was incorruptible. It was also in Ward's files that he had met with Bobby many times to try to bring back the moral sense Bobby once had had, all without avail. That was where the name Wart had come from, Bobby viewed him like a Wart, a bother, and not the brother figures they had once been. This had only egged Ward on. It wasn't until their last meeting, before he had almost killed her at the factory that Ward wrote the final part of his log, "The Bobby Malone that has always, and will always be my brother is dead. This Bobby Malone has lost all sense of moral right and wrong, and continues to try to draw me into his warped and perverted world. I am sure he is not finished with trying to corrupt me, or any mind reader he would be able to reach with his new found skills."

She felt helpless and worse yet, exhausted. She had left the only man that she had loved and who truly loved her, to whatever Bobby had become. Without a trace of him, it would be difficult to discover where either might be. If Bobby had taken Ward with him, then it may be weeks before she would see him again. Jan was sure that whatever happened, Ward would be able to physically and mentally deflect it, but the idea of him going through that torture again haunted her. Closing the one file she noticed another that belonged to Bobby. This file detailed what skills Bobby now possessed. After reading about what he was now capable of made Jan shiver. She also realized after reading that file, he had tried to take over her memories, and plant new ones in her mind. He would have been able to do it if he had had a bit more time, and if she hadn't been as strong minded as she was.

She closed the files and looked for anything that would give locations or numbers of any person Bobby had contact with. In a well-hidden file, using Bobby's activation date as a password, she was able to locate a list of addresses and phone numbers for many people that were probably connected in many ways to Bobby. Most of these people she didn't even know, but one name on the list was all she needed. Bobby Malone's name was there, with a phone number, all typed in red. Placing her head down on the computer desk, she let her eyes close and concentrated on what she had just read. Ward must have felt this way when she had found him that night. She knew what she was going to have to do. The only way she was going to find Ward was to contact Bobby. Jan decided she would make that call it in a minute; she needed just a moment to rest. She had to be completely ready to play his mind games or she would risk losing it all. As she rested, she unknowingly slipped into a light sleep, fraught with worries, and nightmares.

Ward drove up to the entrance of the little development and silently said, "There's no place like home," as he drove through the gates. He was worried. No phone and no way to contact Eddy, or even Jan, to say that he was still alive. He did what he had told Jan to do, and what he told her he would do. He went home. He had planned to meet up with Eddy later in the afternoon, but after the explosion he had made a run for it. The first thing on his list was to find a place to get a bit of first aide. He had been at a disadvantage without his medical kit, and the explosion destroyed what he did have for an emergency. The only regrets he had about the explosion were that Bobby had not been injured any worse than he had been. As the bomb went off Ward jumped and flew backwards with the force of it, and he saw Bobby copy his movements keeping him from grievous bodily harm. Bobby had been closer to the car though, and had been knocked unconscious.

Ward had lain on the ground only minutes before he heard the sirens and pulled himself under the nearest Bronco to hide. He watched as Bobby started to regain consciousness, but it wasn't before the authorities arrived and whisked him off to the hospital. Ward waited until the crowd had built up and then slowly mixed into it. He had given himself a few good bruises, but he marveled at the thought that he hadn't broken any bones. Tomorrow he would be sore, stiff and generally uncomfortable, but he would be alive. If he had thought it through logically, instead of letting his emotions take over, he might have tried to get just a bit farther away before setting off the bomb, but it was too late now for regrets.

As he pulled up to the front of the house, he noticed that Mr. Garcia was not outside. This only meant one thing. She was here. He let himself relax again. It only took moments after he stopped the car and Mr. Garcia was outside to talk with him, his son at his side. Ward spoke fluently to him and asked him the only question he needed to know, was she alone? He received the answer he had hoped for. Manuel took the car he had driven down and Ward gave him instructions as to where to drop it off by the border. Manuel gave him an odd look and Ward waved him away, it wasn't the first time he had stolen a car, but he wasn't going to let Manuel know that it was stolen. It would be found and returned unharmed to its owner, and that was what mattered. Mr. Garcia noticed him limping and stopped him before he went through the patio door, asking him if he was all right. Ward assured him that he was, even though Mr. Garcia didn't look convinced. As he entered the gates to the patio, Mr. Garcia turned and walked back into his part of the house, shaking his head.

She had only had her head down for a couple of minutes preparing for the confrontation, and Jan had drifted off. Then it happened. Slowly she awoke, she knew she could hear thoughts and they sounded like Ward's. At first she thought she might be hallucinating, half-awake and half asleep, so she continued to rest her head on the computer desk. The words and images ran through her head again and again; 'Come get me, I'm right here, and I'm all yours,' Jan thought she just might be going crazy. Looking around, she could tell there was no one else in the apartment with her, she was sure of that. She had checked it thoroughly when she had entered and the visual scan of the place now told her nothing had changed. But still the words and images persisted.

Jan looked around again and saw no one. 'Was she losing her mind?' she thought as she got up to go to over to the phone, and rubbed her temples, 'it must be the mental and physical exhaustion.' If she called Bobby in this state, she was sure to be taken advantage of, and that could not ever happen again. She had no choice, she had to call and find Ward. It was now her job to see to it that he was safe, to end the mission. She looked to the bedroom wondering if she should get an hour or twos worth of rest, and then turned and looked toward the guestroom. That's when she heard it and knew what it was before her brain could register it. It was the scrape of the front door against the floor. This time when she heard a thought, she was sure of who it was.

'Thanks for the chili,' the thought was as clear as any she had in her own mind, and what's more, she could see the diner clearly. She turned slowly toward the front door, and looked, afraid that if no one were there it would confirm what she thought, she was losing her mind. There, silhouetted by the moonlight, was the figure of a man she had come to know, and wanted to take the rest of her life getting to know even better.

"Am I dreaming?" Jan was afraid to ask as the voice and thought left her at the same time.

"Only if I am, and we are doing it together," and he limped into the apartment. They walked into each other's arms, entangling themselves together, and for a very long time, stayed that way. It was over, all of it. Both had made it back home and both now belonged only to each other. She had proved it to him, proved that she was willing to leave the department, never to return, and he had shown just how much she meant to him. It wasn't until she could feel it in his thoughts that the pain of standing was too much. She helped him to the couch, by giving him her crutch and smiling. Once he was sitting, Ward took hold of her hand, and looked at the ring on her finger letting the warmth of his smile travel deep into her thoughts. Then, they kissed. They let their kiss linger and then slowly, she pulled away, "I have to let Eddy know you're here, be right back," she got up and left the couch reluctantly.

As she talked with Eddy on the phone she watched Ward make his way to the bedroom and heard the curtains and the window open. She smiled knowing that the sounds of nature would do more for his healing than any first aide she could give. Water ran in the bathroom, and then all was quiet. Eddy was relieved that Ward was home, and filled her in on the information he had picked up. She stopped him, and thanked him before going on with the conversation.

"Eddy, I think I need to go and take care of Ward right now. He's pretty bruised up. We can catch up on things tomorrow," and she paused smiling to herself, "or the next day."

"Just remember," Eddy cleared his throat, "He needs some rest," and he hung up the phone. Jan pressed end on the phone and then pressed it again to turn the phone off. This time there would be no interruptions.

Walking back into the bedroom after she completed the call, she stood at the door and looked at the figure lying on the bed. He lay half-covered by the sheet on the bed. His shirt was off, and from what she could tell, so were his pants. The sounds of the ocean that had earlier gone unnoticed lapped at her mind and enticed her to relax. Far off in the distance she could just barely make out the sounds of two dolphins in the water. He was smiling. His hands were behind his head and his muscles were finally at rest. His eyes were closed, but he knew she had come in.

"The answers to your questions are, one, I'm okay, sore but nothing broken, and everything seems to be in good working order. After I set off the bomb in the car, I made my way away from the scene when it was clear. No one saw me. It would have been too risky to meet with Eddy, so I came here after I nursed some of my wounds and found a car. Number two, no, Bobby is not dead, and no I'm not sure how I feel about that, but I am willing to deal with that later," there was a long pause. She stayed by the door. He opened his eyes and looked at her for a moment before he went on, "And Babs, the answer to question number three is," and he smiled boldly at her, "what are you waiting for?"

Printed in the United States
91427LV00004B/41/A